The Meri Scott Show

Tori Turnbull

ISBN: 9781726735551

For all women out there; whether you would choose the "dignity" of rising above it or the illicit joy of sweet revenge, and to my best friends, "the Girls," for all the years of friendship, love, laughter, dancing and takeaways.

As always, with thanks to my family for their continued love and support.

Books by Tori Turnbull:

Kissing Frogs

The Meri Scott Show

S-expiry (released 2019)

CHAPTER 1

Boyfriend: It's Time To Celebrate!

I bounced off the hallway walls, clasping my three National Television Award gongs to my chest. I, Meri Scott, was the Most Popular TV Presenter, of the Most Popular Daytime Talk Show, and the Most Popular Factual Programme, as voted by the great British public. The rest of my team was still getting drunk at the after-party.

Usually, Tom, my boyfriend, and I would be the last to leave, working the room and celebrating in style, but he had an important audition for the lead role in a romcom tomorrow, so he'd stayed home tonight to rehearse and get an early night. I'd snuck out of the party early and almost sober, to get home and have a private party with him.

The bonus: I was still sober enough that I'd look good in the after-party photos with my three gongs—*three!*—in tomorrow's newspapers. Three glasses of champagne on an empty stomach and I felt like I was floating like a butterfly, whilst stumbling around like a fool, but I was *a winner.* After years of building my career, I'd finally made it to the top of my industry.

I couldn't wait to share it with Tom.

He'd be so proud. He and my mother were my biggest supporters. They'd been with me since I got my first audition for *The Meri Scott Show*; hell, Mum was there when I was thirteen and got my first break in an advert for cheese strings; Tom since I was a twenty-one-year-old disc jockey in a small mining town in the Welsh Valleys.

The champagne numbness spread to my arms. I struggled to hold my awards and get the key into the front-door lock. Tom and I had moved to London together when I got my big break. My mother had followed shortly after, moving into a flat just down the road. They'd celebrated every success with me. Now I'd officially made it, big time.

The door finally swung open, and I tripped inside, trying not to giggle. It was only eleven, but the lights were out and the flat was quiet. Tom must've already gone to bed. He wouldn't expect me back before three or four in the morning, and with his audition tomorrow, he hadn't waited up. Kicking off my four-inch heels, I dumped my purse and keys on the hall table. Cuddling my NTAs to my chest, I headed down the hall, working the zipper under the arm of my dress. Maybe I'd wake him up and give him a little evening delight. After all, his girlfriend was the *Most Popular* person in town, and tonight I was all his.

I slid the clips out of my mink-black hair and gave it a quick fluff, going for the sexy, tumbled look. Clutching the front of my violet Victoria Beckham dress with one hand, I checked myself out in the hall mirror, tugging the bodice down, tucking the edge under my armpit, making sure I exposed at least some of my minimal cleavage.

Then I leant seductively against the bedroom doorframe, one arm raised above my head, hitched a hip and struck a pose. Hmm, maybe I should have kept my Choos on. Tom had a bit of a shoe kink. I could nip back down the hall to get them… but my feet were sore.

No.

So long as I got naked, and on my knees, quickly enough, he wouldn't have time to care about the shoes. Easing the door open with a toe, I aimed my best slutty-vamp look at the bed.

The door needed oiling; it squealed as I pushed it open. A confusing cacophony of sound and images blindsided me. I struggled to make sense of it. Tom's firm white backside flexed and lunged, his knees spread and braced on the mattress. A pair of skinny San-Tropezed thighs were wrapped around his narrow hips, ankles locked, killer red heels pointing in my direction.

It wasn't the door hinges squealing and groaning. Tom leant over a woman, one hand clutching her hip, the other holding her wrists above her head. Not that I could see him doing it from my vantage point, but I knew anyway. This was our—*his*—favourite position. He lowered his head over her breast, noisily suckling. The woman beneath him writhed and groaned.

I should say something, or do something and let him know I'd caught him in the act, but I was frozen, unable to look away as the pace picked up. Tom's lunging became less coordinated. He started swearing and grunting. Her squeals increased in pitch and frequency.

"Fuck me! Yes! Dig your heels in. Right there."

"Oh, God. Tom!" *No!* I knew that lilting feminine voice. "So good!"

Bile surged up my throat. My stomach pitched. "*M-Mum?*"

Tom stiffened and jerked. "Ungh!"

"Meri?" My mother peered at me over his shoulder, her expressionless medically preserved face, flushed and sheened with sweat, eyes wide with horror.

"Fuuuck…" It was too late for Tom. He'd reached the point of no return and shot his load into my *mother* with a loud groan and a rigor-like stare fixed on me over his shoulder.

* * * * *

"Meri, darling. Listen." Talith, my mother, rushed into the living room. I moved across the room, struggling with trembling fingers, to pull up the zipper at my side. "We didn't mean to hurt you."

I couldn't believe this was happening. My heart pounded, my whole body trembled and the blanket of shock that had covered my emotions started to fray, leaving me feeling disoriented.

Talith reached to grab my hand. Skin crawling at the idea of her touch, I spun away.

It wasn't happening.

It couldn't be happening.

"We didn't think you'd be back so soon."

It wasn't happening.

It… Was… Not… Happening.

"It's only just after eleven. You're usually out much later."

My heart pounded painfully in my chest, my mind throwing up images of Tom staring at me as he came *inside my mother*. Tom had always said my mother's "cougar-ing" was slutish and embarrassing and she should date someone her own age. Clearly, he'd had a change of opinion.

"Meri, Talith is telling the truth. We didn't mean to hurt you…" At the sound of Tom's voice, the final threads of shock and disbelief frayed, anger burning through.

This *was* happening. It wasn't a dream. It wasn't a joke or an episode of my chat show.

It was my life.

This was *real.*

I'd just caught my boyfriend having sex. With. My. Mother.

"It didn't mean anything," Tom added.

I couldn't form words.

It didn't mean anything.

If sleeping with my mother didn't mean anything to him, or to my mother, *I* must mean less than nothing to both of them.

Why would they risk everything for nothing?

"I just… I just… I *needed* someone. You never have time for me anymore." I didn't care that he looked like Chris Pratt's younger, hotter brother. I couldn't bear to look at him; his tousled blond hair and godlike body suddenly turned my stomach.

I should have known what was going on. I should

have at least suspected something. It wasn't like I didn't know the signs. I heard about it nearly every day at work, but… Jesus. These things didn't happen to people like me—I was the Most Popular TV Presenter—it happened to people with low self-esteem and broken families, the kind of people I had on my chat show.

In fact, I'd done an episode on this: "My Husband Is Sleeping with My Mother". Only Tom wasn't my husband. He was my partner of seven years. We weren't married. He didn't want to conform to society's patriarchal repression of women—marriage—and tie me up in bondage.

I wouldn't have minded a little bondage of the matrimonial kind.

So, why wasn't I screaming and shouting and caving his head in with the stone Buddha we'd picked up on our fourth anniversary trip to India, like I watched my guests do whilst my security team held them apart?

I must be the biggest dupe on earth.

My boyfriend and my mother.

I was so blind. So *stupid*. Tom used to love coming to celebrity packed events, getting his picture published in

Heat or *Hello!*. Then suddenly six—or was it nine months ago? Maybe longer—he stopped. I'd worried he was depressed because his acting career had never really taken off, whilst my career had gone from strength to strength. I'd worried he was feeling emasculated, because he was forced to live off my wages. I'd spoken to my mother about it. She'd told me to give him space, not to pressure him and to keep going to the events alone.

Were they screwing each other all that time?

My stomach churned.

Was he going from my mother to me?

If I hadn't caught them tonight, would he have gone straight from shagging my mother to me?

Would he even have showered in between?

Had he done it before? I gagged, slapping a hand over my mouth

"I'm lonely and you're always working, or busy, or out at some glitzy event," Tom said.

What a bloody lame excuse!

He was saying this was *my* fault.

I'd driven him to it.

Tom tugged the waistband of his tartan boxer shorts then scratched his broad, muscled chest. "You know I don't like those things anymore; everyone's fake. The whole time they're talking to me, they're looking over my shoulder for someone more important or popular to talk to, to be seen with. And no matter what they're saying I know they're lying."

They're lying!

"And they're probably—"

"Screwing their girlfriends' mother behind her back?" My words fired out like bullets powered by the fury of betrayal. "My *mother,* Tom? She's fifty-seven."

"Age is just a number, Meri. Your mother is— Fuck! Ow!"

My Most Popular Presenter Award made a satisfying thud as the globe on the top of the smooth, hollow column connected with his shoulder.

I'd forgotten it was in my hand.

Hell, I didn't realise I was swinging for him, until he

screamed and fell to his knees, curling up into the foetal position. I just wanted to shut him up.

I wished it was filled with lead—something heavy and hard… that would hurt more.

I swung again as he huddled on the floor, looking up at me through the shield of his arms.

"Meri, stop it!" Mum's shout turned me from Tom's cowering form. "We didn't mean to hurt you."

"Are you some sort of sociopath? You slept with my boyfriend. In my bed." Rage vibrated in my voice. "How the hell did you think I would feel? Happy? Grateful?" It was surreal; suddenly I felt like I was presenting my show and everything was happening to someone else, and I was just watching and passing comment. "Did you think I'd just say, *Okay, when you're finished with him give him a quick wash and pass him back* like a communal dildo?"

"Don't be like that." Tom whimpered.

Like what? If I still had my pointy shoes on, I'd kick him. "I won three awards. I came home to tell you. To surprise you with a celebratory blow-jo—" I snorted. "I guess you surprised me." Again, I had to force away the nauseating image of Tom watching me over his shoulder whilst he came… In. My. Mother.

"We didn't mean to hurt you."

"Stop saying that!"

"Meri, baby—" The flush on Talith's—I couldn't acknowledge her as my mother right now, not even in my head—face had faded and—thankfully—she'd taken the time to cover her perfect, scientifically preserved and medically enhanced size-eight body. I couldn't handle her postcoital *and* full frontal. Unfortunately, she'd used my favourite Chinese silk throw as a wrap, and her right nipple kept popping out, proudly shouting, *I've been having sex with your boyfriend.* Talith gave up trying to cover herself. There was no containing those seven-thousand-pound DD breasts.

Tom spoke from his position hidden behind her, "Talith and I, we have feelings for each other, Meri. It's no one's fault."

"Yes, it is." Ice dripped from my words. "It's your fault, both of you"—I jabbed my award in their direction—"for acting on it."

"You can't blame the breakdown of a relationship on one person," Talith said.

"I can when he's screwing my mother," I retorted.

"Why don't we all sit down and we can talk this through like adults?"

"I don't want to sit down," I said. "I don't want to talk it through. I don't want to sort it out." My hand cut through the air in a dramatic slicing motion. "It's over."

"Wha…" Tom blinked, eyes and mouth opening and closing simultaneously, like a beached cod gasping for breath. "Think about what you're giving up here, Meri. Our life—"

"I know what I'm giving up here, *Tom*. A guy who's cheating on me with my mother. No thinking time required."

"What about the years we've been together?" His voice rose with panic. "The life we've built?"

"Is that what you were thinking about when you were screwing her?"

"Hey!" Talith snapped, stepping aside and leaving

Tom without cover if I decided to swing for him again. “I know you’re hurting, but we just—”

“Shut up!” I screeched before either of them could say anything else. “Just get out! Both of you. Out! Now!”

CHAPTER 2

Mother: You Ripped Our Family Apart!

Two days later, I was stuck in traffic behind a bus. All afternoon I'd faked a smile with my agent Tony and *Heat*'s editor whilst selecting the best pictures of me on the red carpet, rocking my VB dress. It took real effort to smile and focus on how great it felt to top their Best-Dressed list and not the emotional shitstorm the rest of the night had become. Then I'd answered weird questions about the strangest thing I've ever eaten (fried silk worms in South Korea); whether I'd ever worn something out of the dirty laundry basket (yes, but not underwear); my proudest moment (most popular times three at this year's NTAs); had I ever cheated on anyone (no); my longest relationship, (seven years, *seven long, wasted years with a lying, cheating, money-sucking, mummy-fucking piece of crap.* Okay, so I only thought that bit, I didn't actually say it);

and other fascinating facts that would be spun into a three-page article.

I drummed my fingers on the steering wheel, staring at the back end of a bus and half-heartedly singing along to a country song. I had no idea where Tom or Talith were. I hadn't heard a peep from either of them since I kicked them out. I'd spent the last two days getting my bed replaced and moving all of Tom's stuff out of my bedroom.

The guy in the black Fiesta behind me laid on his horn. The bus driver waved his middle finger out the window, signalling for us to overtake, totally oblivious to the fact the other side of the road was blocked by some arsehole who'd decided to park on a double yell—

Hey! I recognised the arsehole's blue Audi convertible; it was Tom's. A half-mile of traffic built up behind it, tailing back past the traffic lights. The dark wood door to Ottomans restaurant swung open, and out strolled the arsehole, carrying a bouquet of calla lilies in clashing shades of red and orange and a massive brown paper bag of takeout.

My heart tripped, banging painfully off my ribs, and my stomach plummeted. It must be the second Monday of the month. Ottomans was my favourite restaurant. We always got takeout from there on the second Monday of the month.

Reaching his car, Tom dumped the food and flowers on the back seat and jumped over the door, sliding into his seat like an eighties cop show character. He pulled out, whizzing between the static traffic, without so much as a nod of acknowledgment to the vehicles snarled up around him.

"Ottomans and flowers…" He hadn't bought me flowers since my last birthday: brown-tipped roses with curly, wilting leaves from the supermarket sale bin. The bus finally began to move, freeing the gridlock. Without thought, I yanked the steering wheel to the right and, whilst horns blared and drivers gesticulated, swerved into the wrong lane, squeezed between the bus and oncoming traffic with millimetres to spare and floored the accelerator. I blew through an amber, possibly red, light, catching up with Tom as he zipped along the line of standing traffic he'd created.

It wasn't like I was following him, or anything stalker-ish. We were just both headed in the same direction. I slammed on the brakes, cursing as a car pulled out between us, before creeping along the road at five miles per hour.

“Shit!” I slammed the steering wheel with the heel of my hand as I lost sight of him. The creep in front began a ten-thousand-point manoeuvre into a parallel park at the kerb. Breaking every rule in the Highway Code and a couple of traffic laws, I mounted the pavement to get past. Relying on instinct, I made like a NASCAR driver and managed, by some miracle, to get within a few car lengths of Tom.

He was heading towards Regency Street.

My heart fluttered, my stomach warmed with… anticipation… nerves… anger?

Our, *my*, flat was on Regency Street. He had expensive flowers and takeout from my favourite restaurant. Was he coming to beg for forgiveness?

I wasn’t sure if I was ready to see him, or listen to anything he had to say. I certainly wasn’t ready to forgive, and there was no forgetting what I’d seen.

If I was a guest on my show, I’d be screaming and crying whilst Dave, head of show security, prevented me from scratching Tom and my mother's eyes out. But shock had me emotionally numb; that was the only explanation for the fact I wasn't getting violent or weepy. This was my body's way of protecting me. Underneath the layer of numbness was a whole load of hurt and rage just waiting to spill out.

I swung left, careful to maintain two cars between me and Tom. I'd seen cops and private eyes in movies, and they always kept two cars between them and the person they were following.

What was Tom thinking? I wasn't going to be bought off with a takeaway and bunch of flowers.

He turned across Vauxhall Bridge Road onto Regency Street. I accelerated, nearly rear-ending the BMW in front and cutting off a granny in a Ford Ka. Wings beat a nervous tattoo in my stomach. He really was going to the flat. He slowed at the beautiful gated block of red-brick flats we lived in. I pulled up to the kerb and waited. Maybe I'd just stay here and watch him ring the intercom and beg me for forgiveness, whilst sobbing uncontrollably at what he'd lost. *Me.* I could film it on my mobile phone and watch it over and over again.

What the…?

He drove straight past.

Where was he going?

There was plenty of parking out front. Could he not see through the tears of guilt and remorse? Had he changed his mind? His car disappeared around the corner before I could fully grasp what was happening.

My foot slammed on the accelerator, laying down rubber as I pulled out after him. Two near misses, a T-junction and a possible speeding ticket later, I caught up with him. It was harder to keep any cars between us, as he moved onto the quieter roads. My mind spun with confusion. Where was he going?

Another sharp right, and—

Oh my God.

I couldn't believe it had taken me so long to figure it out. He was going to Talith's house.

Tom pulled up to the kerb and leapt out of his car, so desperate to get to Talith that he didn't even bother to put the convertible's roof up. He bounded up the stairs, brown paper takeaway bag in one hand, massive bunch of flowers behind his back. He set the takeout bag on the top step and smoothed back his wind-ruffled blond hair, cocking a designer-jean-clad leg, puffing his chest and leaning nonchalantly against the doorframe.

I recognised that pose, that look. It was the one he used when we started going out. When he was trying to charm me and knew he was going to get lucky.

The big black door swung opened before he could knock.

He whipped the flowers from behind his back as Talith appeared, barely dressed in a black silk and lace peignoir, her ash-blond hair falling in artful waves over her shoulders. She took the flowers and leant in for a deep, open-mouthed kiss. Tom walked into her, backing her into the house, herding her petite form with his big body.

I shivered. I used to love it when he went all macho with me; a little bit dominant—not exactly *Fifty Shades of Grey*, more *Off White*, but still… I should have known he was playing away; it had been so long since he'd bothered.

Talith leant out and grabbed the takeaway bag, her peignoir sagging off one shoulder. Tom's hand slapped down on her backside. Her squeal and giggle floated down the street before she disappeared inside. The door closed.

Black.

Solid.

Final.

With me on the outside.

Alone.

A few minutes later, it started to drizzle, a fine October mist of rain.

Still, I sat in my car, strangely exhausted. My mind and stomach churned. Were they pretend-picnicking on the living room floor like Tom and I used to do? Were they fuelling up on food before getting down and dirty?

Was he feeding Talith little bites from his own plate? Did she have a bottle of icy-cold Pinot sweating on the coffee table ready for them to share, like I always did on takeout night? Was he kissing her between sips from their shared glass?

I sat lost in thought, staring straight ahead, rain blurring the windscreen whilst Jennifer Nettles sang about how *boys can be promiscuous* and she didn't want to be *that girl*, then, without conscious thought, I found my four-inch heels sinking into the tiny patch of muddy lawn outside Talith's house. Back pressed to the house wall, I peered around the edge of the living room window, like a starving orphan at a bakery display.

A car drove past and slowed. I ignored it. It wasn't like I was trespassing. I owned the house. At least, I paid the mortgage and owned all of the furniture in it. Which, to my mind, meant the tiny patch of lawn I was currently irrigating with my stiletto heels was mine.

Irrespective of whether my name was on the deed.

I scanned the open-plan living-dining-kitchen. Tom's shoes were kicked off haphazardly by the door, his leather jacket slung on the stairs. He was sprawled on a plush red sofa cushion. They'd scattered them over the floor, so they could eat picnic style. Talith reclined between his spread legs, leaning against his chest.

Cosy.

Settled.

Intimate.

It was exactly as I'd feared. It was an exact replica of our monthly takeout night. Anger started to boil inside me, flushing my skin. This wasn't a one-off thing. He'd just slotted Talith—she didn't deserve to be called a mother—into my place like we were interchangeable.

Tom took a sip of wine, then put the glass to Talith's full lips, tipping it so she could sip from the same place his lips had touched. She took the glass from his hand, setting it amongst the remains of their dinner. She twisted in his arms, her lush, surgically enhanced body moulding to his. Their mouths melded. Tom arched, twisting to come over her. It was a move I knew well. A quick fondle of her breasts and he'd be gripping her hands above her head, demanding she wrap her legs around his hips and dig her heels in so he could feel the stilettos scoring his flesh.

This wasn't some mistake.

They weren't eaten up with guilt over betraying me.

They didn't care.

Numb, I stumbled away from the window, tripping over the low garden wall and bumping into Tom's car. My Mulberry handbag fell off my shoulder, spilling its contents on the damp back seat. Without thought, I leant over the side of the car, scooping up my purse, a couple of receipts, a stray tampon in a frayed half-open wrapper and a packet of cress seeds.

Then the packet was open and I was reaching across the back of the car, sprinkling tiny black seeds onto the footwell and along the back seat. Everything was already damp from the drizzle, making for perfect growing conditions, but I snapped the top off a bottle of Evian Facial Spray, liberally spraying everywhere the seeds had landed.

By the time I came back to reality, my heart was pounding and I was halfway home. My survival instinct kicked in and I pulled over at a roadside recycling centre to dispose of the evidence, dropping the empty seed packet and spray bottle into the recycling bins before heading for home.

I felt… I felt *good.* A smile tilted my lips and amusement tickled my tummy. It was wanton vandalism. I should probably feel guilty, or upset, even angry, but I didn't.

I felt good. Not quite happy, but good. Amused. Maybe even a little bit proud of myself.

It wasn't like it was premediated. It was a spur-of-the-moment thing. Temporary insanity, maybe. Honestly, no one carried cress seeds around in their handbag, just in case they needed to seek vengeance against their philandering boyfriend. I'd bought them for my godson Owain's nursery project. They were going to make those little egg heads, where you drew a face on the shell, emptied the egg and replaced its filling with damp cotton wool, then sowed cress hair.

Oh my God, wait until I tell Jenn!

Jenn didn't know I'd broken up with Tom yet, about Talith's role in it or that I'd caught them shagging. Twice. I'd been in a shocked haze. I hadn't wanted to talk about it, and besides, Jenn and Owain were on holiday, but suddenly I did want to talk about it. At least, I did with Jenn. Jenn would understand the betrayal. We'd been best friends close to fifteen years. Carrie Underwood launched into "Before He Cheats," and I sang along enthusiastically about smashing up a cheating ex's car. As I pulled onto Regency Street, the happy feeling began to deflate, depression creeping around the edges.

I wanted to feel good again. I deserved to feel good.

None of this was my fault. I'd never cheated. Not with Tom's mother, or father, or anyone. I'd been faithful, for years… seven years. It wasn't like I hadn't had chances or offers either. I had lots of them. I was popular, the *Most Popular*, as voted by the great British public. The more successful and famous I'd become, the more offers I'd had from men: rich men, poor men, fat men, thin men, old, young, ugly and hot, and I'd turned them down. All of them.

Because I had a boyfriend: Tom. I'd wasted years of my life, the best years—my screw-around years—on one man, only to find out he was shagging my mother. My head began to pound.

Tom didn't deserve to be happy.

Talith didn't deserve to be happy, filling my place in Tom's life like I'd never existed. If he closed his eyes whilst he was shagging, could he tell the difference? Did he care? Clearly my mother didn't. Carrie Underwood launched into the final verse of my new anthem. Not that I'd taken a Louisville Slugger to the headlights of Tom's Audi, the Audi I'd paid for, or carved my name into his seats.

I wasn't stupid.

That was criminal damage.

Besides, carving my own name wouldn't exactly be discreet, and, even overworked and underpaid, the police wouldn't have to work hard to find me if I autographed his car.

But I wasn't going to let this go, either. I wasn't going to just disappear like I'd never existed, just move on and pretend nothing had happened. It had happened. They didn't deserve to get away with it.

I'd counselled the women on my chat show against this kind of thing, told them to just rise above it, to move on with their lives and forget about the lying, cheating bastards. But bugger it—this was me, not them, and I wasn't going to let Tom and Talith live happily ever after. .

CHAPTER 3

Are you a real lawyer? Lie Detector Results!

"What's got you all flushed and excited, Marie?"

The deep voice cut through the silent waiting room. I glanced up from *Closer* magazine. A tall, dark-haired man limped into reception, accepted a handful of letters off the receptionist, then propped a jeans-clad hip on the edge of her desk, massaging his left thigh whilst he spoke.

Marie's eyes bugged out as she glanced at me, then back at the man. He followed Marie's wide-eyed gaze and head tilt towards me. I knew what he would see: a slim, black-haired, pouty-lipped, porcelain-skinned woman dressed in designer smart-casual attire. I faked interest in the magazine. I'd been famous long enough to recognise the expression on his face: *She looks vaguely familiar. Where do I know her from?* Usually this morphed into recognition, but not today

“It’s Meredith Scott!” Marie’s tone made it clear he—and everyone else on earth—should know who I was.

He drew a blank. “She’s not one of my clients.”

“From *The Meri Scott Show*?” Marie said, exasperated.

He shook his head.

Still no recognition.

“She’s the queen of daytime chat shows.”

“Christ!” His tone was surly and unimpressed. Not what I was used to. “What has Lia agreed to now?”

Who’s Lia? I wondered.

“Nothing,” Marie whisper-snapped. “She wants a lawyer, Alex.”

“Who’s she getting?”

“You.” He was a lawyer? He was wearing jeans and a North Face t-shirt… his hair didn’t even look brushed.

His gaze shot to Marie, he didn’t make any attempt to control his volume. “No.”

“Yes.”

“Lia can do it.”

“She’s busy with the extra clients she took on when you were off.” I shrank back at the fierce scowl he directed at Marie. Clearly made of sterner stuff than me, she didn’t flinch. “You’re the only one available.”

"I'm busy," he responded.

"Your case finished early," she countered. "You have the rest of the day free."

"But—"

"But nothing. It's been long enough, Alex. Lia needs a break."

He thumped a fist against his left thigh. "One of the others, then."

"Ms Scott?" Marie called. I stopped pretending to be reading and looked towards the reception desk, where Alex scowled ferociously at Marie. She smiled sweetly at me. "Mr Gordon is available to see you now."

Good. I rose from my chair, skirting the surly Alex. He pushed away from the desk. For a second, I thought his leg would give out and pitch him to the floor at my feet. He staggered a step but managed to stay upright.

"This way, Ms Scott." He was Mr Gordon, the lawyer?

He walked away from the reception desk, his gait uneven. "Bring tea and biscuits, please, Marie." I hovered, debating backing out… but I really needed legal advice, and the more lawyers' offices I went to, the greater the likelihood the media would pick up on it. Alex Gordon waved me through the door ahead of him. He was huge, well over six foot. He made me feel tiny. "Lots of biscuits," he continued.

He sank into a big leather desk chair, leaving me to settle myself.

"Are you a lawyer?" I asked.

"Yes."

"A real one?"

"It's not like I'm claiming to be James Bond. Why would I pretend to be a lawyer?"

"You don't look like one."

"It's a curse, but I've learnt to live with it," he deadpanned, then nodded towards the framed certificates lining one wall.

"And those are real qualifications? Legal ones. From the UK." *Not the internet* went unspoken. I crossed to them, spending a bit of time checking out the signatures and holograms in the corner. They looked real.

"I can give you the Law Society's contact details if you want to check me out."

"Okay." I sat down. He pushed the plate of sugary Jammie Dodger biscuits Marie brought in closer to me. I ignored them.

"How can I help you?"

"I don't... I mean, I'm not sure..." I struggled to decide how much to say. I didn't want to give too much away.

Silence stretched.

"Have you been charged with committing a crime?"

I nervously licked my bottom lip. "Not yet."

He scowled. "Do you have reason to think you are going to be?"

"I guess. It depends on whether they catch me." My internal debate on whether to trust him continued. I didn't have a lot of faith in men being honest right now, especially not good-looking ones. And whilst he wasn't in Tom's movie-star-hot league, he was good looking. He looked like he should be shooting on some country estate with spaniels sitting at his feet, not sitting in a stuffy office or courtroom. His t-shirt stretched across his chest and stomach, moulding to his big, solid body.

My mobile started ringing. I reached into my large tote bag to grab it and silence it, and an autographed photo slipped out of my bag, sliding across Alex's desk before I could catch it.

He stopped it in the centre of his desk with one long finger, his gaze flicking from the picture to me and back again. I flashed a smile.

"Your photos are massively airbrushed."

I gaped, gasping like a stunned fish.

Of course they were airbrushed.

He didn't have to mention it.

What a prick. He must be a really good lawyer, because they weren't keeping him around for his personality.

My agent and the studio had been manipulating my publicity shots for years—it was normal in the television industry. Makeup wasn't enough these days—erasing the bags under my eyes from ten hours of filming a day then another four hours of appearances at night, whitening my teeth, slimming or fattening me up depending on the audience—skinnier for women's magazines and strategically rounded for lads' mags. It went with the job description.

TV cameras added ten pounds, twenty pounds and fifteen years of hard living if it was HD TV. I had to look my best, always, even when I'd found out less than a week ago my boyfriend was shagging my mother.

There was always someone—younger, skinnier, prettier and willing to sleep with the producer—snapping at my heels. I couldn't relax and let myself go even for a moment. Still, that didn't give him the right to insult me to my face.

"So, what can I do for you?"

I blinked at him vacantly as he pushed the autographed photo back towards me. Life was nothing but a series of below-the-belt-hits at the moment. Maybe Tom went off with my mother because he was disappointed in the reality of me too.

"You came here to see me," he said, tapping a pen on the arm of his chair, his keen navy-blue eyes assessing me.

"I need a lawyer." I'd barely slept in the three days since I took my little trip to Stalker-town, followed Tom to Talith's house and vandalised his car.

It felt too good getting back at him, but since the adrenaline rush had worn off, I'd had a couple of borderline panic attacks, thinking the police were at my door to arrest me. I couldn't afford to get caught on the wrong side of the law at this point in my career, not with the US networks wanting to take *The Meri Scott Show* stateside. So, I needed a lawyer. A good one. To advise me and keep me on the right side of the law, or close enough that someone could argue my case in court if required.

He nodded. “Then you’ve come to the right place.”

“If you’re a lawyer—”

“There is no *if.* I *am* a lawyer. I specialise in criminal law.”

“So, anything I say to you is secret, right?”

He reached over his desk, swiped a yellow legal pad, flipped it open and set it on the edge of his desk, then watched me expectantly. “Almost.”

“*Almost*? What does that mean?”

“Client confidentially only applies once you have retained a solicitor.”

“For how long?”

“Forever.” Right. Good. Finally, he’d said something I wanted to hear. “Except where I am legally required to disclose the information.” Not so good. “When I have to act in the best interests of my client.”

My best interest was that he kept his mouth zipped. “What happens if you tell someone?”

“Disciplinary action.”

"Is that it?" He broke my confidence and got told off?

"You could sue me."

Better. "Okay, so you can't repeat anything I tell you."

He took a deep breath and let it out in a long, controlled exhale. On a less professional man, one I wasn't paying, I might have thought it was a sigh of exasperation. "There are some exceptions."

"That's not fair."

His lips twitched, and a dimple creased his right cheek. "You don't have to worry about whether it's fair or not, Ms Scott. Unless you're planning on committing a crime which is likely to result in serious bodily harm…" He watched me steadily. I held still, refusing to flinch.

"So, once I get this retainer, I can tell you anything and you can't tell anyone?" This was important. I wasn't going to let him trick me into saying something and then suddenly find some loophole. Lawyers, men—good-looking men—were slippery.

"Client confidentiality applies once you retain—"

"How much will that cost?"

"Depends." He tapped his chin with the end of his silver pen, eyes narrowed. "Have you been arrested or charged with anything?"

"Not yet."

His eyebrow twitching was the only sign what I said surprised him. "Ms Scott, are you about to be arrested?"

"I hope not." It wasn't like anyone had seen me scatter the seeds, and even if they'd sprouted—and the packet said it would take two to seven days for germination—no one would be able to prove it was me. Even if they went all CSI, my DNA and fingerprints were legitimately all over Tom's car. Besides, the police had better things to spend their time on than investigating cress crops.

My chest was getting tight, my heart was starting to pound and a fine sheen of sweat was building up under my arms. I needed a lawyer in case my panic attacks were actually premonitions and I was about to be arrested for vandalism.

"But you have committed a crime?"

"Of course. Who hasn't?" I asked. "Speeding, littering…"

He was tap-tap-tapping his pen again. "You didn't come to speak to me today about dropping a crisp packet, so why don't you explain how I can help you?"

"Like I said, I need a criminal lawyer." Damn it, I should have prepared my story better. He was flustering me.

"Like I said," he mimicked. "Have you committed a crime?"

"Nothing serious yet. I like to plan in advance. To be prepared."

"You're planning to break the law?"

Shit! Not what I meant to imply. "That depends on your advice," I kind of joked. It was one of those difficult-to-answer questions—if someone had asked me a week ago if I would ever sow cress seeds in the back of Tom's car, I would have said no. In fact, I would have bet our first child it wouldn't even enter my mind to do it.

"My advice is don't break the law."

I chewed my bottom lip. I was tired and stressed. Maybe I should hire a female solicitor or just google it. He was a man. He was never going to understand, even if I explained the whole thing to him. “Are there any female lawyers?”

“Thousands of them, but they’re not as good as me.” He didn’t smile. “Nor are the male ones.”

Then how come they’d been busy when I turned up without an appointment and he hadn’t? “I still think I’d be best with a woman.” This guy would probably think I should just *get over it*.

“Well, you’ve got me. So, let’s get down to details. Have you been charged with anything?”

“No.” I rubbed my sweaty palms nervously against my thighs.

“Is there an investigation I should know about?”

“Not yet.” But in spite of my *Orange Is the New Black*-inspired panic attacks, I knew—if the opportunity presented itself again—I wasn’t going to stop at a little bit of cress. I’d enjoyed it too much, even though I had no idea if my impulsive actions had born fruit—or cress, as the case may be. I'd actually woken up laughing this morning, thinking about it. Which beat all the other times I'd woken up from dreams of Tom and my mo—*Talith* having sex.

"Is there one pending?"

"Define pending."

He closed his eyes, taking a deep, painful-sounding breath. He pushed back his chair, pressing a fist against his left thigh, pen tapping against his stubbled chin. The pen stopped.

His blue eyes snapped open and fixed on me, panicking me into speech. "I… I… just want legal advice!" I crossed my fingers. "I haven't committed a real crime." His eyes narrowed, his expression stern. It was a few cress seeds, not grievous bodily harm. "I just want some explanation of a few laws and stuff."

His pen tapping paused. "For a show?"

"Ah, yeah." Shit! Why hadn't I thought of that? It was like the sky cleared and the sun shone through. It was a brilliant cover.

"I'm not interested in being on television."

"You won't need to be on TV. It's just for... advice and... and research and stuff. I just want to have an expert to consult. You know, legal counsel on various criminal matters: vandalism, harassment, stalking... that sort of thing. I want to know what the law is and ... and, ah, any possible loopholes or grey lines," I ended lamely. I could hardly say, *to make sure I don't fall foul of them*.

"Haven't you got researchers for that?" Well, yes. My mind blanked. He let the silence stretch uncomfortably. "I'm pretty busy with real cases and real clients, Ms Scott. How about you call me when, and *if*, you actually need a criminal lawyer?"

A sharp knock cut him off. "Ms Scott!" A woman peered around the door, flashing a dazzling, impress-the-important-client smile. "I'm Lia Lafite, Alex's business partner and a big fan." She cast a steely look of death at Alex, and I found my smile growing in response to his annoyed look. She turned back to me. "It's a pleasure to meet you." Alex scowled as Lia gushed over me. "If you'll excuse us for one moment, I just need to consult with Alex."

Maybe she could be my lawyer. Alex pushed up from his desk, pausing and stretching out his leg before bearing weight on it and following her. They didn't close the door properly, so I listened in.

"What the hell? I thought you were past this. Stop being such a dick to Meri Scott," Lia snapped.

"I'm not up for dealing with anyone else's emotional problems right now, and Meredith Scott has *emotional problem* written all over her."

I shifted my chair so I could see through the crack in the door, watching Marie rush over from the front desk to join them.

"Al—"

"Wait a second. How the hell do you know what I'm being?"

Lia shrugged. "Marie reversed the intercom. Don't fuck this up, Alex."

"If you were listening, you know there's something seriously wrong with her," he said, flinging an arm towards the door and me. Hey! There was nothing wrong with me. That wasn't justified. "I just spent twenty minutes with her, and all we've established is I'm a lawyer. I don't have a bloody clue what she *really* needs a criminal lawyer for."

"She split up with her boyfriend," Marie said. Lia and Alex stared at her. "She let it slip when she arrived." I had? Damn, I needed to get a grip. Loose lips sold newspapers…

"So what?" Alex snapped. "Unless she killed him or beat the crap out of him, that has bugger all to do with me." This guy was a prick—why were they all kid-gloving him?

"She needs you," Marie said.

"It'll be good for you," Lia added. "We've been cutting you a lot of slack since you came back to work, Alex, but it's time for you to step up now."

"She doesn't need me. She needs a relationship counsellor," he responded, but I could hear the resignation in his voice.

"She needs a friend."

"I'm a lawyer, not rent-a-buddy. I have enough problems of my own without borrowing anyone else's."

"I have first-hand experience that being a lawyer doesn't preclude you from being a bloody good friend," Lia said. "You know better than most that sometimes help is the hardest thing to ask for, especially for a seemingly strong, independent woman."

“Fuck. You,” he snarled. “I can’t believe you’d go there.”

“I can’t believe I had to.” Lia shrugged off his rage like it was nothing.

It wasn’t nothing. Clearly, he didn’t want me any more than I wanted him.

Grabbing my tote and coat, I pushed through the office door, seeing the whole of Lia for the first time, taking in her pinstriped suit, crisp white shirt and red cravat. “You look like a real lawyer.”

“Seriously, just because she is wearing a suit?” Alex snapped.

Marie whipped between us, holding a clipboard. Where had she unearthed that, an archaeological dig? No one used clipboards these days. “If you just sign here and here?” she asked.

“Fine,” I agreed, “but I want her.” I pointed at Lia.

“If you just sign here and here.” Marie pointed to a couple of spots, and I signed with a flourish.

“Great. So, I’ve retained you?” I turned to Lia with a

huge smile.

“Nope, sorry. You’ve got Alex.”

What?

No.

My shoulders sagged.

His shoulders sagged.

The disappointment was obviously mutual

My phone buzzed, cutting off my complaint. A reminder popped up, telling me I had to meet Tony, my agent. “Sorry, I’m late. I’ve got to meet my agent.”

CHAPTER 4

You Ruined My Relationship, I Won't Let You Ruin My Career!

Half an hour later, Tony leant across his massive mahogany desk, sunlight glinting off his steel grey hair. "I've been talking with the US networks, Meri. They're still keen on taking the show stateside."

I frowned at his tone. He didn't sound as pleased as he should, given how hard we'd been working to get the US networks interested. A buzz of nerves built in my stomach. "But…?"

"Well, they loved the episodes we sent, and your success at the NTAs really made them sit up."

Good.

"But they still have reservations about your personality."

My emotions, already close to the surface, flared. My throat tightened. “My p-personality?”

“Yes.” Tony didn’t pull his punches. There was no room for sensitivity in the television industry.

“What’s wrong with my personality?” Maybe I was missing something. Was this why Tom and Talith hadn’t cared about hurting me?

“They think you come across as too perfect, pretty and privileged, and US guests and the audience won’t be able to relate to you.”

“Privileged?” I raked a hand through my shoulder-length hair. “Privileged. My father died when I was nine years old. My mother lurched between self-pity, depression and deadbeat boyfriends.” Now was not the time to realise I’d followed in her footsteps with the deadbeat boyfriend. “Our house was repossessed.” My pitch was rising closer to a screech with each disclosure. “We lived in sheltered accommodation—a grotty, mouldy, one-bed flat—in the Welsh equivalent of the projects. By the time I was twelve, I was raising myself. I had to get a job so we could afford to pay our bills and eat and—”

“And buy second-hand clothes,” Tony finished. “I know, honey.”

What he didn't know about were the times my mother left me home alone for days and nights at a time when she went off with whichever boyfriend was on the scene, or the week when she'd gone on holiday with her latest toy-boy, leaving me at thirteen to fend for myself, with no money or food in the cupboards.

"What the hell do these people want?" I jumped from my chair, pacing around his plushly carpeted office. I worked hard. Yes, I was in the public eye, but I was a private person. I didn't like to put my personal life out there for everyone to pick over. I'd been planning to tell Tony about Talith and Tom, but no way was I going to now. Not when I knew he'd manipulate it into a media event to catch the eye of the US networks.

Tony rose too, turning to stare out of the window at the tour boats on the Thames. He didn't have to say anything. He thought I should spill my guts. We'd had this conversation, or variations on it, a hundred times over the eight years since I'd signed with him. "I'm not going to hack off a limb or leak a sex tape just to please the American execs." No one looked good in sex tapes; there was no such thing as a flattering angle in homemade porn. Besides, Tom and I hadn't ever done anything exciting enough to warrant making one to leak.

"Just as well… limb loss might not harm our chances, given the too-pretty issue, but the US networks would not forgive a sex tape," Tony joked. "Anyway, I don't think it needs to come to that."

Damn right it didn't. "I'm bloody good at what I do. That should be enough." But we both knew it wasn't.

"We just need to get more of your personality across, your compassion, bring out some of the tough stuff from your childhood. I'll set up some magazine interviews. Your job is to play up your past."

"But—"

"It's nothing people can't find out with a few internet searches. Most of it has already been published before, but never in one article, and not with an interview from Meri Scott. I know you don't like to talk about it, but if you really want this, you have to play the game. It's not like I'm telling you to lie—just play it up, paint the picture, put some emotion behind it."

"I'm not—"

He didn't give me time to push back. "If you want *The Meri Scott Show* to go to the US, you need to put yourself out there. There are lots of excellent presenters, some of them with grittier backstories than you, some of them cheaper, some willing to do whatever—and I mean *whatever*—it takes to get a chance like this. You have to have something else that makes you stand out."

"And a successful show, three NTAs and a great reputation—" I tried to cut in, but he bulldozed over me.

"You need something that makes people relate to you, and you *have* that in your childhood. You have the fairy-tale rags-to-riches story people love."

I cringed at his description, fairy tales sucked when you were living them. "Fine. I'll do an interview, but only one."

"Great." He turned back to his desk, picking up his phone, getting straight onto making the arrangements. "I'll pitch it as an exclusive. They'll be fighting over it."

"I'm not lying, or *exaggerating*, Tony."

"Fine." He paused mid-dial. "But Meri?" I stopped on my way out of his office. "You need to draw comparisons between you, your guests and their circumstances on the show. Show you can relate and aren't judging them from on high."

"Parallels—like what, Tony? I don't do drugs. I know who my daddy was and who the father would be if I was pregnant now, so no need for DNA." And Talith and Tom didn't need a lie detector test. I'd caught them in the act, and they had no shame about it.

"Show you're human. That you haven't led a charmed life. Let them see there's more to you then a pretty face with a supportive family."

"Ha!" Yep. Such a supportive family.

"What?" He scanned my face, his head tilted to the left. "Are you okay?"

"I just—" I cut myself off. Tony was dedicated to my career, and his ten percent. I couldn't guarantee he wouldn't take anything I told him about my shitty ex and mother and use it to further my career and apologise for any upset later. In fact, I *knew* he would. I'd seen him do it before to other clients. "It's fine. I'm fine. Everything is fine."

CHAPTER 5

You Used Me For My Money, Now It's Time For You To Pay!

"I'm a solicitor, not a pizza delivery boy."

I switched the phone to hands-free, tossed it onto my bed and rolled my eyes, for some reason amused by Alex's surliness. It was a wonder he had any clients. Then again, he was a defence lawyer. His clients were desperate and probably not bothered about his attitude.

"I don't do home delivery."

"What?" I yanked the last of Tom's designer suits and shirts off coat hangers and stuffed them into black bin bags.

"It's Friday night, Ms Scott," he added, as if I didn't already know.

"And…?"

"And I don't work on the weekend."

"That's ridiculous. People only need legal advice during office hours on a weekday?"

"You don't film your show on a weekend. So why would you need my advice?" Shit. I forgot I was going with that ruse. "Unless that was just an excuse all along…"

"Ah, no. No. That's totally what I want you for—"

"Then it can wait until Monday," he interrupted.

"It can't. I hired you because of the show, but that's not why I need you now."

"Have you been arrested?" His tone sharpened.

"No." He was obsessed with me being arrested. Tom was coming around to collect his stuff, and I needed a credible witness, just in case… It was like I'd been stuck in an out-of-body experience since I walked in on them shagging. If anyone had asked beforehand what I would do in those circumstance, I'd have said kill one of them or cry… I hadn't done either.

Yet.

"Detained by the police for questioning?"

"No!" But that didn't make it any less important. I

snagged my phone and stomped into the living room.

"Are you about to be?"

"How should I know?" There was the whole cress thing. It had been nearly a week since I'd sowed the seeds of revenge. They should have germinated by now. So, I needed someone else to witness my *surprise*, just in case suspicion ever fell on me, and who better than a lawyer? "That's the sort of advice you're supposed to give me."

"And I will, on a weekday, when you've explained what's going on. I have plans for tonight."

"It's an emergency." I swiped an array of tacky holiday mementos Tom had collected and lined up on the windowsill into a box on the floor. The silence stretched. "I—I don't have anyone else I can call." I had over two million friends, according to Facebook and Twitter, and was regularly pictured partying with celebrities, but in reality, my friendship circle was small. I'd learnt early on if I didn't want people selling stories about me to the press, I had to keep my "circle of trust" close and keep other friendships superficial. So, my CoT had consisted of my mother, Tom and Jenn…

Now, it was just Jenn.

Unfortunately, Jenn wasn't back from holiday. I'd tried calling, but her mobile was switched off; money was tight as a single mother, so she was probably trying to avoid the roaming charges.

He sighed again. If he kept up like this, he'd be hyperventilating soon. "Fine, tell me where you live and I'll swing by and pick you up."

"Pick me up?"

"I just told you. I have plans. If you haven't been arrested and aren't in imminent danger of being taken into custody, then you're going to have to fit into my plans. Which means I'll pick you up and we can talk about whatever you want on the drive to the restaurant and over dinner."

"I don't want to go to dinner with you. I just want you to come here." It paid to be prepared, and he was my witness of choice.

"And I want food. So, you either come with me and we eat, and you can talk, or you can wait until office hours on Monday and schedule an appointment through Marie."

"But—"

"It's called compromise."

"I'm not hungry." I dragged the huge cardboard box across the laminate flooring, chucking in DVD box sets, a couple of iPads, weights, shoes, books… anything I came across that was Tom's or my mother's.

"You look hungry."

"I'm small-boned!" I snapped, glaring at the phone. "And I'm *not* eating with you."

"I've already given you the options. One: come out with me. You can just sit and watch me eat and pretend you aren't hungry whilst telling me about your urgent need for legal counsel. Or option two: wait until Monday and hope I have an appointment free."

Why couldn't I have retained Lia? She seemed nice. She would have come straight over and wouldn't have forced me to go to dinner with her. "I paid you a retainer."

"No, you didn't."

Well, I hadn't actually paid him anything yet, but the intent was there. "I signed a contract."

"You should check with Marie. As I recall, she handled the paperwork. All I know is any agreement we may have only covers office hours, not eight p.m. on a Friday night."

Clearly, he was one of those hungry-angry—*hangry*—people. "But it's an emergency and you're my lawyer." I was starting to whine.

"You asked me to be an adviser on your show, not a lawyer for you. They are two very different things."

Why did he have to be so difficult? It wasn't like I was asking him for his firstborn. "What do you want me to do, beg?"

"Explain to me what this emergency is and why I should give up my plans?"

Well, that wasn't very professional, but sadly, I didn't have anyone else I could call. "I've split up with my boyfriend, and—"

"I'm *not* a relationship counsellor. I'm a tired and hungry man. I'm not good at tea and sympathy. Believe me, my track record could not be worse." There was something dark and sad in his tone. "Don't you have any friends you can call?"

"Of course, I have friends," I snapped. Just not here right now. And not many flesh-and-blood friends… Well, just Jenn, really. I had another best friend, Ffion, but we'd fallen out a few years ago. She would totally have backed me up. She'd have built a bonfire out of Tom's belongings. "I have more than two and a half million friends and followers on Twitter and Instagram and Facebook." There. I bet he struggled to break double figures on friends.

"So, call one of them; out of that many, at least one of them should be free even on a Friday night. Unlike me," he responded, "Or if it's an emergency, call your mother."

Call my mother? Right. Yes. I'd get right onto that… "He's coming to pick his stuff up tonight, and I, ah… I need a lawyer here when he comes."

"You're scared of him?"

"Well, no, not really." Why would I be scared of him? He'd cowered behind Talith last time he felt the need for protection.

"Is there a chance he may be violent?" Alex asked.

Tom? No. He was way too lazy and worried someone might hit back and damage his face. But Alex seemed to be paying more attention. Maybe I should pretend Tom was the aggressive sort to get him to come around? No, that was too shitty—even in my desperate state, I knew that.

"Because if there is, you should call the police."

What?

What a git!

I'd just pulled my best feeble, trembly voiced *woman in need of help* routine and he blew me off with *call your mum or the police.* "Look, I'm here all alone and I need some support, *legal* support. Please."

"You said he wasn't violent, and from what I've heard about your show, you can look after yourself." The concern in his voice belied his words. He was definitely starting to worry.

"I have bodyguards on my show."

"Then call one of them. Or do they not work weekends either?"

They didn't, but that wasn't relevant. He was supposed to stop me getting arrested, and he couldn't do that if he wasn't here. "How would you feel if this was your mother… or… or do you have sisters?" I took his tense silence as confirmation. "How would you feel if this was your sister, being left alone when she needed help?" An awkward silence stretched, before the phone cut out.

"Shit!" What happened there? Were we cut off or had he hung up on me? I pressed redial. The phone rang and rang and rang. He couldn't have gone far from his phone in the thirty milliseconds since the line cut. He should be able to answer straight away.

His “What?” was neither friendly nor professional, but I didn’t have the time or sensitivity to pussyfoot around him.

“Imagine I’m your sister.”

“No!”

“Do you have any sisters?”

I could hear rustling and movement over the phone. Was he getting changed? It didn’t sound like he was giving his full attention to the conversation. “Thre— *Two*. Which is why I’m not falling for this damsel-in-distress crap. You can’t sucker me in with tears, tantrums or period pain either. I’ve had thirty-four years of it. I’m immune.”

“If this is the sort of support you give them, I feel sorry for your thre-two sisters!” I snapped.

A harsh breath sounded over the line, then nothing. Had he hung up again?

Shit.

I needed to change tactics. You caught more flies with honey then vinegar… but he was a lawyer, so I replaced honey with money. “Fine, I’ll pay you double time.”

“Dinner.” His one-word response sounded final.

The guy had absolutely no flex whatsoever. Of all the solicitors in the country, and there were hundreds of thousands of the heartless gits, why did I have to end up with him? "Fine. I'll come to dinner."

* * * * *

"It's a nice flat. It's got a cosy feel to it."

Half an hour later, Alex seemed surprised as he wandered around my three-bedroom flat, dressed casually in jeans, boots, a white t-shirt and a brown leather jacket. He scanned the rooms, looking out the windows at the gardens and the cobbled court yard. "You struck me as more of a Primrose Hill type, hanging out with the fashionistas like Kate Moss."

His tone wasn't complimentary. "Not unless I'm working. Besides, she got married and moved to the country." Then divorced and came back, but really, who cared?

He shrugged, nodding towards the pile of boxes and bags. His eyes lit up and he bent down to dig through one of the boxes. "Is this a MOXO X-1 portable wireless levitating speaker?" He held the black speaker ball in one hand, moving it around with long, thick fingers as he examined it from every angle.

"Ah… I guess." Tom was always buying electronic gadgets. He *had* to have the latest tech. I never really paid any attention to them. "It's a speaker and it kind of floats above a box thing."

"Is it good? I'm thinking of getting one."

"Tom likes it." Which made me want to pitch it out of the window and stomp the shattered remains into the cobbles below.

Unaware of my thoughts, Alex carefully placed it back into the box and continued his exploration. "Is this all his? It looks like something, or *every*thing, off a bachelor's top twenty must-have gadgets list." He looked at me over his shoulder. "Does he work in IT?

"No."

"Finance?"

"No." He cocked a brow as he continued probing Tom's box of gadgets. I reluctantly added, "He doesn't have a steady job."

His eyebrows rose. "Inherited wealth?"

“No.”

He sat back on his heels, head tipped to one side, watching me intently for a moment, then scanned the boxes and bags again. “No job, no money…” He pursed his full lips in a silent whistle and gave a slow shake of his head. “He saw you coming. How long were you going out together?”

“I’m not talking about this,” I snapped, feeling like a fool.

“He couldn’t have accumulated all of this in just a couple of months. There are several generations of iPad here, but you seem like an intelligent woman, so I’m thinking you would have seen through him in”—his eyes narrowed, and I found myself holding my breath waiting for his assessment—“two years? Three?”

“Seven,” I responded grudgingly.

“You stuck with him for *seven* years, without any commitment?” Clearly his sisters would’ve expected an engagement ring after six months of going steady.

“We were committed. We lived together.”

“You let him *live off* you and didn’t even ask for a

commitment." He made me sound like an idiot.

"Living together *is* a commitment."

"Yeah, right," He scoffed. "Living together is cheap, or in this case, I'm guessing, free. For him."

My cheeks warmed with embarrassment. God, maybe it hadn't just been the last few months Tom had been playing me for a fool. Maybe that was his plan from day one. Maybe everything I'd felt and thought he'd felt was a lie and I was a gullible fool.

"He was using you and you let him." Alex chucked a couple of game cases he'd been looking at into a box and straightened up.

"Marriage isn't the only commitment these days," I said, sounding desperate even to my own ears.

His smile held a mocking edge. "He told you that, didn't he?"

Yes. "Fine. If you know everything about commitment and relationships"—I jabbed a finger in his direction—"you tell me what it was."

"Going out with someone, regardless of the number

of years, isn't a commitment. It's a trial run."

"A trial run for what?"

"Are you sure you want to hear this?"

Now he asked? No, I wasn't sure, but I didn't *not* want to hear either. I needed all the tips I could get about relationships, because I clearly didn't have a clue. "Why ask? You haven't held back your opinions so far."

He shrugged, parking his bum on the windowsill. "The first couple of years are to see if he actually wants to commit. If you aren't engaged after that, it's just somewhere to lay his head whilst he's checking out alternatives."

I blinked, trying to process his take on my relationship. What I had thought was as a long-term commitment was really just Tom looking for something, or someone, better? "What about moving in, sharing a life, monogamy—surely that's a sign of commitment?"

"That's convenience. If a guy wants someone to be available whenever he's interested and wants the perks of not having to travel or work for it, then he moves in without commitment and throws in the monogamy illusion." *The monogamy illusion?* "Women love the whole monogamy thing. Meanwhile, he's probably just too lazy to cheat."

"Ridiculous." But I couldn't stop myself from wondering if that was why Tom had ended up with my moth—*Talith* in our bed. He hadn't had to travel or make an effort to get what he wanted. My heart was starting to pound, and I felt a little breathless. "If dating is waiting for a better offer and monogamy is sexual laziness, what is being engaged?"

He smiled, laughter lines fanning out around his eyes, a dimple creasing his right cheek as he flashed perfect white teeth. "A placeholder for commitment." He didn't give me time to comment. "Marriage is the only real commitment, and even then, sometimes people plan in loopholes."

Seriously? I was not going to ask about loopholes. This was depressing. "You should come on my show and share these… these *insights* with my audience. I'm sure they'd love you."

He shrugged. "It's not really my sort of programme. But you can try tempting me with your best offer when we go for dinner."

"About that—"

"You cancel," he interrupted, jabbing an index finger in my direction, before turning it towards his own chest. "I cancel." He cocked an eyebrow. "No dinner, no legal advice."

"But I'm not hungry," I whined. He eyed me sceptically. "I just have a fast metabolism." I pre-empted any comment on my weight. And I starved myself six days a week and worked out two hours a day minimum, but those were the demands of the industry I was in. I had to look my best. Even an ounce of weight gain showed up on TV.

He shrugged, pushing up from the windowsill and moving towards me. He lifted a hand, tucking a lock of black hair back behind my ear. Warmth bloomed from the trace of his fingertips. "You need to eat, Meredith Scott. You're worryingly thin."

I slapped his hand, spinning away from his touch. "And you're rude and annoying." I sucked in a breath, tamping down my temper. I am not an angry person. Tom and I were together for seven years, and until that last night, we never had a cross word. I made a concerted effort to lower my voice, which had risen to a low screech. “Anyway, I’m not skinny. I’m athletic.”

He snorted. “You are scarily skinny.”

“Yeah, well, you’ve got a limp,” I retorted childishly.

His face blanked. He shifted, stepping back to lean against the windowsill. “Very observant.”

I felt like a bitch. I hadn’t meant to hurt him.

Okay, I had, but not really—I was just hitting out because he was poking at a sore point and I wanted him to stop. “What happened?”

“This isn’t one of your TV shows,” he snapped, crossing to the door. “I don’t have to answer your questions.”

CHAPTER 6

You Cheated With My Mother - Get Out Of My House!

"What time is this ex of yours getting here, Ms Scott?" Alex looked up at me from the courtyard.

I fought an eye roll at his "Ms Scott". "Call me Meri." It had been nearly fifteen minutes and he was still sulking about me questioning his limp. "He should be here any minute." I reached for another bag of Tom's designer clothes, throwing it out of the second-floor window, leaving Alex to catch, or not. I didn't care if the bags split, scattering Tom's clothes across the courtyard and flowerbeds. He'd just have to learn how to use a washing machine. Talith had never mastered the skill, so she wouldn't be able to help him.

Alex grunted, catching the bag and piling it with the others. "So, what made you see the light and split up with the commitment-phobe freeloader?"

I stuck my head back out the window, checking no one else was around and listening in. "I think we already established there won't be any sharing of personal confidences between us, *Mr* Gordon." I might have had to call on him for support, but we weren't friends.

He smiled up at me, flashing a beautiful dimple-crease. "Dumped you for someone else, did he?" I flinched at the direct hit. "You know, if he actually made the effort to find someone else, he'll probably marry this one."

The insensitive bastard!

I grabbed a five-kilogram weight from Tom's collection and hefted it over to the window.

"Ah, ah, ah. I'll take that." Vic, the wiry Irish residence manager, stepped up behind me, sweeping the weight from my hand and placing it back into the box with the others, before heading for the door. "We wouldn't want anyone to get hurt now, would we?"

Alex's laughter was drowned out by the sound of a car.

"Who the hell's he?"

I ran downstairs, arriving in the courtyard in time to watch as Tom jumped out of the Audi, strutting around the car, chest puffed, arms swinging, bounding over to where Alex stood beside his stuff.

“None of your business,” I responded, moving to stand beside Alex.

Tom shrugged and turned to his things, frowning and prodding around like a granny at a garage sale on pension day. Time ticked by, and he didn’t make any move to start gathering his stuff and leave. It was getting close to nine o’clock. Alex’s stomach growled noisily. “Here, let me help you load up your car.”

Tom ignored his offer, turning on me. “Where’s my Wii?”

I shrugged. “Vic liked it, so I gave it to him.” I’d have offered Alex the floaty speaker if he hadn’t gotten personal about my weight.

Tom stormed over to me in three angry paces, towering over me. “You can’t do that. It’s mine. That’s… that’s theft.”

He was so close that his stale coffee breath blasted

me in the face and his chest grazed my breasts. I felt… nothing much, besides mild revulsion that any part of him was touching me.

It was odd. I thought I'd be all trembly and upset, or stab-y and angry about the whole *date night* with Talith as my replacement, but nope. "I paid for it."

"And the rest," Alex muttered, stepping between us, herding Tom back with a hand to his chest. "Ease up there, man."

"It was my stuff. She gave it to me." Tom turned to Alex, looking for an ally.

"Prove it," I said over Alex's shoulder. "Besides, you always said you liked Vic. Think of it as a leaving gift. A thank you for all the things he's done for you." Actually, I gave it to him as a thank you for offering to help haul Tom's shit downstairs so he didn't have to come into my flat to get it.

Tom glared at me, making a visible effort to pull himself back from a full-blown temper tantrum. "Your mother says *hi*," he said snidely. "She wants to know if you've calmed down and are ready to talk about this like an adult yet."

He wasn't even pretending he was sorry, or that he and Talith weren't together. He was making out it was my fault and digging for a reaction. I wouldn't give him the satisfaction. "I was never not calm." If I hadn't maintained my calm, I'd have clawed his face off. "I just don't appreciate coming home to find you shagging her in my bed." Nor did I appreciate her wearing my second favourite Christian Louboutin shoes whilst they did it.

"Jesus!" Alex physically recoiled. "He shagged your mother? Who would brag about that? It's… nasty."

"Talith is more than just Meri's mother," Tom defended. "She's a person with feelings and dreams and rights…"

I was pretty sure that was a quote—with a different person's name—from an episode *Dr. Phil* or some badly scripted romance movie. I should probably be pissed off, but worry over being caught committing vandalism, combined with a strange calm blanketing my emotions, left me in a peculiar Zen-like state. "Well, this has been… *interesting*, but it's time you loaded up and left, Tom."

Alex hefted up a box, shoving it at Tom and letting go. Tom caught it before it could drop to the ground. Alex grabbed a couple of bin bags and headed past him to his car. I reached into the front of the Audi—I didn't want to help Tom, but the quicker he loaded up, the sooner he'd leave—pressing the button to lower the hood. And then stared in open-mouthed amazement.

It was… it was like the health-nuts cress-y version of Willie Wonka's chocolate factory. A thick carpet of bright green cress covered the entire back of the car, seats, foot wells—*everything*. "Ah, Tom… You seem to have grass growing in the back of your car," I said. "Isn't that taking carbon neutral a little too far?"

"It's not grass," he snapped. "It's cress."

"Really?" *I'd never have guessed!* "Here I thought you were more into sowing wild oats than cress," I said. Alex laughed, a deep, rich boom of sound that stroked over me. Tom didn't. "You know what you should get for that?" I asked, on a roll.

"No." He looked at me eagerly, like he thought I could, or would, fix it for him. He loved this car.

"Eggs," I said, straight-faced. "Hardboiled eggs go really well with cress." Alex crowded behind me, a black bin bag of Tom's belongings in each hand, staring into the back of the car in horrified fascination. “In fact, you could go the whole way with the environmentally friendly schtick and get yourself a couple of chickens. You could keep them in the boot of the car and—”

“Did you do this?” Tom snapped. It was so far outside of something I would ever do that I could understand his surprise. If I hadn’t been there, sowing the seeds of revenge, I wouldn’t have believed it was me either.

“Meee?” Gasp, eyelash flutter. I faked innocent surprise. Neither Tom nor Alex seemed to be buying it.

My stomach pitched, and sweat began to bead my brow.

Shit, keep calm.

Keep calm.

They couldn’t prove anything.

Alex’s eyes narrowed, his expression going tight. There was a reason why I was a chat show host and my acting career hadn’t made it past adverts for cheese strings and acne cream. I went for deflection instead, frowning. “Cress seeds need a *damp* environment to germinate. You left the top down all night again, didn’t you?”

"I forgot," Tom snarled, immediately on the defensive. Shortly after I'd bought him the car, he'd gone out and left the top down on one of the wettest days of the year. It had cost me a small fortune to get the interior professionally cleaned and dried. This time, it wasn't my problem. For his sake, I hoped he'd found some acting work, otherwise who knew how he'd be able to afford the… harvesting.

I whipped out my mobile phone. "You don't mind if I take a picture for Instagram, do you?"

Tom knocked my hand out of the way, earning a growl of warning from Alex, but not before I got my picture. "You didn't answer my question," Tom said. "Did you do this?"

"Me?" I flattened a palm against to my chest, feeling my heart pound. "Such a nasty allegation." I shook my head sadly, hamming it up. "And without proof, too. You should be careful what you say. Slander is such a costly thing." I turned to Alex. "By the way, I don't think I introduced you to my lawyer, Alex Gordon."

Tom paled.

I nudged Alex out of the way with a sharp elbow to

the stomach, when he stepped forward, hand held out politely, ready to shake with Tom, like we were at a garden party.

I plucked a couple of shoots of cress, popping them into my mouth. “Hmm. Yummy. So plentiful and mustardy. Is it organic?”

Who’d have thought such a small, impulsive action would give me such pleasure? It was almost worth the nightmares and stress about going to prison. “I’ve got some lovely fresh brown bread upstairs, and it’ll only take five minutes to hardboil some eggs if you want to make a sandwich before you leave.”

CHAPTER 7

Lie Detector Results: Make or Break!

"Next time you're planning some childish prank, leave me out of it." Twenty minutes after Tom had driven off, I sat opposite Alex at a candlelit table for two in Ottomans. We'd taken so long to see Tom off that he'd lost his reservations. He still wouldn't give up on the whole dinner thing, though, so I'd called Ottomans and used my name to secure a table on no notice.

"I don't know what you're talking about." I didn't even convince myself with that feeble denial. Still, I wasn't planning a next time. I'd nearly given myself an ulcer worrying about being arrested over the cress incident.

"Cress," Alex responded flatly, and took a sip of his beer.

"No thanks, I prefer the tabbouleh salad here." I chuckled. He didn't. I sighed.

I needed a wingman. I'd never been alone before. I needed a sounding board until Jenn came back in a couple of days and he was all I had.

His eyes narrowed. "You know exactly what I'm talking about."

I sighed again. He was sucking the joy out of what was a really gratifying experience. "You were laughing about it half an hour ago."

"I didn't say it wasn't funny." He set his beer on the table and leant forward, his intense eyes capturing mine. I found myself leaning towards him. "Just that I do not want to be involved in your immature, publicity-seeking games."

I jerked back. The last thing I wanted was media attention. It was a one-off, spur-of-the-moment thing. I just didn't want to be pushed aside and forgotten, like an unwanted present. I wanted Tom and his older-model girlfriend to at least be inconvenienced. "I don—"

"Don't bother denying it. The timing is too convenient."

"It could've been anyone; one of my fans, for example. Not all of them like the fact I have—*had* a boyfriend. Or teenagers taking advantage of the opportunity when they found a sports car with the top down."

He frowned, but I could see the cress seed of uncertainty had been planted. “Hmm, whatever, but don’t do it again or this relationship is over.”

“We don’t have a relationship. This isn’t a date,” I said, even as a tickle of… awareness blossomed in my stomach.

Alex settled back in his chair, idly straightening his cutlery. “It’s Friday night and we’re having dinner in a nice restaurant with a candle on the table… It could be classed as a date.”

“It’s business.”

He shrugged as if he didn’t care either way. “I don’t work weekends.”

God! I was not getting back into that argument again. Nor was I going to allow anything or anyone to take away the enjoyment of my cressy revenge.

He cleared his throat, drawing me out of my musings. “I guess you can argue reasonable doubt on the cress… Where the hell do you even get cress seeds from?”

I copied his earlier shrug. “How should I know?”

“Don’t overdo it, Meredith.” He levelled a cold, hard lawyer stare at me… and I crumbled.

“Of course, if it was a life-and-death situation and I

had to find cress seeds—"

"Not many people could use the words life, death and cress in the same sentence." He absently rubbed a fist against his thigh, pressing hard against the muscle, as if his leg pained him.

I shrugged again, still wallowing in amusement. "As I was saying, if it was life and death—"

"And cress." His lips twitched.

"—and cress," I said, "I might look in Sainsbury's just down Wilton Road. In the vegetable seed rack. Next to where they sell the lottery tickets, across from the chicken rotisserie."

Thank God for godchildren and nursery school teachers who thought making eggshell heads with cress hair was educational. I would definitely thank Jenn when she got back from holiday. If it hadn't been for her asking me to pick up the seeds, I would never have realised what I needed to do to reclaim control of my life and happy emotions.

"Of course, I couldn't say for sure they would *have* cress seeds there, but that's where I would start my search.

If I needed some." I blinked slowly, trying to make my eyes wide and innocent.

"You wouldn't win any awards for this piece of acting."

The waiter arrived, silently sliding plates of meze off a tray held by another waiter and onto the table between us.

"I can't believe I've just let a pretty face use me as some sort of alibi and I'm laughing about it."

I couldn't help preening a little when he said I was attractive. It made a change from him calling me skinny. Fluttery butterflies of nervous pleasure took wing in my stomach. It was a long time since anyone—who I didn't pay/house/didn't want anything from me—had paid me a genuine, off-the-cuff compliment. It made me feel… hopeful, like maybe he meant it, that maybe I wasn't just a replaceable source of funding. If I could trust him…

The doubts immediately started to build. He was practically on the payroll as my lawyer, after all. Maybe he flattered all his female clients. He hadn't seemed like the type. He wasn't good at it, but you could never tell. "I bet you say that to all your clients."

His eyes shot to mine, surprise clear. "Nope. Some of them are really ugly. Besides, I'm not interested in a sexual harassment charge. Now my *dates*, on the other hand…"

I shook my head, spooning a tiny amount of salad and one olive onto my plate when he gestured towards the food in the centre of the table, muttering, "Just like Tom with the false flattery."

"I'm nothing like your *motherfucking*—and I mean that figuratively and literally—ex," Alex whispered, mindful of the other people in the restaurant. "I don't use women or cheat on them."

"Whoa! You're kind of intense." Okay. So, now clearly wasn't the time to check if I'd broken any major laws with my cressy revenge. I'd put reasonable doubt into his mind with the idea it could be a zealous fan or prankster teens. So, now I needed to wait, to put enough time between him witnessing evidence of my revenge and me seeking his legal advice… for a "show story".

I scowled at the array of food he'd selected. I'd gone for salads and low fat. He'd gone for meat, more meat and a selection of carbs with a side of bread.

"So, how long ago did you two split up?" He ploughed his way through his selection of fat, grease and calories. I watched, with a major case of food envy, whilst nibbling the lettuce from my fattoush salad, *hold the croutons, dressing on the side.*

“Six days.” I eyed the quarter of a dolma I was going to allow myself. The vine leaves were stuffed with white rice and pine nuts. I could only have a small bite if I didn’t want to bloat. So, I was going to make it last as long as possible.

Alex’s eyebrows rose. He forked up the second last piece of basturma, consuming it in one massive bite. I watched him chew, smile and swallow, licking his lips to capture every greasy morsel of deliciousness. My tongue snuck out, mirroring his action. My empty stomach cramped with longing. I was so tempted to eat some.

I forced myself to remember how I’d looked in the plum-coloured suit on the clip of my show they’d used on the NTAs last week. Bloated. Tubby. I sighed, turning my attention back to my practically calorie-neutral fattoush salad minus dressing and croutons.

“You’re a good-looking, intelligent, successful woman.” Oh! Another compliment, even if it was delivered in a *but* tone. “But”—here it came—“from what I’ve seen and heard, Tom didn’t work and wouldn’t commit.” He shook his head. “As emasculating as it is to admit it, he must have been hung like a donkey and porn-star-good in bed."

I snorted. "Nope, and not even on his most inspired days." Like Christmas and my birthday, when he let me choose the sexual position from his full repertoire of "the usual" or missionary.

"What the hell did you see in him for *seven* years?"

"Are you blind?"

He shrugged. "So, he's okay looking, for a total shit."

"Gorgeous," I corrected him. Tom might be a lazy, lying, cheating bastard, but no one with functioning vision could deny his looks. He was like Chris Hemsworth's hotter, younger, way buffer brother.

"Maybe." Alex shrugged, "But I've scraped stuff off the bottom of my shoe with a better personality." He waited, clearly expecting me to say something more. I didn't. He sighed, one of those martyred men sighs when a woman does something they find inexplicable. "And he slept with your *mother*. Which is about as ugly as a man can get." He dragged some bread through the bowl of hummus, before fixing his eyes on me, waiting for a response.

"And it appears he still is." I shuddered. Tom's looks *were* a little tarnished when I remembered, but maybe that was just the angle when he looked back over his shoulder and his "come" face. "Can I sue him?"

"For what?"

"I don't know." I pointed at Alex with my fork. "You're the lawyer."

"The more I talk to you, the more I understand why you need a… *legal adviser* for your show." His hesitation and emphasis on "legal adviser" underscored his doubt in what I wanted him for… which was worrying. "However, as I keep telling you, I'm a *criminal* lawyer. I don't sue people. And whilst shagging your girlfriend's mother should be a crime, it isn't."

I ignored him. A lawyer was a lawyer. They all had the same training. They only gave themselves specialities so they could charge more money. "Breach of promise, or something?"

"I think we already covered commitment and promises, or lack of them, earlier. Tom didn't make any, and you didn't ask him to." Strong white teeth ripped off a bite of hummus-covered bread.

I pushed salad around my plate with my fork. "We'd been going out for seven years, lived together for nearly as many, and… and—"

"And he was screwing your mother."

Ouch. That was blunt. He really didn't care about my feelings at all.

Usually, when people realised who I was, they were nice to me, at least to my face, even if it was just because I was famous and they wanted something from me. Alex, however, had been insulting me from the moment we met.

"Surely, that makes us common-law husband and wife?"

"What it makes you is foolish." He sipped his beer.

"You're not being very nice." Actually, he was being a total arsehole, but I needed him, so I was trying to be polite.

He shrugged. "You're not paying me enough to be nice."

"How much does nice cost?"

He laughed, then jerked as if surprised by his amusement. "You couldn't afford it."

Hmm. Maybe not, with all my dependents and outgoings, but Tony was talking serious money from the

US network. If we took *The Meri Scott Show* stateside, I'd become a very rich woman.

"Besides, I'm only nice to *clients* on weekdays—"

"Between nine a.m. and six p.m.," I finished, rolling my eyes dramatically.

He smiled. "See, now you're getting to know me."

"I don't want to get to know you." I wanted to make sure I wouldn't get arrested.

He sat back. "And yet here we are, on a date."

"It's not a date." I almost screeched the words.

"It sure as hell isn't a common-law marriage."

He was laughing at me! "It's just a working dinner," I snarled. "And you practically had to blackmail me into it."

"We haven't talked work."

Frustrated, I gave in, stabbed the last piece of basturma off his plate and shoved it into my mouth, glorying in the spicy, greasy sausage heaven. "Hmm." Good. So very, very good. I savoured the flavour, chewing until there was nothing left, then licking my lips to be sure I caught every iota of taste. Sighing, I slowly opened my eyes, done savouring. I'd spend an extra half-hour in the gym for the next three days.

It was so worth it.

Alex's eyes were fixed on my lips. I touched them nervously, checking I wasn't drooling.

He waved the waiter over. "We'll have another plate of the basturma."

"No!"

"Yes," he said firmly. The waiter rushed off to do his bidding, more interested in Alex's order than my waistline.

I licked my lips again, getting a bonus hit of greasy goodness. "But—"

"Do you really want to talk about your weight right now, Meredith?"

"Meri," I corrected him. "And no. I thought you had sisters. With comments like that, you clearly don't have a girlfriend. No woman wants to talk about her weight 'right now'… or ever." But most especially not when she was out on a kind-of-date with a good-looking man, or eating, or dieting… or breathing.

We settled into a glare-off, broken when he reached over the table to offer me a bite of falafel dipped in hummus from his hand. That was cruel. Did he know how delicious and *fattening* that was? I'd already eaten a quarter of a dolma and a piece of basturma. I couldn't eat anything else. I tightened my lips, refusing to open them. He kept his hand in front of my mouth, waiting. A waiter paused beside our table with the new plate of sausage. "Great. Thanks. Just put it beside the lady," Alex said.

"No— Umph."

Taking advantage of my parted lips, he shoved the bite of falafel into my mouth. I snapped my teeth, just grazing the tip of his fingers as he snatched them back. Alex's eyes flared, and he shivered, humming with pleasure.

CHAPTER 8

Stop Using Me For Money - Get A Job!

Alex smiled in triumph, raising his thumb to his mouth to lick off a bit of hummus. Dark eyes watched me, as I struggled with the spit-or-swallow dilemma, in the middle of my favourite restaurant, with delicious flavours exploding in my mouth. I gave in, chewed and swallowed, glaring back, too annoyed to get the full enjoyment from the forbidden treat. What game was he playing with the feeding and flirting? I'd been out of the dating game for so long—okay, so I'd never really been in the game—that I wasn't sure if it was real or not.

What I did know was I now had to add another half-hour on my gym routine, for at least three days, probably the cross trainer on level ten. "Bastard."

"And yet you offered to pay me double time to spend

the evening with you." He smiled, forking some basturma onto my plate, in full feeder mode. The waiter rushed over to top up my water glass then melted away. "What would people think?"

"I'm a television chat show host. You're an officer of the court…" I shrugged. "I'm guessing my career would recover from an escort scandal first. Especially as you're the one prostituting your time in this scenario. But we can always test out the theory." I was bluffing. My image was key to my success, but Jerry Springer's career had survived an escort scandal.

"Fair point," Alex responded.

"Do you usually force-feed your dates?" I asked, stabbing each piece of spicy sausage and moving it off my plate, weeping silently inside as I mourned the loss.

"I usually don't have to."

"Because no one will go out with you?" I asked sweetly.

"Usually, the women I date are happy to enjoy my company *and* the food."

"I wouldn't be so sure."

"Well, as you pointed out, this isn't a date; it's business. So why don't you tell me what's going on? Surprising as it is, I'm starting to think my charm,"—I snorted rudely—"good looks and advice for your show are not the main reasons you want a lawyer. So, hit me with it."

My stomach sank, nauseatingly. "I don't know what you're talking about." I didn't bother dressing it up with eyelash flutters, going for a less-is-more approach with a flat-out denial.

"There's something going on," he said. My heart pounded. I felt cornered. "You've been betrayed by your mother and your boyfriend. People you should be able to trust above all others. So, you opted for some petty revenge?" He made it sound pathetic and predictable.

"I don't know what you're talking about."

"Cress."

I smiled. There was no stopping it. The happy hit was still there. Although getting fainter with every passing hour. My mind churned over my next step. I didn't want to be as predictable as he made me seem, but I wasn't ready to just let it go just yet. "Nope, still don't know what you're implying."

“Don’t waste my time.” He was getting grumpy again. I forked a couple of pieces of sausage and some hummus onto his plate, hoping to stave off a full-on moody-man moment. He frowned at his plate, then fixed his eyes back on me. “The cress was juvenile—*funny*, but juvenile. Time to move on now, before it gets serious or gets traced back to you.”

“Whatever.” I’d take his advice on board and probably ignore it. “Suppose, hypothetically—”

“Hypothetically… of course.” His lips tightened, signalling his displeasure.

“Yes. Suppose hypothetically someone was to… to play a few practical jokes on their ex…”

“Don’t do it, Meredith.”

“Is that legal advice?”

“Take it any way you want. Just don’t do anything stupid. The best way to get your revenge is to get on with your life without him. Show him what he’s missing.”

I rolled my eyes at the trite platitude. “He knows what he’s missing,” I snapped. “He had it for seven years.”

"And that hurts. I get it." He shrugged. "Everyone has been dumped at least once—"

"I dumped him!"

"Hmm." His noncommittal tone screamed, *He dumped you first in action when he started shagging your mother.* "You need to move on with your own life. I know it's tough."

"It's only been a week." Nowhere near long enough. I'd wasted seven years on Tom, and who knew how long he'd been screwing Talith. The therapist on my show said people were entitled to one month of wallowing—and an episode of revenge (I added that bit)—per year they were with someone. I'd wasted seven years; that gave me six more months and revenges before I had to move on, and I was going to use every one of them.

"This isn't normal."

What the hell was normal about what Tom and Talith had done? "So, if I sat at home and cried, that would be okay? Because that's how *normal, intelligent* women are meant to respond when their hearts are broken."

"Your heart isn't broken." He sat back, taking

another sip of his beer. "Your pride is bruised, that's all."

He made it sound less than it was. "You don't have a clue what you're talking about. This is the ultimate betrayal. This isn't Tom sleeping with his secretary or someone he met in a bar. It's my *mother*!" I pushed my plate away before I gave in to my emotions and the anger Alex was provoking, and tried to eat myself happy.

"Have you cried?" he asked. I didn't respond. "I thought not. That's how I know your heart isn't broken."

I glared at him. "Not all women cry." He raised his eyebrow. "Just because I don't act like one of your sisters and melt into a weeping mess on your shoulder doesn't mean I don't deserve support or sympathy."

His jaw tensed and his eyes narrowed.

He glared over my shoulder.

The silence stretched.

Finally, he took a deep, slow breath. "Have you thought about getting help?"

I'd done more than think about getting help. I'd sought help. That was why he was here. "You said you didn't want to be involved. Something about your career—"

He heaved out a sigh, jabbing a hand through his hair. "I meant some sort of counselling."

"For what?" I didn't need a shrink. I needed a guaranteed alibi, a lawyer and… possibly someone to hold a stepladder.

"It can be hard to get over the end of a long-term relationship, especially when you didn't see it coming, or one party cheats. I understand."

"How bloody magnanimous of you."

"I'm not being a dick just for the sake of it. I believe I mentioned I have three sisters." His voice broke, and he closed his eyes, taking a deep breath and letting it out slowly, like he was performing some sort of breathing exercise. "They've been cheated on a time or two, had their hearts broken. So have I. It has to be worse in your case, when it was your mother and you're a celebrity."

Ah, well, maybe… It wasn't like I was crying myself to sleep every night, or comfort-eating, or begging Tom to take me back.

“It’s nothing to be embarrassed about, Meredith. Lots of people see counsellors these days.”

“I know. I have an after-care team on the show. More often than not, they tell people they need to work through their… issues. Gain closure.” Which was what I was doing.

“Look.” His large, warm hand covered mine on the table. A quick squeeze and release. “I understand you’re hurt.”

“I’m *not*.” So why was I feeling so… *vulnerable,* all of a sudden? I didn’t want to talk about this. I was fine before he started this conversation. Yes, I was… maybe… strangely… emotionally numb and becoming increasingly fixated on seeking revenge, but so what?

Given the circumstances, I was pretty sure it was a normal, healthy response. There was nothing wrong with not wanting them to continue with their lives like I’d never existed. It wasn’t like I was stalking them and doing weird things; it was a spur-of-the-moment cressing.

“I can see there’s no talking to you,” Alex said.

“So stop trying!” I snapped. He’d managed to suck the last iota of joy from me seeing the cress-mobile.

I was always urging women on my show to *move on* and *leave their losers behind* and *rise above the petty need to hit back*. Of course, now I was on the receiving end of that advice, I could honestly say it was total bullshit.

Outside, horns blared and tyres screamed. We both turned to look out the window. A familiar blue Audi screeched to the kerb. Tom ditched the cress-mobile on a double yellow and jumped out, barging through the door into the restaurant, shattering the quiet atmosphere.

The maître d' greeted him effusively, handing him a big brown paper bag of takeout and pointing in my direction. This was not a restaurant that made takeout—that was something the manager did for me. He liked having someone famous frequent his restaurant. In return, I was always happy to give them publicity and host events with them.

Shit! I slumped down in my seat, praying for invisibility. Tom turned, heading towards me with his takeout. What part of our recent interactions made him think I wanted to speak to him, let alone twice in one day?

The maître d' disappeared.

No cash changed hands.

I frowned.

His dinner better not be going on my account. He wasn't going to cash in on me anymore. He could pay his own way, or ask my mother to do it. In fact, he shouldn't be allowed takeout at all now—that was my special privilege.

"Meri." His greeting was clipped, but friendlier than the cold look he gave Alex.

"Takeout twice in one week?" I responded blandly. One of the worst things about being a celebrity was not being able to say or do what I wanted in public without it being picked up in the media. It meant I could only kick Tom in the balls metaphorically. "Is that wise? You don't have the fastest metabolism." Tom watched his diet almost as religiously as I did, and worked out hard to stay in shape. It was one of the things we'd had in common. He really cared about physical health and looks. He was always the first to tell me if I was putting on weight.

He sucked in his stomach self-consciously. I enjoyed the tiny victory. "Talith loves my body."

"You should go. *Now.* Before your food gets cold," Alex said, before I could speak.

"We've moved in together. Talith's unpacking my stuff, so I thought I'd give her a break and get dinner."

From my favourite restaurant, on my tab? "So kind."

"That's what your mother said," he responded snidely.

Was this his lame attempt to make me jealous? He was sleeping with my mother. It wasn't jealousy I felt—it was nausea. I glanced around to make sure no one was listening in on our conversation. "Don't forget to settle your bill on your way out."

Tom checked out the table. "Business dinner?"

"It's Friday night," I said. "Maybe I'm on a date." Alex was a good-looking, successful man, and I was a newly single, attractive female. Why shouldn't I have fun?

"I doubt it," Tom responded, like I was an undateable workaholic who didn't know how to have fun. "Has she eaten anything other than a couple of dry, undressed lettuce leaves from her fattoush and a bite of dolma?" he asked Alex.

Who had the good sense not to respond.

Instead, he waited until Tom turned away, before raising an eyebrow in my direction.

"Actually, I find my appetite has increased recently," I said. "It's like a nauseating weight has been lifted off me." I forked up a slice of spicy sausage and crammed it into my mouth. My eyelids fluttered at the delicious flavours.

"Anyone else and I'd consider it comfort eating," Tom retorted.

I chewed and swallowed quickly, denying myself the full enjoyment of my illicit treat, so I could respond. "Can't handle the fact I'm not crying and begging you to return?" There was no other reason for his jibes. I was the wronged one in this scenario.

"But it is you," he continued as if I hadn't spoken. "The original frigid ice princess."

"Hey!" I snapped. So, a five-minute weekend special—hands above my head, red heels on—didn't do it for me. I lowered my voice before I attracted attention. "I think you'll find if something this size"—I held up an *index* finger—"can make me come, *you* are one with the problem."

“Even the biggest organ can get lost in a vast cathedral,” he responded.

What. The. Fuck? “Ask Talith. You certainly didn’t come to that conclusion with me.”

“Bitch,” Tom snarled, looming over me.

“Control yourself and take a big step back. Now!” Alex’s voice was deadly. I shivered with… something that wasn’t fear. My skin felt unexpectedly tight and tingly.

Tom shrank back, no more interested in attracting attention and possible negative media than me; he couldn’t have heard back from his audition yet, and was smart enough to know no one wanted a cheating scumbag as the hero in a romcom. “At least Talith *likes* sex. She could teach you a thing or twenty—”

“I like sex, Tom,” I cut in. It wasn’t strictly true—Tom was the only person I’d ever slept with, and it was… okay, but that was beside the point. “Just not with you. Which is surprising. You’d think with all the practice you clearly got behind my back, you’d be better at it.”

“And yet your mother and *Jenn* keep coming back for more,” Tom retorted.

The blood fled so quickly from my head that I swayed in my seat. No. Jenn wouldn’t do that to me.

CHAPTER 9

Did You Betrayed Me? Lie Detector Results!

I grasped the brass door knocker, banging it against the claret-coloured door, then waited in the rain, my dark green full-length trench coat flapping limply against my calves.

I shifted nervously from one foot to the other, praying for Jenn not to be in… praying for her to be in. I'd waited impatiently for two days for her to return from holiday to make this call. I couldn't believe I was doing it. Jenn was my best friend. We'd always been there for each other, no questions asked… but I'd trusted Talith and Tom, and look how that ended. I clearly wasn't as good a judge of character as I'd always thought.

The door swung inwards and light spilled out into the dark, wet night. "Meri! Why didn't you just let yourself in?" Jenn asked, the light behind her casting her in shadow.

I stood on the step, mute. Dripping wet. Unable to take the first step. The silence stretched and still I said nothing, did nothing.

I didn't have to.

The longer I waited, the more obvious it became. "So, it's true. He wasn't lying."

Jenn's smile slipped, wavered, then died as she stared back. The shock of betrayal exploded out from my soul, stealing my breath in a blinding flash. Then numbness rushed in, filling the void.

"Come in," she said quietly. "Please. I can explain."

She could? "I'm fine where I am." The curtains in the ground floor flat next door twitched.

"You don't want to discuss this in the street, Meri," she said. I didn't want to discuss it all. "It's too easy for people to hear and sell to the press."

God.

It was as good as a confession.

A small, desperate part of me had hoped Tom was lying. Trying to hurt me. But I knew in my heart. This duplicity was so much worse than my mother's. Jenn was my best friend. She, Ffion and I had gone to school together. We'd shared secrets and commiserated with each other over failed exams and teenage heartbreak. Ffion had gotten married straight out of school, but Jenn had followed me not long after I'd left the Valley. She was the sister of my heart.

I stood frozen on the step, in the pouring rain, blinking through the water.

Jenn ran a hand through her thick brown hair. The action pulled her dressing gown up, the maroon silk moulding to her ample curves. "It was an accident." Her voice wavered.

"You slipped and his dick caught you?" My heart pounded, like I'd just run a race. "Don't!" I twisted away from Jenn's outstretched arm. I didn't want her touching me.

"*Please*, Meri," she cried. "I didn't do it on purpose. I didn't want to hurt you."

Talith had always been flirty and flighty where men were concerned. But Jenn was rock solid… until now. I shook my head, casting off water like a dog fresh from a lake. "You've had front-row tickets for my show whenever you wanted them for the last seven years. You've been to watch more times than I can count. You *know* I listen to lies every day; I don't need a lie detector test."

Jenn's face crumpled. Tears welled in her large brown eyes, then slipped with silent beauty down her face.

Jenn was gorgeous. She could have modelled for Victoria's Secret. She didn't need to stoop to sleeping with my boyfriend.

"Why?"

"D-don't."

Don't what? "Was it just once?" I asked. She shook her head, whimpering as she pressed her lips together. I swiped water off my face with the back of my hand, probably smearing what little makeup remained. "Twice?" I asked. Jenn stared back silently, eyes pleading. "More?"

"We didn't mean to hurt you." She wrapped her arms across her chest, hugging herself.

"How. Many. Times?" I said through chattering teeth, the torrential rain seeping through my coat, striking cold into my bones.

Jenn sobbed.

I ignored her weeping. Tears weren't going to stop me getting answers. I hadn't wanted to know the details with Talith, but this was Jenn. She knew Tom before I did. She introduced us. When Tom asked me out, I'd checked with her first—making sure it was okay, that she wasn't interested in him—because she was more important to me than any man.

What was it about Tom, or about me that made everyone I trusted betray me? “When? Where? Here?” I flung my arm out, sending a shower of water cascading over Jenn. “In my flat? In my *bed*? Every day? Once a week? Twice on Tuesdays?”

“I can’t.” A pained whisper, like Jenn was the one who’d been betrayed. “*Please,* Meri.”

“Last week? Last month? Last year? For the last two years, three years?” My voice was rising with each word I spoke and each head shake she gave in response. “I’ve known you since I was eleven years old. I’ve dated Tom for the last seven years. Tell me how many of those years you were *accidently* screwing my boyfriend.”

“I ca—”

“Yeahy! Aunty M, Aunty M!” Owain came running down the hall in his blue cotton *Tractor Tom* jammies, clutching Peter Rabbit by his ears, his little-boy voice shrill with excitement. He slid to a halt near the open doorway, momentum sending him skidding a couple of feet along the laminate flooring in his sleep socks. Jenn instinctively put out a hand, placing it on his blond, sleep-tousled hair to stop him toppling over. He leant against his mother’s thigh, arms wrapping around her leg. He looked up at me and frowned, his face crumpling. “What’s wrong, Aunty M?”

He glanced from me to his mother and back again, and his lower lip began to tremble. “Why are you crying?”

Heart stuttering painfully in my chest, I squatted down to match his height, forcing a smile. “I’m not crying, *caraid*.” I used the Welsh endearment for love, and what I told him was the truth: shock had cloaked my emotions, and my eyes were dry. “It’s just the rain.”

He looked up at his mother, seeking reassurance, sensing the tension between us. I stood. There was no point continuing this.

Jenn had slept with Tom.

Did it really matter how many times, or where they’d done it?

Would it be easier to forgive her if it was only once, or one night, or week, or month, or year?

What was my cut off on forgiveness?

Ten times, but not eleven?

I didn’t have the answers.

And now we’d woken Owain. An innocent little boy who deserved to be kept safe from the harsh realities of life. “I-is Mummy crying?”

I left that one for Jenn to answer. I wasn’t lying to my godson, not when it seemed like he was the only person in my life who loved me unconditionally, with an innocent, open heart.

"I, ah… I'm just so happy to see your aunty, honey." Jenn sniffed back the tears, pushing her hair off her face and wiping it dry with the cuff of her silken gown.

Worries allayed by his mother's lie, Owain edged past her, his smile tremulous. His plump little hand reached for me. "I wok-ed up and I heard you. Is it morning? Have you come to play Lego? I was on my holidays."

"Oh, no. It's still night-time. Little soldiers like you should be tucked up with Peter Rabbit catching some Zs… not standing out in the cold in their jammies." I forced another smile.

"Will you tuck me in?"

I clenched my teeth against the refusal on the tip of my tongue. I didn't want to go into Jenn's flat and pretend everything was all right when it never would be again. But I loved Owain. I couldn't hurt him. It wasn't fair to visit the sins of the parent onto the child.

I stepped into the hallway, taking his warm little hand in mine. S*ins of the parent on the child* echoed in my mind, and like mental laser eye surgery, one second everything was blurry, the next, I could see so clearly, I couldn't understand how I'd ever missed it. "Oh, God! Oh, no. No." My gaze swung back to Jenn. "Owain?"

Her trembling hand covered her mouth. Tears poured down her face, dripping off the end of her nose. Her pained look was enough.

Owain was Tom's son.

When Jenn had found out she was pregnant—"the result of a one-night stand"—I'd more than stood by her. I hadn't judged her or pushed when she said she didn't want to talk about the father. I'd been her birthing partner. I'd rejoiced in the new addition to our little "family".

When she'd had financial trouble during her maternity leave, I'd stepped in to support her and Owain. If anything happened to Jenn, I was Owain's legal guardian. I loved him as if he was my own. All this time, I'd supported her, loved her and Owain without question… and all the time, she and Tom must have been laughing through their pillow talk.

I'd seen this a hundred times before, on my show. I'd questioned how any reasonably intelligent person could be so oblivious. And here I was, looking at Tom's mini-me, and I hadn't seen it for four years.

"Why are you and Mummy crying?" Owain's voice wavered. I wiped my face with my wet coat sleeve, moving on automatically, helping him into his racing-car bed, brushing his unruly hair back off his forehead, staring into eyes the same blue as his father's.

I pressed a watery kiss to his forehead, smelling his comforting scent. "It's adult stuff, *caraid*." I blinked back the tears, scanning his familiar room. It hurt to look at him, to see the evidence of how blind and bloody stupid I'd been for so long. Four years—five if I included the pregnancy, and, in this case, I was definitely including the pregnancy and every encounter his parents had had before then. "You go to sleep. I'm, ah… I'm going away for a while." What was one small lie from me thrown in the pot with everyone else's? "I won't be able to see you for the next few weeks."

Owain clutched Peter Rabbit to his chest, rubbing his furry ear under his nose, a comforting gesture he'd developed as a baby, and spoke around the thumb he was sucking. "But you're still gonna watch me in egg and spoon at sports day."

My chest constricted painfully. I closed my eyes, praying for strength. "I don't think I can, *caraid*."

"You promised."

"I…" I loved him, but I couldn't bear to look at him and see the living evidence of what they'd done staring back at me. Calling me a fool.

The pain was indescribable. Not just Tom screwing his way through my best friend and mother, but the fact that what he had done had given—and taken away—the greatest joy in my life.

Owain.

I turned from the plea in his big blue eyes. Jenn stood in the bedroom doorway watching, forcing me to be the bad guy.

No way was I going to break Owain's heart. This was her mess, not mine. She could explain it. "I have to go. Don't forget, I love you. Always."

"Love you too," he slurred around his thumb, eyelids fluttering as he fought and lost his battle with sleep.

I pressed another kiss to his forehead and walked out. Jenn closed Owain's bedroom door and grabbed my arm. "Meri, don't. We've been friends for too long for it to just end like this."

I jerked my arm free, snorting with disbelief. "No. *We* haven't," I said, jabbing a finger at her. "*You* clearly haven't been my friend for at least five years. The proof of that has just fallen asleep."

"It was a mistake."

At least a "mistake" implied she was taking more responsibility for her actions than an "accident". "Are you saying it only happened once, that you were drunk or drugged? That you didn't know who Owain's father was, so you couldn't tell me earlier? Like at any point in the last five years." I turned and made my way back into the cold, wet night, the silence stretching behind me heavy with the truth. "I didn't think so."

Jenn ran to the front door, leaning out to call after me. "Owain doesn't deserve this, Meri. He's just a baby. He doesn't deserve to have you just walk out of his life. He won't understand. He *loves* you. Please, don't hurt him."

"Fuck you, Jenn!" I retorted over my shoulder. Fuck her and fuck Tom and fuck my mother, and fuck *rising above it* like I'd naively advocated to my guests for the last seven years. I wasn't taking this shit with a smile and an open purse.

CHAPTER 10

Daughter, Did You Burgle My House?

Talith reached to cup Tom's cheek affectionately in her hand as the Audi pulled up at a red-light opposite where I was parked. His lips found hers, and he kissed her deeply. I slid down in my car seat, sinking below the dashboard, watching as Talith's hand disappeared from view. Tom's head fell back against the headrest. His eyes closed. His mouth opened.

Jesus Christ! I recognised that facial expression. No prizes for guessing where Talith's hand had just gone.

I shuddered.

My mother was a skank, and my boyfriend—*ex*-boyfriend—*loved* it.

I doubted she'd be so eager to give him a hand-job in public if she knew about Jenn. Then again, maybe she already did. Maybe they'd all romped together *ménage-a-trois* style whilst I'd been at work earning enough money to pay for their lavish lifestyles.

A horn blared, the driver behind getting impatient as the light changed.

They jumped apart, laughing and flushed.

They wouldn't be laughing soon.

Two days ago, after speaking to Jenn, and one day after donning a disguise and going for an STD check-up, I'd cancelled the direct debit from my bank account into Talith's, which covered her mortgage and living expenses. I should've done it sooner, but I'd just been… lost, and I'd been paying for them for so long that I hadn't even thought about it. But I had no legal or financial obligation to pay my mother's way.

I'd also removed the automatic money transfer from my bank account into Tom's. I hadn't touched Owain's trust fund. I'd keep adding to that. It was his for when he was older.

I'd been swamped with a disturbing mixture of guilt and relief as I walked out of the bank having cut all financial strings. Neither Talith nor Tom worked regularly; my mother hadn't worked since I'd started acting in adverts and earning regularly at thirteen years old. She'd just called herself a "momager" and helped herself to my earnings. Tom getting walk-on roles or bit parts in TV shows once in a blue moon wouldn't fund their monthly takeout, let alone make a mortgage payment on a three-story townhouse in Pimlico.

They'd have to step up and earn their own money or sell up, and in this economy, with the speed they'd need to sell at… they'd be lucky to get what they needed to cover what they owed on the mortgage. So, they'd have to take their negative equity and make a new love nest in a disgusting, rat-infested bedsit. A fitting location, given their disgusting, rat-infested relationship. At least then I wouldn't bump into them in my favourite restaurant or find myself accidently following them as I went about my neighbourhood.

The car horn blared again.

Tom pulled out of the junction, swinging left and driving past where I was parked, obliviously.

I waited.

Then waited.

And waited some more.

It was cold outside. Autumn was slipping into winter, and frost iced the air, so I left the engine running and the heating on whilst I waited. The aroma of prawns gradually started to permeate the car. Icky-looking water began to form a fragrant, murky pool in the lid-less Tupperware container in my passenger footwell.

Finally, when I was confident they wouldn't return anytime soon—and I was breathing through my mouth and still gagging on the fishy stench—I turned off the engine and gathered the ingredients of my new Plan of Revenge.

Yes. I had a whole plan.

Not a written plan with actual acts of revenge listed out—I was mad, as in angry, not crazy, as in stupid. I wasn't putting anything in writing for some snoop to find and send to the press or police.

Tom hadn't cheated on me once and then repented. He'd done it at least twice. Probably more. He'd be one unlucky bastard if he only cheated on me twice, knocking up my best friend the first time and having me walk in and catch him with my mother the second.

No. He'd done it again and again…

So why should I limit myself to one almost-accidental act of vengeance?

From now on, when the opportunity presented itself, or just when I felt like it, I wasn't going to rise above it. I was going to grab my little bubble of revenge happiness with both hands and wring every drop of fun out of it.

Today I had a double whammy planned. I slipped stealthily out of the car, head down, casting furtive looks around to make sure there was no CCTV and no one was close by, clutching the fishy container to my chest with my right hand and a bin bag of clothing in my left. I eased the car door closed and headed off down the street.

I'd dressed carefully, all in black, with a baggy coat and a beanie. It was only seven, but the nights were closing in so fast that it may as well have been midnight.

I turned past the junction, where Talith and Tom had played find the chipolata, slinking into the shadows at the edge of the small, fenced park, and made my way cautiously towards Talith's house.

This was where I had to be extra careful; people knew me here. I'd posed for photographs with them and signed autographs for their families and friends. If they saw me, they'd recognise me, stop to talk and *remember*. I paused in the shelter of a leafless London pride tree as I checked out the street ahead in both directions.

Then checked again.

Nothing.

I scanned the neighbouring houses. Luckily, the bitter cold and continuous icy drizzle kept most sane people tucked up inside with their curtains closed and their TVs on.

I pushed away from my tree trunk hiding place and hurried down the street. I slipped the key from my pocket and slunk into my mother's house.

The heat hit me in a suffocating blanket. I blew out a breath and scanned the room. The curtains were closed, so I flicked on a side lamp, and pale-yellow light filled the room—bright enough for me to see, but not so bright it would flood around the curtains and be seen in the street.

Shit!

Now what?

My heart was hammering so hard that black pulsed at the edges of my vision. What did I do now? I hadn't thought beyond buying prawns and making the house smell… I got the idea off a show I'd done a few years ago, only the woman had used mussels and put them behind the boiler…

I looked around frantically for a hiding place for my fishy friends. In order for this to work, the prawns couldn't be discovered for a while. They needed time to heat up, to really begin to decompose and release their full aromatic impact. If there was one thing Tom hated more than monogamy, it was fish—or, more particularly, the smell of fish.

A strip of light flashing around the room and the sound of car tyres swishing on the street had my gaze flashing towards the curtained window. A bead of sweat ran down between my breasts.

It was okay.

I couldn't see anything, or be seen through the curtains… curtains held up by a long brass rail with globe-shaped fitments on the end. *Hollow* curtain rails.

Leaving the bag of clothing by the front door, I made my way quickly into the living area. Detouring to the dining area, I grabbed a chair from the table and dragged it back across the living room and over to the large front window. I toed off my shoes and put the Tupperware container on the floor beside the chair. Climbing onto the wooden seat, I reached for the end of the curtain rail. Dust coated my hand and rained down.

I twisted the knob on the end of the rail, then tugged.

It didn't budge.

I twisted again, putting my weight into it.

Nothing.

I tried again, grunting with effort.

It popped off in my hand like a champagne cork shooting from a bottle. Caught off balance, I pitched off the edge of the chair, a millisecond of free-falling ending when I slammed into the thick, oat-coloured carpet.

Stunned.

Head pounding.

I lay still, struggling to inflate my lungs and assess

my injuries. I couldn't afford to have to call for an ambulance and have them alert the police to my breaking and entering, and I didn't have anyone but Alex law-abiding Gordon for a friendly rescue, which meant I was in this alone. So, it was time to woman up and get over it. I rolled slowly into sitting position, wiggling each joint and limb in turn, checking for injury.

Owee, ow, ow!

I had a second-degree carpet burn on my right hand. My wrist and ankle hurt badly, possibly broken, probably twisted. I wiggled them again, to be sure, whimpering through the pain.

Enough!

I was an agent of vengeance on a mission. I didn't have time to lie on the carpet feeling sorry for myself. I might have broken bones and a mild concussion, but I'd also succeeded in removing the globe from the end of the curtain rail. Hopping on one leg, I gingerly climbed back onto the chair, holding the wooden back with my sore right hand and the Tupperware container in my left hand. Once steady, I selected a stinky grey king prawn and fed it, beady little black eyes first, into the hollow curtain rail. Its sticklike legs caught on the way in, then gave as I thrust it down the tube. My wrist twanged as I went back for a second, third and fourth prawn…

Ugh.

They already smelt pungent.

Given the fact Tom and Talith had the heating running on surface-of-the-sun hot, by tomorrow the aroma would have begun to permeate the room. Another day or two and it would be unbearable.

I picked up the penultimate prawn. "In you go, stinky." I giggled, enjoying myself. It might be painful, but it was fun, too. And, as the saying went: no pain, no gain. I forced prawn number five into the curtain rail, using the crustacean's hard translucent shell to push numbers one through four further down inside the curtain rail, then quickly added number six, poking it down as far as it would go with my index finger. Wincing as my right ankle took my weight, I lowered myself to the floor and picked up the brass knob before awkwardly climbing back up onto the chair and fitting it back into place, sealing in everything but the odour, which would escape through the small holes in the back of the pole that allowed it to be lengthened or shortened to the width of the window.

I grabbed the back of the chair with my left hand and placed it back at the table, before heading back into the kitchen to wash the Tupperware container. I slipped it into the small corner cupboard, alongside my mother's containers. The last thing I wanted was to be caught with a fishy Tupperware. Talith wouldn't notice one more stacked willy-nilly in there with all the others.

All in all, it took about ten minutes. Which was too long. I'd planned to be in and out of the house ninja style within ten minutes, but that was prior to my fall. I gave myself some injury time. Professional athletes got injury time, and I was a novice at this whole revenge thing. Raising my timeframe to twenty minutes, I hobbled back over to the front door. Ignoring the burning of my palm, I grabbed the bag of clothes I'd left there and rushed through to Talith's bedroom. This was a little bonus specifically for Tom. One that would strike at his very core.

His vanity.

I flung open the wardrobe doors. The shock of seeing Tom's designer clothes cuddled up with my mother's rainbow of silk dresses and designer jackets was enough to subdue my happiness.

I was used to seeing these clothes tucked in one side of my wardrobe with mine. It suggested an additional intimacy, a permanency I didn't want to think about.

I tore the first shirt off the rail—Tom's favourite pale pink Ralph Lauren—then opened the bag I brought with me and pulled its replica out, replacing it neatly on the hanger and slipping it back into the wardrobe. I worked methodically through each shirt, for once thankful Tom didn't have a job that meant he had to wear suits. It had been expensive enough to replace all his designer shirts and jeans.

Task complete, a kernel of happiness unfurled inside me as I imagined Tom's horrified and panicked response to getting too fat for his clothes. He wouldn't have the wit to check the labels. I closed the wardrobe. Bin bag of replaced items clutched in my left hand, I hobbled to the bedroom doorway, aching right arm pressed to my chest. I took the time to leave the door a couple of inches open, just as it had been when I arrived. Moving to the front door, I scanned the dining room. The chair was tucked back at the table just as I'd found it. I checked the living room. There was a large scuff mark on the carpet where I'd fallen, right next to my flat burglar shoes. I slipped on my shoes and sank to my knees, shuffling backwards, using my left hand to brush the marks out of the carpet. I kept backing up and carpet-fluffing until my backside hit the front door.

I'd removed all trace of my nefarious presence.

I collected the bag of swapped clothes. I'd drop them into a charity bin on my way home. It was too risky to go into a shop; someone might recognise me and give a tip to tabloids, who would start digging into my reasons for giving away Tom's clothes.

The heat continued to blast down at me. I was sweating. Still, if I was sweating, the prawns must be doing their stinky, rotting version of it too. I slipped out of the house and into the night, hobble-slinking down the steps. I checked no one was around before I set off down the street, not too fast, not too slow, trying not to limp, head down to hide my smile.

Shit! A ringtone shrilled, cutting through the still, dark, formerly silent night.

Shit.

I'd forgotten to put my phone on silent when I'd gone into revenge-stealth mode. I fumbled the phone out of my pocket, swiping the screen to shut it up, and hobble-launched myself the last few steps, beeping the door locks and throwing myself into the car before someone heard and looked around.

Panting, heart pounding, adrenaline flooding my system, I lifted the phone to my ear, whisper-answering, "Hello?" Sobbing and heavy breathing sounded down the line, but no intelligible words. "Hello?" More sobbing. I took the phone away from my ear and checked the screen, seeing a picture of Owain and Jenn eating ice cream in Hyde Park last summer. "Jenn?"

"M-Mer…" The voice trailed away again into incoherent, sobbing babble.

"What?" My stomach plummeted. "Is it Owain? Is everything okay with Owain?"

"I'm s-sorry." Jenn's voice hitched. "I-I d-d-didn't know who else to call."

"What's happened?" *Jesus, please let Owain be all right.* Fear hollowed out my stomach. It must be serious—Jenn wouldn't call otherwise, not after what she'd done. "Where are you?"

"H-he's cheating on m-me… with T-Talith."

Who? "What?" *The fuck?*

"Tom, he's s-sleeping with your mother. I t-thought

he l-loved me. I—"

I hung up then threw my mobile on the passenger seat, before pressing the ignition button and pulling out from the pavement, making my getaway. I shook with a mix of adrenaline, fear and *disbelief* at Jenn calling me for support, like she was the wronged one. It should be me calling Jenn for a shoulder to cry on. What the hell had she expected? Tea? Sympathy? Bonding over Tom's dicking around on both of us?

So, why did *I* feel guilty at hanging up on her?

I slammed a hand against the steering wheel. "Ow!" Pain screamed up my sore arm, bringing tears to my eyes.

Fuck it!

Why was nothing going right for me?

Jenn's call had delayed me. Tom and Talith pulled to the kerb ahead of me and spilled out of the cress-mobile, laughing and touching, in the middle of my route to freedom. There was no slipping down in my seat or turning around and heading in the other direction. I was just going to have to hope the darkness and their focus on each other would blind them to me. I white-knuckled the steering wheel and forced myself not to stare at them… or rev the engine, mount the pavement and mow them both down.

Instead, I drove past them like I had somewhere to be and hadn't just spent the evening breaking and entering in their house. I took a left at the "groping" traffic lights, keeping my speed dead on the limit, even though I wanted to put my foot down and make a speedy getaway.

Breathe. Breathe. Keep calm.

No one had seen me. I was fine. I'd gotten away with it.

Even if I had been seen, I had every right to be here. It was a public highway. I was a member of the public and… and I was nearly home, so I didn't have to panic.

Even if they discovered the prawns quickly, they'd never be able to prove it was me just because I happened to be driving around Pimlico.

I lived in Pimlico.

I lived here first.

I'd paid my mother's mortgage and had a key and an open invitation to go there. So, it wasn't like it was real break-in… Right?

My mind was spinning.

I'd be lucky if I didn't crash the car making my getaway.

If there was an investigation, my fingerprints would be on the curtain pole. But I'd helped fix it to the wall and hung the floor-length curtains for Talith six months ago when she'd picked them. So, there was a legitimate reason for them to be there.

Okay. I had a defence.

I still felt panicky.

What if the police got involved?

What if I was arrested for… for burglary… although I hadn't stolen anything…

What if I was arrested for stalking or something?

I didn't want to spend my prime years in prison, wrinkling away with a bunch of criminal lesbians. Not that I had anything against lesbians. I just didn't want to be forced to have bitch-sex with a butch, violent, criminal lesbian in the communal prison shower. I'd already wasted enough of my good sex years on Tom. My chest went tight. I couldn't catch my breath.

I pulled my car to the side of the road before I killed someone.

My heart continued to pound erratically, beating at my ribs. I'd chosen to take my revenge, but I couldn't help panicking about the repercussions now.

I didn't want to go to prison.

Could I go to prison?

It wasn't liked I'd killed anyone. .

CHAPTER 11

Ex: You're Crazy Stop Now Before You End Up In Prison!

"What the heck is that supposed to be?" Alex asked, his chair squeaking as he slumped with disappointment. I'd called him at two this morning, scared after my fishy felony. He'd agreed to meet me at six forty-five, provided I brought breakfast.

"Breakfast," I responded, sitting opposite him, on one of the two visitor's chairs. He glared at the pot of natural yoghurt and handful of slightly crushed, purple-juice-weeping blueberries I'd put on his desk.

"Not for a grown man."

I rolled my eyes. He was obsessed with food.

"It looks like the scraps from the back of an

anorexic's fridge. I'd have been able to pull together something more appetising if I'd gone dumpster-diving next to a homeless shelter."

I shrugged. "Eat it or leave it. Your choice. I brought breakfast. I upheld my side of the deal."

He sighed. "I hate natural yoghurt and bitter, bruised blueberries." He prodded the yoghurt pot, shoving it across his desk in incremental jabs like a petulant child. Kicking out the bin, he pitched the offending items over the edge, watching them tumble into the bin with a dull thud.

Assuming his man-trum was finished, I said, "I need some of the legal advice I hired you for."

"Yeah. We should talk about that." His stomach growled loudly. "God. I'm starving."

"Focus, Alex," I snapped. "You're in no danger of starvation."

"Are you calling me fat?" He pressed his hand against his stomach. "I might not have a six-pack, but I have a *job*, so I can't work out for hours every day."

I ignored his jab at Tom, who did spend hours a day in the gym—although he didn't have a six-pack; he had an eight-pack. There was no need for Alex to get defensive. He was big, well over six foot, and solid, not fat. "Look, I just want some legal advice."

"You're finally going to tell me what's going on?" He sat up, dragging a legal pad towards him. The silence stretched as I tried to order my thoughts. Alex tap-tapped his pen against an old-fashioned blotter on his desk, counting off the seconds.

"I was wondering… Are there specific laws against… I guess it's harassment?" I was so worried he'd see straight through my question to my vengeful acts that I could barely hold eye contact.

"The Protection from Harassment Act 1997 makes harassment and stalking illegal in England and Wales."

"Oh… Okay."

"Are you being stalked by Tom, or some fan? Is that why you're awake in the middle of the night calling me?" He seemed genuinely concerned, which was a change from the grumpy sod he'd been on the phone when I woke him this morning.

I ignored his question, focusing on my main concern.

"Is it a criminal offense?" I was pretty sure my face was pale, beneath my Chanel makeup mask. "As in prison time?"

"That depends on whether it's pursued through criminal or civil courts," he responded. "If you've got a stalker, there are things we can do." He reached forward, his big, hot hand squeezing my smaller, cool one briefly before lifting away. He ducked his head, trying to capture my gaze, and gave a reassuring smile.

Seeing him like this made me think he was probably a good brother. He exuded calm and caring that made me feel like I could tell him everything and he'd fix it for me. Luckily, I'd had a crash course in not trusting people recently, so I managed to pull myself back from the edge.

"If he's making a nuisance of himself in other ways, like making abusive or silent phone calls—"

"Do they still exist? Silent phone calls. Haven't caller ID and blocking functions made it practically impossible?"

He borrowed a play from my gamebook and ignored my question. "Are you worried about the media finding out?"

Of course. The last thing I needed was to star in a stalking story in some tabloid. That would totally blow my image as an in-control chat-show host.

"You asked me to be with you when Tom came to collect his belongings, if you're scared," he said. No, bugger. This was getting out of hand. "There are laws against domestic violence, revenge porn, ha—"

"I'm not—" Shit! I nearly said, *I am not doing that.* "I'm not going to make a show about that." I needed to pay better attention to what I was saying. "I'm only interested in stalking a-and prosecution."

Alex sat back, assessing me, his pen tap-tapping, a tortuous beat, until I caved and spoke again. "When does just following someone, or leaving… *gifts"*—of the fishy variety—"become illegal?"

"When it becomes a course of conduct—multiple events—which amount to harassment."

Well, that told me next to nothing; if I just did everything once and spread it out, would it be okay? Tiny yellow sticky-note snowflakes piled up on the edge of his desk as I nervously shredded. I dusted them into the bin on top of his breakfast, a delaying tactic whilst I considered what to say next. “How does a person know if they’re… ah, being stalked?”

“Is his behaviour obsessive or controlling?” He pushed up from his chair, limping around the desk to sit to the right of me, on the vacant visitor’s chair. His knee brushed mine, his left leg—the one that seemed to pain him—stretching out. Big as he was, he seemed to surround me in a protective wall of man. “Does it make you feel frightened or distressed?”

Even the most weak-nerved of people wouldn’t feel scared or distressed over cress… or fetid fish. “Surely what’s frightening is different for different people?”

“That’s why the judicial system uses a ‘reasonable man’.”

“What about a reasonable woman?” I asked. “You’re far more likely to find a reasonable woman than a reasonable man.”

Alex sighed and rose, moving back behind his desk. “There’s no need to get offended.” He dropped gracelessly into his seat, pulling open his desk drawer, searching and muttering about chocolate.

"What are you looking for?"

"My emergency chocolate bar." I rolled my eyes. "Why I thought you'd bring a decent breakfast after dinner the other night is anyone's guess." He huffed, trying another drawer. "You clearly haven't had a proper meal in the last decade."

A door banged, followed by the sound of someone moving around outside in reception. "Cassie? Marie?" Alex jumped on the intercom like Rose on that floating door in *Titanic*.

"It's Cassie," came the response. "I didn't realise you were in so early."

"Thank God you're here. Before you take your coat off, can you pop out and pick me up something for breakfast, please?"

"Sure, I'll be back in five, but I'm getting myself coffee and a croissant on your account."

"Sounds fair," he responded, his tone making it clear she could have asked for the limb of her choice and he'd have agreed. The intercom clicked, and he cast a quick glance up, belatedly recalling I was still here. Clearly hunger was affecting his ability to concentrate. “You want anything?”

I shook my head.

“There a surprize,” he muttered.

I ignored him. “Reasonable man…”

“The reasonable man is genderless. It’s a technical term,” he said as he continued his drawer foraging.

“Who makes the decision about what’s reasonable?”

“In a criminal case, the jury considers whether a reasonable *person* with the same knowledge would think the actions amounted to harassment.”

“Not if they were in possession of the facts and were a reasonable woman,” I retorted.

“Okay. How about you give me some specifics from a show you’re thinking of running, and I can give you some legal advice.”

“Yes!” I fixed my gaze somewhere to the right of his shoulder. “So, say a person follows someone, their ex for example”—Alex gave a slight nod—“maybe drives past their home or favourite restaurant…”

"Could be harassment or stalking."

Shit. I winced. "*Everyone's* a stalker, given that example."

"It's not as easy as it sounds. It would have to be as part of a systematic approach."

"So, stalking's—" I had to clear my throat and start again, as I could hear the excitement edging into my voice. "So, stalking's difficult to prosecute?"

"It can be."

Finally, something I wanted to hear. So even if I got caught, the odds were good I'd get away with it. I wasn't malicious, not *really*. Alex studied me a little too closely for comfort.

"What you're looking for is a range of activities that may seem innocent, but when repeated—"

"How frequently?"

He shrugged. "More than two occasions, especially if it makes you feel scared or distressed." His irritating pen tapping started up again. "It's about the *reasonable* person and intent."

I only just managed not to roll my eyes and shout, *It's totally reasonable! He deserves it.* "I just can't see it. I mean it's so… innocent."

"Okay." He punctuated the word with a hard tap of the pen, which sent the pen top flying across the room. I laughed. Alex growled. Hungry men never had a sense of humour. "I can see you need me to paint a picture."

Was he calling me stupid?

"A guy likes a girl, loves her. He sets out to woo her." My lips twitched at the word *woo*. He gave me an unamused lawyer look and continued. "He asks her out. She turns him down. But he knows she's 'the one'. He buys her flowers regularly. Turns up at her favourite restaurants, pubs and nightclubs. He even invites her on an all-expenses-paid holiday…"

"That's harassment and stalking?" I asked. "How does anyone of dating age survive without a criminal record?"

He shrugged one broad shoulder. "If this is about your ex—"

"It's not."

"It's not about your show, either." *What? No, I mean yes.* Yes, it was. My heart was pounding. My stomach had vertigo. "There is a reason why you made it big as a presenter and not an actor," he continued dryly. "You need to keep a record of what's happening. Date, time, place and how you felt. Report every incident to the police, no matter how innocent it seems. This is about a course of events, so you need to be sure it's on record."

Oh, thank God. He still thought I was being stalked, not that I was the one stalking. "So, the police are reluctant to act on stalking complaints?" Maybe nothing would happen even if I was caught or Tom complained. Of course, there was still the risk he would sell the story to the tabloids; the *Mirror* or *Mail* would love it.

"They're stretched to breaking point," he responded. My shoulders relaxed and my stomach unknotted. No way would Tom or Talith record anything—they weren't even organised enough to go to Talith's place for sex so I wouldn't catch them. "That's why you record and report every incident. Whilst they may be able to find an alibi for one or two events, they'll struggle to find one for everything."

Oh my God. I hadn't thought of that. I didn't have an

alibi for anything… seeking my *reasonable* revenge was getting way too complicated.

"So, what could happen if the police did decide there was an unreasonable *course of events*?"

"Well, if he's just—and I don't use *just* lightly—following you and there are no threats or disruption to your work or life, they'd probably tell him to leave you alone and move on. If it escalated, or continued, he could get a formal warning…" Was that it? I could handle a slap on the wrist. It wasn't hard time. "It's not like in the movies. Stalkers are rarely strangers lurking in the bushes waiting for the first person who walks past with purple eyes or black hair. Given your job, it could be a fan, but it's more likely to be someone you know, someone 'normal' like an *ex-boyfriend* or neigh—"

"I get the point." I was pretty confident I could avoid arrest just by applying the reasonable woman test. Cress, a few new designer shirts and some partially putrid prawns weren't going to get me more than a police caution.

I'd sign a couple of autographs and give them free tickets to the show and they'd probably just let me go. Even if they didn't, I could live with a caution, provided none of them tipped off the press.

Hell, even if they did, it would probably just give me more credibility. Ricki Lake had weight issues, Jerry Springer was caught with hookers… and I got revenge against my lying, cheating ex. My audience would probably love me even more. In an ideal world, the US networks would see it as proof I wasn't too pretty, perfect and privileged.

"To be honest, Alex." I was pretty sure he muttered, *At last*. "This all seems a bit tame: a gift, a few texts or phone calls and suddenly I'm a stalker."

"It doesn't feel tame when it's happening to you. Why are you going to such lengths to protect this creep?" he asked. "If you're worried about how it will look, your career, no one would think less of you for speaking up."

"I've already said this isn't about me!" I snapped. "It's for a show."

"Fine." Alex sat back, his chair creaking. "Then I think it's time I actually came along to one of your shows."

A young woman came bustling into the room with a steaming cup of coffee and three Danish pastries on a plate.

“Oh! Sorry. I didn’t realise you had a client this early. There was nothing on the computer.” She flushed, hurriedly dumping everything on the desk.

“It’s all right, Cassie. Ms Scott made a last-minute appointment this morning. I just brought her straight through myself.”

“Can I get you something to drink, Ms… Oh! You’re Meri Scott!” Her voice rose with excitement. She turned to Alex. “It’s Meri Scott.”

I took the opportunity to gather my things to leave. I knew what I needed to know. I was pretty safe, unless Tom or Talith connected everything together, and even then, it would take a while to establish a course of events and link it to me.

“No, thank you. I’m leaving.”

“Do you… Can I… Would you mind—”

I whipped an autographed photograph out of my bag before Cassie had to ask and handed it to her. She clasped it to her chest with an excited squeak.

“Meredith?” Alex had inhaled his first pastry and was already selecting a second. “A little free advice.”

Ha! "I've probably just paid you more for the last hour and twenty-five minutes than most people earn in a week."

"Have a cinnamon-roll and I'll go pro bono."

No! I pushed up from my seat, moving away from the temptation—Three-hundred and sixty-five calories, twenty-one grams of fat. Alex picked up another pastry, consuming half of it in one bite.

"Whatever is going on with you, whether this is research for a show"—he fixed me with an *and we both know that's a load of crap* look—"or something to do with your ex, you shouldn't retaliate."

"What?"

"Cress. You'll just escalate things, and it will count against you if the police and courts get involved." He held up a hand, silencing me when I would have protested my innocence. "I can talk to the police for you, or to Tom as your lawyer. Just because you're in the public eye doesn't mean you're public property." .

CHAPTER 12

You're Pregnant; So Who's The Daddy?

Three days later—just over two weeks since I'd walked in on Tom and Talith, five days since I found out about Tom and Jenn—I walked across the limp, wet grass on the school playing field, hugging my long coat around myself for warmth.

"Aunty M, Aunty M!" A tiny body hurtled towards me. Getting close, Owain threw himself at me. Love bloomed anew in my chest, at his innocent trust that I would catch him. I did, laughing and sweeping him up and spinning him around, whist he shouted and whooped, cheeks flushed with the cold and pleasure. "You came! You said you couldn't. But I knew you would. You promised!"

I hadn't been able to sleep thinking about the tears in

his eyes, the hurt, when I'd said I couldn't come. I'd *promised.* He didn't deserve to be punished because of his parents.

"I *told* Mummy you would come."

I lowered him back to the ground, ruffling his blond hair and sending him back towards the others. I scanned the groups of parent-spectators, making sure to put as much distance between Jenn and I as possible. A race track of sorts had been marked out on the school field. At one end, teachers and helpers were trying, with varying levels of success, to herd overexcited children towards a start line. Why they'd chosen to do this in autumn and not spring or summer was any sane person's guess. Owain skidded to a halt at the start line, facing down the track, jumping from one foot to another and swinging his arms, all the while talking a mile a minute to one of his little friends.

I walked to a gap in the throng of parents and friends strung out along the side-line. It felt odd and lonely to be standing here alone, not snuggled together with Jenn laughing and gossiping whilst we waited, then cheering Owain on like he was going for Olympic gold. Jenn moved uninvited to stand beside me, looking effortlessly stylish in designer skinny black jeans and a sheepskin coat. "I thought you weren't coming."

I considered ignoring her, but just because I was at school didn't mean I was twelve again. "I changed my mind."

"Thank you."

Sod off. "I didn't do it for you, Jenn." I kept my eyes on the starting line and pulled a cold hand out of my pocket, waving when Owain and his friends looked towards me. "Owain's my godchild. I love him. Despite his parentage."

The silence stretched.

Jenn's stare bored into me. I didn't turn to acknowledge her. I might talk to her civilly, but I couldn't bear to look at her. I'd happily never see her again.

We stood side by side. The wind whipped loose blue-black strands of hair from my ponytail to tangle around my face. The sound of mothers and fathers encouraging their children carried on the air.

"I'm pregnant." Jenn's words hit hard, a solid gut blow. My breath escaped in a whoosh. I staggered back a step.

Pregnant.

Finally, sucking in a couple of gasping breaths, I turned. Jenn's full lips trembled. A perfect crystal teardrop clung to her thick lashes. "Four months gone."

My heart pounded. I looked back to the track, hugging my arms across my chest, trying to force some warmth into my cold heart. "Tom's?"

I strained to hear her whispered response. "Yes."

I laughed, a hollow, mirthless sound. They were still at it. She hadn't even had the sense to learn from the first time, even after she'd had to bring Owain up alone, unacknowledged by his father.

I shook my head, dislodging more hair from my hairband, leaving it tangling around my face. It was no wonder Tom never had time for a real job between auditions. He was too busy screwing around.

"Another accident?"

"Yes. *No.* A mistake."

I failed to hold back the fury. "Whilst my choice in friends and boyfriends might be a *mistake*, I've never considered Owain to be one." I turned, stalking off down the field, finding a clear spot to watch Owain.

Jenn followed, stopping in front of me, forcing me to look at her. Her eyes were luminous with tears, her brown hair haloed her face and her cheeks were flushed with windburn. She looked like a model in a shampoo commercial. I stared back. She was gorgeous. She could have had anyone—a prince, an oil sheik, a millionaire—so why did she want an unemployed loser like Tom? Why did she want to sleep with my boyfriend behind my back?

He hadn't done a damn thing for her or Owain since he'd been born. Hell, the closest he'd come to even acknowledging Owain's existence was when I signed his name on whatever card or gift *I* bought Owain for birthdays and Christmas. And yet it seemed Jenn thought he was a good enough father to foist on a second child.

"I don't think Owain's a mistake," she said. "I love him. You know that."

"I guess it's too much to hope you only had two accidental dick impalings with my boyfriend, with a four-year gap between and you just happened to get caught out both times?" Stranger things had happened on *The Meri*

Scott Show. It was amazing how many times someone got pregnant by a man they were a hundred and ten percent sure they'd never slept with, as opposed to one of the three other men they brought up on the stage for testing.

"I'm sorry. It was a"—Jenn searched for a word, then gave up—"mistake."

"Four years between children isn't a mistake… it's family planning." Teachers herded the last few children to the starting line, tying shoelaces and wiping away tears. Owain edged forward, hopping from one foot to another, keen to get going.

"I l-love him. Tom," Jenn said. I laughed bitterly, giving Owain a fake smile and thumbs-up when he glanced over to see if we were watching. "I'm scared, Meri."

For some reason, the name Meri was starting to grate on me. There was something naïve, childish and stupid about Meri. Meri was the kind of person who only ever slept with one man and didn't realise he slept with any woman who'd drop her knickers. Meri didn't realise people were only with her for her money and fame. Meri was pathetic. I was fast beginning to prefer it when Alex called me Meredith.

Meredith sounded switched on, independent, successful and sophisticated. Meredith wouldn't be oblivious to the fact that her boyfriend had been cheating on her with her mother and best friend, whilst she worked like a dog to fund their lavish lives and his children.

"I c-can't afford to go on maternity leave." Jenn gave a hic-sob. Lifting the trailing end of her Chanel scarf, she dabbed delicately at the tears. "And I don't have a birthing partner—"

"That's your problem. Yours and Tom's." Maybe Talith's, too. I wouldn't count on her as a stepmother, though. She'd been a crap mother. "Not mine. Not this time around. I'm done with you all." Jenn delicately, beautifully sobbed, pressing trembling fingers to her lips. "Tell Tom. It's time he stepped up to the mark."

"Owain—"

"Owain is a beautiful, bright, *brilliant* child. He'll be fine." I'd make sure of it. Just because his parents were faithless, lying, money-grabbing sacks of shit, didn't mean he had to suffer. "He'll enjoy having his father in his life. I assume you've told Tom he's the father?" She nodded. "And you've told him about the latest pregnancy?"

"No. I tried, but he was at Talith's."

"Well, you better get on with it." In spite of everything, the part of me that had been best friends with Jenn since we were eleven years old wanted to step in and solve her problems, like I always had. But we weren't best friends anymore. We hadn't been for longer than I cared to know. "You've only got five months, and it will take Tom at least that long to get real a job."

"Meri, *please.* I thought you'd understand. Tom—"

"Don't worry." I hardened my heart. "I'll give you a free DNA test on my show if he decides to play hardball."

"You're so cold." Jenn looked at me, toffee-coloured eyes swimming with tears. "Tom always said… that's why he turned to me for—"

I spun on her, fury spilling out, finger pointing. "That's Tom's excuse. What's yours, Jenn?"

"I love him. I've always loved him, even before you two met… By the time he realised he felt the same for me, it was too late. You two were together… We didn't know what to do. We didn't want to hurt you, but I *love* him."

"Funny, I thought you loved me." I turned back to the

race, giving another bitter laugh. I didn't know why I was laughing; nothing was funny about this. It was desperate and sad and ridiculous. "It seems your love doesn't count for much…" It also sounded like Tom used the same lines on Jenn he used on Talith. The starting whistle sounded. The swell of cheering parents became deafening.

I clapped, my cold hands making a hollow thumping sound. "Go on, Owain!" He started well, streaking to the front of the pack. He turned, waving excitedly. "Run!" I shouted, wincing as he tripped over his own feet and went sprawling across the grass, skidding along on his tummy. A teacher rushed forward, sweeping him up onto his feet, brushing him down and pointing him back towards the finishing line.

"You can do it, *caraid.* Keep going," I shouted, but it was too late. he had gone from first to second to last. A trooper, he put his head down, little fists pumping as he ran through the finish line, all knock-kneed determination. One of the teachers swept him up in a hug, wiping away his tears of frustration and sending him off to pick up his egg and spoon for the second race.

"Do you know where he's living now?" I didn't have to say Tom's name. "That he's with Talith?"

"He said it was just to help her out financially," Jenn responded softly.

She'd talked to him recently, then. Long enough for him to fill her head with more lies. He was an unemployed, narcissistic, selfish git. The only person he helped out was himself. "He's screwing her."

"N-no. That's what I thought at first, but you're wrong." She'd changed her tune from the other night when she rang me sobbing about him cheating. "He said he wouldn't do that to me."

Again, I laughed mirthlessly. "Just to me, right?" Jenn looked away guiltily. "Why do you think we split up?"

"I thought maybe he told you about me and Ow—"

"I caught him fucking my mother."

"No." She stepped back, shaking her head.

"Yes. He could have come to you at any time in the last five years. Hell, any time in the last seven years. He chose not to." Owain picked his egg up off the ground and put it back onto his spoon, clenching his tongue between his teeth, to aid his concentration. "If he's helping someone out financially by living with them, why isn't it you and Owain?" Jenn mouthed *no.* She was living in cloud cuckoo land. "He's screwing her. He has been for years, maybe even longer than he's been screwing you."

"Why?"

"Perhaps he found *you* too cold for his liking, too."

Jenn flinched as I recycled the insult. Hurting her didn't make me feel proud, or happy or… anything.

Done with the conversation, I moved away, taking up position alone further down the track. I cheered Owain through a six-egg-drop egg and spoon race, then stayed long enough to admire his plastic silver medal. I hugged him, breathing in his scent, absorbing his warmth and silently pouring my love into him, until he wiggled for freedom, running off with his friends. We'd have to work out how I could continue to see him, without having to spend time with Jenn. Maybe I'd talk to Alex about it.

I left without speaking to Jenn again.

* * * * *

Four hours later, I heard a key scrape in my front door lock. I hauled the door open without checking the spy hole, which in hindsight was really stupid. I should have checked and then put the security chain on. Hell, I should have made them leave their keys, or changed the stupid lock. Gloria Gaynor had been preaching this to hapless women for decades. I wished I'd listened.

I thought my day couldn't get shittier than finding out my best friend was having a second child with my boyfriend—*ex*-boyfriend—who was currently shacked up with my mother. Then Talith pushed past me, all unnaturally taut and pert with that strange post-plastic-surgery frozen look that meant she could be any age between forty and Egyptian mummy, thick blond extensions swishing around her shoulders and down her back. She marched into the living room, as if I'd invited her in for tea. "You're not welcome here anymore, Talith." I remained at the door, holding it open. "I meant it when I told you to take Tom with you and not come back."

"We need to talk."

"No, *we* don't." There was only one reason for her to be here. I thought it would take longer for her to realise all lines of credit had been cut off.

The Bank of Meri had only stopped trading three days ago. I thought she and Tom would have squirrelled away enough of my money over the last seven years to get through a couple of months at least. Clearly, I'd overrated their intelligence… or they thought I was the biggest sap to ever draw breath and the money would keep flowing.

Talith looked up, eyes pleading, the rest of her face frozen in Botox-induced rigour. In a detached part of my mind, I wondered what she'd look like when the Botox began to wear off—because I wouldn't be paying for it—and her skin started to wrinkle and sag. How sexy would Tom find her fifty-seven-year-old body when a few of the nips and tucks came undone?

"He tricked me, Meri. I never would have betrayed my baby if he hadn't played to my vulnerabilities." She tugged some super-strength aloe tissues from the box on the coffee table, delicately dabbing her eyes. "I'm a forty-seven-year-old w—"

"Fifty-seven-year-old."

Her eyes flashed with anger. "What does age matter?"

I shrugged. "It doesn't, not to me." I watched as she

attempted to pull her argument back together.

"I ah… I…"

"You're a *fifty*-seven-year-old widow…" I prompted. The sooner she said her piece, the sooner she'd leave. "He played to your vulnerabilities."

"You don't understand."

"You're damn right I don't."

"That's because you're young. Still in the first flush of life. You can have any man you want." Except the one I thought I was with, apparently. "When your father left me—"

"He *died*, Mu—Talith."

"He left me all alone with a young child. I had to scramble to make ends meet. I had to work in a *shop*. A shop. On the tills." She said it like she'd had to sell her body on the streets of Cardiff for five pounds a shot. "The best years of my—"

"Life were wasted." I'd heard it a million times before. I moved out of the hallway and across the living room, back to my cup of tea, taking a sip of the lukewarm brew. "You should have given me up for adoption if you felt like that."

"I couldn't." She pressed on hand to her chest. Her usually perfect manicure was looking a little chipped. "You're my baby."

"But you could screw your baby's boyfriend…"

"You're being vindictive. I've sacrificed for you, for the last eighteen years—"

"No." I paced. "For the last fifteen years, since I was a kid, I've worked every hour I could. *I* paid the mortgage on your home and mine. *I* bought *you* everything you wanted."

Talith perched on the edge of the couch, skin-tight jeans and low-cut top hugging her every surgically enhanced curve. "I did it for you, darling."

"You slept with my boyfriend for me? Seriously?" This was the best she could come up with?

"Did you think I enjoyed it?"

"From personal experience, I'd say not much, but from all the noise and the scratch marks down his back?

Yes. Yes, I do." I blew out a harsh breath. "Why don't you just skip to the point? You don't want to be here any more than I want you to be here. So just ask for the money, so I can turn you down and you can leave."

She jerked from her seat, tears evaporating in the face of her temper. "You always were a cold-hearted bitch. Even as a child. You never needed anyone but yourself."

"And yet you sacrificed…"

"You suck the emotion out of other people's lives to put on TV," she said. "You don't care about anyone but yourself." I rocked back on my heels, absorbing the pure venom in her words. "You're an emotional vampire."

"Maybe I'll get a role in the next *Twilight* movie."

"So that's it? You're going to refuse me."

"You haven't even told me why you're here yet."

"You know why I'm here," she snarled. "You've stopped paying my mortgage."

"And your bills and credit cards and the automatic top-up to your bank account," I added with a smile. "You've always said you were an old-fashioned woman at heart. Well, you have a man now. Why doesn't he support you?"

"It isn't like you don't have the money, and I'm your *mother*."

I stared at her, unmoved.

"He stopped loving you and started loving *me*. He wanted a woman, not an icicle in his bed," she snapped, lurching across the room, fury stealing her co-ordination. The scent of Chanel and putrefying prawns followed in her wake. I stepped away, heaving up the sash window and taking a deep breath of traffic-polluted London air. Anything was better than rotting fish. "Tom wants me more than you."

"You and any other woman who'll—"

"Enough! I won't have you talking about him like that. You and he had drifted apart."

"I'm beginning to wonder if we were ever really together in his mind."

"I know how you're feeling." She didn't know anything about feelings. Certainly not the feelings a mother should have for her child.

I'd had seven years of self-centred liars and cheats on

The Meri Scott Show as training for manipulative wheedling like this.

"It isn't like I abandoned you. You're still my baby. You'll always be my baby, just like I'll always be your mother. We're family. And Tom's my partner. That makes him part of our family. So, you have to get along."

With perfect timing, Tom strolled into the flat as if he still lived here and wasn't trespassing. Clearly, I needed to have a conversation with Vic about security. "Talith and I"—he sank down onto the sofa, tugging Talith down beside him—"we're going to get married. I'll be your step—"

"Fuck no!" I lost it. I slapped my hand down on the oak dining table beside me, the sound cracking like a gunshot, shutting Tom up, before he said something I could never un-hear. "Let me make it clear." They both jerked back at the sound. "I will divorce my mother before I accept you as part of my family."

"She's your mother."

"She's your *lover*, Tom," I snapped. "And just so you're clear, there won't be any money coming from me to either of you. So, I guess you'll just have to get a real job and pay your own way."

"Meri!"

"And hers." I ignored my mother's shocked tone. "And it's not going to be cheap. She has expensive tastes, and I hear Jenn has another of your buns in the oven. So, you'll have child-support payments to make for the new kid as well as for Owain."

"What?" Talith turned to him when he didn't immediately deny my comments. "T-Tom?"

"We'll talk about it later," he said.

"You slept with Jenn?" Her voice rose to an unattractive screech. "When?"

"Later, Talith! It was nothing. I—"

I wasn't interested in hearing his excuses. "Just leave, both of you. I'm not interested in having anything to do with you." I crossed to my front door, pulling it open and waving between them and the door, in the universal sign for *get the fuck out of my house*. "You made your choices. Now I've made mine. I'm shedding the parasites in my life. Moving on."

Tom rose from the sofa, pulling Talith with him and

stomping towards the door. "I'm your *mother*. You *owe* me," she shrieked her head turned almost one hundred and eighty degrees, like something from *The Exorcist*. "Don't force me to do something you'll regret, Meri." .

CHAPTER 13

Did You Vandalise My Car? Lie Detector Test

Three days later, I could feel Alex's stare burning into me as we headed into the studio. He was coming along to watch the filming of my show, as part of my *legal adviser* ruse. I'd offered to drive him. Nervous anticipation boiled in my stomach and shivered over my skin.

Part of me wanted to impress him, to show him why I'd won three Most Popular awards at the NTAs. The rest of me was worried about accidently giving the revenge plan away, I was four revenges down: cress, fish, clothes, cash. If I took my "one revenge for every year we were together" theory to heart, and I did, I still had three left.

Embarrassingly, part of me was a bit worried about what he would think of my show.

Some people were snobby about my work. So, I wasn't Jeremy Paxman interviewing government ministers or anything. I was good at my job. I helped people put their lives back on track, so they could try to become valuable, contributing members of society.

Alex continued to stare at me. I loosened my death grip on the steering wheel and touched my mouth and nose, just in case I had something icky on my face. My fingers came back clear. I flipped down the sun visor, checking my face in the tiny vanity mirror.

I looked fine—good, even.

"Brake!" Alex's shout snapped my attention from my reflection to the road, where an SUV had stopped at a red light. He braced himself for impact. I slammed on the brake, wheels screeching as I slid to a stop, millimetres behind the SUV. "For fuck's sake, Meredith!"

I unclenched my jaw. "What?"

He stared at me, breathing hard. "You nearly killed us."

"Rubbish! You're such a drama queen," I retorted, feeling a little shaky, but trying to cover it. "At the speed we were going, at the worst what would have happened was a slight maiming. Why are you staring a hole in me and frowning?"

"You nearly killed us!"

"Because you were staring at me like I had something on my face."

"We nearly died because you're worried about your makeup?"

"No! Well, not just because of that." Admittedly, my concentration was a little frazzled. This morning Tom had tweeted a picture of rumpled sheets with Talith's bare twig-brown leg, right up to the crease of her crotch, sticking out, artfully posed. Not that anyone else would know it was Talith's leg—they'd probably think it was mine. The message read, *Nothing better than breakfasting on my Honey in bed.*

Not breakfasting with.

Breakfasting *on*…

I choked back my own breakfast, which was threatening to make an unscheduled return at the idea of Tom *breakfasting* on my mother. I'd unfollow him, but that would get attention—at the moment, people still thought I was the *honey*. Plus, the only thing worse than seeing what they were up to would be not knowing and being blindsided by it.

"Huh?" Finally, the traffic light turned green. I pulled out carefully behind the still-gesticulating SUV driver. I gave him a super-dazzling, toothy smile, a famous-person version of middle-finger-flagging someone. I didn't want to be photographed cursing. He was totally overreacting. It wasn't like I hit his car. I may have come close, but almost didn't count in car crashes.

I looked at Alex. "So, why were you staring at me?"

"Eyes on the road, Scott!" he barked.

I turned back to the road, rolling my eyes. "Well?"

"Perhaps I like the view."

I gave up. He clearly wasn't going to tell me.

Unless… maybe he was serious? I'd been out of the dating game for a while. Actually, I'd never really been in the game. Maybe he was flirting. He was a good-looking guy, the whole tall, dark and handsome package, with a side serving of sexy and intelligent sprinkles. I'd made top three on the hundred hottest female celebrities in the UK list last year… so I wasn't eyes-bleeding ugly either.

But I wasn't sure I was ready to show him my prepubescent flirting skills, or moving on yet. I turned my attention back to the road. Clicking the volume button on the steering wheel, I started singing along.

"Aren't you concerned this is a little ah… inciting?"

I glanced from the back end of the big black SUV directly in front to see what the Alex was concerned about now. He nodded at the radio where I had my phone connected. The Dixie Chicks sang about killing Earl, an abusive ex-husband.

It was from my recently created "Inspiration" playlist, a.k.a. "women singing about revenge" music. I shrugged off his question. "It's legal." To listen to, anyway. Killing your ex, unfortunately, was not.

"It's insane."

"I don't question your taste in music."

"Because I'm normal."

"My music is normal."

Alex coughed. If he wasn't my lawyer, I might have thought his *cough* sounded suspiciously like *bullshit.*

"All of these people are chart topping."

"So far you've had the Dixie Chicks singing about murder, Pink preaching revenge and some woman singing about getting vengeance on a cheating ex."

"Carrie Underwood, season four winner of *American Idol*." And singer of my favourite inspiration song. Killing Tom—ah, Earl—as per the Chicks, was unrealistic. But Carrie, you had to like her style—a little vandalism and a heads-up to the next girl stupid enough to be taken in by her loser ex. I used the button on the steering wheel to skip back to Carrie and "Before He Cheats" again.

Why, when Tom was deliberately taunting me, when having my mother's *honey* for breakfast was the least offensive thing he had twittered over the last week, was I just letting him get away it?

I needed to crack on with my great Plan of Revenge.

The shock of betrayal was still insulating my emotions, but even so, I had a right to be pissed about this. I had a right to feel. It wasn't good for my health and wellbeing to keep everything locked inside. Any other woman worthy of the gender *would* be crying, shouting, smashing windscreens and carving their name into the lying, cheating bastard's leather car seats. Just like Carrie sang about.

Whatever the consequences may end up being, I was pleased I hadn't just *risen above it* and sat back and done nothing as Tom shagged my mother and best friend and drove around in a car I bought, wearing clothes I bought, smiling smugly with porcelain veneers I paid for.

So why was I just driving to work as normal, when he was publicly bragging about eating my *mother's honey*?

I yanked the steering wheel and shot past the entrance for the studio, cutting across three lanes of traffic and shooting through an amber light.

"What the fuck?" Alex grabbed for the dashboard, slamming to a halt as his seatbelt locked.

The car swerved, wheels screeching. Horns blared and traffic snarled behind us.

"What the hell are you doing?" He craned around, clearly checking for a reason for my erratic driving. "Is it your stalker? Is someone after you?"

"What? No. This isn't an episode of *Law & Order*."

"Pull over and tell me what the hell is going on, then."

I ignored his directive to pull over, but responded, "This morning Tom said he was breakfasting on my mother's 'honey'."

Alex grimaced. "What's that got to do with you causing a five-car pile-up?"

I said nothing.

"Get over him, Meredith." His voice took on his exaggerated lawyer tone. "He's *not* your boyfriend anymore."

No. He wasn't. After seven years, I suspected that should hurt more. "She's still supposed to be my mother, though."

Alex scanned the fairly clear road in front of us, then sighed, a long, painful sound, his head dropping back against his seat. "Why are you so hung up on the guy? You are a gorgeous, successful career woman, and he is an arsehole."

I ignored him. It wasn't a conscious decision. I just found my mind focused on other things at the moment.

Like the fact Tom was suddenly tweeting with the frequency of a Kardashian, with all of his messages targeted to upset me. He'd followed this morning's vomit-inducing *mummy honey* tweet with his philosophy on picking a life partner. *Some people say if you want to know what your girlfriend will be like in twenty years, look at her mother. I looked. I liked.*

It wouldn't be long before the press got hold of their affair. It was a bloody miracle they hadn't already. This wasn't a run-of-the-mill affair that would only get a day or two of media coverage. This was my boyfriend having an affair with my *mother*… this would run for weeks.

Worry bubbled in my stomach. I really needed to talk to Tony about this and how we'd manage the impact. I'd been putting it off, but now with Jenn too…

"Are you even listening to me?" Alex demanded.

"Not really," I responded without thinking.

"Pull over!"

I swerved to the pavement, coming to a halt.

"Where the hell are you going now?"

I shrugged free from my seatbelt, grabbing my handbag and stumbling from the vehicle. Alex clambered stiffly out his side of the car, following as I started to jog.

"Meredith?" At a disadvantage, due to me having a head start and him having a bum leg, he arrived thirty seconds after I reached my destination: Talith's house. "What the hell? Is that some sort of ninja baton?"

I pulled my baton out of my Mulberry tote and extended it police style with a flick of the wrist.

"What the fuck!" He leapt back, only just avoiding my first practice swing. "Where the hell did you get that?" he whisper-shouted, scanning the street for threats and witnesses.

"Online." I hadn't planned what I was going to do, so this was an off-the-cuff revenge, just like the cressing. I took a swing at the front headlight of the cress-mobile.

Alex grabbed my elbow, slowing my swing and knocking off my aim. The baton made awkward contact with the bumper just above the headlight. The impact jarred it out of my hand, sending it skittering underneath the maroon Ford Fiesta parked in front of Tom's car.

"Why the hell are you so hung up on this loser?" Alex snapped. "You're an attractive, intelligent, independent woman. I don't understand why you're being a psychopath about a deadbeat."

His grip on my elbow tightened. I twisted my arm free before he could shake some sense into me.

"This is real life, Meredith. Not some hormonal, whingey country song. You can*not* go about vandalising your ex-boyfriend's car just because he likes someone else more than you."

Falling to my knees, I crawled halfway under the Fiesta, patting down the tarmac, trying to reach my baton. "I can do what I want to it." My voice echoed weirdly under the vehicle. "It's my car."

"What?"

"It's my car. I paid for it."

"You gave it to Tom."

"Semantics!"

"Legal fact!" he snapped.

I wiggled out from under the car, staggering back to

my feet. My handbag fell off my shoulder, tumbling down my arm, swinging like a pendulum into the headlight. The glass shattered. We both froze, staring as glass fragments scattered across the pavement. The car alarm started blaring, and the remaining lights were flashing.

"Shit!" I swung my handbag back onto my shoulder and took off running, shouting over my shoulder, "Run."

"What?" Alex glanced from the glass-strewn pavement back to where I'd been standing seconds before.

"Run!" I repeated, making like Usain Bolt.

Alex ran.

I was breathing hard and digging through my cavernous handbag when he caught up with me back at my car.

"I can't believe you did that!"

"What?" I glanced up.

"Are you fucking kidding me?"

I shrugged. "It was an accident."

"You had a baton and a theme song, Meredith. That

was no accident. You came prepared."

"I didn't come prepared. It was spur of the moment. And it was still an accident."

"Jesus Christ." He threw his hands in the air in an *I give up* gesture.

"It *was*. My handbag fell off my shoulder."

"What the hell have you got in there that can break a headlight and dent the bumper? No!" He held up his hand, traffic warden style. "On second thought, don't tell me. The baton was bad enough. I'll be better off when it gets to court if I don't know what else you have."

"Don't be such a drama queen. I may have gone intending to smash up the car with my baton, but you saw what happened. It was an accident."

"Not for lack of your trying." He started to pace the length of the car, his limp pronounced. "You do realise you just made me an accomplice, don't you?"

"What part of *it was an accident* do you not understand?" I snapped.

He paced, anger and tension radiating off him. "I can

see the *CSI* episode now. They'll trace me through pollen on my shoes that comes back to some rare pot plant I have at home," he muttered, one hand fisted and digging into his thigh, which clearly pained him after the sudden sprint. "Then they'll find tiny fragments of headlight glass in my trouser cuffs." He glanced down and shook his leg, as if expecting betraying splinters of glass to fall out. He didn't even have cuffs on his trousers.

"You're being ridiculous." I pulled my keys from my bag and turned to face him.

He rammed the hand not massaging his thigh through his hair. "You need to get over him and stop this."

"It. Was. An. Accident!" It wasn't a lie. I'd intended to smash up the headlights with my baton, but gravity and Mulberry karma did it for me.

He jerked to a stop in front of me. "What the hell am I even doing here? In spite of the fact you supposedly hired me to advise on your show, I've yet to see an episode, including the one we should be at right now. You're clearly still hung up on your loser ex and… What the hell is the point?" He pulled open the passenger door and slumped into the car beside me. "What exactly do you want from me, Meredith?" .

CHAPTER 14

My Mother Chose Her Lover Over Me!

I glanced at Alex and then back at the road. He was talking like he liked me and was upset I might have feelings for my ex, which was… unexpected. Yes, we'd had dinner together once, he'd been to my house, I'd taken him breakfast at work… and we'd kind of remedial-flirted a bit.

Well, he had.

I wasn't sure. Tom and I hadn't really done the whole tease-y, sexy, kissy, touchy-flirty thing.

But he was my lawyer and I wanted legal advice—not that I needed it in this case. "It. Was. An. Accident," I said.

"There is no talking to you."

Wow. I didn't know what he was so worked up about. It wasn't like I'd planned it out. It was spur-of-the-moment thing fuelled by Tom's tweet and perhaps a little musical peer pressure from Carrie and the girls. Yes, I had my baton, but that was just coincidence. I bought it as part of Tom's RoboCop outfit for Elton John's Halloween party last year, then kept it for self-defence.

Alex thumped his head back against his headrest. "I'm not sure what's going on here, if he's harassing you, stalking you… whatever, but what happened back there… can't. Don't you see this is not moving on?"

I tensed. He was getting dangerously close to realising I was the one stalking and harassing in this scenario.

"Hell, this isn't even sane."

Was he right?

Was there something wrong with me?

From where I was sitting, my response to finding out my boyfriend was shagging someone not just old enough to be my mother, but who actually *was* my mother, was *totally* reasonable. The fact I hadn't gotten over it in the two and a bit weeks since discovery, considering the additional blows of discovering my best friend had cheated with him and so on and so forth… totally *understandable*.

"You're going to ruin your whole life. *You*. Not him." Alex pointed in my direction as I traversed the one-way system back towards the studio. "You. Because what you just did isn't just crazy, it's *criminal*." He gave it a second to sink in. "And it's not just your life. You had no right to bring me into this. None. I could get disbarred, and all because your boyfriend cheated on you. It's ridiculous. It has happened to just about everyone at some time in their lives. Get over it! Get over him."

"It was an *accident*!" I practically screamed at him.

I could almost hear the *tick-tick-boom!* of Alex's temper. "Let me out." He jabbed the release button on his seatbelt, yanking at the door handle as I slowed behind a queue of traffic at some lights.

"What?"

"*Now*, Meredith. Unless you want to add kidnapping to your crimes of the day." He yanked open the door, stumbling out before I even managed to stop properly, which was probably how he'd buggered up his leg in the first place.

I turned, watching him, feeling confused and restless. I was starting to lose control of my life. "What are you so pissed about?"

"It's my job to uphold the law!" he snarled, leaning back into the car.

"So?"

"There's no point talking to you. On the positive side, I think you'll have a legitimate insanity defence. You are nuts." He slammed the door and, ignoring the blaring horns, stalked across two lanes of traffic as vehicles streamed towards him.

* * * * *

"We love you, Meri!"

The shout interrupted my flow, but it was a welcome confidence boost when I was feeling low.

"Thank you." I smiled in the direction the shout came from. The floor guys shushed the audience as I tried to continue to read the autocue introducing my first guests.

"Meri! Meri! Meri!" More shouts and stamping filled the air. I had a lively crowd in today.

Usually I would take a few minutes to chat with them before filming started, but I was running late and, well… it was nice to get some positive affirmation right now.

Alex had no right to shout at me and stomp off leaving me feeling guilty. He'd totally overreacted. It wasn't like I'd deliberately smashed the car headlight with my handbag. That bag cost over a thousand pounds. The last thing I wanted was to scar the leather, especially when I had a baton to do the job.

He was totally exaggerating. *CSI*? Really? Hadn't Grissom from *CSI* gone blind or deaf or something? And the whole cast had something better to do. Like finding a light switch so they didn't have to always walk around in the dark with a crappy bloody torch. So, I was pretty sure we were both safe… Unless Alex sold me out to save himself.

Did client privilege cover this?

Okay, so if I was being objective—which was kind of my job—maybe he had a right to be a *little* bit pissed about being an accessory to a crime, but it wasn't like he was a real accessory. He was more like an innocent bystander.

And whilst I may have gone intending to commit a crime, at the end of the day, it was an accident. So, it wasn't my fault either. Still, I didn't like him being angry with me. It made me feel, itchy and uncomfortable and… sad.

Maybe I should apologise.

"Meri!" Jerry and Mike called me off stage. I met them in the wings. "What's going on?" Jerry asked.

"I… ah, I split up with Tom." I didn't think Jerry was actually asking about my relationship status, more about the fact I'd just frozen up on stage, but the words just fell out of my mouth.

"I'm sorry," he responded. "Sorry I can't say anything but *thank God* you dumped him." Jerry looked like a balding version of those ugly little good-luck Troll dolls with the colourful hair, but underneath the swearing, shouting and bluster, he was one of the nicest men in television. He squeezed my shoulder bracingly. I drew some confidence from the fact it didn't occur to him Tom would have dumped me.

“Guy was an arsehole,” Mike said. “I hope you kicked him out of your flat too. You’re better off without him.” This was Mike’s version of comfort. “Now pull yourself together. We have a show to make.”

“Take five,” Jerry said. “We’ll settle things down, kick a couple of people out, if necessary, and then you can go back out and crack on with the show.”

* * * * *

We were filming the third segment of the day, and I was starting to flag. It was a struggle to keep my mind on what was happening on stage. I kept flashing back to the hurt and temper in Alex’s eyes when he stared back into the car.

My step faltered and my smile slipped. Jenn was in the front row. I thought I’d made it clear I wasn’t interested in having anything more to do with her. I hadn’t thought she’d have the nerve to accost me at work, or I’d have spoken to the studio about revoking her pass.

“Meri.” She leapt up from her usual seat as soon as Mike and Jerry stepped away, snagging my arm. I shook her skin-crawling touch off. “Meri, I just wanted to see how you were doing?”

Who the fuck was she kidding?

She couldn’t care less how I was. She’d proved that every day since Owain was conceived, and for God only knew how long beforehand. I had nothing to say to her. The tide of revulsion and hurt when I looked at her was overwhelming. The time for sharing and caring between us was over.

“Dave?” I called. The head of security wandered over from the wings, all barrel chest and thick arms and legs, his bald head shining.

He flashed Jenn a smile. “Hey, Jenn. Nice to see you. How’s it going?”

“Get her out of here.”

“What?” His head whipped towards me as if I’d just asked him to strip naked and jump into a boiling vat of snake venom.

“You heard me,” I continued, as cold as Tom and his

coterie had accused me of being. “I want her gone.”

“Meri!” Her voice trembled. She’d deliberately approached me in public. In my workplace. Thinking I’d talk to her to avoid a scene. “I understand you’re upset, but I won’t give up on our friendship. Whenever you’re ready to—”

“I want her gone. *Now.*”

I watched dispassionately as she turned on the waterworks, tears turning her doe-like eyes luminous. How had I been fooled for so long? She might be gorgeous on the outside, but inside she was a manipulative, poisonous bitch.

“She doesn’t get back in. Ever.”

“What?” Dave barked out on a laugh, before realising no one else was amused. “Seriously? You two are like *best friends forever*, like sisters…”

What a joke.

Jenn had fallen silent, face pale and streaked with tears. Dave shook his head, looking like I’d asked him to drown a puppy, then gently cupped her elbow to escort her out. “Come on, Jenn, it’s best you go.”

"She doesn't get in here again, Dave," I called after him. "Tell your team. Not her, not Tom and not my mother. Owain is the only exception, and he's not to be accompanied by Jenn." I watched him herd her towards the exit.

"What's going on?" Jerry asked from behind me. "I thought she was your best friend."

"So did I," I responded, turning. "Let's get on with the show."

Twenty-five minutes later, the segment was going well. It was pretty standard stuff: a homosexual man in his early twenties trying to get his mother to understand his sexuality was not a choice. Begging her to love and accept him.

The mother was a sanctimonious bitch of the first order. The audience hated her on sight. It had only deteriorated after she'd refused to be hugged by her sobbing son and dragged her chair across the stage so she didn't have to sit beside him.

"I don't know why you're booing. *It's* an abomination," the mother shouted, to more booing.

"What kind of mother thinks that?" I asked, glancing at my cue card, trying to recall the son's name. Carl. Carl cried. "What kind of mother calls her son 'it'?"

"That's not my child."

"You don't get to pick and choose your children." *You bitch.* The audience cheered, but I couldn't really hear them through the pounding in my ears. "You're a mother! What happened to putting your children first? To loving them unconditionally?" When had mothers become so self-obsessed? Sleeping with their children's boyfriends, disowning their children because of their sexual orientation… "This isn't about you, you selfish—"

"Meri! Calm it down," Mike called in my ear, bringing me back from the edge.

I took a deep breath, focusing back on Carl and Tal—*Mary-Anne.* She was a useless mother, but she wasn't *my* useless mother.

"I love you, Mum. I'm no different than I was last week, before you knew." Carl looked at his mother, tears running down his face.

"Shit, this is good stuff," Mike said in my ear. "Close up camera two."

"There is no defence for homosexuality," Mary-Anne

said. More booing. I shook my head. “It’s an abomination. I don’t know why you are all booing. It would be different if it was your child.” She turned on the audience. Always a mistake. The audience could make or break you on TV.

Forty minutes of sobbing and bitching later, which would be edited into an exciting twelve-minute slot, including an ad break, I handed them off to the Catherine, the after-show counsellor, rushed through my meet-and-greet with chosen audience members and made a run for door.

I needed to talk to Alex before the police did. .

CHAPTER 15

Daughter: Your lover loves me more than you – Get over it!

Oh. My. God.

I couldn't believe she'd done it.

My vision tunnelled.

My head went light.

I stumbled into the wall beside the front door, sinking down to the floor, clutching the newspaper. Three days had passed since I'd declined to re-establish financial connections with Talith and Tom, and Talith made her threat. Here it was.

A two-page article with a full-colour double-page picture of Talith.

Naked.

It wasn't arty or discreet or… classy. It was airbrushed. Talith lounged back on her elbows, breasts standing to attention, nipples pointed to the heavens.

Her back was arched, her head thrown back in mock ecstasy, mouth open, eyes slumberous. Her legs were bent and spread. She wore bright red four-inch heels with peep toes. A framed picture of me was shielding her… between her spread legs.

It was obscene.

It looked like Talith was rebirthing me in photographic form, framed in sterling silver.

How could they do this?

How could it be allowed?

Fingers numb, I fumbled my mobile from my pocket and called Tony. His phone rang unanswered. I called again.

And again.

And again.

Nothing.

I waited through ten rings before it switched to voicemail. "Hi, I'm busy. Leave a message and I'll call you back. If I like you."

"Damn it, Tony!" I rattled off a furious message for my useless, shitty agent. "You're supposed to hear about these things in advance. I'm not supposed to be surprised by a picture of my mum's seven-thousand-pound tits and spread legs before breakfast. How could you let them do this?" Hysteria edged my voice, nausea churned my stomach and anger pounded my pulse. "There's a photo of me between her naked legs. I'm covering her *vagina*, Tony! *Call me!*" I violently jabbed the hang-up button on the screen, breaking a nail.

Heart pounding, hands trembling, I smoothed out the paper on the laminate flooring and began to read. The headline was posed as if it were one of my show titles. *Daughter: Your lover loves me more than you – Get over it!*

Under the massive centre page naked picture, the caption read, *Seductive: Talith says Tom can't get enough of sex with her.*

IN A STORY straight from an episode of her shows, the mother of controversial chat show host Meri Scott has betrayed her daughter by having a four-year affair with her daughter's boyfriend of seven years, Tom Kinley. Here Talith tells us her side exclusively.

Cougar Talith Scott, 48…

She was not forty-eight, she was fifty-seven. Tony could damn well get that corrected.

...started sleeping with wannabe actor Tom Kinley during Christmas in 2014. "I never meant to hurt Meri," Ms Scott says, "but Tom and I have an undeniable attraction. We just couldn't stop." Talith explains how on Boxing Day in 2014, when Meri was working, she and Tom, 34, first got together. "One second we were talking and the next we'd ripped each other's clothes off and we're going at it like rabbits on the kitchen worktop.

"I knew it was wrong. He was my daughter's boyfriend, but the thrill of knowing he wanted me and was willing to give up everything to be with me was overwhelming. It got so sometimes Meri would be in the house and we'd be having sex in the other room."

Suddenly, I understood the meaning of the phrase "killing rage". If either of them were here now, I'd be looking at hard prison time.

"Sometimes we had to be quick. On other occasions, when Meri was out, it could for last hours. I would pretend we were in a proper relationship and we weren't cheating on her.

"I would often say, 'Tom, we can't do this. We have to tell Meri.' He would say, 'I know, I know,' but neither of

us wanted to hurt her.

Talith says things have been on the rocks between Tom and Meri for years, adding: "She's always been too focused on her career. Tom's a virile man who needs regular attention from his woman."

There was a small inset picture of me with Tom and Talith at an awards show in 2016, Talith and Tom were looking into each other's eyes and laughing. The caption read, *Betrayal: Talith knew she was out of order but couldn't stop herself.*

"Sex is so natural between us. We tried to stop, but neither of us could keep away. In 2016, we broke up for four months, but then Tom called and told me I was the love of his life and he couldn't live without me."

Talith admits lying was hard. Speaking about their relationship, she said, "I know I should feel guilty, Meri's my only child, but we never set out to hurt her. We just couldn't stop; we love each other."

In public, though, Tom continued to direct his affections towards Meri, attending award shows and often being pictured by her side in magazines and newspapers. Struggling actor Tom, whose career never really took off—

he has had a couple of bit-part roles in TV soap Hollyoaks *and hospital drama* Holby City*—was with Meri for seven years. In June this year, he said, "She's everything to me. She's perfect. I can't imagine my life with anyone else."*

Meri spoke in an interview in November 2017 of her relationship with the actor: "He's a wonderful man. My rock. He's caring and supportive. I couldn't ask for more." When asked if they would get married, Meri said, "I'm just waiting for Tom to ask. No, I'm joking. Tom and I are committed. We'll get married one day. I've been focusing on my career for the last few years, but I'm thinking more and more of our future. I'd love to have children. I love my godchild, and can't imagine anything better than having little Meris or Toms running around."

Talith and Tom's relationship came to light three weeks ago when Meri returned early from the National Television Awards and caught them together in her bed.

"It was awful," Talith says. "Tom and I were naked and Meri was hitting him with her NTA. Then she threw us out of the house. She refused to listen to our explanations."

Meri—winner of Britain's Most Popular Talk Show, Most Popular Presenter and Most Popular Factual

Programme—has always credited the love and support she's received from Talith and Tom as the key to her success.

Talith says, "I know Tom cheated on Meri, but we couldn't help it. If there had been any other way, we would have taken it, but we couldn't bear to be apart, and there was never a good time to tell Meri. I know he won't do the same thing to me. I trust him one hundred percent. I couldn't be with someone I didn't trust.

"I'm really hurt over the way Meri has responded to our relationship. I understood she was hurt and angry at first, but I gave up my life to raise her as a single mother in a middle-of-nowhere failing mining town. I sacrificed my best years for her and her career. Now she's made it, just because she and Tom are no longer together, she's cut off all my credit. Basically, she's leaving me destitute. I don't want to hurt her, but she's hurting me. She's made me sell my story so I can pay my mortgage, so I can eat."

But Talith says she's not bitter – she just wants to move on with Tom. She admits she feels sorry for Meri. "Until she learns to forgive me and Tom and accept our relationship, she is going to continue to be lost and lonely," she says. "Her show is not going to keep her warm at night.

"I can understand she's angry Tom prefers me to her. It has to be embarrassing for a young woman to know her boyfriend is more sexually attracted to her mother, but she needs to get over it. We're going to get married. Tom will be her stepfather."

* * * * *

"Meredith! Mer—"

I had no idea how long I had been sitting on the floor, staring at the picture that accompanied the article, insides trembling with shock, but I flinched back as my front door swung open and Alex appeared. What was the bloody point in paying to live in a secure complex if people just buzzed anyone in off the street? Alex slouched in the doorway, looking hot, in a rumpled, strangely relieved way, and studied me, as he caught his breath.

"Shit!" He slapped a rolled newspaper against his jean-clad thigh. It was the first time I'd seen him for days. He'd been in court when I went around to his office to apologise, and he hadn't taken my calls since. "You've already seen it. I hoped I might get here first. Break it to you gently." I tried to stare him down, but had a disadvantage, given I was sitting on the floor at his feet. "Up you get," he said gently, snaking a strong arm around me. My emotions seesawed for a second. Tears surged forward and I thought I would cry, but then Alex hauled me to my feet, tucking me under his arm, against his side, and I felt his strength infuse me. He guided me down the hallway to the kitchen. I guessed he'd forgiven me, then… An unexpected warmth flowed, warming the cold pit inside me and spreading out to encompass my whole body.

"I tried calling. When I eventually managed to get through, your phone was answered by some woman who wouldn't tell me anything."

"I-it wouldn't stop ringing, so I diverted it and my social media accounts to Allie—she works for Tony, my agent. It's standard practice when the shit hits the fan." I must've looked really rough, for him to be so gentle. "Can I sue?"

"For what?"

"Slander."

Parking me on a stool at the breakfast bar, he rounded the counter, dumping the plastic bags and his copy of the newspaper. "It's libel if it's written. And no. You can't sue someone for having no taste or morals. There's nothing in that article about you that isn't true. Is there?" he asked, his navy jumper making his dark eyes seem even darker. I shook my head. I didn't think he'd care that Talith lied about her age. "And whilst it is stomach-churning, it's just your mother talking about her sex life."

I nodded, deflated.

"It's bedlam outside. Looks like the press and some fans are camping at the gate. Vic is in full Rottweiler mode. I didn't think he was going to let me in at first." He started removing items from the plastic bags, and chocolate bars began to pile up—white chocolate, milk chocolate and dark chocolate.

"What's all that?" I asked.

"Chocolate and ice cream, crisps, cookies…"

"It's amazing you aren't the size of a house," I responded. "All you do is eat."

He scowled. "I bought them for you. I wasn't sure what your comfort food of choice was… so I brought some of everything my sisters like. Wine, too, if you want to drink your troubles away, just this once."

My stomach dipped and tears welled. No one had ever done something like this for me. I couldn't—I *wouldn't* eat it… Getting fat wouldn't make my life any better. But my heart bounced and swelled at the kind gesture.

"I don't—" Prickles of panic chased across my skin as he pushed the overflowing bags towards me.

"I got the low-fat versions… and the high-fat ones, so you can pick. I'll eat what you don't want."

Of course he would. I hic-laugh-sobbed, grabbing some kitchen roll to wipe my eyes and nose before things escalated into a full-on emotional meltdown. This wasn't me. I wasn't the weepy type… it was just the shock of everything. I felt like I'd lost control over my life, and it was a scary place to be.

Alex crossed the kitchen, yanking open each cupboard in turn, searching. I watched him, my mind lurching from one thought to another. "Do you think I should get a boob job?"

"Ah…" He stared into the last cupboard as if seeking

divine inspiration from two tins of mung beans and some powdered slim-line mushroom soup.

"I paid for my mum's, and they look good, even in a grainy newspaper photo." I chewed my lip. "I don't have very big bre—"

Alex slammed the cupboard door. "There's nothing wrong with your breasts. If you get breasts like that"—he nodded at the newspaper I'd spread out on the worktop, tits up, without even realising I was doing it—"you'll look like someone stuck a couple of beach balls on a toothpick."

"Hey!"

"And you'll keep falling on your face."

"Shut up!" I huffed. "I don't pay you to insult me." I slumped onto a barstool.

"That comes for free, princess." His lips twitched and his eyes sparkled with suppressed amusement.

I was surprised by the endearment, but ignored it. "That implies you're willing to lie for a cost."

"I'm a lawyer." He shrugged, crossing back to the breakfast counter and pulling out a stool. He sat opposite me, turning the newspaper, his hand stroking over naked Talith as he eased the wrinkles out of the article.

"Stop touching up my mother!" I slapped his hand off the paper, then glanced back at the picture, examining Talith's body. "Do you think I'm boring in bed?"

"Well now." Alex pulled a pen out of his pocket and tapped it against the counter. Hadn't anyone any one ever told him how irritating that was? "That's not something I could comment on with any authority without some prior carnal knowledge of you."

"I must be." I tugged the pen he was tap-tapping from his hand and flipped the lid off, using it to add black nipple tassels and a skirt that obliterated my rebirthing photo to Talith's picture. "Boring, I mean. Tom and I never had sex on this counter." Alex pulled a face, rearing back and wiping his hands on his sweater. "Or in the hallway or even the shower…" A couple of chin hairs and a nose wart made the picture closer to my mother before surgery. "If my sex life with Tom had been anywhere near as exciting as the one Talith sold, I might have been able to overlook the fact he slept with her." Okay, that was a lie. I blackened Talith's porcelain veneers.

“So, your mother’s had more sexual experience than you.” He made a drumroll with his index fingers—which was even more irritating then the pen tapping. I glared him into silence. “She is twice your age and has no morals.”

“Yes,” I agreed, finding his assessment soothing.

He nodded at the picture. “Try a moustache—something long and feathery that will disguise whatever she did to her top lip.”

“Fillers,” I responded without looking up.

“Is that like Botox injections?”

“Sort of. It’s collagen injections.”

“It’s disturbing.” He looked closer. “It looks painful. Was it painful?”

“She cried for a week.” And I made her smoothies five times a day and brought her cream to numb her lips… Hell, I bought her lips, too. He was right, though. They looked like tyre inner tubes. “You need to go now.”

“I just arrived.”

“And now you need to go.” I felt the urge for revenge coming on. I’d hosted a show on trolling and viral emails once, the ones with video clips. I'd helped to keep a young computer geek out of jail, sent him to boot camp, got him a job… He'd always said if I needed any help, anything, no questions, no fee, to go to him. Maybe I'd get him to set up some sort of viral email or trolling campaign against Tom and Talith… I didn't know exactly, but Neil would know what to do.

Alex made no attempt to leave his stool. "I thought you might want someone to keep you company, seeing as how none of your two and a half million 'friends' are around right now."

"They're probably all screwing Tom," I responded absently, giving Talith's moustache a little curl at the ends. "Or selling their s-exploits to the tabloid newspapers."

"I'm not."

Not yet, anyway. "That's sweet, but I don't need you. Not if there isn't anything you can do legally about the articles."

Alex rounded the counter, cupping my cheek in a large and surprisingly warm palm and turning my face away from the newspaper and up to his. A fine tremor lifted the hairs on the back of my neck and pebbled my nipples. I leant into his touch. His thumb stroked my cheek. "I know you're upset, Meredith. What your mother and Tom have done is unforgivable. This article is beneath contempt. If your mother has money troubles, she should do what the rest of the world does and work to support herself." He stared into my eyes. My eyelids felt heavy. I swayed towards him. "If you need me, and I don't mean for legal advice… If you need a friend and the other two million, five hundred and fifty-four thousand are busy, call me." He must've checked me out online to know exactly how many friends and followers I had.

"How much do you charge for friendship?" It emerged as a whisper.

"For you? I'll do it pro bono." He stepped closer, bending to press a warm kiss to my forehead. My eyelids sank closed and my breath stalled. He straightened, swept the newspaper off the counter, tossed it in the recycling bin and headed for the door.

"Oh fuck! Sorry, mate. I didn't expect the door to open just then. I almost knocked in your face." Short, stocky and grey-haired Tony barrelled into my flat, his East End accent thick. He didn't have his hands full of comfort food or flowers, he didn't even bother with a "how are you doing?"

I'd only known Alex for a few weeks, but he thought of me first. Not my career or image… me.

Tony clapped a friendly hand on Alex's shoulder as he barged past. Alex planted himself at the door, narrowed eyes fixed on Tony. "Are you the new boyfriend?"

I didn't give Alex time to answer, rushing over with the crumpled-rescued-from-the-recycle-bin newspaper in hand. "Where the hell have you been?"

"I could have done with a heads-up on this one, babe," Tony said.

"You could have?" I snapped. "That's what I pay you to do for me, Tony. I've been calling you all sodding day. Where the hell were you? Couldn't you have pulled some strings and kept it out of the press?"

"Sorry, I've been trying to sort this shit out all morning. The wankers didn't even let me know it was coming. Apparently, it was a condition of Talith's when she sold them the story. We'll never give them an exclusive again." He spoke rapidly, pacing around my living room. "It won't happen again… I've been doing damage control and dealing with the press all day. It's why I missed your calls."

"Hmm."

"You didn't think you should tell me you'd caught your mother screwing your boyfriend and kicked them out?" he asked.

"I wasn't exactly shouting it from the rooftops."

"I'd have been happy if you just whispered it in passing, babe. I can't do my job if you don't tell me what's going on."

"I know. I just… I wasn't ready." I was still trying to sort out how I felt about it all.

Tony's sharp blue eyes focused on Alex, who hadn't managed to escape yet. "What do you do? Sport, presenting, singing, acting? You help us and—"

"None of the above," Alex responded coolly.

Tony glanced between Alex and me, his gaze finally settling on Alex. "You and Meri are friends?"

"Yep. I'm number two million, five hundred and fifty-four thousand-and-one," Alex said.

"He's on retainer," I said, glaring at Alex. The smart

arse was never going to let the friends thing go.

"Yeah, about that—"

"You single?" Tony didn't wait for Alex's response, turning to me. "You need a love interest to distract people. He's not as fit or good looking as Tom, but he's all right, and he's got a job." He turned to Alex, asking, "You have a job, right?" Alex nodded, and Tony turned back to me. "I'll pitch it as you growing up, trading up, going for maturity and intelligence over looks." .

CHAPTER 16

Girlfriend: Stop Faking!

An hour later, Tony barrelled out the door with the same energy he'd entered, his mobile phone glued to his ear as he barked into it. Silence settled and stretched. Alex stared at me across the living room.

He'd stuck around but, from his expression, wasn't impressed. "All that man cares about is *The Meri Scott Show* and his percentage. Where's the concern for Meredith the woman who's just had the foundation of her world rattled?" He shook his head. "Where are your friends, Meredith, the ones who care about you the woman, not the fame and money?"

I… I didn't have any, but I wasn't going to admit that. "So, I was thinking," I said, "I know you weren't keen when Tony mentioned it earlier, but… maybe… it doesn't have to be real… We-should-start-a-fauxmance." My words merged into one nervous rush.

"Wha—?" He inhaled and choked on laughter.

"A fauxmance," I repeated. "Why are you surprised? You had the same idea."

"No." He cleared his throat, the amusement fading from his eyes. "I did not."

"You said I should *rise above it, m*ove on."

"And…"

"So, I am."

"Nowhere did I say anything about a *faux*mance." He shuddered. "Besides, you wouldn't want to be stuck with an ugly pretend boyfriend."

I rolled my eyes. "Tony just meant you aren't movie-star-hot like Tom. There's nothing wrong with the way you look."

"Gee, thanks for the compliment. Get a real boyfriend."

"It takes time to meet someone and have a romance."

He shrugged. "You're a smart, successful, gorgeous woman. You don't need to go faux."

"I've no time to do it the real way."

"You're what? Thirt—" I glared at him. "Twenty-five?"

"I'll take that." If he wanted my real stats, he could look them up on Wikipedia, like everyone else did.

"You're attractive, and unless you've got something terminal I don't know about, you have time to get over your ex and meet someone and have a *real* relationship."

"I need someone now." And he was the only someone I could kind of trust. "We've gotten along fine today." In fact, there had been that moment when he touched my cheek and I felt like I could melt into him, and I was pretty sure his eyes smouldered before he forehead-kissed me. Yes, he harped on about me being skinny, but I thought there might be some sort of attraction there.

I shifted from my chair to join him on the sofa, sliding closer until I practically sat on his knee, burrowing under his arm so he had to wrap it around my shoulders to sit comfortably. His body warmth and ocean-fresh scent wrapped around me, and I found myself leaning into him.

"You putting the faux-moves on me, Meredith?"

I tipped my face up to look into his. "We wouldn't have to spend too much time together. Just enough to get some photos in the newspapers and on social media."

He frowned as his dark eyes narrowed. "The public birth of a fauxmance?"

"Yes." My cheek rubbed against his chest as I nodded. "Then the press can fixate on our relationship, instead of who Talith and Tom are shagging." An unexpected warmth began to swell inside me. A fine tremor ran under my skin as I imagined Alex in a naked newspaper spread. Actually, given what I suspected he was hiding under his clothes, we could aim much higher than some tatty tabloid. No one would believe Tom if he said I was frigid then. "We could sell the story to *Heat*, or some other magazine… maybe even *OK!*"

He shook his head. "You lost me at fauxmance."

"Pleeease. There's no one else I can ask." I wasn't too proud to beg.

He pressed his lips together, his eyes intense, but surprised me by not giving an immediate refusal. Instead, he grunted. "How faux would this *mance* be?"

"What do you mean?"

"Do we hold hands?"

Sure, why not. I nodded.

"Kiss?"

A shrug and more nodding.

"With tongue?"

Ah… I swallowed, "I guess, I mean it needs to be realistic."

"How far are you willing to take this, Meredith? Sex?"

My tummy felt strange, tickly and sinking. "I… I don't know." I bit my cheek. What was the right answer? Did he want me to say yes or no? Did *I* want me to say yes or no? "No?"

"You say that like it's a maybe."

It *was* a maybe. "No. No. I… I just…"

He sighed, looking off across the room for a moment, before sighing again and looking back down at me. “You need a friend,” he continued before I could respond. “I don’t mean followers or Facebook friends or acquaintances or financial dependents. I mean an honest-to-goodness, flesh-and-blood, put-you-first friend.”

God, yes, I did.

No one ever told you how lonely being Most Popular was. I was famous and award-winning and I didn’t have a single friend I could trust.

“There must be someone you can trust not to sell you out. Someone who sees Meredith, not Meri Scott, and can call you on the fakery and fauxmance shit before you harm yourself?”

“I…” I struggled to think.

“Someone from before you were famous?”

“There was Ffion, but we… lost touch.”

“What did you fall out about?” he asked.

“Her husband got laid off, and she hadn’t long given birth to their second child.” The story spilled out. “I was living in London. I'd just signed up for my third series of the show. I offered to help them out financially. She refused. We argued…" Ffion refused to "put a financial value on our friendship" or borrow money she couldn't guarantee they'd be able to pay back. I said she was being stubborn and proud, letting her house be repossessed when I had money and was already helping Jenn and my mother out. I didn't care if they never paid me back, but Ffion did, and she didn't take kindly to me "trying to buy her friendship". "We made up, kind of. We exchange birthday and Christmas cards, but I guess… I'm in London, she's in Aberdare, in Wales." I shrugged. "We just drifted apart."

"Hmm." He nodded, almost as if he heard the words I didn't say. "What about the woman in the photos, the one with the child?" He nodded to a picture of Jenn, Owain and I holding hands, ice-skating and laughing at the Hyde Park Winter Wonderland. I'd positioned it so Jenn was obscured by a coloured glass vase. Alex had clearly been snooping.

"We're not friends," I responded. "So…?"

"I'm not fauxmancing you," he responded evenly. My heart sank. I felt sick and clammy. I didn't realise just how badly I wanted it to be him. Now, I'd have to let Tony to set me up with some reality star or wannabe actor who was willing to pretend for the media exposure.

"But I will date you."

"You'll date me?"

"Yes," he answered. "Real dates. Real kisses." His voice was deep and husky and made me shiver in spite of the warmth he was radiating.

"That sounds"—*hot*—"nice." I felt lightheaded and trembly with a strange mixture of excitement and anticipation. Beneath the palm I pressed to his chest, I felt the steady, strong beat of his heart. His head dipped towards mine. My eyelashes fluttered closed and my tongue sneaked out to moisten my suddenly dry lips.

His lips pressed against the warm curve of my neck, featherlight kisses, whispering just below my ear. Shivers raced from the contact. My mind blanked and I arched into his touch. "And if we ever get to that stage, Meredith, we will be making love, not faking it, *any* of it." Strong teeth tugged my earlobe.

Oooh.

My nerves short-circuited. I knew I should say something, do something, but I couldn't concentrate. My lungs ceased as my heart seemed to swell before taking off, hammering and banging around my ribcage erratically. His tongue flicked out to soothe the sting of his teeth. Shivers of sensation raced across my skin, causing my nipples to tighten. He pressed kisses across my throat and around the curve of my jaw. I leant into him, making sounds of pleasure. Kissing with Tom had never felt this good, this all-consuming, and we hadn't even locked lips yet.

Finally, his lips met mine. Firm and sure. A shiver rushed up my back and down my arms. His tongue stroked over my lips, running along the seam, seeking entrance. He raised his hand to cradle my head, holding me still. A sound of pleasure rumbled in his chest, vibrating through every point of contact.

I'd become good at faking during the years with Tom's lacklustre moves, but this was the real deal. Sensations overwhelmed me. The rough scrape of his stubble across my palm. The firm, moist pressure of his lips. The friction of his tongue brushing against mine. The strong tug of his fingers pushing into my hair. Twisting. Holding me.

Heat flared in my stomach. I dissolved against him.

He slid his free hand down my back, cupping the curve of my bottom and hauling me onto his lap. I curled my hands around his nape and pressed my aching breasts against the hard wall of his chest.

He groaned.

I arched against him, squirming. My head felt light and lust hazed my vision. My blood zinged and fizzled around my body. My heart was bouncing in my chest and ears.

My mind was spinning wildly.

I was going to have sex.

I'd only ever been with Tom. I had wasted years on boring sex with one man. I'd never experimented with different positions and men.

That was about to change!

I wanted hot, hard, sweaty, *good* sex, and I was going to get it. No more wasting years on mediocrity; no more working my arse off so everyone but me could have a great life. I was going to look out for number one.

I was going to have an orgasm, and then we'd go out somewhere so people would see us. I shivered as his lips moved to my neck. "S'good. We'll have sex and then go out, so the press can see?"

Strong hands pushed me back, stiff arms holding me away so he could look into my face. "No."

No? "What about my orgasm?" His lips twitched, and he vibrated with suppressed laughter. *Bugger*. I'd said that out loud. I sagged, defeated. "D-don't you want me?" What was wrong with me? My boyfriend picked my mother over me, and now I was offering no-strings sex, and Alex wasn't exactly jumping at the offer.

"I'm a man, not as good looking as your ex—apparently." His ego had definitely suffered a blow there. "But you, you're a gorgeous, warm, willing woman." He shook me, gently emphasising his words. "Of course I want you."

I slumped back on his lap. His words and actions weren't matching up. "Then what's stopping you?"

He squeezed my hip comfortingly. "You're not in the right place."

"We can have sex any place you want," I offered. "I just want good sex for once. A real, flesh-and-blood, *man*-provided orgasm."

"Jesus!" His breath hissed between his teeth and his eyes squeezed closed. "I meant mentally, emotionally. You're not in a good place emotionally."

"Hmm." I wasn't the daughter of the UK's most prolific cougar without having learnt a move or two. I pressed my breasts against his shoulder and ran a hand slowly down his chest, before slipping it underneath the hem of his jumper, finding the fierce heat of his skin.

Alex groaned, his eyes closed, his head tipping back against the sofa cushion. He clamped his hand down on mine, stilling it, before he pulled it out from under his jumper.

"Stop it, Meredith."

It wasn't fair. "So, Tom can have it. Talith can have it… but not me?" I struggled to get up.

"If you were over them, you wouldn't care what Tom or your mother or anyone else was doing. You certainly wouldn't be thinking about them whilst you were with me, or any other man."

"My mental and emotional state is none of your business," I snapped. "This is just about sex and publicity. If you don't want it, someone else will."

Alex captured the hand I'd been jabbing towards him, preventing me from jumping off the sofa and stalking off.

“If a man on your show tried to rush a woman into meaningless sex and spoke like you just did, you and your viewers would vilify them. Just because you’re a woman and I am a man, doesn’t mean I don’t deserve the same respect, Meredith.” He stood, tipping me off his lap, and strode across the living room. Hauling the front door open, he paused, head lowered, and sucked in a deep breath. “I’ll pick you up tonight, for our first real date. If you can wait that long before finding a faux replacement. I’ll even take you to that event Tony was harping on about.” .

CHAPTER 17

I'm Not A Stalker - Leave Me Alone!

Alex was running late.

I should have insisted on the limo and picking him up. At least then I could have been waiting in comfort for him. Instead, I was heading down the stairs to wait on Regency Street. The police had come and cleared everyone away earlier, so the coast was clear. It went against my principles, but he'd said he was on his way, so I'd decided to head on out and meet him on the roadside.

This was our first public outing, and if it took him much longer, I would miss my red-carpet photo opportunity on the arm of "a mystery hunk". Turning up with him would earn me magazine covers. It would allow me to be the one to control the media around my breakup with Tom and show I was in demand. Not sitting at home crying my eyes out or slinking around London, carrying out my revenge.

Well, not crying, anyway.

People would be too busy guessing who Alex was to care about Tom or Talith's fifteen minutes of fame.

I tapped out a WhatsApp message to my friendly IT geek Neil as I walked. *Can I call in the offer of a little IT help? Something*—I tried to think of a palatable word for "probably illegal"—*clandestine?* I pressed send, and a millisecond later, two grey ticks appeared, almost instantly going blue. Message sent, received and read. My heart rioted in my chest.

Oh my God, I shouldn't have sent it. Now someone other than me knew. It could be used against me in evidence. My phone chimed three times in quick succession. I checked the messages, worried they would say something along the lines of *Your message has been intercepted by the police. You have 24 hours to hand yourself in. Do not run. We will find you.*

Instead, Neil's name appeared on screen.

Babe. Good thinking on WhatsApp. Its encrypted. Delete all messages sent and received in this thread after read.

God, I was starting to sweat. I was hyperaware, checking over my shoulder and jumping at every sound. This was all feeling a bit *Mission: Impossible*. This message will self-destruct in five seconds.

Read the news article. Bastards.

Follow this link to dark web... Put what you want in basket. I have payment/delivery channels that can't be traced.

After you've used link, follow these steps to delete search history. Message me if any problems and I will wipe for you.

Laughter floated across the yard; a family clattered down the stairs. Heart pounding, I locked my phone and tucked it away, slipping through the big black security gate and into the street.

Alex better not have lied about his expected arrival time. I was ready, in full makeup, with my hair styled in a high, slick bun. I was wearing another fabulous VB dress: a flattering, bright red floor-length dress. I'd doubled my gym routine and cut back my calorie intake for the past week to do the dress justice. The neckline was cut in at the shoulders and high at the front. It didn't flash boob, but then, I didn't have boobs to flash. I left that for the trashy reality TV girls and Talith. After the financial investments they'd made in their breasts and lips, they needed all the media coverage they could get.

A car slowed. I ducked back into the archway, hiding as it did a drive-by. The last thing I needed was to be photographed looking like I'd been stood up. It slowed. I peeked around the edge of the red brick archway to check if Alex had finally arrived.

Shit!

I jerked back out of sight.

It was the cress-mobile. Tom was driving, Talith in the passenger seat. They glanced up at my flat. The lights were off. The windows dark. They didn't see me hiding. They were too busy staring up at my flat. Tom said something, Talith laughed and they drove on.

Tom seemed to be spending a lot more time with my mother than he ever had with me. He'd always maintained his own space. He said he needed to be alone, to concentrate on his art… I'd always thought he meant acting. Now I knew he'd been practicing his love scenes. Unfortunately, in his case, practice hadn't made perfect.

But why the drive-by? What were they up to?

I hitched the skirt of my dress up, glad Victoria had gone for thigh-high splits this season instead of streamlined sophistication.

Without conscious thought, I unhitched a London bike from the hire rack, hiked up my skirt and pedalled after them.

The light at the end of the street changed to green, and Talith eased the cress-mobile out onto Vauxhall Bridge Road. The light was amber when I approached, red when I shot through it. Brakes squealed, car horns blared and an array of swear words fouled the air. I pelted up the road, eyes fixed on the flashing red tail-lights of the cress-mobile. They swung right, heading up past Pimlico Underground Station.

My heart was pounding, my breath panting, VB dress flapping in the wind behind me. I pedalled as hard as my three-inch Choos allowed. The traffic began to thin as we moved deeper into Pimlico. I hung back, recognising the direction they were heading in. They were going back to Talith's house. I swung my bike between the large iron gates and into the public garden in the central square, nearly falling off as I bumped up the kerb in the fast-falling night. Ditching the bike, I pushed my way in behind some shrubs as Talith and Tom got out of the car.

"I swear I saw something." Talith's voice cut through the gathering dusk. "Someone was following us."

"On a bike?" Tom scoffed. "They were probably just headed in the same direction. A lot of people live in Pimlico, honey." I growled. My mother shivered, and Tom wrapped his arm around her. "Why would anyone follow us?"

"Did you hear that?"

"What?"

"I thought I heard something growling."

"It's probably one of Mrs Coe's horrid little dogs."

"Maybe." Talith sounded doubtful. She snuggled closer to Tom.

“Come on. It’s getting late. Let’s go inside and get dressed.” Tom pulled the house keys out of his pocket and unlocked the door, ushering Talith in ahead of him with a palm to the small of her back. “Home sweet— Oh!”

Talith gagged.

Tom coughed.

Both of them flinched back from the open doorway. “Oh, God! It’s getting worse.”

I hunched down, biting my finger to stop the laughter. It was worth the mad dash across Pimlico to see this.

“It smells like something died in here.”

I pushed deeper into the shrubbery so I could see better.

My mother buried her face against Tom’s chest. “I can’t understand it. We’ve searched everywhere.”

“Maybe a rat died under the floorboards… Je-sus.”

“Make it go away,” Talith snapped.

“How?” He sounded exasperated.

“I don’t know. *Do* something.”

Tom was gagging now, but trying to be macho about it. "Let's leave the door open. I'll get the windows before you come in."

"You need to fix it."

"Me? It's not my fault. It's your house." Tom sounded resentful.

"It didn't smell until you moved in!" Talith retorted.

I pressed my lips together, holding in the laughter. It looked like there was trouble brewing in paradise.

Tom covered his nose with his arm, as if heading into a burning building, and rushed into the house.

A squealing sound, followed by the clanking of metal gates and a lock being thrown, cut through the cool night air. I pushed back through the bushes, gripping the hem of my dress to keep it out of the mud, walking on tiptoes so my Choos didn't sink into the compost. I hit the grass square at the centre of the park, just as the parks van pulled away from the street.

Leaving me locked inside the small, dark, shrub-filled park.

I gripped the bars on the gate, pushing and pulling, but it was locked. With me inside…

I scanned my surroundings frantically. The park was small, only an acre or so. It was surrounded by a black five-foot metal fence with spikes on top. I was five feet, two inches. Even if I wasn't wearing a VB dress and Choos, I'd never be able to climb out.

Oh my God. I was stuck! I'd have to wait until morning when they unlocked the gate. I squealed, ducking and running for cover when a door opened across the road. I waited. The door closed. My phone vibrated. I pulled it out of my purse. Alex's number flashed on the screen. I hit answer. "Where are you? Did you go without me? I was only five minutes lat—"

"Help!" I whispered. .

CHAPTER 18

Help! My Crazy Ex Is Stalking Me

My hands shook, and a fine trembling took my body. I felt excited and nervous and sick. I'd decided to follow Neil's link whilst I waited for Alex. I pushed myself further back into the bush, tipping my phone to reduce the risk of anyone seeing the light.

It was an STD shop!

A shop that sold STDs, for you to give people.

You could actually *buy* sexually transmitted diseases online.

Most of me was horrified by the idea, but a small part of me giggled manically and rubbed my hands together… Even as angry as I was, I skipped the deadly and incurable, hand shaking and mind swinging in the *yes-no-yes-no* dilemma…

I stabbed the screen, tagging crab eggs and dropping a dose of public lice into my shopping cart. Heart pounding, blood roaring in my ears, I stared at the screen.

I shouldn't do this.

They totally deserved it.

I closed out of the link, following the steps to delete my search history. I opened WhatsApp to message Neil to check them out.

This was bad.

I shouldn't do it.

They deserved it.

Should I get him to check it out…

No-yes-no-y—

Poop, someone was coming! I slipped my phone away and stealthily crawled forward to see who approached.

"What the hell took you so long?" I said in a harsh

whisper as I peered between the bushes and the black iron railing. "It's formal dress. Are you wearing a dinner suit?"

"Jesus." Alex closed his eyes, looking strangely pale and… scared? "I think you have bigger problems than my outfit right now, Meredith."

"Yes, but—"

"Don't worry, I won't embarrass you," he snapped. "I wish I could be as confident about the reverse."

Well, that was rude. If I didn't need his help, I'd tell him where he could go. "Step into the light where I can see you,"

He stepped into the yellow glow of a historical replica street lamp. Wow. He cleaned up well. His dark hair was styled back off his face. He was dressed in a black dinner suit with satin lapels and bright white shirt. He was *Great Gatsby* hot. He turned around, a full three-hundred and sixty degrees, arms out at his sides. "What the hell's going on?"

I snapped out of my gawking. "Shh!"

He turned back towards the park, frowning as he peered into the bushes. "Why are… we whispering?"

I gave him credit for not asking why I was hiding in the bushes. “I don’t want anyone to see me.”

“That explains why you’re hiding in the bushes. Which was not the question I asked. So, instead of seeing you in the bushes, they can see me, standing under a lamp, looking like a crazy man spinning around and talking to myself.” He stepped back into the shadows, leaning against the fence within touching distance of my hiding place. “Why are you hiding? Are you scared?” His voice carried a lethal undertone that was as sexy as it was deadly.

“Ah…” My mind blanked. “No comment?”

“No comment,” Alex repeated, heaving a massive sigh. “Where. Exactly. Are. You?”

“Behind you.”

“Give me coordinates.” He looked around again. “This is the weirdest first date I’ve ever had in my life.”

“It’s a faux-date.”

Another sigh. “In that case, I’m going home. I didn’t sign up for faux anything.”

“No!” I snaked a hand through the railing, grabbing his pant leg. “Please. Don’t leave me.”

“I’ve got better things to do than hang around talking to shadows ahead of a faux-date.”

"No! Please." I made like a limpet and clung to his leg. "Why are you being so mean?"

"You just rang for *help* and scared the shit out of me. My heart is still pounding so hard that I think I fractured a couple of ribs." He shook his leg, like he was trying to kick free from a humping dog, but I clung on. "And you're playing some psychotic game of hide and seek and denying our date. Come. Out. Where. I. Can. See. You."

I rustled my way out of the shrubbery, thankful the lighting was dull. "I'm here."

Alex blinked a couple of times as he stepped closer to the park railings, gripping them in his big hands. "Jesus. What happened? Are you all right?"

"Keep your voice down!" I glanced around desperately. I couldn't sense any movement across the street, no one had noticed yet. "No, I'm not all right. I'm stuck."

"Did he kidnap you? I'm calling the police." He reached into his pocket for his mobile.

"No!" I shook my head frantically, dislodging some hair, which had already been loosened by several trips through the bush.

He stared at me steadily for a long beat. “How did you get in there?”

“Through the gate.”

“Then can I suggest you use the same gate to get out?”

“The warden *locked* the gate.” Honestly, did he think I was an idiot? Why would I be in here if I could just walk through a gate?

He white-knuckled the railings, the only outward sign he wasn’t as calm as he was pretending to be. “Why didn’t you ask the park warden to let you out?”

“I, ah…” I struggled for a plausible excuse. “Would you believe I came out for some fresh air and fell asleep on the bench?” I didn’t think now was the time or the place to tell him I was stalking my ex as part of my Plan o’ Revenge.

“No.” His tone was cold. He spun away from the fence, looking out into the street, then spun back, snapping, “Stand up.”

"Someone might see me," I said.

"Yeah, well, if someone sees you squatting down there with me standing over you, they're either going to think I'm taking a piss on you, or you're giving me a blow-job. I'm guessing neither scenario will look good in the newspaper." .

CHAPTER 19

Ex: I've Moved On You Should Too!

I sprang up, heart pounding as I looked around, checking for paparazzi.

"Why is it so hard to find low-maintenance, sane women in London?" Alex muttered. "I wish I was one of those guys who didn't give a damn about a damsel in distress..." With his job, he'd be used to hearing about the worst things in life. He took a deep breath. "What's going on?"

"I'm trying to get out of the park."

"Don't dick me around or I'll leave you here. Where's your stalker?"

"I don't have a stalker." I had a mother and an ex across the square with all their windows and doors open.

"So why are you hiding in a bush, when our date was supposed to have started forty-five minutes ago?"

"Forty-five minutes?" I wailed.

"That's the least of your problems."

"I haven't broken any laws."

"I hear the same refrain every day from my clients, most of whom are lying."

"The reasonable woman is totally on my side."

"Jesus Christ!" I could almost see him mentally playing back all the times I'd sought out his legal advice on stalking and harassment, the late-night phone call desperate for a breakfast meeting, the cress and the car headlight… "Are you the stalker in this scenario, Meredith?"

"No! No. Not really *stalking*," I said, feeling sick as nerves beat their wings in my stomach.

"Bloody hell. You're lying. I was so dazzled by your looks and fragility and my own problems that I totally missed it." He heaved another sigh. Much more of this and he'd be hyperventilating.

"Can we save the chat for later? How am I going to get out of out of here?" I asked, too scared of being discovered by the media to panic about the fact Alex was getting dangerously close to discovering my revenge.

"You tell me."

"I don't know." I almost whimpered. "I pay you to help me."

Alex moved along the fence, looking for a way to get me out. "You couldn't pay me enough to deal with this crap."

"Pleeeease."

"I should've held out when Lia and Marie foisted you on me, or at the very least tripled my fee."

"With your attitude, it's a wonder you get any work at all," I snapped.

"Tell me what's going on, or I leave—or I place a missing-person call in to the police." I gasped, horrified. "We have a date, and you're a no-show, after all."

I spoke in a panicked rush, "I saw my mother and

Tom and I just, I…"

"Followed them into the park?"

"No, I followed them home. They're living together." I pointed to a house. "Over there."

"Why can't you just get over the arsehole? I've yet to hear anything good about him, but you seem totally fixated on the loser. Whilst I can understand you're pissed, what with his new girlfriend being your mother, you can't have been surprised by the breakup. There wasn't any real commitment."

"We were going out for seven years." I pressed up against the fence, glaring at him. "We were in a monogamous relationship."

"Not Tom."

I flinched from his words. That was shitty, even for him.

"I just don't get it."

"You make it sound like there's something wrong with me."

"I just found you in a bush, Meredith. You're fixating

on your ex and your mother when you should be going out with your friends and getting over them."

I didn't have any friends. I didn't have anyone. My life that had seemed so perfect just a couple of weeks ago was disintegrating, and the only person I had to cling to was one I had on retainer.

"Unless don't you have any friends?"

"I-I've told you before, I have over two and a half—"

"Where?" His tone was gentle, even as his words were harsh. "Where are they all now, or even one of them? Because they're not here stopping you from making a fool of yourself."

I winced, looking away. "That was mean and unnecessary. It's not my fault the park warden locked up without checking the park properly. I'm not paying you to say mean things."

"You're right. I provide the good sense for free."

"It's not free. I pay you a retainer."

"You would pay a retainer if you were retaining me as a lawyer, not a *date*."

“I’ve got a hundred in my purse. How long will that shut you up for?”

He shrugged. “About twenty minutes.”

“You charge three hundred pounds per hour to say nothing?” I gaped at him. “That’s… that’s criminal.”

“Yet I’m not the one behind bars.”

I suddenly remembered where I was and started to panic again. “Get me out of here.”

He was tempted to go… but I could see something was stopping him from walking away. “Okay. Pass your shoes over. You’re not going to be able to climb in them.”

I slipped my shoes off and handed them through the railings. The loss of three inches might not seem like a lot, but as I topped out at five foot two and was wearing a floor-length evening dress, it might as well have been a mile.

“God, you’re tiny. Was your dad a hobbit? We’re going to have to go straight to plan B on this one.” He took off his suit jacket and folded it into a long pad. he laid the pad along the spiked top of the rail. Gripping the top of the fence between the spikes, he hauled himself up, putting one foot on a sign warning of fines for dog fouling, hoisting himself over the fence and into my garden prison, wincing as he hit the ground.

I surged forward, slamming into his safe, solid form. “Thank you for not abandoning me!” I tightened my arms around his waist and pressed my face against his chest, breathing in his rich, warm scent. He wrapped his big, strong arms around me, holding me tight, as if he was equally comforted by the gesture. He held on for a couple of seconds then leant back.

I burrowed deeper, clutching him harder, still trembling.

I hadn’t realised how scared I was that he wouldn’t come. That I would be alone. He relaxed, letting me snuggle back in for a few minutes.

“Okay, now, princess, melodrama over.” He pulled back as far as my arms would allow, plucking a couple of bits of moss from my hair. “Let’s get out of here. You still owe me a date, and I’m looking forward to meeting Penny Shepherd.”

I shoved him away. “What the hell makes you think that overblown tramp will be there?”

He laughed. He seemed to do that frequently around me. "Come on, bunny boiler, let's go." He grabbed my waist from behind and lifted me, grunting as he took my weight. "Put your hands on top of my jacket. Be careful of the spikes." His voice was strained with the effort of remaining standing and holding me up. I placed one hand as instructed, and with the other fiddled with my dress, holding the skirt up. "Stop being a princess and hurry up! Swing your legs over and I'll drop you to the pav— Ah!"

I fell back against him. He staggered, clamping me against his chest. Then we were falling over a park bench. Alex hit the ground with a grunt.

My nose smooched up against his armpit. I sniffed spicy aftershave and hummed. Alex took a deep, pain-filled breath and pushed back to his feet, hauling me up with him. He staggered back to the fence.

"Are you okay?"

He ignored my question. "Brace yourself. I'll boost. You put your foot on the rail and hop over."

"Wait! Wait, my dress. I can't hold it *and* the fence. It'll get ripped."

"Tuck your skirt up into your knickers and out of the way."

"What? No. I can't."

Alex closed his eyes and tipped his head back to face to the heavens. "Please tell me you are wearing knickers."

"Of course I am. I'm not a Kardashian."

"What's your problem, then?"

"They're just tiny and lacy and… they won't be able to take the strain."

"I know how they feel," he snapped. "I don't know how much longer *I* can take the strain, either."

"They're—"

"Don't say another word," he said through his teeth.

Lowering me back to the ground, he steadied me with my bare feet on top of his shiny black shoes. "Careful. You don't know what might be hidden in the grass." I huffed, shuffling around, no doubt crushing his toes, clenching his shirt for balance.

"I'll tuck it up," I said. "They'll either take the strain

or they won't."

"Ready?"

"As I'll eve— Wait! Wait." I grabbed his arm, tugging him down behind a bush as the door to one of the houses slammed behind a couple.

"What now?"

We crouched behind a bush. Talith and Tom came down the steps into the street.

"I don't care about burglars, Tom. The windows stay open. That stench has to be the most effective anti-theft device known to man."

"What is it?" Alex whispered, correctly reading that this was a whispering situation—not a huge leap of intelligence, given we were crouched behind a bush, in a park, in the dark.

"Tom and Talith." I dug my nails into his arm. "I don't want them to catch me here."

"For once, we're in complete agreement."

We waited, Alex awkwardly hunched beside me, as they clambered into the cress-mobile and took off down the street.

Finally, done with creeping around and hiding in bushes, Alex straightened, hauling me up by the arm. “Right, since you’re incapable of doing this in a way that won’t put my back out, or snap my leg—or your knicker elastic.” He laughed at my embarrassed squeak, slipping his hands under my armpits. “I’m going to swing you over the fence. You need to lift your legs and get ready to land on the other side. I won’t be able to hold you up for long.”

Three swings later, I was slipping back into my shoes. Alex hauled himself over the railing.

“Shit!” I said as a door across the street opened. A little dog ran out yapping. An old lady followed, shouting for her pet.

For the second time in a week, I snapped, “Run!” And took off like a cheater hunting prey, leaving Alex in the dust.

“Wha—”

By the time he caught up with me, I was standing beside his car, dusting muck and moss off my dress.

“How the hell can you run in those heels?”

I shrugged. “Your limp is worse.”

“Is that why you left me in the dust to face the hound of the Baskervilles? Survival of the fittest?” He beeped the car doors open.

I laughed. “It was a Shih Tzu.”

“I’m amazed you noticed at the speed you were going.”

“I’m not that fast. It’s just because you were hobbling.”

“Yes, well, that’s because I just spent the last thirty-five minutes hefting you over a fence.”

I settled in the passenger seat of his silver Porsche. “Is your leg hurting?” I felt a pang of guilt for making him perform acrobatic feats of park escapology.

“There is nothing wrong with my leg,” he responded, but the fact he slid the driver’s seat back a little as he said it underscored the lie. “There is something wrong with your mental state.”

“What?” I jerked towards him. “That’s… that’s slander.”

"Not if it's true." The car purred away from the kerb. A couple of turns later, we merged into traffic on Milbank Road.

I looked out of the window as we crossed the Thames on Westminster Bridge. "Hey, where are you going? I need to go home and get cleaned up."

"We're nearly an hour and a quarter late, Meredith." He kept his eyes on the road, but yanked down the passenger sun visor. "Use the vanity mirror to tidy yourself up the best you can."

I gasped at the horrific sight reflected back. My blue-black hair stuck out at strange angles from a messy, lopsided bun, and loose strands hung in limp, tangled ribbons around my face, moss and leaves decorating it. My makeup was smudged, and green-brown dirt marked my face and arms. The bodice of my sexy, sophisticated red dress was skewed and creased.

"Oh my God!" If I was the fairy-tale princess Alex kept alluding to, now was definitely time for my fairy godmother to step in for a magical makeover. "I can't go like this."

"Can and will," he responded without looking away

from the road. "There are wet wipes in the glove compartment, and I'm pretty sure one of my sisters even left an emergency makeup kit in there."

"I'm not using someone else's makeup."

He shrugged, still not looking at me. "So, use a wet wipe and go makeup-free."

"You can't be serious."

"I can."

Fifteen sullen minutes later, when we arrived at the venue, I looked… *reasonable*, provided the lighting was bad and the viewer partially sighted. "We're going in the back entrance. No way am I risking the Z-list time slot on the red carpet looking like this. I don't care if I miss getting photographed with a mysterious hunk." My huffy tone made it clear I minded—a lot.

Alex's chest swelled and his shoulders went back. "I'm hunky?"

I rolled my eyes. "You're not ugly."

"Let me enjoy my ego boost. I deserve it after Tony's not-so-flattering comparison between me and your ex. I'd have thought being photographed showing up late looking like you've had a quickie with a *mysterious hunk* on the way would be just what you and Tony were trying to pull off." He reached forward, plucking a leaf from my hair.

"True." I still looked slightly rumpled, but otherwise not much of the misadventure showed. "Come on. We'll let some enterprising paparazzi hanging around the back door, where there aren't as many lights, get the exclusive."

Alex manoeuvred his leg out of the car, slowly straightened it, then rounded the car to help me out. The central locking beeped as we headed towards the bouncers covering the back door.

"Isn't it all a bit predictable and childish?" He captured my hand, threading his fingers between mine.

"What?"

"The whole faux thing."

I shrugged. Conceding, "Maybe you're better than the alternative." His brows rose in silent question. "Faux going out with an up-and-coming model or actor or hot felon and getting pregnant or married within a month of the breakup."

"Wow."

"Yeah. I'm not ready for a convict's kid just yet."

His lips twitched. "Give it a week or so." He was on a roll. "Can't you just take a timeout? Go on an expensive, luxurious holiday somewhere sunny, wear a skimpy bikini..." He glanced down at me, with—I thought—a warm glint of appreciation in his eye.

"No. I can't."

"Why not?"

"Because... because..."

"Because?" A smile spread across his face.

"I'm in the middle of filming. I don't have the time to pick some guy up and... and I loved him." I flashed a smile and our VIP plastic wristbands, and the hulks at the side door let us slip in.

"Of course you did," he said, but his tone disagreed. "Not only is Tom a total arsehole, the guy's an idiot. He should have married you—"

I looked up at him, flashing a dazzling smile. "Thanks, Al—"

"Then his gravy train wouldn't have had to end. He

could have taken you for half of everything *and* tried for maintenance. Throw in a kid… Then again, the idiot thought you were in love with him."

"I was."

"Nope," He responded, popping the P.

I turned on him, whisper-snapping, "Don't tell me what I feel."

"So, you're going to start crying any second now over your lost love?"

I thought about it and blinked a couple of times, trying to force out a tear, but nothing happened. "I'm being brave."

"Of course you are." He laughed. "Maybe one of your fans will nominate you for a George Cross for such a feat of heroism and courage."

I stopped, Alex halted beside me, but refused to let go of my hand.

"Your heart isn't broken, Meredith. Your pride's dented, and you've got enough to survive a dent or two."

I sucked in a sharp breath, my eyes narrowed.

"God, you're stunning." He seemed surprised by the fact he'd said the words out loud. "Even with the temper and mossy head decoration." He plucked more moss from my hair and swiped a thumb over my neck just below my ear, wiping off a smudge of dirt.

"You're a sucky date, Alex Gordon."

"I'm better than spending the night alone in a bush, Meredith Scott." .

CHAPTER 20

Did You Have Sex With Me When I Was Drunk?

The sun glared around the edge of my blinds. I pulled the covers over my head and buried my face in my pillow. Every part of me ached, every bone and organ, even the roots of my hair. It could have been due to the escapology escapades of the night before or the four glasses of champagne I'd had on an empty stomach.

I whimpered into my pillow. I felt sick and depressed and worthless. What was the point in getting up and working out, dieting, going to work as if nothing had happened, as if my life was normal?

I'd just stay in bed, sleep until I could remember why I cared so much about looking good and succeeding in my career.

It wasn't fair.

I didn't want to be alone anymore.

I wanted to be part of a pair.

I wanted to be snuggled together for a lazy Sunday morning, daydreaming about our future whilst buses rumbled by outside and the occasional siren blared.

Maybe I *was* selfish. I hadn't thought about how Tom felt. He was struggling in his career, whilst I raced ahead with mine.

I missed Tom and my mum and Jenn.

No.

No. That wasn't right. I didn't miss them; I missed the life I used to have—or at least the one I thought I had. I'd never lived alone before. I missed the comforting familiarity of having someone around, of coming home to find Tom and my mother watching Corrie on the TV. Although, now I thought of it, they were probably postcoital, which took some of the rosy glow off the memory.

A lonely, probably hungover, part of me wished I'd

never walked in on them, wished I'd never found out and things could've just rumbled on as they were. Ignorance is bliss and all that.

Maybe I should just have accepted his infidelity. Plenty of people did in my business—they had *open* relationships or a *don't ask, don't tell* marriage, and they weren't alone in bed, feeling like shit and struggling to name a single friend to call so they wouldn't be alone. I sniffed and snuffled and smelt… bacon?

I didn't eat bacon.

Tom *certainly* didn't eat bacon.

You didn't get an eight-pack eating bacon.

So… why could I smell bacon? I glanced towards the window, to see if Ashley, the estate agent who had the flat beneath mine, was polluting my environment whilst cooking her Sunday brunch, but the window was shut. Which meant the smell was coming from inside my flat.

I flopped back against the pillow, my tired, hungover mind shuffling through possibilities… I was pretty sure burglars left before daylight and didn't bring fatty, cholesterol-heavy food with them. I didn't smell putrefied fish, so Talith and Tom were out. As Alex was so fond of pointing out, I didn't have any flesh-and-blood friends…

Alex.

It was Alex.

I kind of, sort of, *thought* I remembered asking him to stay last night. I remembered leaving the charity gala, a photographer taking photos and me giving an Oscar-worthy fauxmance performance, draping myself all over Alex, laughing and giggling like fourteen-year-old flirting with the captain of the football team.

I was exhausted—okay, still drunk—after our date, when I begged him to stay. I couldn't really remember what I'd said, which was probably just as well…

My body flushed, at the same time as the blood drained from my head. Had I had sex with Alex and been too drunk to remember?

I lifted the duvet; cold air rushed over me. I heaved a sigh of relief at the sight of my shorts and camisole PJs. I squeezed my thighs together and did a little pelvic floor clenching, but nothing… unless he wasn't that impressive, we hadn't had sex last night.

Was I relieved or disappointed?

I may have been out of the dating game for a while—okay, I was never really in it—but I wasn't a first-date kind of a woman. Actually, now the panic was over, I kind of remembered stumbling into the flat and walking through to my room, deciding to change into something more comfortable and… Nothing.

Poop.

I should probably get up and say something, do something… ideally kick him out, but I was guessing from the fact he hadn't already left, had found a radio, had obviously been shopping and was making himself breakfast that he wasn't in any rush to leave.

I slumped back against my pillow, closing my eyes. I felt a little dizzy and spin-y. Maybe I was still drunk. I needed to sober up. I didn't like myself much in my half-drunk, half-hungover state. I was a contrary wimp. Five minutes ago, I was bemoaning my loneliness and lack of flesh-and-blood friends, and now I was complaining because one—albeit one I was paying—was in my flat.

"Brunch, Meredith!" Alex called, simultaneously banging against my bedroom door. A splintering sound preceded the door swinging open. “Sorry! I was using my foot to knock and must’ve kicked it harder than I thought.” He looked worried as he stood in the now-open doorway holding a tray.

Why in God’s name had I just wasted an hour wishing for company?

“I made you breakfast.”

“Is it natural yoghurt and chia seeds?” I asked hopefully.

“Hmm. Close. Crispy bacon, scrambled eggs and toast. Hangover food.”

“I’ll pass, thanks.”

“You need to eat something. You can’t just lie in bed and waste away.”

“I’ll make myself something after I get up and fix my bedroom door lock,” I responded sarcastically.

Alex crossed the room, placing the tray on the bed beside me. It smelt… delicious. There was a croissant. He hadn’t mentioned the croissant. My mouth watered. He crossed back to the door and poked around at the lock for a second. “I can fix this in five minutes. I’ve just popped the lock; it won’t take long. Eat.”

“Where did you get this… stuff?” I asked, as he returned to sit on the edge of my bed. “I know it wasn’t in my cupboards.”

“I went to the corner store. They’d just got a bakery delivery in.”

“How did you get in?”

“The store was open.”

I rolled my eyes. “To my flat.”

“Don’t you remember? I brought you home last night.”

I remembered that bit; I was asking about after he’d been shopping, but now was probably a good time to fill in a couple of blanks from last night—like: what did we do? “And spent the night?”

“Uh-huh.” A smug smile. “And what a night. You sure know how to show a guy an interesting time.”

My heart was hammering. My skin felt clammy, and darkness edged my vision. Probably overreacting, but I’d stopped taking the contraceptive pill when Tom walked out. It made me bloated. Plus, I was pretty sure we hadn't slept together from the old pelvic floor test, but maybe we had and he really was just under-endowed… It was a depressing thought.

"If we'd made love last night, you'd remember. As it is, I don't have to take advantage of senseless drunk women, even hot ones." Alex rolled his eyes. "You are the cheapest date I've ever had. You didn't eat a thing and got drunk on three glasses of champagne."

"It was four," I said. He laughed. "Go away!"

"Enjoy your breakfast." He stood, still laughing, and pressed a swift kiss to my forehead. "I have to get going. I need to shower and change. I wouldn't abandon you, but I've got to meet up with my family."

"Good." I pushed the tray of hangover temptation away.

Alex paused. "Let me see you eat something."

"I'm not hungry. I feel sick," I responded, not entirely untruthfully.

"After you've eaten, have a shower. Then you'll feel

better."

"Go away and then I'll feel better."

"Here, why don't you enjoy this whilst you eat your breakfast?" He slapped a folded newspaper down onto the bed between us, before walking out whistling. I quickly unfolded the paper, staring at the picture. It was taken inside the club where the gala was held. We were on the dance floor. I was wrapped around Alex, one thigh practically hooked around his waist. His hands were firmly clamped to my backside, my back was arched and we were gazing intensely into each other's eyes. It looked like a still from the underground club scene in *Dirty Dancing*. Hot. As. Hell. .

CHAPTER 21

Caught in the Act!

The next morning, I sat in the makeup chair and reluctantly looked in the mirror, then wished I hadn't bothered. Dark shadows ringed my bloodshot eyes, my skin was sallow and greasy and my hair hung limply around my face. I'd already apologised twice to Evie in makeup. It was going to take hours, a lot of skill and a miracle to make me look like anything but an extra in a zombie movie.

Champagne hangovers were the worst, and this was day two.

I was pathetic.

I'd already copped a talking to from Jerry, who'd greeted me with: "What the hell happened to you? It looks terminal."

"There you go, hon." Evie, my blue-haired forty-something makeup artist squeezed my shoulder comfortingly. "You're done. Rest up here with hot stuff and drink lots of water."

Alex rose from the dressing-room sofa and came up behind me, leaning over my shoulder to get a better look.

It was take-two on the whole legal adviser for my show thing. Part of me wondered why I bothered continuing with the lie. He obviously suspected I was lying, and the last thing I needed was to prove it to him, but I really wanted him to see me in the one area of my life where I was still in control, strong and successful… The exact opposite of my spiralling personal life.

"Evie's done a good job." He sounded surprised.

Clearly having sisters growing up taught him nothing about women. "My eyes are red."

"You look fine." *Liar, liar pants on fire.* I scowled at him. He shrugged. "It's not permanent."

That showed what he knew. "My shows get broadcast all around the world. This show will be repeated for years to come… and my hair's lank and—" Alex dropped his forehead against my shoulder, groaning in despair. "It's no wonder Tom went off with my mother," I lamented. "Look at me."

"Hey!" he snapped, glaring at me over my shoulder. "Stop it! There's no excuse for what he did. And it had nothing to do with the way you look, or anything you could have, should have, or would have done."

"But—"

"Shh." His lips swooped down on to mine. I shivered out a breath of surprise. The warm, firm pressure of his lips brushing mine sent tingles of desire pulsing through my body. My eyes closed. The tip of his tongue slipped out, tapping against my top lip.

Hmm. My hand fluttered up to stroke his cheekbone down to his firm, square jaw. Light stubble scraped my fingertips. A fine tremor shook me. Alex pulled back. My eyes opened. His strong, handsome, passion-flushed face gazed down into my…

Yeah, I didn't want to think about what my hangover face looked like right now.

A small smile tipped his lush mouth, and his pupils

grew. His warm palm cupped my cheek. I shivered with expectation. His thumb rested beneath my bottom lip, pulling gently downwards, tugging my mouth open, ready for his kiss.

I gripped his broad shoulders, anchoring myself and preventing him from pulling away. My heart pounded; my stomach dipped. His head lowered. My eyelids sank closed again; our mouths met. A hot, wet exploration.

I arched into his kiss.

His other hand settled in the dip of my waist, big, hot, steady. My skin jumped, pebbling in response to his touch.

Good, so good.

“Meri! Time to get on se— Ooooh!” The work-experience kid skidded to a halt halfway into the room, face scarlet, as she stuttered, apologised and backtracked. I reluctantly stepped away from Alex.

Cool air, sanity and doubts rushed in between us. What the hell was I doing, kissing him?

This wasn’t public or a photo opportunity. I was at *work*.

Yes, Alex said it was real dating, not faux-dating, but Tom and I had only been split up for a few weeks. I'd never kissed Tom at work not once in seven years… That made me pause halfway down the corridor on my way to the stage; why had I never kissed Tom when I was at work? If my kiss with Alex was anything to go by, we'd definitely been missing out.

The applause and cheers were deafening. I winced, feeling a little shaky. It was strange how my hangover had disappeared when I was kissing Alex, but was back with a vengeance now. Still, sufficiently buoyed by kiss endorphins and rapturous applause and shouts of "Meri! Meri!" I stepped out for my usual walk through the audience, shaking hands and high-fiving people.

One second, I was moving with cool confidence, the next I tripped over… air… or my own foot… or *something*. As I pitched forward, my hand, raised to high-five a grey-haired lady in the audience, slapped her across the face.

"Agh!" she cried, dramatically cupping her face.

"Ooof." I landed arse up across the lap of the obese thirty-something guy sitting on her right, my face in the crotch of his pubescent neighbour.

“Jesus Christ, Meri!” Mike yelled into my earpiece. “What the hell was that for?”

“It was an accident,” I said, muffled by the fact I was still face-crotch-ing an audience member. I struggled to get back on my feet.

“Stop sniffing his balls and get up.” Jerry was laughing so hard that I could hardly tell what he was saying. “You better have gotten that on camera for the outtakes show.”

“No,” I yelped. Strong hands wrapped around my waist from behind, lifting me, as the teen began to shift uncomfortably beneath me and the obese guy patted my arse.

“Hands off,” Alex snapped at the arse patter. “And you,” he said for my ears only, laughing as he settled me back onto my feet, “stop molesting the poor kid. He’s going to be jacking off on this for the next decade.”

“Get a first aider out there, stat,” Mike said, ever the professional. “We’ve got a gusher.” I might have given two guys the experience of a lifetime, but it looked like I’d broken their grandmother's nose in the process.

Twenty minutes, half a dozen autographed pictures and a promise of backstage passes and private health treatment later, and I ditched the remainder of the walk-through and went straight onto the set.

Mike and Jerry checked me out on the viewing screen, calling wardrobe over, pointing and muttering. Feeling self-conscious, sick and bloated, I tugged uncomfortably at my skirt's waistband. It was cutting me in half.

Jerry shook his head fiercely and then turned to Steven. "Get in there and do something with her fucking hair." Steven rushed forward, sighing and smoothing and pinning back my half-limp and half-static black mop.

Louise from wardrobe skittered over to my other side, tugging at the skirt she'd poured me into earlier, undoing the button and pinning me in with a couple of safety pins. "How you holding up, babe? You know, if you need someone to talk to or anything… I never slept with him." She didn't have to say who the *him* was. I also knew I couldn't take the risk. Louise was sweet, but she liked to gossip. "I didn't know, or I would've told you what a sleaze he was."

"What's taking so long?" Mike snarled. I breathed a sigh of relief at his interruption.

"There, that should give you another inch of breathing room," Louise said. Steve finished pinning and spraying my hair and stepped away. Louise hovered, waiting until he had disappeared before asking in an excited whisper, "Have you got some news you want to share?"

"What?"

"Well, I saw a picture of a good-looking man in the papers this morning." Oh God. Was Tom sleeping with men, too? "A man you were practically climbing… who happens to be sitting in the audience today." Oh, oh. Thank God. "And you're feeling sick and I'm having to let your skirt ou—"

"What? No! God, *no*!" I practically screamed, weathering the cursing of the sound man as he ripped his headphones off. "I got drunk. I'm hungover. I am *not* pregnant. Not even maybe."

"Ah, okay. If you say so." Louise edged away,

looking at me like she feared I might have had some sort of mental breakdown. The audience started whispering, as people debated whether I was fat or pregnant.

Mike consulted a clipboard held by this week's work-experience girl. I'd pushed hard to ensure they gave opportunities to disadvantaged kids when I first made it. I remembered what it was like to wish I could be part of something, but worry that "someone like me" would never get an opportunity. "Okay, Meri. Just read the Autocue; keep your tone low and smooth, like usual, doll. And stop all that swallowing if you can. You look like you're going to be sick."

I was.

I swallowed again, listening to his continued directions through my earpiece. Maybe this wasn't the best time to have Alex here watching how strong and in control and generally brilliant I was at my job. Honestly, if I didn't go for a second round of crotch surfing or puke before the end of today's show, I'd deserve another award.

"Ten seconds to rolling!"

"Five!" Mike counted down.

Swallow.

"Four."

A deep breath.

"Three."

A smile.

Mike hand-signalled the last two numbers.

I checked the Autocue, introducing the guests as they came on stage. Then I flicked a look at the running card in my hand, working out what today's story was about. Usually, I would run over the background first thing in the morning before filming, but I'd needed the extra time in makeup and hadn't been up to it today.

I moved to my second point, sinking down onto the top step when I couldn't find anything to lean on or stop the shakes. Maybe I should have listened to Alex and eaten something when he'd stopped at a bakery on the way in this morning.

I squinted, trying to focus on the words on the Autocue.

"What the hell is wrong now?" Jerry barked. He was

a grumpy git, but he was good at his job. "Do you need glasses?"

I shook my head minutely in response, trying to focus on what my guest was saying so I could follow up with a reasonable question.

"Then stop frowning."

I gritted my teeth, at the words in my ear, nodding encouragingly at my guest, whilst mentally reminding myself I loved my job.

The Meri Scott Show was everything I'd worked for. Of course, now there was the potential of taking it to the US, too. But what I enjoyed most was being able to help my guests, knowing that, along with my crew of after-show professionals, we really did turn people's lives around. There was nothing better than receiving a letter or update from a former guest about how, thanks to the show, they'd conquered their addiction, reunited with their family... Nothing beat receiving those letters.

Well, okay, winning my three Most Popular NTAs was better, but I'd never admit that out loud.

"Meri? Meri, what the hell is wrong with you?"

Damn it, I'd totally phased out in the middle of the segment. Even Mike was mad now, and he rarely lost his temper.

"Take five," he snapped.

Ugh. I stepped to the edge of the stage as Mike, Jerry and Evie rushed over to join me. "Please, tell me I feel worse than I look," I said.

"No can do. Sorry, hon." Evie dug through her kit, looking for something with better coverage and applying it liberally under my eyes and across my cheeks and nose. She leant back, squinting, then pulled out some powder, applied it to my nose, squinted, assessed again, then leant back in and applied some more, tutting. "It's not great, but it'll have to do. That's as good as she's getting, Jerry."

"Fine, I'll work with what I've got, but you need to pull yourself together." Jerry turned to me. "This is turning into a total clusterfuck. You want your new boyfriend to see you making a fool of yourself?"

"What? Who? Alex? He's not—" I gave up when Jerry stomped over to the viewer, ignoring me. Mike shrugged, slapped me on the back, nearly pitching me headfirst off the edge of the stage, then headed for his perch off set. I stumbled a couple of steps forward, landing on Alex's lap in the front row of the audience.

Meanwhile, Jerry had obviously had time to check me out on the viewer. "Wardrobe!" he snapped. Clearly, he hadn't realised there was no making me look decent today. "Find her something to wear she might actually fit into. I don't want her bursting out of her skirt."

I hunched down against Alex. "Fucking ridiculous," he growled. "I'm starting to understand where your warped ideas about food and weight come from."

"I'm—"

"There's nothing wrong with you that eating a bacon sandwich every now and then, and not drinking on an empty stomach, wouldn't fix."

I blinked, taken aback by his furious response. "It's television, Alex." I patted his chest soothingly, enjoying the feel of hard muscle and crisp hair through his t-shirt. "People make comments about presenters' appearance all the time. It's normal in this environment."

"It's not normal in any environment."

"Back to it, Meri," Mike called.

I gave Alex's chest one last stroke and pat, oddly reluctant to stop, like I was leaving behind some therapy pet, then headed back to the stage, running through the rest of the segment. It was a typical episode. Stuart, a small, lean man in his forties—who looked about sixty—was suspicious about whether his stunning twenty-three-year-old girlfriend of three years was cheating on him.

I started with Stuart, alone on the stage, setting the scene, talking about how great his relationship was. How much he loved his girlfriend.

"And you have a young daughter together?" I asked.

"She's my little angel. She's perfect. I love the bones of her." He started to cry. I motioned off set for a box of tissues.

"Why are you crying, Stuart?"

"Because… I need to know."

"Know what?" It was my job to get to the emotions and make sure the guests painted a story my audience at home could follow.

"If my girlfriend's cheating on me… " An *ooooh* of gleeful shock sounded from the audience. My heart twanged… I knew what it was like to have your partner betray you. Shitty, with a capital SHITTY.

“What makes you think she’s cheating?”

“She goes out shopping and then has a shower when she comes in. She never used to do that.”

“Did you ask her about it?”

“She said she was hot.”

“Sounds reasonable.” If you weren’t on *The Meri Scott Show*… It was a rare day people were reasonable on my show. Reasonable didn’t make for good television. “What will happen if she is cheating?”

“I don’t know.” Stuart sniffed, covering his face with a trembling hand. This was how I thought I would react when I found out about Tom, instead of my little trip to revenge-ville. “I love her. I don’t want to lose her.”

“So, you’ll forgive her?” My temper started to simmer. Why was he letting her do this to him? I wanted to shout at him to stop being a sap.

Instead, I invited Sarah-Jayne to join us. She entered stage right, a petite blond bombshell dressed in mile-high stilettos and a red body-con dress. She looked like Hayden Panettiere. When she sat down next to Stuart, she looked like she could have been his granddaughter.

Stuart reached for her hand. Sarah-Jayne tucked it away before he could latch on. I'd seen this before. It didn't look good for Stuart.

"Sarah-Jayne, welcome to the show."

"Thanks, Meri."

"You heard what Stuart said from backstage—"

"I'm fed up with him," she responded before I could ask her if she was cheating. "He's always accusing me. It's over. We're not even having sex anymore, which is no great loss. He's crap at it anyway." There were some hisses and shocked giggles from the audience.

"I love you," Stuart said. *Have some pride*, I wanted to snap. *Don't give her the satisfaction of knowing she's hurting you!*

"I don't care." This woman was C.O.L.D. We talked through a few questions and allegations, but it was clear she held no finer feelings for her boyfriend of four years.

"Why are you with him?"

She shrugged. "Money."

Oh. Okay. At least she was honest about it.

"You took a lie detector test this morning." I opened the envelope with the results. "It says here you refused to take the test." Stuart turned, staring at her. "Why is that?" I asked.

"Because I don't need one. I am cheating on him with Adam."

"Who is Adam?"

"My son!" Stuart's face paled then flushed an alarming red. He white-knuckled the arms of his chair.

Before the dust settled from that revelation, Sarah-Jayne pulled the pin and tossed the real emotional grenade. "Ellie may not be Stuart's daughter; she might be his granddaughter."

"What!" Stuart jumped to his feet. "Where's that bastard?"

A young man strutted onto the stage, walking over to Sarah-Jayne and locking lips.

"I'm going to kill him!" With a roar, Stuart launched himself at Adam. Dave and Nobby ran onto the stage, forcing the men apart.

It took ten minutes to get things calmed down. Stuart's chair was moved to one side of the stage, Sarah-Jayne and Adam's to the other. Nobby stood, thick arms folded, legs braced, a man mountain between them.

I opened the paternity test envelope, not enjoying this show. It was far too close to my own story to be entertaining.

"The results are in. Stuart, Ellie is…" I dragged out the dramatic pause, using the excuse of pulling the card from the envelope to build the tension. Shit. My stomach dropped. I didn't want to read it, but I did. "I'm sorry, Stuart. Ellie is *not* your daughter."

Stuart jumped from his chair, running off the stage in floods of noisy tears. Sarah-Jayne began screaming at Adam, telling him he needed to step up and stop being a deadbeat father.

I could have told her he was a deadbeat without meeting him. If he was willing to sleep with his father's girlfriend, he'd never care about anyone but himself.

Twenty minutes of backstage hysterics and I passed everyone to the backstage counsellors.

"That's a wrap." Mike's voice was still echoing in my ear as I kicked off my high-heeled shoes, whimpering as my feet hit the ground. Every part of me hurt. I thought hangovers eased off as the day progressed.

Alex walked over, joining me. He lifted an arm, and, without thought, I tucked myself under it, leaning into his warm strength. As if it was totally normal. "Where the hell do you find these people?" he asked as we headed for the car together.

"I don't." I shrugged. "They find me. What did you think?"

He gave me a level look that didn't bode well. "You're taking advantage of them when they're vulnerable."

It was nothing I hadn't heard before. "Says the lawyer."

"I don't take advantage of people for other people's entertainment."

"You just do it for money. So much more noble."

“It’s not about the money—”

“If they’re innocent, do you still charge them?”

“I do some pro bono.”

“And I reunite people with their families when they have given up hope of ever finding them. I help people find out the truth and children find out who their fathers are. I hold interventions for desperate families and find places in rehab centres. I resolve access issues and family arguments.” I pushed away from his side. “So, I do it on a TV show. How else would they get help? It’s not like it’s just floating around out there for free.” I was disappointed in him for judging me without looking beyond the surface. “It’s easy to dismiss the value of the service my show provides without thinking about it, but I’d have thought you’d have been willing to look deeper, given you are a lawyer and all.”

Alex sighed, reaching to pull me back to his side. “Fair point, Meredith. I shouldn’t have judged. It was unfair.”

“Yes, it was.”

“I’m sorry. Can we stop arguing now?” he asked.

"Please. I am genuinely sorry."

"I don't get why you rile me up so much. I've argued more with you over the last few weeks than with Tom over the whole seven years."

A slow smile brought out the dimple-crease in his cheek, as he if was pleased by the idea.

Weirdo.

"Interesting," he responded, irritatingly.

I ground my teeth. "How about you focus your opinion on my show to the legal advice I pay you for?"

"You haven't paid—"

"You haven't done anything."

"Based on what I have seen today, the best advice I can give you is not to face-molest male audience members… Present company excepted, of course. You can explore my crotch with your face—with any part of your body—whenever you want." .

CHAPTER 22

Rebound Relationship Or The Real Thing?

"What?"

"Hmm?"

"Why are you staring and smiling?" Two days later, I stood beside Alex in the lift on the way out to dinner, for a date. Not a work event, or a "just to be seen" photo opportunity, but an actual date.

"I'm just enjoying going on a date with you. A normal date. One where I picked you up at home, not out of a bush in a park."

I glared at him. He seemed to get hotter each time I saw him, but then he opened his mouth and I couldn't understand why I was letting my growing fascination with him distract me from my Plan of Revenge.

"You look stunning without the moss and grass stains, by the way."

I rolled my eyes, even as a flush of pleasure at his backhanded compliment tinted my skin. It was the Wednesday after he'd attended filming of my show and kissed me, a panty-melter of a kiss, one I'd dreamed about for the last two nights. I'd spoken to him both days on the phone, just chitchat, nothing important. He'd called me between court cases and when he was having lunch, but I hadn't seen him. He'd been busy with work. It was new for me having a boyfriend who worked and wasn't sitting around at home playing video games… and shagging my mother.

Whoa! I took a sudden step back, banging into the side of the lift, as my mind flashed on the fact I'd just thought of Alex as if he was my boyfriend, my *real* boyfriend, not my lawyer or faux-boyfriend.

"Are you okay?" He stepped forward, looking concerned.

Was I painting rainbows around this fauxmance?

Yes, Alex had pushed back on the faux label, but we both knew that what it was, right?

Was I so desperate for affection, or at least the illusion of affection, that I was building sandcastles in the sky?

When Alex had asked me on a date tonight, I'd suggested a couple of work events we could go to, but he insisted on a *real*, non-work-related date, just the two of us, where I didn't have to worry about who I was talking to or what I was wearing.

"Are you still stressing about missing the work events?" he asked. "You can't work all the time. Life's short, Meredith."

"Not that short," I scoffed. "I'm not even thirty yet."

"Painfully short," he countered. "You have to take time off to relax and have fun. You deserve to be happy."

"We've already had this conversation." I rolled my eyes. We'd compromised: a non-work date, but at a celebrity hot-spot restaurant, because I still needed to be "seen", more so now that Talith had sold her story, so people didn't think I was sitting home alone motherless, boyfriend-less and—not that they knew, I hoped—friendless.

Thankfully, Alex was single and hot, and I was desperate enough for company that I wasn't even worried I may let something slip about my Plan of Revenge.

"I'm fine. Fine," I stammered, avoiding eye contact. I smoothed a hand down my short navy dress, fluffing the flirty peplum at my hips, checking everything was in place. I glanced to the brushed stainless steel at the back of the lift, seeing our wavy, scratched images there, me small and blue, Alex tall and solid, cream chinos hugging his long legs and a blue short-sleeved shirt stretching across his broad chest and wrapping around his firm biceps, highlighting his stunningly-hot arms.

"There's nothing wrong with the way you look, Meredith."

"Then why—"

"You look beautiful."

Anticipation built; tension snapped and crackled with his gruffly spoken words. He pushed off the lift wall, one stride had him in front of me. I fell into his hot gaze.

Time stretched.

The lift continued to whirr, gears grinding as it ascended. The sound became muted, then disappeared. Everything in me slowed and focused on Alex. My heart whooshed in my ears, blood pumping, and my breathing grew laboured. His exhales became my inhales. One large, hot palm cupped my hip; the other slid slowly up my arm, raising goose bumps along its path to my throat. Tingles bloomed across my skin. His fingers pushed through my thick, loose hair.

The air thickened. I sucked in a desperate breath. His thumb stroked the soft, tender skin behind my ear. Deep inside me, something fluttered, followed by a sinking, tingling heat. A fine, trembling weakness invaded my limbs. I shivered, my hands rising to settle against his chest, then sliding up to grip his broad shoulders.

His head bent to mine.

Yes.

I'd been waiting for this, missing this, wanting this. Wanting him. My eyelashes fluttered closed as his lips brushed mine. Delicious. I sighed. A small sound, almost a whimper, escaped me, and then I collided with his hot, hard body. I looped my hands around his neck and stretched against him, rising onto my tiptoes to reach his lips. Alex chuckled, breath puffing over my mouth. I flicked the tip of my tongue out, touching his top lip.

He growled, and his hold tightened, making my skin burn. His mouth fused with mine. My thoughts blanked; my lips parted. Alex tilted his head, improving the fit. Our tongues tangled, battled. My breasts pressed against his chest.

Red-hot need exploded.

A bell dinged—a splash of ice-cold reality slicing through my lust haze.

My lashes rose, but my lips remained parted as I panted for breath, staring up into Alex's deep, dark eyes. The lift doors slid open. I tore myself from his arms.

I ran a trembling hand down my dress, checking it was fastened and in place. I honestly wasn't sure. My mind was still foggy, my heart bouncing around uncontrollably.

People turned and peered in at me.

I looked towards Alex.

What the hell? He was gone.

How?

Where?

I headed blindly out of the lift, staggering, heart pounding, head floating, lips tingling. The sounds of music and people talking and laughing assaulted my ears.

"Hi, Meri."

I snatched my fingers away from my lips and blinked at the man who'd spoken. I had no clue who he was, but from the way he was looking at me, I knew I should at least recognise him.

My mind was dazed over the whole lift-kiss thing... Alex had said there would be kissing, *real* kissing, and that was as real as it got. It made the work kiss feel like a brotherly peck.

Tom and I weren't into public displays of affection. We'd never done more than hold hands when we were outside, and even then, it was always me who instigated it. For some reason, that made me sad. I'd wasted my best PDA years on a man who was more interested in my mother, my best friend, his Xbox—hell, his own belly button—than me.

"Don't worry. I'm not some weird stalker."

What? Oh, the guy I should know, but didn't, was standing beside me, looking expectant. I mustered up a smile. On closer inspection, he was gorgeous in that fit, healthy, model-like way of so many guys in entertainment.

Alex had definitely got me messed up if I not only missed the fact Ben Affleck's younger, sexier lookalike was eyeing me up, but also didn't care. I didn't feel flutters or tingles or… anything.

"Oh, that's a relief," I said.

His lips twitched with amusement. He continued checking me out with subtle, but obvious appreciation. "You look great."

I did a quick head dip and scan, making sure I was still put together enough to appear in public. I looked fine. A little creased, thanks to the lift gymnastics, but good all the same. "Thanks, ah…?"

"Tiger Lyons."

Ah, yes. How had I forgotten that name? He was one of those ex-special forces guys, who got dumped in canyons then drank his own pee and ate raw eggs to survive… whilst the cameras rolled. After they stayed in five-star hotels, complained their Wagyu beef was overcooked and the air conditioning wasn't strong enough. His television show had won an award at the NTAs.

"Can I—"

"Sorry for the delay, princess." Alex's voice rumbled over my shoulder. "I got you a drink." He stepped up beside me and handed me a glass. Leaning down, he whispered, "Virgin G&T," warm breath puffing against my ear, reigniting tingles and sending them shivering across my skin. He settled his hand at the small of my back, in a possessive, territory-marking gesture.

I glanced up. Alex's dark, impenetrable eyes were fixed on Tiger, who melted away like butter in a hot pan. I'd have thought he'd have more staying power… Clearly there was a reason Tiger was now a TV presenter, instead of a special forces soldier.

"You didn't have to scare him off," I said.

"I didn't like him," Alex muttered.

"You didn't even speak to him."

"I didn't have to. Cat-boy was looking at you like you were catnip."

I rolled my eyes at his petulant tone. "Cat-boy? And you called me princess, and it's not the first time. I didn't realise we have pet names now."

He smiled, following the waiter, guiding me through the discreetly placed tables in the crowded restaurant to our seats. London skyline views were visible on three sides, and an open view of the kitchen on the fourth side.

"You look like a Disney princess," Alex said. "All blue-black hair, milky-white skin, violet-eyed and petite—like Snow White or Belle."

"You like Disney movies?" I couldn't imagine such a big, serious guy watching Disney cartoons.

He shrugged. "Three sisters." His face blanked, his amusement disappearing, his eyes dulling. "Two. Two sisters."

I turned to him, but he kept walking, hand to my back, eyes fixed straight ahead, clearly not willing to talk about whatever had just happened. I waved at Kate Turner, an up-and-coming country singer, and her author boyfriend, nodded at a newsreader I knew, and gave a fake smile to a vlogger who ran a celebrity gossip column, making sure to slow down enough so they could get a good look at Alex.

Talith and Tom were getting more press coverage than me recently. I was happy to fly under the media radar some of the time, if it meant I could enjoy my vengeance, but a mention of my date on a vlog wouldn't go amiss.

Finally, we arrived at our table. I settled on the chair Alex held out for me.

"Can I get you another drink, Ms Scott?" the waiter asked. "We have great cocktails tonight."

"Thanks. I'll have a vodka and Slimline tonic."

"And for you, sir?"

"I'm fine with my beer for now. Thanks," Alex said.

I glanced around the dimly lit restaurant, crumpling and releasing the tablecloth as the silence stretched. It had been years since I went on anything close to a *proper date*. Tom and I had never really dated. He was a struggling drama school dropout and I was a low-on-the-totem-pole presenter when we'd met. We couldn't really afford to date. He took me to McDonald's the first time we went out. We both got chicken salads… and split the bill, kind of. Tom didn't have enough for his half, so I paid for most of his too.

I should have known then he was a cheapskate dirtbag.

My heart, which had just calmed after the whole excitement of the lift kiss, kicked back into overdrive, this time with nerves.

I didn't know how to date. Before Tom, my dating highlight had been sitting on a park bench and sharing a bag of chips with my teenage boyfriend during the school lunch break.

What was I supposed to do?

What should I talk about?

How should I act?

Did I mention the kiss, or would that make me look clingy and pathetic?

Should I pretend it had never happened, or would that stop it ever happening again? I definitely wanted it to happen again. What if it didn't happen again? He'd run off as soon as the lift doors had opened, and now he was staring off over my shoulder.

I felt anxious and panicky, which was crazy.

We weren't even on a real date. Even though it wasn't an official function, this was my work, being seen out and about. Tony had insisted I kept my profile up. And Alex was my lawyer. I paid him a retainer.

Oh God.

I'd paid him.

Did that make him an escort or a gigolo?

What did they call people who paid for dates and sex? The person giving sex was a prostitute, the person running the prostitute was a pimp or a madam… the people hiring them were… *losers*.

I was a loser.

"Ten minutes." Alex's voice cut through my panicked contemplation.

"What?"

"Actually, it's closer to fifteen minutes," he responded. "That's how long you've been avoiding eye contact and fretting over… What? The kiss?" His smile held masculine pride. "I've been told I'm a good kisser, but most women recover the power of speech after around five minutes." He glanced at his watch.

I snorted. "You weren't that good." He was spectacular, but that kiss was at least half me, right? It took two to tango, or in this case tongue-tangle.

"Uh-huh." Hot, dark eyes slid down to my chest, where my still-tingling nipples pressed against the bodice of my dress, playing peekaboo with the little ruffle top. "Your, ah"—he saw sense and changed whatever he'd been going to say as I glared daggers at him, crossing my arms over my chest—"*silence* says otherwise."

"I feel queasy," I retorted.

"No wonder. That's a large drink, and you haven't eaten more than a couple of slices of cucumber today." He waved over the waiter. "What would you like to eat, Meredith?"

"I'm not hungry."

"You need to eat."

"I've got a horrid taste in my mouth."

"Meredith."

I flinched guiltily. It wasn't his fault I was a

mistrusting dating novice. “Sorry, I’m just…” I trailed off without saying *scared and confused.*

Alex relaxed back in his chair. “I can understand that you’re having problems coming to terms… with your attraction to me.” His eyes sparkled. “My kisses have that effect on women.”

My lips twitched at his cockiness. “And yet you’re single.”

“It’s your lucky day.”

I snorted, before giving in to my amusement and laughing.

A wine waiter appeared at the table. “Red or white wine?” Alex asked.

“I’ll just stick with the virgin G&T I already have, thanks.” I wanted to wake up without feeling or looking like death tomorrow.

Alex waggled his eyebrows and twirled the ends of a fake moustache, like an old film villain. “Here I had all sorts of ideas about getting you drunk and taking advantage of you.”

"In your dreams." I laughed. Given my response in the lift, there would be no taking advantage. He'd be lucky if I didn't jump him in the taxi on the way home.

"Every night in glorious Technicolour, princess."

The waiter discreetly stepped away from the table.

I leant forward, closing the distance between us. "You really fancy yourself, don't you?"

"*Fifteen* minutes of stunned silence after I kissed you," Alex reminded me, then called the waiter back before I could respond.

I bit my lip. I'd learnt the hard way never to say anything I didn't want published in front of waiters or bar staff… or anyone, really.

"We'll have the chicken liver parfit and the lobster claw with lemon and fennel for starters. If there's any oil or dressing on the lobster, can we have that on the side, please? Then for mains, one seabass with clams and asparagus. Again, please can you hold off on any oil, butter or dressing? And one beef filet with truffle hollandaise."

"Of course. Thank you, sir." The waiter swept away from our table grandly, leaving me staring after him.

"Wait. Did you just order for me?" I asked.

"Yep," Alex responded. "I'm not giving you the chance to order a bowl of hot water 'soup' for a starter and a green salad without dressing for your main. I've stuck with seafood and no heavy sauces, but you need to eat something. It's a key part of going out for dinner with a date."

There was nothing I could say without sounding like a diva with an eating disorder. I loved seafood, but I *had* planned to order a thin soup. Miso if they had it. If I didn't have to watch my weight, I would have picked the seabass. I wouldn't have picked a starter or dessert, though.

The food going to other tables looked and smelt fantastic. My stomach growled embarrassingly. A well-known catwalk model at the next table asked her companion if he'd heard the thunder.

Alex pushed the bread and vinaigrette towards me. I managed to hold out until the second rumble. I gave in. Tearing a one-centimetre piece off the crusty bread and dipping it in the vinaigrette, I barely managed to stop myself from groaning in pleasure. I couldn't remember the last time I'd eaten bread.

* * * * *

"So, she was a four-by-four."

An hour later, I sat back at the table, comfortably full, chatting away with Alex, my nerves about what I'd say long forgotten. The food was fantastic. I'd made a point of Instagramming pictures of every course as it arrived and even ate a third of both the dishes.

"A car?" Alex asked. I'd been talking him through a recent episode of my show.

"No, it means she had four children by four different men."

"Right."

"Of course, she was on the show for a DNA test. She swore child number four was her current partner's and she'd never cheated, but there were three guys there for testing…"

"Of course," Alex said, but he was smiling at me, not mocking. He was listening and interested in my work.

"Who was the daddy?"

"No idea! None of the three who were there. She's asked us to bring in another three to test. Although she still swears she hasn't cheated."

"She sounds like some of my clients. It doesn't matter if the police catch them driving away in the stolen car—they still say *it wasn't me.* So, which of your shows is your favourite?"

"Paternity programmes are the viewers' favourite, and I think children deserve to know who their fathers are. As well as mothers deserving financial support to raise their children."

"She doesn't sound like much of a mother, needing to test six men for one child."

"So, it's all right six different men slept with her without caring whether they impregnated her, but not okay for her to sleep with them?" I asked.

"They're not mothers to three other children."

"Don't say that like it makes perfect sense, when it plainly doesn't," I snapped. "I don't get why men manipulate these things so they're always in the right, saying one thing and doing the other. One minute he's telling me I'm the love of his life, the next he's screwing my mother and best friend, because I was always working."

Alex snagged my hand with his, covering it on the table. The warmth from his touch travelled up my arm, filling my chest and spreading out to cover my whole body. "Stop tarring me with someone else's brush and stop thinking about that *arsehole* when you are out with me." He clamped down when I would have pulled my hand back. "Smile. You can even kiss me if you want; there's a guy over there taking photos with his mobile phone." He nodded to his right, where the skinny, black-haired vlogger fiddled with his phone.

I leant across the table, staring into Alex's eyes. "I'm sorry, I'm… I… I'm really enjoying tonight. It would probably rate as the best date I've ever had, if I put aside the couple of times you were a bit of a dick." Alex huffed at my compl-insult. "I know, I'm paying you to be here, but I still… You're doing a tolerable job of being a decent human being… for a lawyer."

"Maybe," Alex said, flashing a shark's smile. "I'm just lulling you into a false sense of security in the hope you'll introduce me to your mother."

I hesitated, before it dawned on me he was joking. “You actually think you’re funny, don’t you? Tom broke my heart,” I added, hoping to make him feel bad.

“He dented your ego, princess,” he responded calmly. “People whose hearts are broken don’t plant cress in their ex’s car and Snapchat it.”

“You have *no* proof I did that.” I tugged my hand free and glared. Sod the photos.

“You didn’t hire me for my good looks.” He shrugged. He was right. I’d hired him because he was one of the best, and his partner Lia wouldn’t take me on, and I was desperate. “You’re lucky the snap-happy creep has gone and won’t catch that glare you’re shooting me right now. So, most people who see the pictures will think you’ve gotten lucky, moved on and traded up.”

“You really rate yourself, don’t you?” I asked. I was enjoying myself. Alex was amusing and kind and interested in what I said.

“Hey, I’m employed, solvent, happy to foot the bill for our *date*—and the idea of shagging your mother gives me erectile dysfunction. That makes me the best date you’ve ever had.” .

CHAPTER 23

My Girlfriend Is Sex Obsessed!

Alex insisted on walking me to the door, protecting me from the handful of "Meri" supporters who had gathered outside my flat after Talith's story was published. He was totally overreacting. They were sweet. I'd done the whole autograph and selfie thing with them on the way out earlier and soaked in their praise for me and vitriol for Tom and Talith.

Once I opened my door, I reached up to give him a kiss on the cheek at the same time he leant down.

I tilted my head left.

So did he.

I missed his cheek and found his lips. Neither of us pulled back or adjusted to any of the platonic landing zones.

Alex took control swiftly, backing me into the wall beside the door, hands on either side of my head as he devoured me.

Then our clothes melted. I was pretty sure it was from the blazing heat of his kisses.

I whimpered, shivering at the delicious sensation of his mouth on mine. He hauled me against him, lifting my feet from the ground, his lips never leaving mine. Like my clothes, I melted. My breasts flattened against his warm, hair-roughened chest as his hands slid down my back, gripping my hips. The ridged length of his erection pressed against my quivering stomach. My breasts swelled, nipples hardening into tiny pebbles of need, heat building between my legs.

He tore his mouth from mine, feathering kisses across my jaw, pausing to tug my earlobe with his teeth. "You need a law-yer." His voice cracked.

Huh? "Wha—"

"You need a lawyer."

"I want you."

"The feeling's mutual, princess." He pressed open-mouthed kisses along my collarbone. "But not as a lawyer."

I arched against him. "I have to make"—kiss—"a really clear distinction here." Another kiss. "For both of us, because"—kiss—"if this carries on the way we're going—and it will—I'm going to have ethical issues." His sexy sea-spray scent and body heat wrapped around me, cocooning me in Alex.

"Later," I said, need and pleasure building low in my belly, desire skating across my skin, leaving goose bumps.

Seeking something solid to hold on to, I fluttered my hands against his pecs, covering his nipples before sliding up his muscled arms to curl around his neck, holding on to him as the world began to spin around me.

Alex exhaled a harsh, shaky breath as my fingers fisted in the hair at his nape, tightening. His cock continued to harden, and he grunted, shivering against me.

Excitement sizzled over my skin; the wet heat of desire built between my shaking legs.

"Open your legs for me."

I followed his directions. He pushed one thick, seriously scarred, thigh between my own. I rocked against him, desperate to ease the pressure, desperate to increase the friction. He was driving me crazy.

I struggled to pull in a breath of passion-heavy air. I'd never felt this out of control with Tom. Not even in the early days.

That scared me. If I was this… crazed with the need for revenge over Tom's betrayal, what would happen if I let myself be sucked under by Alex?

I wasn't a casual-sex person.

"Uhmmm."

I was inexperienced… not just sexually—relationships, too. Tom was my first everything, and looking back on it, he hadn't even had to put any effort into catching me; he'd just flashed his smile and his eight-pack abs and dazzled my dangerously inexperienced and desperate-for-love self with his boyish charms. I'd been blind to his selfish ways.

Alex wasn't like that; even just kissing him was heart-palpatingly, leg-tremblingly, skin-shivering-ly good.

I was scared to lose that.

"Come back, princess." Alex's fingers halted their tingling path up my outer thigh. I was straddling his thigh. Seconds before, I had been riding him, like some sex-starved nympho. What the hell was I doing?

Oh, we'd stopped kissing. A flush of embarrassment warmed my neck and face.

"I've lost you. I thought it was going well, and then you just spaced out. What happened?" He cupped my jaw, his thumb feathering my cheek. His other hand remained steady on my hip, holding me when I would have slid off his leg and put some space between us.

"I think maybe we should stop here."

"Why? Did I do something wrong?"

"No, it's just…" Sex had never really been all that for me. I didn't really get what all the huffing and puffing and screaming was about in the movies.

Sex with Tom was… boring. No big O—hell, no little o either, but that could have been my fault more than his. He was experienced in ways I wasn't… Maybe he'd looked around because I wasn't very good at it.

"Can you let go? I think—"

"I must have done something wrong if you were thinking instead of just feeling." He leant in, his lips moving down my neck, teeth nibbling.

"It was just… It was too much."

"Hmm-hmm," he mumbled against my throat.

"I'm just, ah…" My head rolled back, giving him better access. "Well, sex wasn't that good with Tom, and—"

"No." His head snapped up, his dark eyes intense. "You are not going to think about that useless motherfucker when you are in bed with me."

"Technically we're not in bed, yeeeeeee—"

I squealed as he picked me up and hauled me the three steps into my bedroom, throwing me down on the bed.

Cold air rushed over me, and still he didn't move, staring down at me. Had he felt my hips? Was he worried he would impale himself on them? Nerves and embarrassment built. Only one man had ever seen me naked… and he'd traded me in for an older, used model. Alex was always saying I was too skinny. I rolled, reaching for the edge of the duvet to cover myself…

Alex's head tipped, his eyes narrowing. Suddenly he moved, yanking the cover off me, exposing me to his passion-filled gaze. "You're perfect," he said as he crawled over me, taking the place of the cover, bracing himself on his elbows over me, keeping his weight from crushing me. His head dropped, his lips finding my ear. I shivered with each puff of air. "Now, tell me what's going on. What happened? I thought you were into it?"

"I'm"—I twisted, trying to put some space between us—"suffocating," I lied.

"Liar." But he rolled to my side, one thigh hooked over my legs. "Talk to me, Meredith."

"What if I'm not very good at it?" I blurted.

"At what?" He slid his fingers up the inside of my thigh, higher, combing through my curls, finding my wet heat. He groaned, his fingers slipping and sliding as he explored between my legs.

"Sex!" I gasped, shuddering at his touch.

He caged me with his body. "Oh, princess, you passed *good* eons ago. Together, we are going to be way better than good. We're going to be incendiary." His thumb found my clit, pressing and rubbing as one finger found my entrance and slipped inside. I arched involuntarily, desperate to feel his heat and weight against me.

Why had I pushed him off?

Why were we talking when we could be having sex? Or at least… "Maybe we should just keep it to kissing and fondling and stuff."

"Hmm." His lips skimmed the sensitive skin of my neck, his teeth nipping, his lips sucking, all of which I knew would leave marks. His tongue was soothing, and goose bumps tingled and prickled all over my body. All the time, his fingers explored between my legs.

Internally, my muscles clamped around his fingers. I was desperate for more. Something to fill me. "Please."

His thumb continued to circle my clit, teasing around the edges, until I was squirming and begging. Something was building inside of me, I couldn't stay still. I felt like I was going to explode. Finally, he stopped teasing, and a second, long, thick finger sank inside me.

I moaned. Loudly. It was so long since anyone had spent time on me, learning my body, seeking my pleasure before theirs. Maybe Tom had the first time… I couldn't remember. Certainly, for the last few years, it had just been "assume the position", wham bam… *Are we finished? Oh, right, I'll put the telly on, then.*

I'd never felt this hot and desperate and passionate and out of control before.

Finally, Alex's thumb stroked over my clit, and a shock of pleasure zinged through my body. A sharp, tingling pressure began to build inside me, radiating outwards.

"That's it, princess."

I couldn't hold on to my thoughts… couldn't process everything that was happening inside of me. I was too full of feelings, and yet they continued to build, to fill me…

I was panting, whimpering… arching into his touch. His thumb continued to press and circle my clit. He curled his fingers inside of me, pressing against… something.

Pleasure ignited, exploding in blinding waves that had me crying out, writhing across the bed, my whole body shuddering.

"There you go, beautiful," Alex growled, lightening his touch and gently stroking me through my orgasm.

As soon as I caught my breath, he reared back onto his knees, gripping my waist and flipping me over onto my tummy. Ignoring my squeal of shock, he positioned me with urgent hands, pulling me up onto my knees. "Have you done it like this before?"

"N-no." My body felt lax and tingly. I didn't know how long I could stay in this position before I dissolved into a heap of post-orgasm jelly.

"You're going to enjoy it. Every stroke is going to hit your g-spot, and I can go deep from this angle." His hand smoothed down my spine and over my bum. "And I get to hold your perfect peach of a behind, as I watch you take every single inch of me."

I moaned. My skin prickled. I loved the idea he was behind me. Watching. He would have control over everything.

I heard the sound of a packet opening. My heart was pounding. A condom wrapper fell onto the bed beside me. Puffs of breath caressed my exposed nape. I clawed at the sheets, desperate for something to hold on to. His heat blanketed me as he bent over me, his hips pressing against my behind, his thick cock sliding through the wetness between my legs.

He groaned, sliding back and forward, small movements, tapping my clit then sliding back to notch against my opening, spreading my wetness as he teased us both.

"Please!" I flailed back with one hand, grabbing his thigh, nails digging deep, trying to force him forward. "I need—"

"Take it easy." He peeled my nails free, placing my hand back against the sheet, his big body pressing my chest and cheek down onto the mattress.

"Hurry."

"Shh. I want to make this good. No rushing. I want us both to enjoy it."

I pressed my hips back into the cradle of his, impatient.

"I promise it will be worth it."

His words whispered over me, chilling my sweat-dampened skin. Without haste, he slid his hands back up my outstretched arms, then around to my sides to cup my breasts. His big hands engulfed my small peaks, fingers gripping and tugging my pebbled nipples.

Pleasure and pain shot out from my nipples, on a direct path to my clit. I screamed, rearing up and back against him. Wetness flooded between my legs. I bucked and writhed against him. "Alex!" I wailed. "Please. Now!"

"So sensitive, so—"

"Hurry the fuck up!" I snarled.

He laughed. “So moody.” His big body prevented my attempts to force him to move.

My hips rocked against him, and I pressed my face into the pillow, moaning a desperate plea. His teeth scraped my skin, then bit down on the curve of shoulder and neck. My breath sobbed out. I was too far gone to do more than tilt my hips, trying to ease the burning emptiness.

Alex’s chest lifted off me. He shifted back on his knees, his cock sliding back to my opening. One hand slid down and around, smoothing over my stomach before dipping between my legs.

His long, blunt fingers parted my folds, his finger playing over my clit, pressing and circling as he slowly pressed his thick cock into me, stretching me. He hissed a breath. “Oh, princess. That’s it.”

“Please, please.” I panted, riding him, pushing him deeper and quicker. Pressure built again, a scarily intense tide I couldn’t help reaching for, fighting for.

He moved. His hips pumped, hard, fast, deep. Again and again and again. “Come, Meredith.”

“Again?” I asked, disbelieving, even as I surged back

against him, screaming into the pillow as the tide built. My whole body began to shake.

"Fuuuck," Alex said, his hips pumping faster, thrusts going deeper, harder. I tightened around him, muscles clamping down as he drove me straight back up to the precipice of pleasure.

"I can't…" It was too much, almost painful. The headboard banged against the wall. He thrust deep, hard, again and again, and… I came with a high whimpering sound, body rippling, muscles gripping and releasing, taking him with me.

He sank down over me, pressing a kiss to my nape as he turned us. His arm banded against my stomach, holding me against him as he spooned me.

I sighed, snuggling into him. Best. Sex. Ever. It was amazing. I could definitely get used to this…

My muscles locked.

My eyes shot open.

I'd just slept with my lawyer.

Were lawyers allowed to represent people they were

sleeping with?

I didn't want to have to start afresh with someone new.

What did this mean for my Plan of Revenge?

This was totally going to complicate our fauxmance. I needed to kick him out and regroup. Then I could pretend this never happened… Wait, did that mean I wouldn't get any more orgasms? Maybe I would pretend it was all part of the whole not-fauxmance package, an orgasm bonus. He said I would get real kisses, real sex… Boy, had I gotten real sex.

I felt Alex's smile blossom against my shoulder a second before he said, "You can stop overthinking and praise me now."

What? What the hell was he smiling about? This was a disaster. I could end up in prison, and all because of his hotness melting my clothes and giving me the big O… and my Plan of Revenge was jeopardised. "That wasn't supposed to happen." I was starting to panic. I rolled, turning to face him. His hair was mussed, his face was passion-flushed, lips swollen and his dark eyes lambent.

"Orgasms are always supposed to happen, Meredith." He spoke seriously, but his eyes sparkled with… amusement? Pride? Passion? "Now, I'm ready for my praise."

"You should praise me," I snapped.

He reached out, gently stroking my hair back. Damn. Why had I turned to face him? I probably looked a mess, all sweaty and sticky. I probably had a death mask of smeared makeup, and my hair would be a bird's nest. "You only gave me one orgasm," he responded. "I gave you, like, five or six."

"Two," I countered—or possibly three, my first real-life man-given orgasms, but his ego clearly didn't need stroking.

He smiled. "That was multiple orgasms right there, princess." He tapped my bare bottom for emphasis. "Right now, I'm hungry. I'll need to eat before round two. Let's push for at least three orgasms for you this time."

"Round two… Three…?" I wasn't sure if I was excited or scared.

His hand hadn't left my backside. He continued to

stroke and squeeze. “Oh, yeah.”

“I need a shower first.” But I was too tired to move.

“You get the shower going. I’ll order dinner then join you.”

What? Hang on a second.

He didn’t give me time to protest. Leaping naked and unconcerned out of bed, he padded out of the room to the hall, searching for his phone.

How did I end up powering up for round two and a his-and-hers shower when I was going to kick him out, regroup and somehow work orgasms into a fauxmance, with no real anything… except orgasms?

The orgasms had to be real and multiple. .

CHAPTER 24

I Slept With Your Boyfriend When I was only Seventeen!

I held my pose beside Alex, smiling for a photographer, as the entertainment journalist asked, “So, Meri, who’s the handsome hottie with you tonight?”

I leant into Alex, as he slipped his arm around me, placing my palm over his heart, feeling the strong, steady beat. My fingers slipped under the silky lapel of his sharply cut navy suit and over his crisp white shirt. His body heat warmed my fingers. His skinny navy tie matched my long dress.

I snuggled into his side, still smiling even as the camera flashes blinded me. I couldn’t keep the smile off my face. I’d had sex with Alex. Not just once, either—

three times, and not boring, ordinary one-"usual"-position sex; we'd totally Kama'ed that Sutra.

Best. Sex. Ever.

Granted, I didn't have much to compare it against, but if this was the kind of sex other people were having, the world should have ground to a halt years ago, because no one would have been willing to get out of bed.

I felt fantastic, buoyant and… sexy.

I glanced up at Alex's surly expression. It would look great in print, a brooding Heathcliff. "That's for me to know and you to find out." I laughed, looking under my lashes coyly as I responded to Ryan Jones, the tall, good-looking celebrity interviewer, who was eyeing Alex like he wanted to eat him up.

"Ooh, do tell."

"Sorry, but you understand I want to keep him to myself for a little longer," I said over my shoulder as I steered Alex away, before he could say something like: *I'm her lawyer, Alex Gordon. I'm trying to keep her out of prison for harassing her ex, and doubling up as a faux-boyfriend so she doesn't look friendless.*

We'd get more positive press if I kept the celebrity journalists guessing. I didn't want them to find out straight away I was dating a lawyer. It was fine for George Clooney with Amal; she was a human rights lawyer, which just built up George's good-causes side. As soon as people realised Alex was a criminal lawyer, they'd start asking how we met and what I needed a criminal lawyer on retainer for.

"Meri!" Clare Winters, my least favourite entertainment journalist, called, before continuing snidely, "Nice arm candy."

I felt Alex tense beside me. The petite blond was dressed in gold, glittering like an Oscar. I'd tried to avoid her, but she locked in on us and wouldn't be deflected.

"How do you feel about Tom and your moth—"

Alex's arm tightened around my waist, and he practically lifted me off my feet, twirling me away from Clare mid-question and walking us away without a word.

"Alex!" I said, even as relief swept over me. "She'll write something bitchy and horrid now."

"She was going to anyway."

True. It wouldn't matter whether I trotted out the line

Tony and I were using in all statements: *Meri and Tom are no longer together. They have both moved on. Tom is now seeing Talith. Meri wishes them every happiness they deserve in their life together*—a.k.a. nothing but misery and perhaps a dose of the clap.

We continued to move along the red carpet, pausing to give time for photos. I laughed up at Alex even though he hadn't said anything funny, holding on to his arm whilst I pretended to untangle my dress from my heel. I almost kissed him when he bent down to help me. I could practically hear the female journalists start ovulating at his gentlemanly action.

Finally, after faking and posing and dodging the bitchier and more interrogative journalists down the red carpet, we made it into the massive function room, where white and red swags hung from the ceilings and adorned the walls and chandeliers lit the room. People in evening dress milled around, laughing and drinking.

"Wow," Alex said as we paused at the top of four stairs leading down into the sunken ballroom. "It's like Christmas."

"Glitz and glamour?" I asked.

“Fake and tacky,” he responded. My laughter at his refreshingly honest assessment of the celeb party was cut short as I realised the group of people off to one side were talking about me.

“She totes rigged the vote.”

“Meri?”

“Yes. No way is she that popular. Three awards? *Please*.”

It wasn’t the first time this had happened, and it wouldn’t be the last, but still my heart sank a little, and a bit of the gloss wore off the night.

I turned to see some nineties rock star’s offspring holding court with several socialites and a couple of reality TV babes and bitching about me. It didn’t say much for a person and their life and achievements when they were in their twenties and still identified only by what their daddy did.

“I bet she paid her date, too. He looks like a model or an esco—”

“Hey,” I snapped. I would have shrugged it off as petty jealousy and continued walking, but Alex didn’t deserve to be denigrated. "That sounded remarkably like slander to me." I turned to Alex. "You're a *lawyer.* We have witnesses—"

"We were only joking." She looked Alex up and down, like she was a tiger and he was prey. "I'm sure he's flattered." Yeah, right, because calling someone a prostitute was flattering… "I heard about you and Tom breaking up." She gave a fake sympathetic smile. "Obviously, we all saw that coming." *Obviously,* it was just me who didn't, then. "But when I read he'd traded you in for your mother…" She sucked in a breath through her teeth, eyes wide with fake concern.

"Why have a pale imitation when you can get the original?" one of her sycophantic little friends asked, almost echoing one of Tom's tweets.

"Why indeed?" I asked, without emotion. They wanted me to get upset, to shout or cry, but I honestly didn't feel anything other than a bit of embarrassment that if I hadn't walked in on Tom and Talith, I would still be gushing about how great they were and paying their way.

"Wow. You really don't care, do you?"

Genuine emotion showed on her face—confusion and hurt. Which didn't make any sense, unless…

"He said you worked all the time, you were never home. He was lonely." He didn't have time to be lonely; he was juggling my mother and Jenn. "He said you were a frigid bitch." Tears flooded her eyes, but she blinked them back determinedly. Her "friends" watched from the side-lines gleefully. "But he couldn't leave you because your finances were intertwined, and you loved him and he didn't want to hurt you."

God, the poor kid. She couldn't be more than twenty years old. Tom was a dirty, lying, cheating bastard.

"He gave me this for my birthday." She held up a small silver locket.

And possibly an STD as well, given the increasing numbers of his conquests. I hoped she had the sense to get checked out. "I'm sorry if he lied to you and used you and hurt you," I said, reaching out to squeeze her hand. "You deserve more, better than he'll ever be."

"I'm fine." She shrugged me off, sniffing back the brimming tears. "I don't need you going all chat-show host on me." I stepped back, letting her have her pride and leaning into Alex. His arm immediately settled around my waist. She looked between us. "Maybe I'll have ride on this one too, wh—" The flash of white-hot rage nearly floored me.

"Thanks for the offer, but I'm not interested in bitchy little girls," Alex responded, clamping me to his side. "I already have a real woman."

I relaxed and rolled my eyes at him, but couldn't hide my smile. "Come on now, Twinkle. Don't be mean. *I* didn't sleep with your boyfriend."

Alex barked out a laugh, then looked to me. "Seriously?"

"Real name," I said. Yep, the girl was really called Twinkle, it should be treated as a form of child abuse giving children weird names.

"Meri, darling." Rock-star daddy stepped up beside his daughter, slipping an arm over her shoulder, giving me a *kids-will-be-kids* look. "You're being sooo brave. It can't be easy knowing your boyfriend prefers your sixty-year-old mother to you." He spoke through a smile, but his cold eyes showed his real intent.

I couldn't expect people not to talk about it; on the one-to-ten good gossip scale, this was one hundred and ten. So, I let it go and sought enjoyment from the fact no one believed Talith was forty-seven years old.

"I see they're here tonight," he continued.

I glanced in the direction he'd indicated, but a crowd of people obscured the view. I should have known they'd be here; Tom would no doubt be big-upping his "acting career" to anyone who would listen, whilst my mother revelled in the glitz and glamour and bitching. It would take a while for the connection to my fame to wear off and for their invites to stop coming.

"I don't know why she stayed with him so long, or what her mother sees in him." Twinkle had turned back to her friends and was, from her bitchy tone, obviously trying to bluff her way through the vulnerability she'd shown earlier. "He was the worst lay I've ever had."

"It was probably the lack of inspiration," Alex responded coolly, to the laughter of Twinkle's "friends".

"She's right," I responded. "He was the worst I've ever had too."

I could see the second my meaning hit home. I'd only ever slept with two men; Alex seemed to grow as pride swelled his chest. He smiled, his arms tightening around me. "You're my number one too, princess." His warm breath puffed against my ear as he whispered, turning us to walk away, "You know, he might have given her a locket you probably paid for, but you know what he didn't give her?"

"An orgasm."

"*Multiple* orgasms, princess," he said. I laughed. I'd just found out my ex cheated with a third woman, this one barely out of the school room, and I was laughing. "It's interesting to see you in your element," he continued, "but I don't think much of your friends. You should cull all five of them from your two and a half million. You won't miss them."

I rolled my eyes. "They're not my friends. No one here is really friends. We're colleagues at most. It's like me saying your clients and the other solicitors you work with are your friends."

"They are. Well, not my clients, but Lia and Marie and the others."

"Okay, Mr Popular, no need to rub it in." I pouted. I felt different. Lighter somehow. Stronger. It was nice to smile again, and not just because I'd sought revenge, but because I was enjoying myself with Alex. "I'm sorry about the way they're talking about you, objectifying you…"

"Don't worry. They may be bitches, but they think I

am hot, *a model*," he said, mimicking Twinkle.

"Or an escort," I added, feeling a spurt of jealousy. Every woman we passed was eyeing him up. He was mine, and they needed to keep their eyes and everything else to themselves. Well. Not actually mine, but he was my real-faux-boyfriend, and they needed to back off.

"Don't try to kill my happiness." He puffed his chest and struck a model pose, before sweeping a couple of glasses of champagne from a passing waiter's tray, handing me one. He scanned the next waitress's canapés, taking one of each, charming her into waiting so he could go back for seconds of the filo prawns with sweet chili. "You want one?"

Yes. They looked delicious. "No." It was bad enough I was drinking empty calories. I didn't need to eat them too. My dress was form-fitting. I didn't want tomorrows lead story to be about my "baby bump".

Alex stared at me, seeming to see right inside me. "Yes, you do." He plucked another filo prawn off the tray, dipped it in sweet chilli and held it in front of my mouth.

I firmed my lips, refusing to open.

He waited me out.

A bead of sweet chilli dip swelled on the end of the prawn, building into a big, fat, sticky drip. My dress had been lent to me by the designer; it was worth more than I wanted to think about. "It's going to dr— Umph."

"There you go. Delicious!" He popped the prawn into my mouth, forcing me to either spit it out in public, or chew and swallow it. The waitress read my look correctly and swept off to a safe distance, leaving Alex staring forlornly after her. "I'm starving. I should have had fish and chips before I came," he said, turning back to me.

"That was deep-fried, Alex! Do you know how many fat grams there were?"

He shrugged. "Neither know, nor care. As long as it tastes good."

"I care."

"You shouldn't. You could stand to put some weight on. Besides, you ran a four-minute mile in those stilettos twice last week. You're clearly fit and healthy. One filo prawn is not going to change that."

"I put ten pounds on every time I step in front of the camera," I snapped. "You saw me last week; they had to pin my skirt." I didn't go into the fact that it was because of my hangover bloat.

"It's a shame it isn't fifteen pounds and permanent," Alex said, scanning the room, no doubt looking for another circulating platter. "Good God, who, or should I say *what*, is that?" I followed his gaze across the room. "She looks like Gollum's mother."

The *what* he referred to stood in front of the large floor-to-ceiling windows, framed by the London skyline. She was the deep mahogany of fake tan. Her bleached blond hair had been scraped back so tightly that it was a miracle she could blink. Her skin had been stretched, her face lifted, lips filled. Cheek implants gave her the profile of a mannequin, and her nose looked like it had been borrowed from Michael Jackson's corpse. She was wearing a VB cocktail dress, too short, too tight and *mine*.

"Just call me Gollum, then."

I pounded Alex's back as he choked on air. "That's your m-mother? You don't look anything like her. Hell, *she* doesn't look anything like her. She must have slept with the photographer on that newspaper."

I smiled, silently accepting the compliment and carefully sipping my champagne. Now I'd had the prawn, I needed to make this one glass last all night. "We looked similar BS."

He flashed me a confused look. "BS?"

"Before surgery."

"She *paid* to look like that?"

I shrugged. "Almost. *I* paid for her to look like that."

He laughed. "You got your revenge early. You must have really hated her."

"Actually, she picked all the parts and the surgeons. I just paid when she asked me to."

"I can't believe he left you for her." He continued to stare at my mother. "Is she rich?"

I appreciated his disbelief. "No."

"She must be amazing in the sack."

I punched him in the arm. Hard. "You were doing so well at making me feel better, right up until the end."

"Shit." He turned towards me, putting his back to my mother. "Don't look now, Gollum, but you mother is headed this way with her orc in attendance."

What could she possibly think we had to talk to each other about? She must've felt confident, safe she could say whatever she wanted in public and I would listen, because I wouldn't want negative publicity.

"Meri, dah-ling!"

"Talith." I stepped back, avoiding her hug and air kiss. Alex moved to my side, blocking my mother's second attempt.

"Who's your delicious new man?"

"Don't bother. He's not interested in elderly women."

I was pretty sure Alex muttered, "Or bestiality," but his face was suspiciously blank when I glanced at him.

From across the room, it would look like we were all having a civil conversation. We faked smiles and kept our voices low. I could feel all eyes on us, and the conversation in the room dipped as people struggled to listen. Some edged closer.

"Don't be bitter, Meri." I cocked an eyebrow, even as I smiled, wide and toothy. I knew it annoyed Talith when I did this, her eyebrows being frozen in place halfway up her forehead.

"I'm not bitter. I'm better… better off without you."

At first, I felt kind of lost, angry and stupid that the people I'd trusted and depended on could do something like that to me and I would be totally oblivious.

Now I felt… relief. It was like a weight was lifted off my shoulders when I cut the ties. I was enjoying myself with Alex and my Plan of Revenge. I couldn't remember the last time I only had to worry about myself.

"She's always been cold." Tom wrapped an over-muscled arm around Talith, the bulge of his bicep threatening to hulk through his suit jacket. "That's why she felt she had to try to buy my love."

"Ha!" I barked. "Believe me, even if you'd charged by the minute for your 'love', you'd have gone bankrupt buying the condoms." Alex laughed. Tom didn't. I continued, "You'd have had to pay me if you'd charged by the orgasm."

Tom's hands fisted at his sides, his face going puce at the slight to his sexual prowess. He snarled, "Your mother doesn't have to pay. Any time we spend together is priceless."

Gak.

I wasn't going to have to worry about the deep-fried prawn calories; if he kept talking, I was going to empty my stomach. "How is the money situation? Have either of you managed to get a job yet?"

Alex edged between us.

“I thought you could be mature about this,” Talith said.

“Clearly not,” I responded.

“I thought as you’d moved on, we could heal the rift.”

I laughed again. “You should take this comedy show on the road.”

“I’m your mother.”

“Pity you didn’t think about that when you were screwing my boyfriend.”

Talith stepped closer.

Alex stepped back, taking me with him. “Meredith, princess, why does your mother smell of Chanel and death?” he asked.

“Well, in spite of the surgeons’ best work, Alex, she’s not getting any younger.”

Talith gasped with outrage, as we continued ignoring her.

“Hmm, just goes to show the old saying, ‘you’re only as young as the one you feel’, isn’t true.” Alex tipped his head in Tom’s direction. “He smells the same.”

“Maybe they’re just rotten at the core?” I said.

“Unquestionably.”

My gaze flicked back to Tom. “You’re filling out a bit there, Tom. If that shirt was any tighter, it would cut off your circulation.” His gasp of outrage caused a straining button to explode off his shirt, hitting me on the chest. “Ow! If that bruises, I’m suing.”

“You should try working out,” Alex said. “You don’t want to let yourself go at your age. Not when your livelihood depends on you being attractive enough to be able to live off women.”

I sniggered. Alex could hire himself out as a white knight. I couldn’t have planned it better if I’d told him what to say.

“I can see you’re clearly not ready to be mature about this.” Talith turned on her heel, stalking across the room, Tom and the unpleasant odour of rotting fish trailing in her wake.

I watched them slink off, relishing the way the crowd opened up to let them through, whispering and waving hands to dissipate the smell that followed in their wake.

“Can we go now?” Alex asked. “I’m hungry, and I

think you've achieved all you set out to."

He stared into my eyes, his palm warm against my cheek as a camera flashed. The picture would make it obvious we were lovers and would be in half the newspapers tomorrow.

"Haven't you filled up on hors d'oeuvres?" I asked.

"It isn't possible to fill up on those things. I want fish and chips. Actually, I've gone off the idea of fish, thanks to smell. It'll have to be pizza." .

CHAPTER 25

Affairs Exposed - Lie Detector Results Show

"Hey, what are you doing here?"

Three days later, Alex nudged me out of the way, walking into my flat. He dropped a black duffel in the hall and headed into the lounge.

"I came to see you. It's what normal people do when they're dating," he said as he plugged a flash drive into my fifty-two-inch curved-screen TV, another hangover from my Tom days. I decided to give up on protesting his presence. I didn't have the energy to go into the whole fauxmance thing again, and it would be nice to have some company. I wasn't used to being alone all the time. "Go to each other's houses and hang out. All we seem to do is go to events. I thought it would be nice to spend some time together without press and fans watching."

"Netflix and chill?" I asked, going to join him in the living room.

"If you're lucky," he said, winking. "But first, I downloaded the NTAs. I thought we could watch you win and win and win together. I know shit kicked off later that night and you didn't get to celebrate your success, so I thought it might be nice for us to change the ending and celebrate together."

My heart kicked hard against my ribs, and tears pressed the back of my eyes. I blinked them back. He wanted to watch me win. "I'm not paying you to watch TV with me."

His eyes hardened, but his tone was still jovial when he said, "I'm willing to do this one pro bono. Consider it charity."

I scowled. "Whatever. It's not like anyone else is queuing up for the honour."

Alex mumbled something that sounded suspiciously like: *They're probably busy screwing Tom.*

"What?"

He pulled a tube of salt and vinegar Pringles and some toffee popcorn from a stripy plastic bag. "I bought Scooby snacks."

"Are you sure you want to do this?" I asked. "It lasts for ages, and it'll probably be boring for you."

"Are you kidding? You won three awards; of course I want to see."

"Why?" I was genuinely confused. Tom was in the entertainment business, but even he only went to events when he thought he could make good contacts. He would never watch the playbacks of anything with me.

Alex laughed, sobering quickly when he realised I was asking a serious question. "Because I like spending time with you. And because a good boyfriend celebrates with his girlfriend when she's achieved something." He pulled a bottle of champagne from his coat pocket and lifted the four-pack of beer in his other hand, waggling it in front of me.

He must have thought my silence was because I was going to kick him out, not because I was choked up, because he continued to sell his presence. "You can take a picture of us watching together and Instagram or Snapchat it."

I blinked rapidly. I was not going to cry because someone was being nice to me. I'd spent years working for those awards. I'd been devastated when Tom and Talith and Jenn all had reasons why they couldn't come to the awards show with me. Now here was Alex, wanting to share my moment of glory with me.

"Okay, Miss Popular." He sank down onto the sofa, right beside me. The sofa tipped, tilting me into his side. I relaxed against him as he hit play, and was instantly pulled back to that night.

"Look." I pointed at the screen with my glass, champagne slopping over the edge. "I look bloody great in that dress. You can barely see my stomach."

"You don't have a stomach." Alex slouched back against the sofa, one arm thrown across the back of the cushions, his fingers hanging millimetres from my shoulder.

"Everyone has a stomach."

"Only if they eat. But you're right. You look really hot in that dress. You look even more stunning naked."

I slapped a wet, winey smooch on his cheek. Alex kicked off his shoes, crossed his feet on my coffee table, popped the top on his beer and opened the bag of toffee popcorn. He shook the bag under my nose. I pushed it away with a scowl. He shrugged, scooping up a massive fistful and dropping them in his mouth, munching contentedly, attention on the screen. "When do they stop with all the boring posing bits and get on with the awards?"

"She's not forty-seven years old, she's fifty-seven," I said, out of thin air.

"Penny Shepherd?" Alex turned from drooling over Penny on the red carpet. "No way. She's thirty, max!"

"No. No, not Penny. My mother."

"You're still thinking about the newspaper article?" He made it sound like I'd been mulling it over and wittering on about it for months. He reached into his pocket, pulling out his phone. Probably calling for a taxi so he could get away.

I glared at him.

He played around with it briefly then handed it over to me. "Here, maybe this will cheer you up."

"Unless they've printed their obituaries, I'm not interested."

"Don't be a baby. Here." He slapped his Samsung into my hand. "Scroll down to the comments section. See what the readers think about your mother and Tom."

Bobbi Smith

8:55PM

*What a b*tch. She's obviously lying. Why would Tom pick her over Meri Scott?*

I smiled. I liked Bobbie's train of thought, though, unfortunately, he was wrong. At least partially. My mother wasn't lying. I still had flashbacks to prove it. I scrolled down further, whilst the TV prattled on in the background about dresses and awards and Alex sat beside me crunching popcorn, hoping for another perv at Penny Shepherd and drumming his fingers on the sofa armrest.

Name Withheld

8:23PM

This comment is under review.

Under review? Under review by whom, for what? "Why is this under review?" I shoved the phone under Alex's nose, bumping his hand away from his mouth and sending popcorn raining across the sofa and floor.

He wrapped his hand around mine, holding it steady whilst he read the message. "It must have had something offensive in it."

"Like what?"

"Well, it could have been sexually explicit or had profane or unacceptable language."

"Oh…" Someone saying nasty things about my mother's article, or my mother, or Tom? I wished they'd left the name up so I could message them and ask what they'd written.

Jo Fletcher

7:44PM

Stupid old ho. She looks like she was made by Mattel. Is anything about her not fake? She's just cashing in on her daughter's fame.

Jon Gibbs

7:18PM

Silly slag, anything to get a few quid for herself

Cat Essex

7:08PM

She'll be on Celeb Big Bro next year. Hope she's proud. Old ho. Shame on you for paying for her story and printing it.

Penny Parsons

5:25PM

SHAME ON HER. Hope she is happy with herself, go get yer own man, then again will any bloke want u after this?

Laura Coe

4:10PM

Serves Meri right. Can't stand the beyatch. Like mother like daughter. Perhaps she'll be nicer to her guests now she and her mother have proven how skanky they are.

What?

That ruined my happy reading. How was I a skanky beyatch when my mother slept with my boyfriend—the only one I'd ever had—and posed naked, birthing me in celluloid form in a national newspaper? It wasn't fair to blame the victim.

"Who the hell is that?"

"Laura Coe. I don't know her. I don't think. Unless she came on the show sometime. It's been a long time. I can't remember everyone. I guess I could check her out on Facebook or ask my researchers."

"What?" Alex tore his gaze from the TV and cut me a confused look. "Why would you do that?"

"You asked—"

"Are you still reading those?"

I lowered his mobile and followed his extended finger to the television screen.

"No, I meant that." He tipped his head, frowning at the TV, which showed Chole Allen off *The Only Way Is Essex*. "She looks like my five-year-old niece did her make up with her Crayola crayon set."

"She's off TOWIE."

"What's Toe-ee?"

"TOWIE. Have you been living in a cave?"

He stared back coolly, waiting for an answer. It probably worked really well in court. It was fairly effective on the sofa.

"It's an acronym; *The Only Way Is Essex*." Realisation did not dawn. "It's one of those docudramas… reality TV."

He held up his hand. "Enough said. When will they pan back to the beautiful Penny Shepherd?"

I rolled my eyes, returning to his phone and the reader comments.

Abby King

3:50PM

I cannot get over how these silly trampy wh*res tell the world and his mother how cheap and nasty they are like its smart or clever to spread your legs for anything with a c*ck

Name withheld

2:19PM

This message was left by a user who has been blocked by our staff.

Damn it. Another good one. It had to be good if they'd blocked it. Maybe I could ask Neil to hack into the newspaper's internet account and uncover what was written.

Yes. That was what I would do.

I just needed to find an opportunity to sneak away from Alex… and I also needed to decide on the whole "seafood" shopping: to check out or not to check out the crab eggs. I'd been vacillating for days. It was strange; I had my mental Plan of Revenge in play, so why didn't I have the burgeoning excited feeling I got from my other activities?

Maybe… possibly… was it a step too far?

Could I be getting over it?

Was Alex having a good effect on me?

Whatever it was, it seemed wrong to plot to break the law when he was sitting right beside me. It wasn't just "seafood" shopping; even hacking into the newspaper felt wrong, and that wasn't a direct physical attack against a person.

The punishment wouldn't be severe.

Would it?

It wasn't like hacking into the CIA, or stealing people's bank details. It was just a few comments from people whose opinions were so strong that they were withheld by a newspaper that pretended to represent the moral majority when it actually just sold stories with pictures of naked women sprawling across two pages.

I sighed, mourning the loss, and turned back to the phone. There were only a few more comments left.

Dale Wilcox

1:52PM

I'd do her.

Who? Talith? He'd do my mother? He must be sick, or blind. I scrolled down. Jim was no better. Rhapsodising about my mother's seven-thousand-pound breasts.

Jim Wannamaker

12:43 PM

Go Cougar mum. Nice t*ts.

Name withheld

12:41PM

This comment was left by a user who has been blocked by our staff.

Zoe Mason

12:40PM

Serves the sanctimonious b*tch right. Maybe she'll be more understanding to her guests now.

B*tch? What happened to girl power and the sisterhood? Zoe was the bitch. I hoped *her* boyfriend shagged *her* mother *and* her brother.

Clare Wilson

12:22PM

Can never understand why these women tell the world what cheap whores they are… wait until he does to her what she did to Meri. She'll be selling her story to another rag then.

Jenny Fletcher

11:52AM

She's only selling herself because Meri stopped paying for her. If she had any class (which she clearly doesn't) she would take her implants out and sell those before she sold out her own kid

Name withheld

11:22AM

Only one step away from prostitution. Slag.

I scrolled through the messages one last time, counting. One, two, three… twelve messages in my favour—I included blocked messages—versus four for Talith. “How do I post one of these?”

Alex tipped the popcorn bag into his open mouth, pouring the crumbs in. “You don’t,” he said as he munched. “You can get sued for libel.”

“I’ll do it under someone else’s name.” I thought about it for a second. I was already logged in as Alex. A contented smiled tipped up my lips. “Yours.”

“No, again.” He swiped the phone from my hand. “I’m not getting disbarred because you’re having a hissy fit. Let it go, princess.”

I lunged at him, trying to get the phone, but Alex held it out of reach. He swooped forward and pressed his lips to mine, then slipped his free hand behind my neck and into my hair, cupping my head and holding me to his mouth. His lips moulded to mine. My hands came to land on his hard chest. The warm pressure of his mouth sent tremors of desire skating across my skin.

My eyelids sank closed. My tongue captured the sweet toffee flavour of his lips.

I felt his smile against my mouth, a second before he pulled back, his looking down into my eyes. “I thought it would cheer you up.”

“Hmm,” I responded happily. The kiss had totally cheered me up. If we’d kept it up and his hand had gone for a little wander, I was pretty sure, given previous experience, it could lead to him giving me a very happy ending.

“Thanks, princess.” He laughed, swooping in for a little more lips-on-lips action. “But I was talking about seeing the comments, not the kiss. The majority of them are in your favour. Who cares about a couple of ignorant people writing stupid things?”

What? “Me!”

He sighed. “It’ll only get blocked before anyone gets to see it.”

I sank back onto my side of the sofa, pouting. "But writing it will be cathartic." He cocked an eyebrow. "The counsellors on my show always suggest guests write letters to dead relatives, or letters they'll never send, and pour all their emotions out. It helps them get closure and move on."

"Of course, it does," he responded dryly.

"It does." I'd always thought it was a load of mumbo jumbo, but given it worked in my favour right now, I was all for it. "They're qualified counsellors. They know more about these things than you do."

"Uh-huh. You're still not using my phone, or email, or name. Look." He turned his attention back to the TV, tucking his mobile out of reach in his pocket. "Here's the award for Most Popular Talk Show. Didn't you get nominated for that?"

"I won it."

"Damn it, Meredith! I hate it when people give away the ending." He threw himself back into the corner of the sofa. "There's no point in watching now."

I rolled my eyes at his amateur dramatics. "I'll make it up to you by letting you hold my gongs later."

He waggled his eyebrows and leered, turning my totally benign offer into something else entirely. My face flushed. I was saved from some salacious remark when he said, "Either this is a really shitty massage chair or your phone's vibrating."

I hit pause o and swiped the screen to answer when Tony's name showed. "Tony."

"Babe, I'm hearing there's going to be another story."

"About what? Talith's shown everything God and plastic surgery gave her already. What more could she have?"

"They're keeping pretty tight-lipped on the name, but it seems like there was another woman. I need to know what you know, babe. It's the only way to get us one step ahead."

"He slept with Jenn, too," I said.

Alex's head jerked up. He didn't pretend he wasn't listening. "You sure know how to pick 'em, Meredith."

"Jesus, I always wondered if Owain was his," Tony said at the same time. "He looks like a mini-me."

"I didn't pick my mother, Alex," I snapped, then turned back to the phone conversation. "Thanks for the heads-up on your suspicions about Tom's *mini-me*, Tony." Sarcasm may be the lowest form of wit, but it got my point across. I could practically see him wincing on the other end of the line. "She's pregnant again."

"Jesus!" Alex said.

"Is someone else there?" Tony asked.

"My lawyer," I said.

"You have a lawyer?"

"Yes."

"I've got Richard on payroll; he's always handled all your contracts. You're not thinking of jumping ship, are you, Meri? I admitted we slipped up on Talith, but we won't make another mistake, and I'm millimetres from closing the deal with the Americans—"

"He's a criminal solicitor."

"Shit," Tony said. "What's going on?"

"Nothing you need to worry about," I responded.

"Now I'm really scared."

"Don't be. What you don't know won't get you arrested."

Alex frowned. Tony choked and spluttered. I smiled.

"Don't do anything stupid, Meri."

"I won't." Stupid would be getting caught.

"So, the new bun in Jenn's oven—it's Tom's?"

"Yep."

"You think it's her? Do you think she'd sell her story?"

"I would have said no, but then, I didn't think she'd sleep with my boyfriend and make me godmother to their lovechild, either. And she's going to need a financial cushion to see her through maternity leave."

"Hasn't she got a private income? What did she use last time?"

"Me. But I'm all out of charity."

"Oh-kay!" Tony blew out a long breath. "I'll get Danni onto it. I'll work on your response myself. I'll give you the heads-up if we hear anything else."

"Fine. Thanks." I couldn't drum up any enthusiasm. Somehow the promise of a heads-up next time someone sold a sex story about my ex didn't fill me with joy. "He slept with Twinkle, too."

"The pop brat? Jesus, she's, what, fifteen?"

"Twenty. Old enough to consent."

"Thank God. No one will care about that. It's nothing compared to your mother and best friend."

"Yeah. Great. Thanks." *For nothing.*

"If it makes you feel better, we've dropped Tom from our books. We only had him on as favour to you. The boy can't act, or present, or do much of anything, really. He looks pretty, but there are hundreds of pretty boys who *can* act. No one will hire him for anything… Well, maybe a reality show where he has to eat grubs in the jungle. Rumour has it he only got those bit parts because he slept his way into them. The bastard can't be any better at fucking then he is at acting, because he wasn't invited back for an encore."

God. It was just wonderful to hear Tom's slutting around extended from the personal into the professional sphere.

Was everyone laughing behind my back?

Was I the only one who didn't know?

I should've been the first to know.

I should've recognised the signs.

I was always telling my guests and audience they should pay attention to the little changes… and yet I'd been blind, for *years*.

"Let's just say his bit parts are probably more impressive than his bits," I retorted miserably. God, I was pathetic. At least most of the other women only slept with him once; I kept going back for more, and paid for it.

"Well, no reputable agent's interested in picking him up, and your mother's no good for anything but stories about her s-exploits, and warning posters or YouTube clips against plastic surgery."

"So, they'll both be on *I'm a Celebrity* next series, then." No way could either of them survive in the jungle.

Tony laughed. “Probably. It’s been running for so long now, they’ll take anyone they can get. You, however, are hot stuff at the moment, what with all the awards and your mother selling herself to the highest bidder. This could get rough, but—”

“Will it affect the US deal?” My head fell back onto the back of the sofa, and I stared at the brilliant white ceiling. At some point, Alex’s hand had settled on my thigh, warm and steady. Every now and then he gave it a comforting pat or squeeze.

“If I spin it right, we can use it in your favour. The networks should be happy enough, so long as you keep your nose clean.”

“Easier said than done.” I had a shopping trolley full of pubic-lice eggs waiting for checkout on the dark web.

“You’re only human. It’s normal to be upset. Just don’t sink to their level. Everyone’s been cheated on. It makes you seem more human. The audience will relate to you better. It could actually help with the US negotiations. Just remember, you need to maintain your integrity, so keep cool.”

Being cool wasn’t the problem. Keeping my hands clean… problem. “What should I do about the article?”

"Nothing. I'll handle it." His wheeler-dealer tone softened. "I gotta say, I'm disgusted your mother and Jenn would do this to you, and I've been in this business long enough to have seen just about everything. You've supported them for years, and Tom's a loser."

"They're desperate, lonely women, Tony." Or, at least, that was what they'd told me.

"They're backstabbing bitches, Meri. Don't just roll over, babe. You don't want to be a doormat. It won't be good for your image. I can get some dirt published on the bastard. Just say the word."

"No. Don't do that. Tom will love the publicity. He won't care whether it's positive or not, so long as he's getting attention." He must still be in the running for the romcom role, or he'd have been flashing his arse next to Talith in the newspaper.

"We could sell your story, give you control over what's written. It'll take the bite out of anything else your mother has, and you can pre-empt Jenn."

"No." I sighed, rolling my head so I could look at Alex. He smiled and winked. "It'll just escalate things, and then Tom will sell his story too, and it will never end."

"Good," Alex whispered. "Show some class and rise above it." I rolled my eyes at him.

"I thought you'd say that," Tony said. "Do me a favour though, babe: think about it. People will relate to you if you show some vulnerability, let them see your heartbreak."

Alex didn't bother hiding the fact he was listening in on the call, and snorted his opinion of my heartbreak.

"People already relate to me, Tony. I got voted Most Popular three times at the NTAs. Speaking of which, I have to go. I'm watching with Alex, and they're starting the awards now. I need to Insta a picture of me snuggling with my hottie on the couch."

"Great. Allie can pick it up at this end and work it into a few stories, tweets, etc."

I ended the call. Alex lifted his arm, slinging it around my shoulder. I snuggled in, whipped out my selfie light and stick, worked out my best angle and snapped a picture of us looking cosy, then posted it. Alex pressed play.

"You kept quiet about the fact he knocked up your friend."

"It wasn't relevant." I took a swig of wine. "At least my mother's too old for me to have to worry about someday being a big sister to my ex's kid."

"Your life is like one of those tabloid magazines old women read in coffee shops and train stations. You could sell your story for five hundred pounds."

"I could sell it for a hell of a lot more than that. There I am." I pointed at the TV. "They're about to start the next award."

The screen filled with the image of me squeezed into a seat between Mike and Jerry, who spilled over his chair and took up half of mine. Jerry turned to speak to me, and the camera panned over the crowd. I remembered it so clearly it was like I was there.

"Nervous?"

Yes. *"No. It's just the cold. You?"*

Jerry smirked at my obvious lie. Okay, so I was eating myself up inside. I really, really, really *wanted to win the Most Popular Presenter this year. It was my turn. Tom and Trey had won so many times that they were thinking of renaming it the Tom and Trey Award.*

"You've got a good chance. People are getting bored of perky, perpetual little-boy presenters."

No, they weren't, but I appreciated the lie. I kissed Jerry's cheek, smoothing his tufty hair back from his shiny face.

"And next, the nominees for Most Popular Presenter..."

I sat up straight, trying not to look like I was hyperventilating, flashing a smile as a camera zoomed in to catch my response.

Let it be me.

Let it be me.

Let it be me.

I'd practiced my happy-loser face in the mirror before I came out, but I was a presenter, not an actor. It wasn't going to hold up to close scrutiny. So, I needed to win.

I wanted to win.

I had to win.

Mike and Jerry sat on either side of me, holding our awards for Most Popular Talk Show and Most Popular Factual Programme. We'd done well, but it wasn't enough;

if I won this, it would be about me. This was entirely in my control, the result of my hard work alone—not the whole show, just me, and it would be an NTA hat trick. The pinnacle of my career.

I couldn't take much more of this. The camera angle tightened, projecting a massive image of me looking calm and professional, whilst practically peeing myself with nerves. "Let's take a look at Meri in action." The big screen lit up with a clip from my show.

Finally, the clip ended, and David made a big deal about opening the envelope. The camera zoomed in for a painfully tight shot, projecting me and the other nominees on the big screen. They were hoping for shots of one of us swearing or crying if we didn't win.

"And the winner of Most Popular Presenter is..."

I fixed a smile on my face, but I was trembling with nerves. Inside, I chanted, Me, me, me! Let it be me…

"Meri Scott!"

It was me!

I'd won.

I was hauled from my seat by Jerry, hugged and thrust stumbling towards the aisle. Somehow, I made it to the stage in a blur of lights and cheers and catcalls from the audience.

"Thank you. Thank you." I held on to the podium with one hand and my NTA with the other. I felt like I was going to float away; life didn't get better than this. "I, um... I... only wrote one acceptance speech, and you've already heard it. Twice." Catcalls from the crowd. Yeah, I was bragging. "So, I'll just thank my crew, again, who make me look great even when I'm not, but mostly I want to thank my mum and my wonderful boyfriend Tom—who have loved and supported me since before there even was a Meri Scott Show. *Without their love and support, I wouldn't be here. Without them, I'd still be living in a small Welsh village, dreaming one day I would stand here, accepting this award. This is for my mum and Tom for their unstinting love and support. I love you both."*

Ick. I scowled, turning the TV off, unable to watch myself gushing over Tom and Talith. What an idiot I was, so desperate for the perfect life that I'd fooled myself into believing I had it. "Whilst I was saying that, they were shagging around."

"Forget about them," Alex said. "I'm thinking *we* should celebrate your win."

Tears welled in my eyes. "Thank you," I whispered, voice breaking. "Thank you for… caring."

"Of course I care! My girlfriend is the most popular times four."

"Times three."

"Four." He held up four fingers. "Most Popular TV Presenter, Most Popular Daytime Talk Show, Most Popular Factual Programme, and Most Popular Sexy, Successful Woman, as voted by me."

"Sounds like an important award." My lips trembled with emotion and tears… happy tears. My heart felt painfully full.

"Hmm." Alex twisted off the couch, moving to kneel between my legs. He winced, changing position to straighten his left leg. Then he pulled me to the edge of the sofa cushion and wedged his body between my thighs. My muscles clenched with anticipation.

He leant forward. I met him halfway, our mouths brushing then lifting away. His tongue stroked the seam of my lips, seeking entrance.

I kissed him back, desperately.

"Nuh-huh." He pulled back. "You already did the hard work by winning the awards. I'll take care of the *celebration*."

Picking me up, he strode, with barely a limp, through to the bedroom. .

CHAPTER 26

Help! My Girlfriend Is Starving Herself To Death

"I'm sorry, Vic," I said to my apartment manager. "I've tried everything. I can't get rid of them." I winced as Team Meri, the ever-increasing group of Meri Scott fanatics, who'd set up camp outside the gates to my apartment building, started chanting my name.

"It's all right, Meri. I don't mind your supporters—it's the scummy paparazzi trying to squeeze in the gates every time they open, ringing random intercoms, trying to get people to let them in." He shook his head. "Did you get the newspaper I left outside your door this morning?"

"Yeah, thanks." I didn't sound as grateful as the words would suggest, but given the contents of the newspaper he'd left—yet another of Tom's lovers selling her story—Vic wouldn't take it personally. Besides, I was still in credit with him for gifting him Tom's electronic goods.

"That bastard didn't deserve you. And don't get me started on your mother."

The last thing I wanted was to get him started on my mother. He hadn't liked Talith since he got drunk one Christmas and hit on her, and she knocked him back because he was "*just* an *old* odd-job man". Now he thought she was lower than dirt, and he was happy to expound on it.

I closed the door behind him and stared around the flat. I felt trapped and… alone. It had been nearly a month since Tom and I split up and my circle of trust imploded, and even though I had Alex, I felt lonely.

Usually, if I argued with my mother, I'd have Jenn or Tom—although he wasn't much of a listener—to talk to, or Jenn to talk to if it was Tom who was irritating me. I'd gone from feeling safe and snug in the cocoon of my family, in an industry where true friendship was rare, to having no one.

For the past three days, every day I'd opened the newspaper and felt panic fist my chest. I dreaded seeing Jenn's story. The final betrayal. To read how she and Tom laughed about how gullible I was as they rolled about in my bed and I looked after their lovechild, oblivious.

Heart pounding, hands shaking, I opened the paper.

Each day there was a different woman proving just how low she was willing to go.

I wandered through the living room to stand by the window. Lifting the edge of the blind, I looked out across the court yard to the big black gate railings to see just how bad it was.

“Meri!”

“How do you feel, Meri?”

It was bad.

“Team Meri!”

“We love you, Meri.”

“Come and talk to us.”

Really bad.

“Tell us your side.”

“Shit!” I winced as the noise level ratcheted up.

Shit, shit, shit.

I shouldn't have looked. It would take hours for them to settle back down now.

"What the hell? Why did you do that?" Alex stumbled into the room wearing grey sweat pants and a t-shirt, rubbing a hand over his sleep-flattened hair.

"I wanted to see."

"Why didn't you just use the video button on the intercom?" Alex's remark proved why he was a successful, highly paid lawyer, and I presented daytime television.

Putting his words into action, he crossed to the intercom and watched Team Meri pushing and jostling with the paparazzi, whilst they chanted and ad-libbed surprisingly accurate songs about Tom's lack of prowess in the bedroom.

"You could have seen them without stirring everything up."

Alex hadn't left since we'd watched the NTAs together; when I'd woken up the next morning, he was still there, pulling clothes from his black duffel and strutting around like he owned the place. When I questioned why he was there, he smiled and said, *Because that's what good-*

not-faux-boyfriends do.

I sighed and turned back into my dark cave of a flat. At this rate, I was going to end up with rickets from the sun deficiency. Team Meri had started out as a few dedicated fans wanting to show their support after Talith published her story. At first it had just been t-shirts with *Team Meri* printed on them, but now there was a website, a whole range of clothing, hats, even knickers…

Celebrities had been pictured showing their support for me; it was *the* in thing to do. Alex had been the first to bring it to my attention, turning up with a picture of Penny Shepherd, her boobs distorting the catchphrase into *eam Mer*. He'd torn it out of the paper and folded it into his wallet, pouting when I refused to ask Penny to autograph it for him. Penny started a celeb craze, and soon everyone was proclaiming their Team Meri status.

I wandered nonchalantly over to Alex, wriggling up against him, so I could watch the show on the intercom screen over his shoulder whilst sliding my hand under the hem of his t-shirt and copping a feel of hot man. Team Meri had sold out of merchandise within hours. Some guy had tried to cash in on Team Tom, but they couldn't give the merchandise away. In fact, just the other day, a man wearing a Team Tom t-shirt in public had been set upon by a mob of angry women.

I had, of course, given a statement to the press and tweeted, appealing for calm and asking Team Meri to *pity, not harm anyone stupid enough to purchase Team Tom merchandise…* whilst secretly being proud of them.

A few days ago, Talith and Tom had been pictured out together in matching Team Love shirts… Euch!

Still, from the look on Talith's face the next day when the first of the "other" women got their stories published, Team Love wasn't as exclusive as she'd thought.

It was day three of the campout. My neighbours were complaining, filming was on hold whilst security was beefed up and I was stuck in my flat going stir crazy. I wandered back to the couch and unrolled the papers, scanning for details on today's offering. She was some bit-part actress. It didn't matter anymore who they were, or even that I was starting to think some of them were making it up. One of them had said she had an orgasm… so she was definitely lying. They all just seemed to want their five minutes of fame by selling their pitiful s-exploits with Tom.

I knew without reading, and regardless of what they said, that their sex lives were pitiful. I'd been with Tom for seven years; if he'd had any sexual skill, he'd have used it on me at least once, even if it was a fluke or one-off stroke of sexual genius, but no. It never happened. The latest article came complete with naked photo shoot. Thankfully, this time my photograph wasn't being used as a vaginal screen. This one had gone for a "classier" photo than my mother, sitting on the edge of a bed with a plush towel artfully clasped to her chest.

Jesus! My breath caught.

I reread the paragraph.

Then reread it again.

How could people sell their private lives like this? Like Jenn, this one had gotten pregnant by Tom, only she'd taken the abortion route and was telling everyone and her grandmother about it.

I tossed the paper aside to join the others. Someday, I'd have a massive bonfire with them, burn an effigy of Tom on top and invite Team Meri to roast marshmallows with me.

But not today.

Today, I was stuck in my flat again, or at least within the back courtyard, behind high walls and away from the gate and Team Meri and the press. The police had had to set up a cordon to enable residents to get in and out of the gate and make sure Team Meri didn't spill out into the road and block traffic.

Alex had disappeared for a few hours on Saturday morning, then turned up wearing a baseball cap and shades, carrying two suitcases. He'd been closely followed by a Sainsbury's food delivery van. He'd immediately made himself at home, and I'd… let him.

Finished with the paper, I trailed him into the kitchen. He smiled at me, dimple flashing in his right cheek. "You want some breakfast?"

"I guess." It wasn't like there was anything else to do with filming postponed. I'd sulked in bed all day yesterday, so I was too restless to sleep today, which only left eating to break up a tedious day stuck in what was beginning to feel like a very small flat. He'd suggested I move to his flat, but he didn't have a courtyard or security, and he liked his neighbours, so I didn't want to inflict my suddenly crazy life on them.

I slouched onto a stool at the breakfast bar. Alex placed a bowl of little round glazed things in front of me and took a seat, digging in to his own bowl. “What are these?”

“Honey-Coated Puffs,” he said with his mouth full.

“Are someone’s kids coming around for breakfast?” I asked.

“No.” He pointed with his spoon, frowning as I pushed the bowl away. He expected me to eat this crap?

“You do realise Puffs have no nutritional value at all, don’t you?” I said. They were just carbs and sugar. One twenty-nine-gram bowl of Puffs contained almost ten per cent of a person’s daily carbohydrate requirement and one hundred and ten empty calories.

“Honey-Coated Puffs?”

“Yes!” Given my maximum eight hundred calories per day and Alex’s serving being nearer to one hundred grams than the recommended twenty-nine, just sitting this close and watching him consume nearly four hundred calories—without accounting for the full-fat milk—was probably putting weight on me.

Alex finished his bowl quickly, then hooked a hand around my bowl and dragged it across the counter. "Are you going to eat these?"

"No!" Hadn't he just listened to what I said? "*No nutritional value*, and don't even get me started on the sugar content."

He huffed. "Whatever. You shouldn't criticise a man's breakfast." He wrapped his arm fully around the bowl, using it as a shield, clearly scared I was going to lose my mind and snatch the bowl back.

"It's reconstituted rubbish. There's nothing natural in them."

He swallowed. "There's honey."

I had my doubts. "Grown men do not eat Honey-Coated Puffs."

"They do, too." Alex swiped the box off the breakfast bar, tucking it behind him on the worktop. I followed the action, suddenly realising just how full my usually neat, empty kitchen was. Danish pastries sat in little plastic containers on the worktop, and several sharing bags of crisps were stacked on top of the fridge, which I'd already seen was stuffed with red meat, chocolate, beer and wine.

I started to sweat and shake and crave things I'd never let cross the threshold into my home before. It was like Oscar Wilde said: *I can resist everything except temptation.* A cinnamon whirl begged me to eat it. I half jumped, half stumbled from the stool, edging out of the kitchen. "You need to get all this crap out of my house."

"What crap?"

"This." My heart was starting to pound. I gestured around the kitchen, taking in all the fat, sugars and carbs in their bright, shiny eat-me wrappers, displacing my fruit, salad, lean meat and brown rice.

Alex shrugged. "You don't have to eat it." Yeah, right. When it was right there calling me?

Tempting me?

He thought I'd just be able to avoid it?

"You need to eat something more than cardboard flakes. I don't know if this is a control thing or an appearance thing, but it's not healthy. Most men, most *people*, want their partners to be fit and healthy, not emaciated and exhausted. There's nothing wrong with a few curves to snuggle up to."

"Then find yourself a curvy girl," I retorted, turning away. My stomach felt heavy and tears pushed behind my eyes. Why couldn't I be good enough the way I was?

"Hey." He pushed up from the counter, snagging my hand and pulling me back to face him, then tipped my face up to his. His eyes darkened to an impenetrable navy, searching my face. "You are gorgeous. Every part of you is perfect." He wiped a stray tear from my lash with his thumb, then brushed my hair off my cheek, looping it behind my ear. "Well, your mind is possibly warped, but I am *not* interested in anyone else. I'm just worried about you, princess. You've been slim since I met you, but you've lost weight you couldn't afford to lose in the last few weeks. You need to eat if you don't want to end up in hospital."

"I'm fine," I snapped. He didn't have a clue about my industry. I forced myself to step away from him, when all I really wanted to do was curl up in his arms.

Alex sighed, picking up the breakfast bowls and rinsing them before stacking them in the dishwasher. "So, what are we going to do today?"

"Well, given what's going on outside, my choices are

somewhat limited…"

He smiled. "I can think of a few things to keep us entertained."

"And risk impaling yourself on my hipbones?"

"Some risks are definitely worth taking."

"And some aren't," I countered, still not willing to forgive him for the skinny jibe. A cherry bakewell tried to launch itself off the counter at me. I ducked. "I need to get out of here. I'm going to the gym. I don't care how you do it, but you need to get rid of this crap before I get back."

* * * * *

Humming under my breath, backside wiggling from side to side, I pounded and sweated my way through a full-body workout on the elliptical trainer. "Work it, princess!"

I jumped, then stumbled, fumbling to catch myself on the hand bars. How the hell did Alex get in here?

It was residents only.

"What are you doing here?"

"I thought I'd join you. Work off the sugar and carbs you were so worried about me eating earlier."

He set my spare key on the shelf by the door and moved into the room, checking out the machines. He was wearing a faded blue-grey University of Cambridge t-shirt and blue sweatpants. I watched in the wall of mirrors as he moved through some stretches, his left leg significantly less flexible than his right.

I wondered what had happened to his leg… a fiery car crash, rescuing puppies from a train track, fighting off armed muggers to save a defenceless granny on pension day…

Sigh.

I liked those ideas a little too much.

Reality would be something dull or embarrassing, like running to the loo with a dodgy stomach and tripping over his shoelace.

I'd probably never know. He was supersensitive when I asked about it. It wasn't like I was asking for a penile measurement or function test. I already knew he topped the scale with both of those. I just wanted to know what had happened to his leg.

He winced through another stretch, and I couldn't hold my silence. "Are you sure you should be doing that?"

"What?"

"Stretching your leg like that. It obviously hurts."

"Get on with your own workout, Meredith."

Oh-kay! Well, I'd tried. If he did himself more damage, it was his fault. I pushed through a fast legs-only section of my workout programme and watched via the mirror as he kneaded the muscle just above his knee. I knew from the times I'd seen him deliciously naked that he had angry red operation scars running down both sides of his thigh. "Seriously, Alex—"

"If I need medical advice, I'll call a doctor," he snapped, fitting the earbuds attached to his phone into his ears, signalling the end of the conversation. He ignored me, starting off at a brisk walk on the treadmill.

Forty-five minutes later, I was starting to feel lightheaded. My vision dimmed, and I started hallucinating about Nando's barbecued chicken smothered in medium-hot sauce, followed by Krispy Kreme glazed donuts.

I'd seen some donuts in a box beside the nearly empty fruit bowl in my kitchen. Another hour on the cross-trainer and I could have quarter of one.

I'd skipped breakfast, after all.

I swallowed before I started drooling.

If I wanted to make my own fitness DVD in the New Year, I needed to shift the last three pounds clinging to my hips.

Alex appeared behind me in the mirror looking *hot*—and not just sweaty like me. He lifted the edge of his shirt, dabbing the light beading of sweat off his forehead and flashing a tanned, toned belly; no six-pack, but by no means fat. I'd felt that firm, warm skin with its sexy sprinkle of dark hair that clung to my fingers.

"Shiiit."

The black edging my vision expanded, like a black hole sucking everything into it. I was going to pass out. I felt like I was moving in slow motion. I stumbled, reaching out blindly, slapping ineffectually in the general direction of the emergency stop.

"Agh!" My feet tangled. My legs jellied. I wobbled off the back of the machine, slumping down in a heap beside the mirrored wall. "Ump. Owww."

"Jesus, Meredith! Meredith?"

My vision slowly cleared. I rolled onto my side, on the floor.

"Are you okay?" Alex was crouched beside me. I blinked up at him, bringing him back into focus. "What the hell? Are you trying to kill yourself?" He frowned, pushing my limp, sweaty fringe back off my face.

Taking a shaky breath, I used the wall and his arm to crawl painfully up to half-standing, half-crouching position. Alex rose smoothly beside me, hauling me the rest of the way up. I sagged against him, whimpering. It wasn't so much the impact with the ground—yes that hurt, a lot—but… I felt kind of shaky and queasy and off. If he moved away, I'd be back kissing the floor almost immediately.

He watched me, his expression morphing from concerned to angry. Any second now, he was going to start reading me the riot act. It wasn't like I'd deliberately thrown myself off the climber to disrupt his workout.

I caught my reflection in the mirror and shuddered.

I looked like crap, ghostly pale, with red blotches, shiny with sweat, panda-eyed from last night's mascara, with limp hair scraped back into a ponytail without the use of a brush. My fringe stood straight up like baby-chick fluff haloing my face, gelled with drying sweat. Behind me, hovering, like he thought I was about to pass out on him, was Alex, a vision of solid, broad-shouldered hotness.

His narrow-eyed gaze swept over me. A swift, hard assessment from top to bottom. I might be feeling dizzy and sick, but I wasn't so far gone that I didn't remember to suck in my stomach. I attempted a wobbly smile. He frowned. "Are you trying to kill yourself?"

What? "You surprised m—"

"You're blaming me?" He shook his head, then continued before I could say *yes*. "This isn't about me. It's about you. All you need are a couple of flies and you could model for an Oxfam appeal on famine relief."

"That's offensive!" Couldn't he see the last three pounds dimpling my thighs?

"You didn't eat any breakfast. You just worked out

like you were going for Olympic gold. If you keep exercising like this and not eating, you're going to kill yourself."

"Thanks for the pep talk. Are you done?" I shook off his hold, stumbling when my legs had to take responsibility for holding me up, then stalk-tottered as best I could to the exit. Blackness was expanding across my vision again.

"I haven't even started." His voice echoed strangely in my ears, like he was speaking from a long way away, or down a kitchen roll tube, like kids did. "If you end up dead or hospitalised, everyone is going to think you did it because you couldn't get over Tom. Is that what you want?"

"I've finished," I said, ignoring his question. "I guess I'll see you back upstairs." If my vision cleared.

I could feel the heat of him behind me as he trailed me to the exit. He reached over my shoulder, opening the door for me, snagging our keys and my mobile phone off the shelf on the way past. "When was the last time you had something to eat?"

"Breakfast," I mumbled through numb, rubbery lips.

"No. You watched me eat. You didn't eat. Too worried about carbs and sugars."

I staggered and bumped him. His hand settled on my hip, steadying me. I didn't have the energy to shake him off. "I was up before you. Maybe I ate breakfast then."

"Really." His tone said *liar*. "What did you have? A box of raisins? Half—no, no, a quarter of an apple? Peeled."

"Cereal." Forty grams of bran flakes with water, not milk. I'd weighed and measured the portion out. I'd sat down to eat it, but then Vic had called to say he was bringing up the newspaper, and I'd lost my appetite.

"There's nothing in your fridge I didn't buy and put there."

"I had bran flakes in the cupboard." And a multitude of plastic packets of premade food from Nutrition Chef in the bottom draw next to the oven.

"Uh-huh." He pressed the button for the lift. I edged past him, heading for the stairs. Alex wrapped his arm around my waist, sweeping me up and dumping me in the lift beside him before my legs had time to protest my stupid pride.

* * * * *

Twenty minutes and two crackers and cheese later—which Alex had prepared, then stood over me until I'd eaten it—I crawled out of the shower, sagging onto the toilet seat and nursing my bruised knees, hip and shoulder. Finally, I managed to work up the energy to hobble into my bedroom. I dragged on the first clothes I could find: Victoria Beckham navy wide-legged trousers, with a blue and white spotted sweater, and collapsed on my bed, exhausted.

I groaned as Alex knocked on the door. "Meredith?" I ignored him in the vain hope he'd go away. "Meredith? Are you okay?" He knocked again. "Either you answer or I'm breaking in."

No. I'd just had the door fixed from the last time he broke it. I hauled myself off the bed and yanked open the door, slumping against the frame when the world went dark from my swift transition from horizontal to vertical. I stared in the general direction of where I thought he was. "What? Can't I have five minutes without someone hounding me?"

"I'm hardly hounding you."

"Haven't you got somewhere else to be?" The black started to recede. Alex's large silhouette began to take form.

"Nope, not this week. Lunch is ready. I cooked burgers."

I trailed him to the kitchen. At some point, he'd showered; his dark hair was still damp and spiky. He sat at the breakfast bar. I stood and stared at the processed crap masquerading as meat and yellow, plastic-looking cheese in a white bun he'd put on two plates, then back at him.

"I can't eat that."

"Yes, you can. Just open your mouth, bite and chew." He demonstrated on his own burger, after toping it with a healthy dose of mustard and ketchup. My stomach was cramping. It felt like it had caved in. I definitely needed to eat something. I reluctantly headed for my stash of nutritionist-prepared packet diet meals. I selected the coq au vin, snipping the top of the packet and slipping it in the microwave.

“Let me rephrase. I’m *not* eating that. Apart from anything else, no matter what they put on the packet, there’s a high chance it has horse in it.”

He made a *tasty* sound and took another big bite. He swallowed, then said, “Either you eat something, or—”

“I’m *eating*.” I pulled the packet from the microwave, gave it a stir and then put it back in for a final blast, as per the instructions.

“How many calories are there in that?”

“I don’t know.”

“Yes, you do. You don’t eat anything without knowing exactly what is in it. Besides, it’s written on the back of those shiny little packets your food is delivered in.”

“Two hundred and twenty-four.”

“Jesus, princess.” He closed his eyes, and his lips moved silently, as if he was praying for strength. “I am going to ask again, and I am being serious: are you trying to kill yourself?”

“Says the man who’s eating horse-offal-and-processed-additive burgers with plasticky synthetic cheese, smeared with sugar and wrapped in a bun with the nutritional value of bleached cardboard."

"You worked off more calories in half an hour in the gym. You have to start eating properly. You were skinny when we first met. You're starting to look like Skeletor's sister now."

"Who?"

"Skeletor."

The microwave pinged, and I poured the coq au vin into a bowl. "Still, who?"

"The skeletal baddie from *He-Man... Masters of the Universe*?"

"Nope."

He looked me up and down, like I was some alien specimen. "Everyone's heard of— Fine." He grabbed the steaming bowl out of my hand and dropped it into the sink, running the cold water onto it when I tried to snatch it back off him.

"Hey! I was eating that."

"You need a proper balanced meal, one with grease and fat. As you're not keen on what I made you…" He grabbed his mobile phone and punched in a number. "Vic? It's Alex. Time for a Steve McQueen." There was some mumbling on the other end of the line. "Thanks." He hung up.

"Isn't Steve McQueen dead?"

Spinning me around, he shuffled me through to the back bedroom then yanked open the sash window.

"What are you doing?"

"Taking you out for brunch. Steve McQueen is code for a great escape, like the movie."

"Out where? Wait, when did you and Vic have time to work out a secret code?"

"It took five minutes. We had a quick chat when he brought the newspapers up yesterday. It wasn't hard. Everyone knows that movie. We thought it would be useful to have something in place, given how many people there are hanging around trying to get to you."

Eh. Must be a man thing… secret codes and escape plans, a hangover from boyhood. "We could've just called for a car and had the police keep people back."

He stared at me like I was suggesting something ridiculous. "We're going to the corner cafe for a full English, and if you don't, at the very least, eat an entire bacon sandwich, I am passing your case on to someone who's used to dealing with people with mental capacity issues."

"Oh, right." I felt a strange tug of… disappointment. I thought we'd moved past the lawyer and faux thing and were dating, but clearly not if he was thinking about passing me on.

He kept shuffling me forward, as I tried to come to grips with our relationship status… or lack of status.

"Get a move on, Skeletor."

"You're not endearing yourself to me."

"I'm not trying to." He nudged me forward. "Time to get your peachy behind moving. Unless you're scared?"

I cut him a scathing look over my shoulder. "Really?"

"What?" he asked.

"You think calling me chicken will get me out there."

"Seems like it," he responded smugly.

"Huh? Oh! Right." Somehow, I was stepping off the last rung of the ladder supported by Vic, who then manoeuvred the ladder against the back wall of the courtyard. I'd been so busy bickering with Alex that I hadn't even realised what I was doing. "Well, it had nothing to do with what you said."

"Whatever makes you happy, princess." Alex smirked, slapping a baseball cap on my head and handing me some sunglasses, the most obvious disguise on earth. People may not recognise me, but they would take a second look just to see why I was trying to hide my identity.

"You've already had lunch."

He shrugged. "An appetiser. This can be the main course. Who knows what deliciousness I might get for dessert." He joined me on the pavement outside the courtyard, as Vic pulled the ladder back over the wall. "No! Not that way," he whispered, scanning in both directions. "Do you want to get caught?" Snagging my hand, he tugged me behind him, moving fast in spite of the fact that all the climbing and jumping seemed to have aggravated his limp. "If we cut across the park here, then pass the next two blocks of flats and down Page Street, we'll come out at the cafe, without Team Meri or the paparazzi following."

I stumbled after him, out of breath. "What, do you work for MI6 in your spare time?"

He shrugged, flashing a boyish smile. "I like Matt Damon films." .

CHAPTER 27

Intervention Special - Save My Girlfriend!

On the wall behind the counter, a massive blackboard was covered with white writing, listing a hundred ways to block your arteries with deep-fried, calorific delights. I searched for something that wouldn't add half a stone of blubber on my stomach, thighs and bum. Bacon, egg and sausage roll, full English breakfast, complete with black pudding and fried bread…

The smell of freshly baked bread and crispy bacon permeated the air, making it difficult to concentrate. My stomach cramped and grumbled, and my mouth watered… If Alex asked, I'd say it was nausea, but I could admit to myself it was hunger.

"Hurry up and choose something, or I'll order for you," Alex said.

God, no! I'd seen what he ate. He wasn't putting that on a plate in front of me. "Don't they have vegetables or salad?"

"Fried tomatoes."

"Something that isn't coated in grease and fried?"

"It's a greasy spoon."

"So?" I said. There was no reason for him to say it like I was an idiot. A lot of people didn't want to eat a heart attack on a plate.

"So, no. They have bacon, sausage, egg, black pudding, hash browns."

I clutched my stomach. "Stop. You'll make me sick."

"That's not sickness, Meredith. It's hunger." He pushed me forward as the queue moved up. "Have you decided?"

"Ah, I'll have an egg-white omelette," I said grudgingly. I couldn't afford to pass out again, and I was genuinely hungry. I could see Alex was going to be stubborn about this, and to be honest, it was nice to be out of the flat. It was starting to feel like a prison.

Silence fell.

The chef turned from the grill, staring at me like I'd just asked him to boil his own mother. "What?"

"I'm not ordering that," Alex stated.

"I'm not *cooking* it," the chef muttered.

"Why?" I said.

"Because life's too short to separate the yolks out of eggs," Alex responded.

"Amen," the chef agreed.

"The yolk is the best bit," Alex added.

"It's full of cholesterol," I countered.

"Uh-huh." Alex shared a look with the chef. "Why don't you go and sit down, and I'll order something for you."

"No way. This isn't the Victorian days. I'll order for myself."

"I'll get you a sandwich."

Bread? I couldn't eat that. Knowing Alex, it wouldn't

be a slice of organic, gluten-free soy bread. It would be bleached white, thick-cut, over-processed wheat. I'd be bloated for a fortnight.

Bacon sizzled, sausages spat and eggs were cracked onto the grill as the chef raced through orders.

"You get us a table whilst I order," Alex said.

"I don't wan…" My words trailed off at his glare. My stomach growled. I was bloody hungry, and Alex was a stubborn mule. We could face off forever over this. I would just make the best of it. There would be something I could salvage from whatever he ordered. I reached for my purse. "Here."

Alex pushed my hand away. "I brought you out. I'll pay. I'm not Tom. I can pay for things."

"We can go Dutch and split the bill." Why was I pushing this?

"I'm not Dutch," he said. "Why don't you get us a table before they're all gone? I'll join you once I've ordered and paid. For. Both. Of. Us."

Should I continue to protest?

Just put my money on the counter?

I wasn't used to someone else offering to pay. I should be ordering lobster and champagne and making the most of the moment. But our argument was starting to draw people's attention, and Team Meri and the press were less than a kilometre away. That was less than six minutes if they ran, and they would. My luck was not good at the moment. "Fine!" I nearly bit my tongue off stopping myself from asking for egg whites only. "One egg."

I watched Alex heft his breakfast roll to his mouth.

Oh… My… God!

I wouldn't admit it under pain of death, but the smell…

My mouth watered.

My eyelids fluttered shut.

I imagined taking a bite: flavours exploded in my mouth. Bacon, sausage, egg yolk, grease, tomato sauce. It was good. Sooooo good. Better than sex… well, sex with Tom, anyway.

My eyelids slowly rose.

Alex stared at me, his breakfast roll suspended on the way to his mouth.

"What?" I asked.

He blinked back to attention. "Smells good, huh?"

I shrugged, refusing to give him the satisfaction of knowing just how good. A small smile tipped his lips, before he practically dislocated his jaw—in the fashion of a snake swallowing a small deer, whole—to take a massive bite of his roll, humming his appreciation as he chewed.

"Here." I handed him a tissue. "Clean yourself up."

He wiped his fingers and dabbed his lips. "You're such a snob, princess. Eat up."

I looked down at my own plate. A brown-bread roll the size of child's head filled the plate; half a pig worth of crispy bacon and sausage stuck out the sides over a fried egg-white skirt.

"No!" He held up a hand. "I don't want to hear whatever lie you're conjuring up. I just watched you practically orgasming over the smell of it."

"Do you know how much—"

"Don't know," Alex said, showing how well he knew me. "Don't care. And you shouldn't either. It's not like you do this every day. It's a one-off. Everything is good in small doses, and I'm saying this because I care, Meredith: you need to put some weight on."

Was he kidding? "The camera puts on ten pounds."

"So you've said before." He took another bite of his own roll, chewed and then swallowed. "It's a shame it doesn't put on twenty. At least then you'd be closer to a healthy weight."

"Are you saying I'm—"

"A bag of bones. All sharp edges. Skinny…"

I looked away, feeling self-conscious. Was he disappointed with my body when we made lo—*had sex*? Had he not enjoyed it as much as I did? No. I wasn't going to let him make me feel self-conscious, lacking… I already had enough people formerly in my life doing that. "What kind of man takes a woman out for lunch and then insults her?"

"The kind who won't sit by silently whilst someone

he cares about is killing herself slowly, playing with her food and refusing to eat even though she's starving. I'm not saying this to hurt you or because I find you anything other than gorgeous. I'm saying it because I… *care.*"

"I'm not anorex—"

"*Prove* it."

"You can't trick me into—"

"Look at your plate, Meredith."

I looked. At some point whilst we'd been speaking, I'd deconstructed my roll. My plate was now divided into sections. Section one contained three slices of bacon. I'd cut as much of the fat as possible off the meat, heaping it onto a napkin on the table and leaving it looking like a GCSE science lesson on dissection. Two sausages, cut into halves, lengthways, occupied the second quarter. I hadn't cut anything out of those, because really, what was the point? The whole thing was fat-infused. A double-yolked—I was sure the chef did it deliberately—fried egg sat in the third section. Yolks separated from the white, two deserted yellow islands. The grease- and sauce-coated roll mounded up on the remaining portion of the plate.

I clutched a wad of paper napkins, which I was using to blot the grease off the egg white… clearly hoping to salvage something edible from the meal.

My heart leapt, then settled uncomfortably back into beat. I hadn't realised I was doing it. Still, that didn't mean I had a problem. I could eat if I wanted to. I was just being healthy, protecting my heart and waistline. There was nothing abnormal in that.

Alex hiked an eyebrow. *See? Eating disorder.*

Scowling, I cut the bread down so it was half the thickness—without grease or sauce—and, using the degreased egg white and one slice of the now-fatless bacon, reconstructed a marginally healthier—significantly less enjoyable—sandwich and took a bite, chewing it thoroughly before swallowing. "See? I eat."

"After a fashion." He rolled his eyes, "Baby steps." He finished his own sandwich then stole the sausages off my plate. .

CHAPTER 28

Family Secrets, Exposed!

Once we finished eating, we made our way home from the cafe, walking through the back streets. Alex grunted, wincing as he stepped awkwardly on the uneven pavement.

"Now we've bonded over heart-attack sandwiches, and you've gotten personal over my weight *again*, will you tell me what happened to your leg?"

Denial was written all over his face.

"Was it something embarrassing? Did you slip running for the toilet?"

He scowled at me. "No."

"Was it a feat of heroics; did you save an abandoned puppy from on-coming traffic?" He didn't respond.

"Please. I don't understand why it's such a big drama, but it clearly is."

He looked away, shaking his head. His pace picked up. I had to take two strides for his every one to keep up. His reticence made me feel nervous, and lunch began to weigh heavy in my stomach. Maybe I shouldn't push… but I thought we were starting to trust each other, to build something.

Just when I thought he was going to ignore my question, he said, "Does it bother you, that I limp?"

What? "No. But whatever happened clearly bothers you. You can't bear for me to mention it, even when I just want to check you're okay, because you're obviously in pain." I slipped a hand around his elbow, tugging him to my side and slowing his pace. I was breathing hard, and so was Alex, but I didn't think it was from the brisk pace. "I can tell it's a big deal in your life…"

The silence stretched.

I waited him out. My mind churned. This was something major.

He stared up to the heavens, sucking in a deep breath and letting it out slowly. "It's not like it's a secret," he said. "It's just when I'm with you, I don't have to think about it, or know you're thinking about it, or changing the way you act when we're together or being afraid to call me on being a dick because of it… God, I sound like a selfish bastard."

"No, you don't," I said, mouth dry with nerves.

"Kathy was my sister, my Irish twin. We were just eleven months apart in age, and we shared a room until we were eight." His voice was strained, and he didn't look at me as he spoke. Nervous dread warmed my stomach. "We were best friends."

I slid my hand down his arm to clasp his. Alex wrapped his fingers tightly around mine and held on. I steered us into one of the small parks littering London, tugging him down onto the bench beside me. "Sit down. I don't want to upset you. If you don't want to talk about it…"

"It's hard," he said. "Kathy was different. Special. When we were kids, she used to take us on the best adventures. One summer, we built a raft and launched it on the Thames… It floated just well enough to get us into serious trouble, then sank like a stone. We had to be rescued by the river police."

I laughed nervously. "That sounds terrifyingly fun for a kid, a nightmare for your parents."

His smile died. He stared down at where his hand rested in my lap. "Eighteen months ago, she hung herself from a beam in her kitchen."

His words exploded in my head, a roar of sound my mind tried to make sense of. She'd killed herself? Suicide.

"Life was hard for her," Alex continued. "She felt more than other people. She had severe anxiety, depression. It led to anorexia"—I jerked—"self-harm." His voice broke. He cleared his throat. "She had medication, counselling. We grew up. She moved in with her boyfriend, felt better, didn't think she needed the medication, didn't like the way it made her feel."

I leant into his side, sharing my warmth.

He blew out a short breath. "She struggled with work. She fell out with her boyfriend, James. They made up, fell out, made up. He couldn't cope and finally called it quits. He's a good guy." He glanced up, eyes dark with pain and grief. I nodded, giving a small, tight smile and a reassuring squeeze. "I spoke to her on the phone that morning—she *wasn't in the mood to talk*, and mumbled something about staying in bed, but I was half focused on what I had to do at work. I just grunted at the appropriate points and told her I'd go over with takeout later, and went on with my day."

His heart was hammering in his throat, and his skin looked clammy. “By six o’clock, she was dead.”

It was… incomprehensible.

“I failed her.”

“No, you didn’t. You have a job and a life that’s not failing.”

“I went to her flat. Let myself in…” He swallowed convulsively, then continued setting out the facts in short choppy sentences. “She was hanging. Dead…” My heart was pounding. Alex was breathing hard. “I still see her… sometimes, when I open doors, for a second… It’s normal. According to my grief counsellor, anyway.” He rubbed his eyes with a thumb and forefinger, roughly pressing back tears.

His words rushed out when he started to speak again, as if he wanted to get it over with. “I grabbed a knife and a chair, cut her down. The d-dead weight of her falling knocked us off the chair. We landed on a marble side table… my leg broke.”

My grip on his hand tightened.

“A displaced femoral shaft fracture. I’d broken it before playing rugby. There was a weakness. The bone tore my quad, just missing the femoral artery and nerve”—he gave a small, sad smile—“but caused significant soft tissue damage and bleeding." He looked away, pressing his lips together. "I developed compartment syndrome, resulting in insufficient blood supply and tissue necrosis. They had to operate more than once… There were complications, infection… non-union of the fracture." At my frown, he explained, "The bone wasn't healing, due to the disruption in blood supply… without the complications, the break would have healed in six to eight weeks—with the complications, I still have a limp after eighteen months. I'm still getting physical therapy every couple of weeks, gait re-education and a bit of hydrotherapy. It will get stronger and the limp will fade over time." He stared off into the middle distance. "There was no chance to say goodbye… If she'd been ill, we could've said goodbye, prepared to grieve, but she's just… gone."

"I'm so sorry. I… I had no idea." My throat ached with tears for him and Kathy, for all the times I must've upset him asking about his limp or commenting on his sisters.

"I can remember every argument we ever had, every time I should have said sorry, or listened or cared more… I… feel guilty. Apparently, it's 'normal', but nothing about this shit is normal. It'll never be normal. I didn't even want to hear her name for months after it first happened, I was so angry, but now, I just…" He rubbed his eyes, then pressed his hand back through his hair. "Maybe it was a cry for help, and if I'd gotten there earlier, I could've saved her, I should've listened on the phone. I could've heard something or said something or done something… to change things."

"You can't think like that." I didn't know what the right thing to say was. I was scared of hurting him, of making it worse somehow. "You said you went to counselling."

"Yes. We're all trying to figure out how to say goodbye. We were a family of six, now we're five… able to fit into a single car for the first time, but travelling with a gaping hole beside us. So, we go to counselling, the whole family together, in groups, alone… It dulls the raw edges."

I squeezed his hand and turned on the bench so I could look into his face.

"I don't want to talk about it anymore," he said.

"Okay, but if you ever do want to talk… or just sit in silence… or anything, I'm here for you. I—"

"Thank you."

"And I want you to know—no matter how crazy you think I act sometimes—"

"Sometimes?" He huffed out a watery laugh, swiping at the dampness in his eyes.

"I'm not. I'm justifiably angry and upset. I'm not mentally ill. I don't have any desire to hurt myself. I promise. I understand now why you moved in, why you kept checking on me even when you didn't know me. I may be hurt and angry, but I am not in any way a risk to myself."

His shoulders sank, tension draining, at my words. I don't think he'd consciously made the decision to watch over me because he was scared not to be there for another person when they needed him. "Thank you, princess." He pressed a quick, hard kiss to my forehead, then swiped a thumb over my cheek, capturing a tear. "Enough for today. Let's get back to the flat and just be normal... or as normal as you can be." .

CHAPTER 29

Help! My Past Is Destroying My Future

Five minutes later, we were walking silently down Page Street towards my flat, emotions hanging heavy between us.

"I need your advice," I said. I'd been mulling things over in my head during lunch. I hadn't intended to say anything, but Alex clearly needed the distraction.

He gave me a side look. "Why? You never listen."

"Because I'm paying you."

"Will you quit harping on about paying me? I am not Tom."

"You're my lawyer," I responded.

"I'm your friend."

"I need—"

"A friend. You need a *real* friend, not a lawyer."

"But—"

"If you get arrested, or have a reason to think it might happen, I promise you'll have the best lawyer I know to represent you."

"But I want you!"

He laughed. "And you've got me, Meredith. As a friend. So, make the most of it."

"I was thinking… Say hypothetically—"

"Jesus," he muttered, somewhat discouragingly.

I pushed on, walking through the cool, sharp autumn afternoon, still holding his hand. "Someone played a… a prank, on someone." I paused, trying to find the right words.

"Uh-huh."

My stomach fizzed with nerves. "For example, if someone… hypothetical, hypothetically—"

"I've got the hypothetical point," he interrupted

dryly.

I ignored him, continuing in a rush. "—went online and bought crab eggs and, ah, gave them to their ex…" *And their skanky mother and anyone else stupid enough to still be sleeping with their skanky ex.*

"What's the legal advice angle?" he asked. "Were they stolen?"

"What? No. I didn't steal them. I bought them." Well, not yet, anyway. They were in my shopping cart. I still hadn't WhatsApped Neil the go-ahead. I was struggling. This wasn't cress seeds or prawns… this crossed a line I wasn't sure I was comfortable crossing.

"Hypothetically," he said, with a smirk, even as he frowned.

I was too far gone to hear him. "I'm not talking hard-shell, nippy-claws, rough-day-on-the-beach-type crabs here, Alex. I'm talking about buying and giving Tom pubic lice."

"Jesus Christ!" he cursed, jerking against my hand. "Yo-u—" He cleared his throat. "You're sick. You know that, don't you?"

"It was a hypothetical—"

"I hope for your sake—and Tom's and your mother and half the females in London—it bloody well is. This is *not* normal."

"I'm asking for legal advice, not comments on my mental health you're not qualified to give."

"*Fine*. If I was your lawyer right now, I'd advise you against any action of this nature. *Hypothetical* or otherwise. It's assault: a criminal offence. As your *friend*, I am telling you this is crazy." Halting, he tugged his hand from mine, pushing it back through his hair, frustration and anger vibrating around him. "They hurt you. I get it. But you need to get over it—"

"Get over it!" I shrieked.

"Yes!" he snapped back, loudly. "Fauxmance or romance someone for real. *Whatever*. But keep away from this hypothetical bullshit." God, the sanctimonious arse. He caught my arm as I went to stalk off. "This is fully-fledged bunny-boiler stuff."

"It was a joke," I lied.

"There's nothing funny about deliberately giving

someone a sexually transmitted disease. It's a crime."

"It's not like it can't be treated."

"It can also be passed on to his partners and his partners' partners. Jesus, Meredith. You're talking about giving your mother public lice, and Jenn… it could be transmitted to Owain."

"No, I'm not. I'm not forcing them to sleep wi—"

"Enough!" he roared. I ducked my head, as people looked out of their windows and turned to see what the shouting was about. He lowered his voice. "There is no justifying this. Tell me you haven't done it already." I refused to fill the silence. "Or any other crazy *Single White Female* stuff."

I shrugged. "I'm going to plead the fifth."

"*Shit.*" He tipped his head back, as if talking to God, squeezing his eyes closed and talking several deep breaths. "This is real life. Not some American cop show." He opened his eyes, glaring down at me. "We do not have *the fifth* for you to plead." What? People always pleaded the fifth in TV shows and movies. That wasn't fair. "This is crazy stuff, princess."

I ignored his softer tone. “You don’t have a clue what you’re talking about. I thought lawyers were supposed to support their clients.”

“Not when they’re breaking the law. Not when they’re going to intentionally harm another person. Not when they are being made an accessory to a crime.” His voice was rising.

“I haven’t done it, yet,” I snapped. “What happened to innocent until proven guilty?”

He glared at me. “That’s in court. You better stop now and hope it never gets that far.”

Well, that sealed it. I’d had a few doubts myself… I’d stocked the online cart to overflowing, but I’d been vacillating over the whole checkout bit for days, still… “There’s no way anyone would connect it with me. It’s not like either of them are faithful. The chances are one of them already has crabs anyway.”

“This is not normal. Two wrongs do not make a right.” Eh. It was a few more than two wrongs at this point. “It’s *enough*, Meredith,” Alex said softly, sounding exhausted.

We weren't far from home; I was walking fast, trying to work off what felt like the twenty pounds of lard currently churning in my stomach.

"You've had your fun—"

"Fun!" I slammed to a halt, staring at him open-mouthed. "Fun?"

"The cress."

"I never admitted that."

Snagging my hand in his, he dragged me back into motion beside him. "It's time to forget him and move on."

"He slept with my mother, the woman who birthed me. He fathered a child with my best friend, and they have another on the way." Did he not get the magnitude of what Tom had done? What I was doing was *nothing*. A little karma to keep the universe in balance. "He let me be his secret child's godmother, all the while suggesting we wait to get married and have children until he 'made it' in television. And God alone knows how many other children he has. He screwed around with the women I work with. You don't know this industry. They've all have been talking about me behind my back, saying how stupid I was to stand by him, feeling sorry for me. Hell, from what I've been reading, along with the rest of the British public—my *viewers*—he probably shagged the mother of the man you just paid to clog our arteries."

Was he being deliberately obtuse?

Was it a man thing?

Did he really not understand the betrayal?

"He probably lay in bed afterward—with half of my colleagues and all of my family and friends—laughing about how stupid I am."

Alex shrugged—*shrugged!*—his hand tightening around mine when I tried to yank free and stomp off. "So why would you want him back?"

Was he crazy? "I don't want him back!"

"Then why are you wasting time on him? He's used you for years, lived off you, and you let him like some sort of sap—"

I punched his arm. Hard. He grunted, rubbing his bicep and muttering about assault. "No, I didn't," I snapped.

"He didn't have a real job the whole time you were together."

"He's an actor." He'd acted his way through our entire relationship.

"Other than a walk-on part in the background of a few soap operas—which anyone can get—tell me one thing he has acted in."

"Ah—" I racked my memory, coming up blank.

"Something where he actually earned enough money to support himself, or you," Alex said, sharp blue eyes glaring at me over the top of his Oakley sunglasses.

"He supported my… career." I dug deep for that one and couldn't say it without wincing at the lie. Still, Alex made me sound like a fool for sticking with Tom, and I had enough people thinking I was a fool. I was already feeling like one.

"By shagging your mother?" Given his scathing tone, maybe, despite what he was saying, Alex did understand why I was pissed off. He stopped in the middle of the pavement, turning me to face him. His hands wrapped around my upper arms as he gazed down at me. "Let it go, princess. This kind of anger is not good for you."

"I'm not angry."

"Happy, balanced people don't sow cress in their ex's cars." His tone was sympathetic. "Or—"

"I object!" I'd watched *Perry Mason* and *Ally McBeal* reruns; I knew how lawyers spoke. "That's supposition."

He laughed. "They only say that on American TV shows. Not in real life." He turned serious again. "You deserve to be happy, and you can't be happy until you let it go, let him and the others go and move on with your life."

I looked away, gazing down the side lane that led to the back wall to the flat, listening to the rumble of voices, paparazzi and Team Meri. I stopped, turning to Alex. I couldn't just "let it go". "They turned me into an episode of my show. I can't just let go and pretend everything is fine. Mothers shouldn't do that."

Alex's fingers entwined with mine again. He turned, tugging me along with him. "Where's your father?"

"If you ask my mother, he abandoned us."

"I'm asking you."

We were almost home. Team Meri launched into a bad rendition of CeeLo Green's "Fuck You". "He went off to work one morning and never came home. He crashed his car through a fence into a field. He didn't have a seatbelt on. He went through the windscreen. It turned out he was still technically over the drink-drive limit from the night before when he and my mother had gone out."

"I'm sorry."

"It was a difficult time. Talith had never worked and had no desire to get a job. Dad didn't have any life insurance. He thought he was too young to need it. The debts spiralled pretty quickly." I remembered being scared and missing my dad and wondering if we would lose our home. "I had to get a job when I was thirteen so we could afford to live." A small smile tipped my lips; work had been my saviour. I loved it. "I acted in adverts for cheese strings, washing powder, face wash and sweets. I got onto a regional Welsh-speaking kids weekend show, presenting, that kind of thing…"

Alex's mobile phone appeared in his left hand. He called Vic as we reached the back wall to my flat, where we'd climbed over earlier. The ladder appeared almost immediately.

"Up you go."

"Hey!" I snarled, kicking back as he patted my backside. He laughed. I struggled to balance on the ladder. I still felt about eight months gone with a food baby.

"Nice view."

I glared at him from the top of the wall. He was definitely tactile. He didn't care about being in public, either. Tom wouldn't even hold my hand in public, probably because he didn't want his endless string of girlfriends to see. Leg on either side of the wall, I looked down at Alex. He leant against the ladder, watching me, the breeze ruffling his dark brown hair.

My heart jolted, and my breath caught in my chest.

I wobbled on my wall perch, suddenly lightheaded.

I couldn't look away from him. My skin grew tight and prickly. Tingling heat spread from my stomach, causing a fine, trembling weakness to invade my limbs.

Alex's hand circled my ankle, sliding up under my

wide-legged pants, skin to skin. “Meredith?”

I shivered, electricity zinging up my leg, sparking erogenous body parts to life. My nipples peaked; my heart fluttered. I blinked away the fuzzy, funny feeling. “Huh?”

“You okay, princess?”

“Y-yes. Just indigestion. All that grease…”

“Uh-huh.” He winked. His hand slid further up my leg, and he squeezed my calf before starting up the ladder.

My heart skipped again and goose bumps raced up my leg. I growled, bracing a foot against the top rung of the ladder, tempted to push it back off the wall, with him still on it. He was too cocky by far, and if he stuck around, I’d be the size of a house with clogged arteries within a year.

Team Meri started a hideously out-of-tune, slightly reworked, version of “Amazing Grace”—*Amazing Meri, how sweet is she, that suffered a wretch like Toooooom…—r*eminding me of what my life had become and why I couldn’t seriously maim or kill Alex.

He was my get-out-of-jail-not-quite-free card and faux-boyfriend. I might not get another one willing to overlook the mess my life had become.

“So, I’ve been thinking,” I said.

“Give me a minute.” He joined me at the top of the wall, pulling the ladder over and passing it down to Vic on the other side. A second later, Alex was on the ground, tugging my ankle hard enough that I toppled, squealing, off the wall into his arms.

Alex jostled me against his chest, laughing. I struggled out of his arms, batting away his hands and straightening my clothes.

“So, anyway—”

“Not yet.” He nudged me ahead of him up the ladder, back into the flat, following close on my heels, this time without comment or a helping hand to my rear end.

I started as soon as he cleared the windowsill into the spare bedroom. “I think—”

“Not yet,” he repeated.

What?

Why not?

“What’s wrong?”

He pushed through the door into the living room. I followed. He crossed to the bookcase, where he'd set up a mini-fridge and fully stocked drinks cabinet. "I need to get a drink," he said with his back to me, snagging a beer from the fridge. "Whatever you're about to say, if you've been *thinking*, I'm pretty sure I don't want to hear the outcome sober."

I rolled my eyes, shaking my head when he offered me a drink.

"There's bottled water. I'm pretty sure it's calorie free."

"I'm not thirsty."

He sank down onto the sofa, patting the space beside him. "Why don't you tell me what you've been thinking about, or should I say, premeditating?

"Oh, right. Yes." I perched on the edge of the sofa, leaning toward him. "So, you paid for our lunch."

He shrugged. "Yes."

"Are we real dating or fauxmancing?" My heart was pounding and I was nervously chewing at my lip.

"We've had this discussion before, after I met Gollum."

My lips twitched at his nickname for Talith; there was something sexy about a man who compared my mother to a hideously twisted, crazy beast. He slipped his right arm about my waist, pulling me over on to his lap. I sank against his solid warmth. Alex ran the tip of his nose up the side of my neck, inhaling my scent. His face was buried in my hair, warm breath puffing against my neck. He wrapped his arms around my waist. I shivered as he smoothed his palm over the dip of my waist then back up over the outside curve of my breast.

"Will you just forget the fauxmancing 'Real' Housewives of who the hell cares shit!"

Oh! Alex was mad. Not only was he swearing, he did that air quotes thing with one hand when he said *real*; no straight adult man would do that unless they were under duress.

"You think I share a bed, breakfast, lunch, dinner, Netflix and chill with everyone I represent? I'm not your lawyer."

"But I am paying you."

"No. You. Are. *Not.* You haven't paid a penny for my time."

"I signed contracts."

"Don't get me started on the fact you signed things a random stranger shoved at you without even reading them."

I stared at him, confused. "What did I sign?"

"Autographs for Lia and Marie."

"Wh-what?" I screeched, scrambling futilely to get off his lap. "You're not… I could've told you things in confidence."

Oh shit!

What had I told him?

Had I admitted anything?

"At least then I'd know what you're up to."

I shrank away from him.

"In all honesty, princess, when you left that day, I had no plans to see you again, let alone represent you. Then you called because Tom was coming around for his stuff and… I've represented hundreds of people, possibly thousands, but I've never met anyone who needed a friend more than you did." His grip tightened, holding me still on his lap. "The more time I spend with you, the more time I want to spend with you. I like you. It's that simple."

I stared at him, his words sinking in slowly. "So, no fau—"

"So, no fauxmance. I know you've not long been single and you've got issues. So, we'll take it at your speed, but this"—he squeezed me—"you and me spending time together, it's the real deal, romance."

My lips formed the word *romance*. Testing it.

"Well?"

I jumped up from his lap. "Fine. Fine. I guess." I hurried through to the kitchen, looking for some space to process, covering by grabbing a bottle of mineral water. I had a boyfriend. *Alex* was my boyfriend.

Suddenly, he was there in front of me. "There's no 'guess' about it, princess. When we kiss, they're real kisses; when we make love, it's *real…*"

He closed in on me. My back hit the kitchen counter. Big hands caged my hips. His body heat hit me, his salty scent wrapping around me. He lifted me onto the work surface. He gripped my knees, spreading my thighs, then moved between them.

My stomach muscles clenched. A fine tremble racked my body. My breasts tingled. Alex's pupils dilated as his head lowered towards mine. My eyelids sank closed. His mouth brushed mine once, twice, teasing then lifting away. His tongue stroked along the seam of my lips, seeking entrance I gave.

A growl of pleasure rumbled in his chest, vibrating through every point of contact, lips, hands, breasts, coalescing in my belly, and lower.

Heat flared.

I slid my hand from his hair to cup his bristly jaw. His stubble scraped my palm, shooting tingles up my arm. I struggled to open heavy eyelids so I could watch his response. My body sank into his. He pulled me in tighter, mashing my breasts against his chest. A hungry whimper escaped. This definitely didn't feel like faking. If this was a sample of Alex real-romancing, it could definitely work.

Shivers of heat swelled my breasts and flipped my stomach. He pulled back, breathing heavily. His eyes burned over my face, and he swept his thumb across the curve of my bottom lip.

I shivered.

“We need to sort out your replacement lawyer.”

“Hmm.” I nipped his full bottom lip, relishing his shiver.

“I’ll call Lia now.”

“No. No. I told you before, I don’t want anyone else. I want you.”

“The feeling is mutual, princess.” His smile was lopsided. He smoothed my hair back from my face. I turned into his palm, snuggling. “But I have serious ethical issues where you’re concerned.”

That wasn’t what I wanted.

I pressed against his chest, pushing him back, slipping off the counter—when had I ended up on the counter?

Straightening my clothes, I put some space between us.

"I don't want another lawyer." Alex knew too much about my life now, how I'd grown up, what Tom and my mother and Jenn's betrayal had done to me. I suspected he suspected some of my acts of vengeance, but was cutting me some slack.

If the only way to have him as my lawyer was to keep things strictly professional, then that was what I had to do. I didn't want to—the idea of not having him around, not being able to touch him, was painful, but… "I need… I want you as my lawyer. If that means the faux"—he glared—"the romancing has to stop, then it does."

"Mer—"

The shrill of the door buzzer cut off Alex's words. I leapt on the excuse to get away from him. I didn't know how long I'd be able to resist if he put up an argument. If he kissed me again, it would be an embarrassingly short period of time.

Hurrying into the hall, I answered the intercom.

"Ms Scott?"

I didn't speak. I didn't recognise the voice, and I wasn't letting slip it was me to some paparazzo.

"I'm Detective Harris, and this is Sergeant Remia."

I peered closer at the slightly blurred image on the intercom. They looked like police officers, and they were showing blurred identity cards of some kind to the camera.

"We'd like to come in and speak with you."

My heart pounded, my suddenly sweaty finger slipping off the intercom.

Shit!

Shit, *shitshitshit*.

Did they know what I'd done? Alex loomed behind me. Thank God.

He was a lawyer.

My lawyer.

"Do I have to let them in?" I whispered in panic, even though, without the intercom on, they wouldn't be able to hear me.

"Why wouldn't you?" he asked.

Ah… several reasons, starting with a cress crop and culminating in a shopping trolley full of STDs. I didn't respond quickly enough. He reached over my shoulder, pressing the door release.

A light sweat sprang up on my face. I slumped against the wall to stop myself falling to the floor.

"What the… Damn it, Meredith. You have thirty seconds, maximum, to tell me what you did that has you hyperventilating."

Thirty seconds? We'd never get it covered in thirty seconds. "I… I don't have to admit to anything, right?" I grabbed his arm, hanging on to him desperately.

"Shit." Alex closed his eyes, rammed his hand back through his hair, then sighed, eyes opening as a knock sounded on the door. He fixed me with a hard look, none of the flirting or humour I was used to. "Let me do the talking. Say *nothing* without my say-so, and you might, *might*, get through this without your mug shot appearing in tomorrow's papers." .

CHAPTER 30

Ex: Admit What You've Done Before It's Too Late. Lie Detector Test!

"Your mother's and your ex-boyfriend's house has been vandalised."

"What?" I glanced from the cops sitting opposite me to Alex, beside me on the sofa, vacillating between fear I was about to be arrested and confusion. I hadn't vandalised anything… unless… Was it the prawns?

Had they found the prawns?

Could you be arrested for creating a stink?

"Someone egged their house," Harris said.

I laughed, relief flooding me. Eggs, not prawns. I wouldn't have to act innocent; I actually hadn't done this.

"Rotten or fresh?" I asked. *Please let them be rotten.* If it had been anyone but the police telling me, I'd have updated my joke. *You know what goes well with eggs? Cress!*

"I hardly think that is relevant, Ms Scott," Harris responded.

At the same time, Remia said, "Rotten."

"Wow! That must have kicked up a stink." I laughed again, this time at my own joke.

Alex elbowed me gently, whispering, "Shut up."

"Do you find this funny?" Harris barked.

Yes. I did. Hilarious, in fact. However, the detective's tone and expression said admitting that would be a mistake. I tried to smother my amusement and look like I was taking the eggy vandalism as seriously as the policemen and Alex obviously thought I should. Pressure built in my chest, before bursting out in a wet, snorting exhale of amusement.

Alex elbowed me. Hard. Stealing my breath. The policemen waited in silence, staring at me. What? Oh yes, they were waiting for an answer. I faked a solemn look and serious tone.

"Ah, no, it's not *really* funny." If you had no sense of humour, or the "victims" were decent people who hadn't cheated on you. "Do, ah… do you have photos?"

If there were photos, I wanted them. I could tweet and Snapchat them to Team Meri. They'd see the humour in it.

"It's not a laughing matter, Ms Scott."

"It doesn't have anything to do with Ms Scott, either, detective," Alex said.

Earning his retainer.

If I'd paid him one.

Eh, we could put it on credit for sexual favours. I shivered, liking that idea. I was pretty sure Alex would too. I snuggled against him, smugly watching the police. Alex frowned down at me, then turned back to them. "You said this happened this morning around nine thirty?"

"That's right."

"Meredith and I had an early breakfast and then were in the gym from eight until after ten. The CCTV in the courtyard and fifty or so of Team Meri outside, as well as the two officers keeping the road clear, will be able to corroborate. Then we—"

"*Talked*," I cut him off. Alex frowned at me. Police officers sold stories to the press all the time. The silence stretched. I shifted on the sofa.

It wasn't exactly a lie; we'd talked and done other stuff, like eat… and kiss, but the police didn't need to know.

"This isn't the first attack against Mr Kinley and Mrs Scott," Harris said.

“There’s more?” I asked enthusiastically. “What else was egged?”

“I’m not talking about eggs.”

“Oh?” I leant forward, desperate to hear more.

“There was cress.”

I snorted with laughter at his serious tone. This interrogation was doing nothing for my in-control, composed image, but it was funnier than the last stand-up show I’d seen. “Wow. All he needs is a couple of slices of bread and he’ll have a really nice sandwich.”

Alex curled his fingers around the back of my trousers, yanking me back from the edge of the sofa and muttering for me to *shut up*.

Remia showed his humanity and smiled. “The cress grew in the back of Mr Kinley’s car.”

“Tom was always keen on going green and offsetting his carbon emissions.” I fluttered my eyelashes with exaggerated innocence. It was worth a try; men fell for it in low-rent movies.

“Scott,” Alex said. Surname only. I was in big trouble. He turned back to the police, “When Tom came to collect his things, he said he’d left the top of the convertible down.”

I sagged against Alex. “Was there anything else?”

"An unpleasant odour in the house," Harris said.

"The eggs?" I played dumb.

The craggy-faced detective smoothed a hand over his thick, greying hair. His lips compressed, but he continued, tone serious. "Mr Kinley's clothes no longer seem to fit properly."

I shrugged. "Is gaining weight a crime?"

"There's also been some online activity."

"Tom's watching porn?" How was that relevant?

"Offensive postings online."

"Not from me. My agent is handling all my social media." Still, I'd look the messages up later.

"And Ms Scott is not responsible for the writings of her fans," Alex responded. "I'm sure you walked through Team Meri outside and got a sense of their… devotion."

I glared at Alex, daring him to cast aspersions on Team Meri. "People have a right to express their opinions."

"Within reason, Ms Scott, and it is not just offensive postings on social media," Harris said. "There's a YouTube video."

"Of what?" If Tom had secretly filmed a sex tape of us, I'd bury him.

"Mr Kinley, ah, er, dancing."

I shrugged. "Who cares?"

"In the nude. He recalled you had such a video on your phone."

"Someone's posted that on YouTube?" I was genuinely surprised. It wasn't me. Had Neil hacked my phone and gone rogue? Even if he had, there was no way I'd give him up; we were in this together. "I want to see it." I needed to be sure it was my video. Plus, people may have posted comments. "They must have hacked into my telephone… or Tom's. I WhatsApped it to him. At the time, he thought it was funny."

"He doesn't now."

"I didn't share it. I advocate against revenge porn." Even if I didn't, I wouldn't do anything that gave Tom exposure and might boost his career.

"There's also a website. Rate the Rat," Harris said.

Oh! I was vibrating with excitement. This was better than Christmas. My iPad was on the coffee table. I could almost reach it, if I just stretched a little… maybe edged off the sofa for a second or two.

"Women are rating Mr Kinley's sexual performance," Remia added.

Oh. My. God. I *had* to see this!

"Ms Scott?" Harris said.

"Just a second. Please." I grabbed my iPad.

"Ms Scott!"

"Wait. Wait. I'm almost ready." I didn't know which site to go for first. Okay, I totally did. It had to be the video footage. Even when I'd loved Tom, this video made me cringe. He certainly didn't look sexy. This was the death knell on any remote hope he had of landing a leading man role on a television series or in movies.

I opened Google, typed in *Tom Kinley + Willy Dance*… and there it was.

It already had over a million hits. How had more than a million people known about this before me?

I clicked on the link. A circle of dots moved around on screen. I waited. Nothing happened. I pressed play a few more times. "How do I get it to play?"

"You've clicked on it too many times," Alex responded coolly. "Now you'll have to wait for it to open a dozen times and buffer."

Fine. I'd check out the ratings site whilst I waited. I open another tab, ran a Google search and voilà… The Rate the Rat site was brilliant in its simplicity. The scale was one to five, with one being *No skill* and five being *Best I've ever had*. There were only four areas for women to rate

Tom's sexual performance against: technique, stamina, assets, which had its own ranking from Teeny-Weeny-Wiener to Foot-Long-Donkey's-Dong, and up for a repeat performance, which just had a yes/no response.

A dashboard collating the average scores was provided at the top of the screen. Technique had scored *Must try harder*—a two on the one-to-five scale. Stamina was *No Skill*—Ouch! Assets: *Teeny-Weeny-Wiener*, and Up for a Repeat Performance: *No*.

Thirty-eight women had completed the survey. Tom had told me I was only the third woman he'd slept with. If they were all real entries, and I had no reason to doubt it, he'd clearly made up numbers, if not skill, since we got together.

For women who hadn't had the pleasure—or lack of pleasure, as the ratings showed—of sleeping with Tom, there was a section where they could vote on whether they would *shag*, *marry* or *avoid* him. Thirty-one thousand, one hundred and ninety-three people had voted; two hundred and five wanted to *shag* Tom; forty-one *marry*—they needed help. Psychological help. But thirty thousand, nine hundred and forty-seven voters had confirmed my faith in humans' ability to learn and evolve, and voted to *avoid*.

I hit *avoid* and bumped the tally up by one, then jumped to the five detailed questions and rated him a one for all of them, before finishing off with a no on *up for a repeat performance*.

"Meredith!"

"What?" I glanced up at Alex. Shrugging off his and the policemen's disapproval, I flicked back to where the video clip had been buffering.

"Oh! O-o-oh. My. *God!*" I grabbed Alex's arm, grounding myself against the surge of excitement and making sure he was seeing the same two-minute, thirteen-second clip I was.

Tom.

Dancing. To Psy's "Gangnam Style".

Naked.

His little willy was wobbling; he always said he was a grower, not a shower, but really, he was just a disappointment all around. The video ended with Tom, hands behind his head, thrusting his hips.

"Wow! I guess I wasn't the only one of his women who he treated to his naked dancing." This, combined with the rating website, was so far out of my revenge league. Pure genius.

I couldn't top it. The Rate the Rat website had already gone viral.

"This has nothing to do with me. It's not my video, and I didn't post it. You can check my phone." I ignored Alex's warning sound, handing over my mobile. I'd deleted all contact with Neil, and there was nothing else remotely dodgy on it. "There's nothing libellous in forwarding this, is there?" I asked Alex. "I mean, it's true his willy really is that small, and it's definitely him dancing."

"That's Ms Scott's idea of a joke," Alex said, directing a quelling glare at me, before turning back to the police. "She is not suggesting she would share revenge porn on her ex."

Poop, no. "Of course I wouldn't. I just want to reach out to my fans, let them know this type of"—*pure genius*—"persecution is not acceptable." There, that sounded suitably pious.

"Why do you still have nude videos of your ex?" Alex asked, his tone surly.

"I forgot. There's nothing pornographic about it. It's a total passion killer." My words didn't seem to appease him. I turned to the cops, who were checking out the video on my phone. "I forgot it was there until you mentioned it. You can delete it."

It looked like one of Tom's other exes had decided to take her own form of revenge. If the police really wanted to find out who it was, they needed to ask Tom to identify the woman's bedroom… if he could remember. Given the numbers, it might be a challenge. That said, I wasn't going to give them any help. I was happy to support my fellow woman scorned.

"I think it's clear from Ms Scott's… *reaction*"—Alex confiscated my iPad from me, powering it down and placing it out of reach—"and technical inability that she wasn't behind this."

"And yet she had a lawyer conveniently at hand," Harris said.

"Believe me, no one is unhappier about that than me."

My heart twanged with hurt at Alex's comment. I gritted my teeth and said, "It's possible Team Meri decided to take matters into their own hands. They were very upset at Talith's newspaper article."

"Which article would that be?" Harris asked.

Who was he trying to kid? "The one where my mother posed naked in a national tabloid, wearing my photo like an obscene sanitary towel," I responded dryly, "and told everyone she'd been sleeping with my boyfriend."

"The cress incident occurred before Mrs Scott sold her story to the papers." Harris said.

"Did it?"

"Yes. And you have motive."

"Ms Scott is not the only one," Alex said. "Tom has played a dangerous game with many women."

Harris rose. "Thanks for talking with us, Ms Scott. We've got everything we need for now. I'll be in touch with you—"

"I can be reached through my lawyer," I said.

"I'd appreciate it if you didn't stir things up with your fans. I wouldn't like anyone to get hurt, or into trouble because—"

"I'm not the one at fau—"

"She won't," Alex said, giving me a stern look as he showed the police officers towards the door.

"Oh, one more thing, Ms Scott," Harris said. Oh my God! It was like being in an never-ending episode of *Columbo*. "Do you have a list of the names of the women Tom had affairs with?"

"No. Ask Tom. I wouldn't be surprised to discover he had a little—make that a *big* black book with names and dates. If Tom can't help, just keep buying the tabloids and I'm pretty sure you'll get most of the names from there."

"You don't seem surprised or upset, Ms Scott," the detective said over his shoulder from his position halfway down the stairs. "I thought you'd be heartbroken; the love of your life is sleeping with your mother and your best friend."

"He wasn't the lov— Oh." I froze with confusion. Was I over Tom? .

CHAPTER 31

Girlfriend: Get Over Your Ex, Or Lose Me Forever!

"I. Cannot. Believe. This. Shit," Alex said, about sixty seconds after the police left. "What the hell have you been doing, Meredith?"

"Hey! Why do I have to have been up to anything?"

"Don't insult me!" He towered over me. "Don't try and give me the same shit you just served up to those policemen." He spun, pacing across the room, before turning and pacing back, clearly unable to stand still. "It's not a huge stretch of the imagination to go from hypothetical crabs to *actual* cress and smashed car headlights and… what else? The smell, the nudie video."

"I had nothing to do with that video. You saw the police delete mine from my phone." He spun away from me again. "Come on, Alex. We don't have time for this. We're supposed to show face at the *Sunday Fun* wrap party tonight."

"Ah yes, another fauxmantic night out. What the fuck is wrong with me that I ever thought this was real? What a colossal moron." He shook his head, "How the hell did I get mixed up in this crap? To think I felt sorry for you. I thought you were alone and vulnerable. I was worried you might do something… reckless and hurt yourself. I…"

"I'm not your sister. There is nothing wrong with my mental—"

"But you're not vulnerable, you're psychotic," he continued, getting more and more irritated. "You're bunny-boiling Glenn Close in *Fatal Attraction*."

"You're being ridiculous," I snapped, as my temper rose to match his.

"Says the woman who sowed cress in her ex-boyfriend's car, did something to make him and your mother stink, gave them an STD, for Christ—"

"That was *hypothetical*!"

"And whatever the hell else you've done." He rammed both hands through his hair, clutching his head as if he was trying to stop it exploding.

I pushed past him, heading into the kitchen. He stomped after me. I put the marble counter between us, wanting to avoid this ridiculous conversation. Alex leant over the counter, eyes narrowed, mouth tight. "I cannot believe this. This *isn't* normal, Meredith."

I shrugged. Who wanted to be normal?

"What happened to innocent until proven guilty?"

"So, he's good looking. Clearly Mother Nature took pity on him when she ran out of brains and gave him a double dose of looks, but I thought you had more depth to you. Get over it, over *him*. He's a useless fuckwit!"

"Wow. It's amazing… I wonder why nobody thought of it earlier. All you have to say is 'get over it' and"—I snapped my fingers in his face—"miraculously, poof, there it is. Gone." I was breathing hard. "There's no way they'll connect it to me."

"Tell me you didn't actually give them crabs."

I sucked in a breath. "They deserve it."

"Meredith!" he roared, actually roared. "This is fucking ridiculous. That's assault!"

I rolled my eyes like a thirteen-year-old girl arguing with her mother about the length of her skirt. "Fine! I stocked my online trolley with little eggs, but… I couldn't do it. I couldn't actually check them out."

"Thank God." His eyes sank closed and he shook his head. "You need to see a psychiatrist."

"What?" I jerked my gaze from the window, where I was checking out Team Meri, who huddled in small groups to keep warm, between bouts of singing and shouting encouragement.

"Someone who can help you work through your emotions and deal with the betrayal."

"Rubbish." I snapped.

He reached over, stroking the back of my hand where it was fisted on the countertop. I shivered, ever-responsive to his touch. Maybe if I responded to him even when we were fighting, I was over Tom.

"You need to get over this absurd notion of revenge. You're so worried about what other people think of you and appearing anything other than perfect that you bottle all of your emotions up. Then it gets too much for you and explodes out in these… these *psychotic* actions, days or even weeks after it happened."

"Hey! I—"

He ignored me. "If you admitted to how you feel, let the emotion flow in a normal fashion, I think you'd already be over this whole… whatever the hell it is you're doing, quicker. Like, before you're arrested."

"I'm not seeing a psychiatrist." I folded my arms over my chest, leaning back against the counter and glaring at him. "I don't need to."

"The guy's a worthless piece of shit. He couldn't even please you in bed. And it isn't like you're hard to please; you go off like a rocket every time I touch you. No." He cut me off before I could say anything. "That's a compliment. This obsession is *not* normal. For God's sake. Get drunk…"

"I don't drink."

"Because you might risk putting on a couple of well-needed pounds?"

"That's—"

"Normal. It's *normal* to get drunk when you break up with your boyfriend or girlfriend. Get drunk, leave insulting or sobbing messages on their phone, delete his pictures from your Instagram, change your status on Facebook to *single*… throw all his clothes into the street and tell your friends he had a small penis and didn't know what to do with it. All of that is *normal*." He rounded the counter towards me, his fury clear. "I get it. You are pissed off. Hurt. You have a right to be."

"So good of you. To understand and give me *permission* to be angry and upset my boyfriend shagged my mother and best friend. In. My. Bed."

"That still doesn't give you free rein on vengeance!"

"You have no proof I did anything; for all you know, it was Team Meri."

"Save your lies for the police." He slapped his palm down on the counter. "Do you think this is attractive to prospective boyfriends, faux or real? Because it makes my balls shrivel just thinking about what would happen if you ever decide you have a grudge against me."

"That's ridicu—"

"And if the papers got hold of it! What do you think that would do to your career? Your moral high ground? You might not give a damn about how I feel, but I thought you cared about your career." He shook his head.

He was being totally unreasonable. My breath trembled. Tears edged my lower lashes. "What the hell do you want me to do, just let it go? Forgive and forget?"

"Yes!" he roared. "Jesus, someone should add the award for most obvious question ever asked to all the others you've won."

"It's not like I've killed anyone."

"I thought you were being stalked by a crazy ex—or fan, but you're the crazy stalker in this scenario—"

"I'm not stalking them. It's not like I hang around outside their house or—"

"Hide in the bushes in the park and watch them," he interrupted. He was shaking his head, his hands fisted on the counter. He took a couple of deep breaths, then continued with forced calm. "It makes no sense. From what I can tell, you didn't even like Tom much, let alone love him. You aren't crying into your pillow at night, missing him."

"I—"

"Hell, I don't think you liked your mother much either, and I don't blame you. No one would. But this..." He threw his hands out. "This isn't about a broken heart. You're angry and embarrassed."

"I don't have to stand here and listen to this."

"That's right. Exit stage left. There's no after-show support here to pander after you... and I don't think the paps out there have your best interest at heart."

"Get out!" I shouted, stamping my foot and pointing to the door dramatically.

"Finally, a reaction that's normal. Dented your pride, did I? You paid for Tom and your mum to live free for years whilst you worked fourteen-hour days and they cheated on you, and you can't—"

"Get out!" I screamed, shouldering past him into my bedroom. Going for a dramatic full stop to my exit, I turned, glaring at him as I slammed the door. Hard.

It hit the doorframe with a thundering, wall-shaking bang and bounced back.

Hitting me in the face. The force of the hit and shock had me stumbling backwards, crashing into my bedroom wall. "Jesus! Ow!"

"Fuck. Meredith!" Alex rushed into my room, scooping me up off the floor, cradling the side of my face. "Let me see, princess."

"G-ho aw-ay." I dry-sobbed, batting half-heartedly at his chest.

He ignored me, tugging my hand from my face. "Holy hell, that had to hurt." He winced as he checked out my rapidly swelling cheek and eye. "Damn. You're going to have one hell of a shiner there." He stroked a gentle finger over my hot, puffy cheek, his temper forgotten. "Let's get some ice on you."

"No," I snarled brokenly.

"Yes. You need to sit down and ice that, whilst I cancel the car for tonight."

"No!" I grabbed his wrist. "I have to go out. I have to be seen."

"Your eye—"

"Is fine. Nothing ice and makeup won't cover up."

"So instead of being a rational person who may not want to go out all the time as you recover from the betrayal and the breakdown of every significant relationship in your life, you want to look like a domestic abuse victim?"

"I'll cover it with makeup."

"That might hide the bruise, but not the swelling. You'll look like the elephant woman… like you've been crying over Tom for a month." He ruthlessly targeted my biggest worry and exploited it.

My eyes skittered around the room frantically, as I searched for a response. "Just go, Alex. I'll be fine by myself."

"You could put out a tweet and ask one of your millions of *friends* to come over and look after you, but I'm pretty sure you don't want them posting pictures of you looking like this."

"I don't need a lawyer right now anyway." I continued, as if he hadn't spoken.

"You need a psychiatrist," he retorted. "I'll go. I've had enough of this shit, anyway. I'm not a masochist." He grabbed his half-unpacked duffel from just inside my bedroom door and stalked out of the bedroom. I heard the sound of the fridge being opened—was he taking his food?

He returned. "Ice it." He dropped a bag of frozen peas wrapped in a tea towel beside me. "You know what hurts, Meredith? Thinking you have a chance with a gorgeous woman, only to realise you're just the rebound guy. You are so blinded with Tom and your petty need for revenge that you don't even care who you're hurting or what you're throwing away." He didn't give me a chance to respond, heading back out and down the hall. "I hope you find your happiness wherever it is, princess, because clearly it's not with me. Here. Now." He pulled open the front door. "A tip from me to you, as one *boyfriend* helping out the next: it's off-putting when the woman you love is too busy going *Fatal Attraction* on her ex to emotionally invest in the present."

CHAPTER 32

Your Friends Are A Bad Influence!

"He's passed me off to you?"

An hour and a half later, still feeling sick and shaky from fighting with Alex, I stood in my doorway, one-eyed glaring at Lia. "He can't do that." I flinched as the screaming and shouting from Team Meri outside ratcheted up. "*He's* my lawyer."

Lia huffed. "If by lawyer you mean *boyfriend*, then yes."

"So—"

"I'm here as a friend."

"We're not friends." I sounded petulant, but I was borderline concussed and my heart felt painfully bruised.

"I have wine." Lia held up a bottle enticingly. Oh.

Maybe we could be friends.

"I've got prosecco and the telephone number of a Thai restaurant that delivers."

A tall, curvy brunette walked out of the lift, looking rumpled, dirt and grass stains on her jeans, her hair in a lopsided ponytail.

I recognised Kate Turner. We'd met a few times. Kate had been interviewed on *Before Breakfast*, the morning show aired before mine. Her mother had run an advertising campaign to get her a date. She'd become a media darling; her music career was taking off, and we were invited to a lot of the same parties.

"Ah. Hi, Kate."

"Hey, Meri," she responded, then waited expectantly.

"I don't mean to be rude or unfriendly, but are you here to see me?"

"Yep," she responded cheerfully. "And let me tell you, it wasn't easy. I've been trying for days. After the leprechaun guarding the gate refused to let me in"—I smiled at her description of Vic—"I had to get TJ, my best friend, to boost me over wall into the garden." She smirked, a mix of pride and pure evil. "I created a distraction by getting my boyfriend to go to the front gate and ask for *Tom*." She started to laugh. "You probably heard Team Meri's response…" Kate pulled a ringing mobile from her purse sending it to message service. "Once I was over the wall, TJ was supposed to run around to the front gate and save Mark."

I winced. "Team Meri can be vicious."

Kate shrugged. "Given he's burning up my phone right now, I am guessing he survived."

"Do you want me to call down and let him in?"

"Nope. It's probably best to let him cool off. Plus, it's all part of my revenge for the two months of dating hell he put me through."

"Oh!" A short redhead cleared the top step, then hesitated. "Sorry, I—"

"Ffion?" My heart swelled, "Ffi…"

"Hey, Meri." She hung back, looking nervous as Lia and Kate turned to check her out. My chest tightened. I desperately wanted it to be like it was before. I wanted to rush forward and hug her, be hugged…

"What are you doing here?"

"I saw the article in the paper, your mother. The others… I called Jenn." Ffi scrunched up her face, so I knew Jenn had told her story. "The *bitch*!" she snarled. "So, I told Alfie he had kid duty, took a couple of days off work and hopped on a train. I just thought… Maybe you needed a friend. But… I, ah…" She began edging back towards the stairwell. "I can see—"

I threw myself at her. "Oh my God. I missed you so much." Tears pressed the back of my eyes and throat. I'd been crying on and off since Alex walked out; somehow, with the dam broken, they flowed much more easily.

Ffi gave me a squeeze then broke our hug, stroking a finger over my swollen cheek. "I brought wine, crisps, pretzels, gin and chocolate," she said. "Girls' night in a bag."

"Let's move this show inside." Lia motioned everyone into my flat.

It seemed I was about to have an impromptu party. "I guess I'll get glasses."

"Great," Kate responded. "I'm dying of thirst. Sorry."

She pulled her continuously ringing mobile from her pocket, swiping to answer.

"What the fuck, KT?" The bellow was loud enough that we all stopped and turned to listen.

"Damien," Kate responded.

"You liked Damien!" the disembodied voice retorted. "And it was a speed date. It was so short it barely counted as a date."

"That's why I only waited ten minutes—the length of a speed date"—Kate winked at us—"before I sent TJ to rescue you. If it was punishment for Romeo or one of the other dates you and Mum blackmailed me into, I'd have left you to fend for yourself without remorse. Now suck it up, big boy. I've got alcohol and ex-bashing to get on with."

"You set me up to be attacked by a mob of angry women. They could have killed me," he said. Kate snorted. "They ripped half my clothes off, KT."

"Stalker John stole my handbag."

"KT—"

She disconnected the call, switching the phone to silent before she put it away.

"Oh my God, you're KT Turner, of KT Turner and the Boot-Scooting Band," Ffi gushed. "I love that dating song you did on YouTube. It had millions of views… 'Kissing Frogs!' Are you and Meri friends?"

"Yep," KT responded, and I felt a small spurt of something… warm and comforting. A real, flesh-and-blood friend.

"What was the phone call about?" Lia asked.

Kate rolled her eyes. "I was blackmailed into some dates a few months ago. I'll tell you about it sometime, but not today. Today's about Meri."

* * * * *

Two hours later, we were sitting on cushions on the floor around the coffee table, my revenge playlist on in the background. Mostly empty Thai takeout trays and wine bottles littered the table. I was trying to forget my argument with Alex and filling the girls in on what had happened with Tom.

“I thought it was a squeaking door hinge or something, and then I saw him. A rear humping view; it wasn’t pretty.” Maybe it was the alcohol, or the fact everyone had already sold their stories, or maybe it was having girlfriends to talk to, but I found myself sharing. “And then, as I stood frozen in the doorway trying to understand what the hell was happening, Tom came. In. My. Mother.”

Kate choked, spluttering wine. “He did not.”

“He did. There was groaning, swearing, moaning, then he unloaded into my mother. Whilst looking at me over his shoulder.”

“That’s sick!” Kate said.

“What a supreme arsehole,” Ffion added.

“From the view I had, I can tell you there is nothing special about his arsehole,” I said.

“Eww! What did you do?” Kate asked.

“How come I’m not defending you on a murder

charge?" Lia asked at the same time.

"I'd gut Alfie and burn his precious fishing rods in front of him as he bled out if I walked in on him screwing someone else. Let alone my mother!" Ffi added.

"I was in shock." I crunched on a stray bean sprout. "Numb. I just walked. Of course, they followed. You should've heard them. *We didn't mean to hurt you. It didn't mean anything. You never have time for me, anymore. I'm lonely…*"

"Oh my God." Ffi gasped, wine sloshing over the rim of her glass as she gestured towards me. "It sounds like an episode of your show."

"You watch it?" I asked, oddly touched by the idea she'd kept up with my career even when we weren't talking.

"Damn right. I record it so I can watch it uninterrupted when the kids are in bed."

"I watch when I'm off work sick… or hungover," Kate said.

"Me too," Lia said.

"Thanks. You're the best." I felt emotional, probably because I was still reeling from falling out with Alex. "I'm filming later this week. I'll save you front-row seats if you want to come." I touched my cheek self-consciously. Jerry was not going to be happy if the swelling hadn't gone down.

"What happened to your face?" Ffi asked.

"A door."

She shot to the edge of her cushion. "Don't give me that *walked into a door* crap, Meri Scott. If he hit you—"

"Alex wouldn't—" Lia and I said at once.

"Who's Alex?" Ffi asked. "I was talking about Tom."

"He's my lawyer."

"*Boyfriend,*" Lia said.

"I was arguing with him. I slammed my bedroom door as part of my grand exit… it bounced back and smacked me in the face." The girls winced. "It wasn't my finest moment, but it was self-induced."

"Arguing and door slamming sounds more girlfriend-boyfriend then lawyer–client," Kate said.

"Agreed," Ffion said.

Lia laughed at my scowl. "Now we've got that sorted. I'm totally up for coming to a recording of your show," she said.

"Me too," Ffion and Kate added.

"You're onto bigger and better now," Lia said. "Alex is one of the best."

"Yes," I agreed dully, not denying our relationship. What was the point? They were right: Alex had been my boyfriend. We'd laughed and loved, but now he'd dumped me. I stared down into my wine, blinking back the tears. "I didn't know sex—*everything*—could be so good. But…"

"But?" Lia asked.

"He hates me now." My eyes welled and my lip trembled. "We fell out."

"He doesn't hate you any more then you hate him," Lia said, poking around with her fork in a tub of chilli, ginger and garlic prawns.

"Why did you fall out?" Kate asked.

"I, ah…" Should I tell them about the revenge? What

if they thought I was wrong too? Then again… the whole *reasonable woman* thing. “He said I needed to get over it.”

“Over what?” Kate asked.

“Tom and Talith and Jenn and every woman in London.”

“Present company excluded,” Lia added.

“Insensitive git,” Kate said. “Men have no clue.”

“Don’t you get one month for every year you were together before you have to get over it?” Ffion asked. I shrugged.

“Your mother’s the worst,” Kate said. “I thought my mother was bad, but at least she has my best interests somewhere close to her heart… She’d castrate any guy of mine who hit on her. She wouldn’t shag them and sell her story in the newspaper.”

“She was wearing my shoes whilst he was screwing her,” I said.

“The bitch!” Ffi said.

“She was wearing your boyfriend, too. How come you aren’t whinging more about that?” Lia asked.

“Well, I, ah… Alex says I didn’t love Tom,” I replied.

“What do you think?”

“I don’t want to say he’s right.”

“I don’t blame you. Men can be such smug bastards about the whole ‘I told you so’ thing,” Kate said. Ffi nodded enthusiastically.

“Yes… but well, I, ah, I think I might have been over Tom about six years ago,” I admitted.

“What?” Kate and Lia asked at the same time.

“I thought you were pining over him. Isn’t that what we’re drinking and binge-eating over?” Kate asked.

“I’m hurt and angry and I didn’t let them get away scot-free…” I skirted my revenge antics. “But I wasn’t… I’m not heartbroken. I’m not sobbing into my pillow at night over them.” I glanced up. “I don’t think I loved him… He was just a convenience. No. He wasn’t even a convenience. He was just a… a—”

“Another money-sucking dependent,” Ffion added, her singsong Welsh accent making me feel homesick.

"Like your mother and Jenn. Living off the back of your hard work."

"Tell me you didn't just let them get away with it," Kate said. "When you found them. What did you do?"

"Made like Babe Ruth, swinging for the outfield and beating him with my Most Popular Presenter Award." I smiled at the memory. My mobile lit up, the vibration causing it to rattle across the coffee table. Jenn's name and picture appeared on the screen.

Ffion picked it up, flicking it onto speaker. "This better be about Owain," she said. I smiled, not at all bothered by Ffi answering my phone. It was good to have my bossy, protective friend back in my life.

"Ffion? Why are you answering Meri's phone?" Jenn asked.

"I'll tell you what I'm not doing: spreading my legs and auditioning to be Tom's next baby momma."

"How dare—"

"Get lost, Jenn, and leave Meri alone unless there's something to say about Owain."

"We're friends," Jenn snapped. "I made a mist—"

"You made more than a mistake: you made a baby—*two* babies—and ended a friendship. Meri doesn't need you. She has real friends. She has me and Lia and Kate. We're able to get our own men. Hot men." The girls cheered in agreement. "And we pay our own way. She doesn't need you leaching off her anymore." Ffi hung up the phone to more cheers.

"That was awesome," Lia said, clinking glasses with Ffi. "I have to bring my friend Harriet over next time we get together," she continued, making it clear girls' night wasn't just a one-off thing Alex had fobbed off on her. "She's a real fighter, a martial artist. She'd show you how to kick Tom's arse so he's never capable of dicking around on a woman again, and if you went too far, she'd help you hide the body. No. Questions. Asked."

"Alfie and I have a couple of acres of remote woodland near Haverford West if it ever comes to that," Ffi offered.

"Call me in on the legal side, not Alex," Lia said. "He's a bit of a straight arrow, whereas I'd totally get it and I can work the female jurors."

"I *knew* a reasonable woman would understand. I told him," I explained whilst Ffion topped up everyone's glass.

"I think you've been really restrained. I'd totally have *Snapped Women Who Kill*-ed Mark and my mother."

"I, ah…" I downed the rest of my wine for courage, before whispering, "I might have done a few things…"

"Yes!" Ffion screeched.

"Details," Lia said, snagging a cold spring roll off the table.

"You're an officer of the law," I said. "Shouldn't you be admonishing me and warning me about the reasonable man and being law-abiding?" That was what Alex did.

"Nuh-uh," Lia said, munching her spring roll. "Not when I'm drinking with my girls."

"There's no such thing as a reasonable man," Kate added.

"Okay. So…" I took a deep breath for confidence. "I may have accidently spilt some cress seeds in the back of Tom's car and then tried to clean up the mess with a re-hydration spray, which may, unintentionally, have created the perfect growing environment."

"The cress-mobile!" Kate laughed. "I saw on Instagram. It was brilliant."

Buoyed by their support, I gave a quick summary of the highs and lows of my revenge, to giggles and cheers.

"I'm proud of you," Kate said.

"I can never understand on your show when you tell people they should 'rise above it'," Ffion said. "I say sink down into the shit with them and hold their heads under until they drown."

"Calm down there, killer." I patted her arm. "But you're right about the 'rise above it' rubbish."

"Talith's been living off you since we were kids. She won't have a clue how to earn a living of her own."

"Hence the newspaper article."

"And that freeloading bitch Jenn," Ffi snapped. "When she told me Owain was Tom's…"

Kate's eyes went wide with shock. She glanced at Lia, who shook her head, indicating she hadn't known either. "What happened to the girl code?"

"Hey, don't just be hating on the women. Tom is the king of the bell-ends in this," Lia said. "I don't like it when women only blame women and never men in cheating situations."

"I am an equal gender hater," I said. "I… felt like I lost everything, my family, my dreams of a family with Tom and my friends in one swoop."

"You didn't lose any friends, Meri," Ffi cut in. "Real friends give and take, not one doing all the giving and the others doing all the taking."

"Is that why we fell out, because I offered you money?" I asked, tears welling.

"No," Ffi responded. "We fell out because I needed you to listen to me whinge and give me emotional support; emotionally, we can give and take equally. You just wanted to sweep in and add me to the list of people *taking* money from you. I'd have felt indebted to you forever."

"I just didn't want to see you and Alfie and the kids homeless, and I had the money to help. I-I just wanted to h-help because I love you." I started crying.

"Do something." Kate waved her wine glass at Lia.

"Me?" Lia snagged a box of tissues and shoved them at me, then patted my back awkwardly, repeatedly hitting me with the last bite of spring roll, which she still held.

"She's fine, probably just hungry." Ffi pushed the prawn crackers towards me. "Eat something more than beansprouts, Meri. You are sooo skinny!"

"I can't," I said. "I'll get fat and lose my job."

"Oprah and Ricki Lake didn't lose their jobs, and they weren't skinny. Don't get sucked into the *woman have to be skinny* stuff. Stand up for yourself and for all the women and girls who watch the show and look up to you. They don't watch because you're thin." Ffi continued pushing the last spare rib towards me.

I smiled through my tears. "I can't believe I forgot."

"Forgot what?" Kate asked.

"This." I indicated the three of them with a wave of the prawn cracker Ffion had shoved into my hand. "This is what Alex was saying, but I didn't get it. I didn't remember how much better it is to have one real-life friend than millions of virtual ones."

* * * * * *

"Team Meri!"

"Say something, Meri."

I squinted at Jerry whilst Evie took the opportunity to powder my nose and listen in to our conversation.

"About what?" I had a feeling I knew. He wanted me to address Tom and Talith and the other affairs, but just in case I was wrong, I wasn't going to offer it up. The girls had come to the show this morning. Given the energy and enthusiasm from the audience, I was pretty sure it was going to be a good one.

Jerry gave me *the look.* "It's practically a lynch mob out there, and there are more of them on the street. I don't want things getting out of hand. I'm worried about the safety of the men on set if those women get riled."

Team Meri started up another chant, this one to the old camping song "Build a Bonfire".

"Build a bonfire, build a bonfire, put Tom and Talith on the top. Build a bonfire, build a bonfire, and burn the bloody lot."

It was actually quite good. If it came out on iTunes, I'd buy it.

"The US distributors have asked to see these episodes as soon as they're filmed, Meri. You need to be on top of this. You need to show them what's happened in your private life will make you stronger."

Damn it.

My mother and Tom had ruined the NTAs for me. No way was I letting them ruin the possibility of going to the US too.

"Fine." I stepped away from Jerry and Evie and took a deep breath before heading out on to the stage.

Ffi, Kate and Lia sat in the front row laughing and singing along with the rest of the audience. Spotting me, they waved and screamed. Fake smile wide, I scanned the audience, raising my hands to quiet the cheers before addressing the vast sea of Team Meri and camera three.

"Thank you. I appreciate your support. As many of you know I have been"—what could I call it? Fucked over? Shafted?—"going through a difficult time recently."

"We love you, Meri."

I tried not to laugh at Ffi's shouted declaration, which stirred up a new wave of cheering.

"Thank you." I mock-glared at my friend, gesturing for everyone to calm down again. Having the girls here for support gave me the strength to take a breath and speak from my heart. "It's been a dark time for me recently. Like many of you here today, on my show and in my audience at home, I have been betrayed by the people I should be able to trust."

"Tom's a bastard!" someone shouted.

"Give that woman free tickets for life!" Ffi shouted back. Lia and Kate dissolved into laughter. My lips twitched. I gave up trying to suppress my smile.

"Castrate him!" someone shouted.

"*Meri!*" Mike said through my earpiece. "Don't incite them."

"Please." I raised my hand to quiet everyone again. "Whilst I appreciate your support, I don't want anyone to do or say anything… harmful. As I say every day on this show, we have the right to be angry, upset, when we are betrayed, but it harms us more than the guilty party if we retaliate."

And it was funny, because whilst my revenge had fuelled me through the first days of betrayal, and I regretted nothing of what I had done, not being able to let go had cost me Alex, and suddenly it—revenge, getting even with Tom—just didn't seem worth the cost.

"So, whilst I really appreciate your songs and letters, emails, tweets, etc., my show is and always will be about non-violent forms of resolution. I do *not* want anyone to hurt my mother or Tom or any of the legion of… women who Tom has slept with, to burn them or even castrate him."

"How about poison?" someone from the back shouted. I choked off a startled laugh. I'd already beaten them to that, not in a *till death do us part* way, more of an *I hope you bought a bumper pack of quilted toilet roll* way.

Tom's sports formula had been delivered to my address last week, before I'd forwarded it on. I *might* have mixed a little something extra in. It wasn't like it was an illegal toxin or anything, just a pack of powered laxatives.

The audience continued to shout out suggestions for revenge. I shook my head and stood in silence, and they began to fall quiet. “I understand where you are coming from. Most people who’ve been betrayed have felt the need to strike back, and I admit, I’ve felt the same.”

“For fuck’s sake, don’t stir them back up,” Mike ranted in my earpiece.

I continued, “But these are people I loved once, and I don’t wish them any physical harm.” Emotional torture was something else entirely… “I really do appreciate your support, but let’s keep it peaceful.”

After I’d calmed the audience down, I did the usual walk-through of the audience, high-fiving and shaking hands with various people and managing to avoid assaulting anyone or crotch-surfing.

“From the top,” Mike said in my ear as I hit my mark on the stage. I turned to look into camera one, running through the Autocue. We were filming a segment for “I’m my secret brother’s mother”. I settled in an empty seat on the stage and talked through the background with my first guest, Debbie.

She was twenty-five, well dressed, articulate and employed, a rarity on *The Meri Scott Show*. She talked about how she’d been a daddy’s girl, how her father worked hard, but their family was tight.

None of which was going to grip my audience, but it set the scene. Still I prompted her to get onto the good stuff.

“Then, two years ago, there was an accident. He was in a car accident. He was k-killed.”

I waved a runner over with a box of tissues, feeling a pang of sympathy. I reached over, squeezing her hand. “I lost my father in a car crash when I was young too. I understand how devastating it is.”

Debbie dabbed her eyes. Camera two zoomed in for a close-up. “There was a woman with him.”

“I know this is difficult for you.” The audience started muttering, anticipating. “But what came next was more difficult.”

She nodded, and the tension built in the studio. “It turned out he had another wife.”

“Your father was a *bigamist*!” There was a hiss of surprise from the audience.

“He left us with nothing.” Not quite nothing, or this wouldn’t be half the story I knew it was.

“What happened when the police came to tell you your father had died?”

“It turned out he and his, ah… *wife* had a son. Steven. He’s five years old.”

I paused for the audience to *aaaah*, as the screen on the back of the stage flashed video of cuteish—his head was a funny shape and he had pointy elf ears—little Steven playing with a Spider-Man toy backstage.

"Jesus Christ! It's yoda's half-human love-child." Jerry said in my ear piece, sending the crew into a round of quickly stifled laughter.

Debbie continued talking about how difficult her relationship with her mother had been since she took on guardianship of her half-brother…

I struggled to concentrate between the laughter off set and my mind continually flashing to my argument with Alex. He wasn't just angry over my actions; he seemed genuinely hurt by my "obsession with Tom". My heart ached when I recalled the look on his face when he walked out of my flat. He thought I was endangering his career and our relationship. And I was.

I hadn't thought about his emotions—or my own, really.

I'd been so wrapped up in getting revenge on Tom and his ever-growing harem that I'd torpedoed my chance of moving on with a genuine, fun, hot guy.

"Meri!" Mike brought me back to the present. Debbie had finished whatever she'd been saying. Her mother was screaming and shouting from backstage.

I checked the Autocue and summarised what I'd missed. "So, on the day your father died, you and your mother—"

"Traitorous bitch!" the mother shouted from backstage.

"Hey! Cut it out," I shouted back, which wasn't my usual style, but I wasn't feeling particularly sympathetic right now. "I'll get to you in a minute." I turned back to Debbie. "At the same time you discovered your father was dead, you found out he had a second family and you were listed as your half-brother's guardian. That must have been difficult for you—"

"What about me?" A middle-aged woman came stalking out on to the stage, index finger waving, straggly, grey-streaked hair flopping around her face. Dave and Nobby intercepted her before she could potentially launch an attack on her daughter. "I'll *never* forgive you!"

"Wha—"

"You betrayed me, taking in that little bastard. After I…"

Five minutes of fury and vitriol, and I couldn't take it any longer. I didn't want to turn into this bitter, vengeful woman. Yes, her husband was a faithless bastard, but she was taking her anger out on the wrong person and pushing her daughter away.

Was that what I'd done with Alex, by fixating on Tom and my Plan of Revenge and putting him in an impossible situation?

"I know what it's like to be betrayed." The words burst from me. The audience fell strangely silent, no shuffling or coughing. Even Mike stopped speaking in my ear. "I'm not going to tell you to choose dignity and rise above it, or that the best revenge is success…" The best revenge was revenge, and, well, in spite of what I'd thought previously, falling in love with someone far better and just not giving a shit anymore. "I'll leave that to the after-show support team." I reached out, taking Debbie's mother's hand. "I understand what it's like to be betrayed by the people you are supposed to be able to trust beyond all others. I know how it feels to want to do something to get back at them, to make them suffer…"

Lia coughed a warning not to confess my revenge publicly.

"I also know what's it's like to feel like you have no one. No one to turn to. No one on your side. But you need to look past yourself and your pain. It's amazing who is out there rooting for you. What I'm trying to say is, I am also lucky enough to know what it's like to have people who love and support you in spite of that."

I glanced to my friends in the front row, even as my heart pined for Alex.

"But you have the strongest supporter here in your daughter. She's loyal. She hasn't betrayed you. Hell, she's so loyal to her family, she is raising a half-sibling she knew nothing about. Don't punish her."

Twenty minutes of sobbing and lamenting later, I handed them off to Catherine, the after-show counsellor, skipped sucking up to the audience and waved to my girls to follow me backstage. I needed a sounding board to figure out how I was going to make up with Alex. .

CHAPTER 33

Make or Break - Last Chance For Love!

“I came to apolo— Oh!”

I rushed into speech as soon as the door began to open, I stumbled to an awkward halt when a glamourous, petite older lady filled it.

“You’re not Alex."

She smiled. “No, I’m not.”

“Sorry. I, ah…” I looked around, confused. It had taken me three days to make my plan and work up the courage to come and see Alex, and this was the address Lia had given me. Unless I’d gotten it wrong. “I must be at the wrong place. I was looking for Alex Gordon.”

She stepped back, opening the door wider. “Come on in.”

"Ah…" I hovered, unsure of what was going on. The girls' advice had spanned Ffion's *just jump him; sex will make him forget he was ever angry with you*, to Lia's *Alex is a cerebral, emotionally intelligent guy; talk to him*, to Kate's support of Ffi's *jump him*. Even Lia had agreed that if talking didn't look hopeful, jumping him would probably work.

My heart was practically arrhythmic with fear he'd turn me away. And he wasn't even here.

"It's okay. I'm Alex's mother. Lizzy." She held out a hand.

I took it, feeling dazed.

This wasn't the way I'd planned this.

Alex was supposed to answer the door, then I'd quickly apologise, but not for taking revenge. I wasn't going to lie and pretend I was sorry. It was cathartic and I enjoyed it. But I *was* sorry for dragging him into it and jeopardising his career, and for putting getting back at Tom before our relationship.

Our *real* relationship.

Then Alex would instantly forgive me and we would

fall into bed for more amazing sex.

"I'm Meri. Meredith Scott."

"I know. I've seen you on television. It's nice to finally meet the woman who put a smile back on Alex's face." Ah… was she really talking about me? "Come on in."

I hovered on the doorstep, my mind fluctuating between being polite and going in and turning to make a run for it. "I don't want to disturb you." I took a step back from the door. "I'll come back later."

"Who is it, Mum?" Alex appeared from down the hall, dressed in blue jeans and a black t-shirt, his hair sexily rumpled. His smile dropped. He didn't seem pleased to see me. His mother must be wrong. Maybe this wasn't going to be as easy as I thought. "Oh."

"It's Meri, darling," his mother responded, turning back to me. I'd frozen mid-retreat on Alex's arrival. "Join us. We're having Sunday lunch."

"I don't think so," Alex said, echoing my thoughts. "She doesn't eat."

The git! "Yes, *thank you*, Lizzy," I responded,

blinded by a flash of anger at Alex's snarky comment in front of his mother. I forgot I was trying to escape and that I'd come around to make up with him. "I would *love* to."

Lizzy closed the door behind me, relieving me of my coat then passing it to Alex to put away. I followed them silently down the hallway, second thoughts battering my mind. I'd never had a family roast dinner before. It wasn't something my mother or Tom were interested in. Plus, Alex and I weren't talking. I could feel the tension radiating off him.

I should never have said yes. Now I was going to have to sit down and eat stodgy food to prove Alex wrong and not upset his mother.

We arrived in a large living room, decorated in creams and browns, with a huge L-shaped leather sofa. A curved-screen TV hung on the wall showing a football match. A blue-haired teenage girl turned from the TV to check me out.

"Well, that explains why you have so many episodes of *The Meri Scott Show* recorded on your cable box." She wriggled around to kneel, looking over the back of the sofa at Alex. "Is it inspiration for the solo, one-handed version of Netflix and chill, bro?"

Alex stepped forward, palmed the back of the girl's head and pushed her face into the sofa cushion, holding her there whilst she struggled to escape and gave muffled squawks of outrage. "Shut up, Smurf," he said casually, as if he wasn't suffocating her in front of witnesses.

"Children, that's enough."

I started, as a grey-haired older man rose from a recliner in the corner of the room, where I hadn't seen him.

"Mum!" The girl ducked out from under Alex's hand, looking for sympathy. "He's messed up my hair and makeup."

"Vanessa, don't embarrass your mother or I'll let your brother suffocate you." He arrived beside me, blue eyes twinkling from within a round, jolly face. "I'm Martin. Alex's dad. Now you can see where my boy got his good looks from." He held out his hand. "As you can see, he's worth hanging—" He flinched at the word, and Lizzy touched his arm in comfort. "He's worth *holding* on to. We only look better with age." He flashed a smile, then cast a wink in Alex's direction. "It's nice to finally meet you in person."

“Stop flirting, you old goat,” Lizzy scolded, shaking her head in mock exasperation. “The lazy whatsit that hasn’t made it off the sofa yet is my youngest, Nessa.”

Nessa finished checking out her makeup and hair on her phone and jumped up from the sofa, making her way quickly across to my side.

“What’s going on? Lunch is ready?” A tall woman strode into the room, dressed in jeans, a knitted sweater and a naked-man apron with a rolling pin covering his dignity. I guessed this was Alex’s older sister.

“Nessa is about to embarrass herself by fan-girling over Meredith and begging for an autograph,” Alex responded.

“No, I’m not,” Nessa said. “No one under fifty asks for autographs.” She scowled at Alex, before turning back to me and holding her mobile phone up. “Can I get a selfie of us for Instagram?”

“This is Mary, my oldest daughter and our chef,” Lizzy said. “Mary, this is Meri. Alex’s, ah… friend. She’s joining us for lunch.”

Nessa did a quick lean, pose and pout and snapped

her picture, posting it before I had time to make sure the lighting was okay and she'd caught me at a good angle.

"Great. Hi, Meri," Mary said. "I hope you're hungry." I ignored Alex's scoffing sound. "Lunch is ready. If you've finished messing with filters and posting pictures, Ness, why do you go and add another place at the table."

I tried to catch Alex's eye, to see if we could speak now, but he turned away with a blank look. "Alex—"

"Let me help you carry the food through, Mary," he said. "Mum, you can seat *your* guest."

I deflated, stomach sinking despondently. He was obviously still angry.

This was going to be fun.

Not.

"I can help," I said.

"Oh no. You're the guest," Alex said, walking away and leaving me with his mother. This wasn't going to be as easy as I'd hoped. It certainly didn't look like I was going to be jumping him anytime soon.

I trailed into the dining room and tried to position

myself so I could sit next to him, but he manoeuvred so I was between his mother and Nessa, who spent the entire time, whilst we passed around platters of beef, potatoes, vegetables, Yorkshire puddings and gravy, pumping me to find out if I knew random people from *Love Island* and various other reality shows.

Alex watched every morsel I put on my plate, his eyebrows getting higher and higher, a smirk on his face.

Riled at his clear mockery of the fact I was sitting down to eat, without calorie checking or requesting the fat-free option, I loaded far more than I would ever be able to eat onto my plate. I'd been trying to eat more and not worrying too much about whether I put on a couple of pounds recently. I was still being healthy and still exercising, but I wanted to loosen up a bit, not control everything and to enjoy life more, so his smugness was annoying.

"Have some more beef, Meri," Mary said.

"Well, thank you, Mary. I don't mind if I do," I replied, watching with mild horror as Mary loaded another two thick slabs of meat onto my plate. "Thank you. That's… that's"—*half a cow*—"great. Thanks."

Alex, hearing my panic, snickered.

“Maybe we could all do something, like play a board game later,” Mary suggested.

“Yeah, sure,” Nessa responded. “I’ll give Jay a call and he can hitch a lift over here on Noah’s Ark to make up the teams.”

“Be nice, Nessa,” Lizzy said. “Not everyone needs to spend twenty-three hours a day hooked up to their phone. Some people actually interact with their families.”

Nessa rolled her eyes and nudged me, inviting me to join in mocking the oldies. I laughed. It was nice to be invited to play with the cool kids. I looked up to catch Alex watching me. He lifted an eyebrow and nodded at my plate of food. I cut a chunk of beef and a piece of Yorkshire pudding and popped it in my mouth, staring him down as I chewed.

Flavours and textures exploded in my mouth. My eyes widened with surprise, then fluttered closed, so I could focus my senses. It was fantastic. It wasn’t just I hadn’t eaten a roast lunch before; this was a sensational roast lunch. The beef had some sort of horseradish crust on it, and the potatoes had a perfect crunch into a fluffy middle.

Lizzy followed the direction of Alex's gaze, catching my enjoyment of the food. "It's delicious, isn't it? Mary's a chef. She works at a Michelin-starred restaurant."

I could believe it. "Oh my goodness. How do you feel about coming to work for me as my personal chef? If not, you could just do me takeaway boxes. I don't think I have ever tasted anything—"

Alex slammed his balled-up napkin on the table and pushed back his chair. Stalking around the table, he snagged my elbow and hauled me out of the room. I'd just picked up a bottle of wine to top up my glass, and didn't have time to put it back down, so clutched it to my chest. I may well need it.

"We need to talk."

"Now? I got the distinct impression you didn't want to talk. And now you can't wait until we finish lunch?"

"Pack it in, Meredith. If you think I am sitting across the table from you, with my mother and sisters watching, whilst you make sex sounds and act like you're orgasming over lunch, you're even crazier than I thought." He dropped my arm and spun away, adjusting the front of his jeans as he stalked a few steps from me.

I smiled, realising the direction of his discomfort. Maybe jumping Alex wasn't such a far-fetched idea. "I like your family. Your sister's a great cook." And, to be honest, I was closer to an orgasm eating Mary's roast then I'd ever been having sex with Tom.

"Spit it out." He spun back to face me. "Whatever you came to say. It must be important if you would risk eating and putting an ounce of weight on."

"Don't be snarky and mean. That's not you. That's not how Lizzy and Martin raised you. I came to apologise, to…" I fidgeted, nervous but resolute. "I know you think I'm a blind idiot because I didn't realise what was happening under my nose, but… what you have in there with your family. That's what I wanted; what I tried to make with my mum and Tom and Jenn. But I couldn't… I couldn't create even a fraction of that. I couldn't even hold together the crappy replica I did have, not with love, not even with money." I laughed without humour. "Not when I was the only one who cared."

I looked away, my throat tightening so the words came out strained. "That hurts. So, I couldn't just turn the other cheek, rise above it, etc., not even when I had something, *someone*, better. So, I sought my revenge."

Even now, my lips twitched with the amusement my revenge memories produced. “I’m not sorry. I didn’t physically hurt anyone or do irreparable damage. I didn’t break the law—”

Alex’s eyebrows shot up. “Ah…”

“Fine, so I maybe bent the law a bit. Stretched it…” At his level stare, I tried again: “Circumvented it. It doesn’t matter.”

“The best revenge is success.”

“Rubbish! That’s like saying *time heals all wounds*, and we both know it doesn’t,” I snapped. Alex would never get over the death of his sister, and I wouldn’t expect him to. I’d also never dismiss his very real feelings. “Maybe, in the long term, success is the best revenge, but in the short term… I’m *not* sorry for what I did, not the cress or the prawns or the laxatives or the car headlight or cutting off the funds or anything else… *none* of it.”

“Jesus, M—”

I held up my hand. “It made me feel better. It let out the anger and hurt and gave me something to focus on other than the fact I was all alone and everyone I loved in the world fucked me over without a care."

"No one's life is perfect, Meredith."

"I didn't want perfect. I just wanted that." I threw a hand in the direction of the dining room. "What you have in there. And I tried so hard, for so many years."

"They're very likable," he agreed on a sigh. "Even Nessa, on a good day." He glanced across his living room, eyes hard. "Go on, then."

"What?" I edged forward, hoping from his softening tone that he was finally ready to forgive me.

He looked down at the pile of papers on his coffee table. Just when I thought he was going to ignore me, he looked up, his eyebrows arching. "Apologise."

"I don't take orders."

"You don't take suggestions or legal advice either," he responded dryly. "I assumed you came here to apologise."

My smile slipped. Well, I had, but… "I thought I just did."

"Think again."

Maybe if I had a drink, a little bit of Dutch courage…

Alex stalked forward and removed the bottle from my hand before I could drain it, sliding it onto a nearby bookcase.

Why couldn't he just accept my apology? Why did he have to get all pernickety and lawyer-y about the actual wording?

I should have ignored Lia's advice and just jumped him.

Although I couldn't really do that in front of his family.

"What are you waiting for? Spit it out or go home, Meredith." He leant back against the wall in a casual pose, but I could see the bunch and flex of muscles in his sexy arms as he fisted and released his hands.

"I don't know where to start." I'd been planning what to say, but my scenarios focused mostly on the jumping him part, not the actual words.

"You're sorry for jeopardising my career, for lying to me and stringing me along because you aren't over your ex."

"I'm over Tom. I've been over him for years," I responded. "You were right when you said I wasn't in love with him. I was just clinging to the dream, the family fantasy." I looked away as tears pressed the back of my eyes. "I *am* sorry. More than you will ever know. I would *never* want to hurt you."

"Good."

I'd missed him, and it had only been three days since I saw him. "I… I cried into my pillow over you. You always said I couldn't have loved Tom or been broken-hearted because I didn't cry, but I've cried every night since we fell out." I gave a wobbly smile. "I miss sitting cuddled up on the sofa, bickering over who's ogling which hot celebrity… I love you."

I blinked in shock. Of course, I felt it. Bone deep. I just hadn't planned on putting it out there like that.

Alex stared at me, impassively.

Nerves started to build, bubbling from my stomach.

Why didn't he say it back?

You were supposed to say *I love you* back when someone said they loved you, except if you didn't and you were one of those brutally honest people who didn't care about your partner's feelings, or the possibility they'd never sleep with you again. Then you said something like *me too* or *I care for you deeply*.

"Well, what about you?" I snapped, feeling panicky, heart pounding, breath coming short. I began edging towards the door, in case I needed to make a run for it. He was going to reject me. This was my worst-case scenario. I didn't want to start crying and embarrass myself in front of his family.

The silence stretched.

"Are you worried about what might happen if you ever cheat on me?"

"I imagine I'd get a case of crabs, or prawn pole or foliage growing in my back seat…"

The breath I'd been holding huffed out in a laugh. "And that's just for starters."

"I'm not worried, princess." His expression lightened. I could see the relief and hope I felt reflected in his eyes. "I won't cheat, so you'll have no cause."

"But—"

"I also know your tells. If you start listening to country revenge songs, I'll call your security team for protection and your after-show counsellor, and we can talk it through." He took a deep breath, pushing away from the wall. "I think we've got real potential for something good here, *if* you're honest and you let Tom and Talith and all that shit go. Think of it as something that brought the best thing that ever happened into your life. *Me*," he joked, eyes glinting, like sun sparking off the sea. "I won't spend longer than you primping in the bathroom. I have a good job. I make good money. I don't need yours. I'm interested in you for *you*, not anything material you can give me."

He reached for me, pulling me into his strong, sexy arms. His thumb rested beneath my bottom lip, pulling gently downwards, tugging my mouth open.

My breathing grew fast and laboured, tingles spreading out from my tummy.

His head lowered towards mine, in what seemed like slow motion. My tongue came out to wet my suddenly dry lips.

Finally, our mouths met. There was no easing into the kiss, no holding back. It started out a hot, wet, fierce claiming on both sides. I arched into him. His hands ran down my back, over the curve of my backside, tugging me against the hard planes of his body. Tremors ran over my body, and my head spun.

Gasping for air, we pulled apart, breath coming hard, arms still wrapped around each other.

"Right, Meredith," Alex said, voice rough with passion. "Deal is, we're going to be upfront and open. No more revenge or lying and sneaking around." I nodded, joy bubbling up inside me. "And I need you to look after yourself better; take time out from work for yourself, go out with me and your friends for *fun*, not publicity opportunities; eat more… I'm not talking about eating rubbish or piling your plate with a meat mountain to make a point. You can be healthy, but you have to eat more even if you put on weight. Your fans will love you whatever size you are. *I* will love you whatever size you are—"

He loved me. Tears flooded my eyes and ran down my cheeks. My heart was so full it felt like it would explode. "If it tastes like what Mary made, I can do that."

His smile slowly reached all the way into his deep blue eyes. "Speaking of that, you can only make sex sounds over food when we are alone. I am not sitting at the table fighting a hard-on with my family looking on again."

I laughed, reaching up onto my tiptoes to kiss him.

Nessa snuck around the door, paparazzi style, snapping pictures on her phone "OMG. They're so cute. I'm totes posting this on my Insta timeline,"

I jumped, pulling back. Alex clamped me against him, looking towards the living room doorway, where his family was crowded, listening in. "Way to kill the romance, brat."

"This is a total slap in the face for those trolls who said it was a showmance. There's nothing faux in this romance."

The End

OTHER BOOKS BY TORI TURNBULL

Kissing Frogs

The Meri Scott Show

S-expiry (Released 2019)

If you enjoyed this book, please recommend it to your friends and followers on social media and leave a review at the site where you bought it. .

ACKNOWLEDGMENTS

First, a big thank you to you for buying this book, I hope you enjoyed Meri and Alex's story. I love to talk with readers. You can find me on Facebook @toriturnbull.author, follow me on Twitter, @ToriTurnbull or contact me through my website at ToriTurnbull.com.

A lot of my time writing is spent alone (well, just me and my puppy), but it is not an entirely solo endeavour, so, I want to thank everyone who has played a part in helping *The Meri Scott Show* become a reality. Most especially, thank you to my beta readers Sunami, Katia and Jennifer, who, with blunt honesty and laugh-out-loud challenges, have helped me to make this story the best it can be; Debbie for the medical perspective on Alex's injury, treatment and recovery; Moumah for the fantastic cover art; and Arran McNicol at Editing720 for proofreading.

I hope you enjoyed reading *The Meri Scott Show*. If you did, please take a moment to visit the site you bought it from and leave a review and recommend it to your friends and followers in real life or on social media!

Tori

12431865R00303

Printed in Great Britain
by Amazon